THIEVES' WORLD™

is a unique experience: an outlaw world of the imagination, where mayhem and skulduggery rule and magic is still potent; brought to life by today's top fantasy writers, who are free to use one another's characters (but not to kill them off . . . or at least not too freely!).

The idea for Thieves' World and the colorful city called Sanctuary™ came to Robert Lynn Asprin in 1978. After many twists and turns (documented in the volumes), the idea took off—and took on its own reality, as the best fantasy worlds have a way of doing. The result is one of F&SF's most unique success stories: a bestseller from the beginning, a series that is a challenge to writers, a delight to readers, and a favorite of fans.

Don't miss these other exciting tales of Sanctuary: the meanest, seediest, most dangerous town in all the worlds of fantasy. . . .

THIEVES' WORLD
(Stories by Asprin, Abbey, Anderson, Bradley, Brunner, DeWees, Haldeman, and Offutt)

TALES FROM THE VULGAR UNICORN
(Stories by Asprin, Abbey, Drake, Farmer, Morris, Offutt, and van Vogt)

SHADOWS OF SANCTUARY
(Stories by Asprin, Abbey, Cherryh, McIntyre, Morris, Offutt and Paxson)

STORM SEASON
(Stories by Asprin, Abbey, Cherryh, Morris, Offutt and Paxson)

THE FACE OF CHAOS
(Stories by Asprin, Abbey, Cherryh, Drake, Morris and Paxson)

WINGS OF OMEN
(Stories by Asprin, Abbey, Bailey, Cherryh, Duane, Chris and Janet Morris, Offutt and Paxson)

THE DEAD OF WINTER

Edited by
ROBERT LYNN ASPRIN & LYNN ABBEY

ACE FANTASY BOOKS
NEW YORK

THE DEAD OF WINTER

An Ace Fantasy Book/published by arrangement with
the editors

PRINTING HISTORY
Ace Fantasy edition/November 1985

CONTENTS

Dramatis Personae, Lynn Abbey x

Introduction, *Robert Lynn Asprin* 1

Hell to Pay, *Janet Morris* 9

The Veiled Lady,
  or A Look at the Normal Folk, *Andrew Offutt.* . 39

The God-Chosen, *Lynn Abbey* 75

Keeping Promises, *Robin W. Bailey* 102

Armies of the Night, *C. J. Cherryh.* 134

Down by the Riverside, *Diane Duane* 176

When the Spirit Moves You,
  Robert Lynn Asprin 225

The Color of Magic, *Diana L. Paxson.* 240

Afterword, *Andrew Offutt* 266

1. Sanctuary
2. Old Ruins (First Settlement)
3. Ranke (Capital of Rankan Empire)
4. Ilsig (Capital of Old Kingdom)
5. (6) Contoured cities, now in Empire
6. Death's Harbor
7. Scavengers' Island
8. The Forgotten Pass

N
W ← → E
S

wanderings of the people
the great road
small roads
caravan routes
the generals' route
cliff
mountains
ocean currents
steppes
forests
swamp

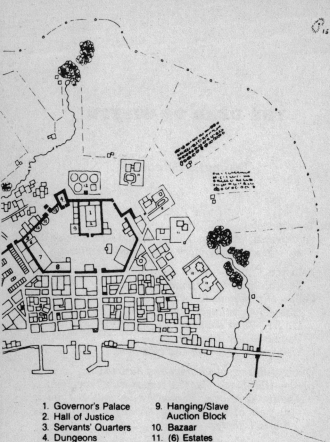

1. Governor's Palace
2. Hall of Justice
3. Servants' Quarters
4. Dungeons
5. Officers' Quarters
6. Armory
7. Barracks
8. Stables
9. Hanging/Slave Auction Block
10. Bazaar
11. (6) Estates
12. (4) Granaries
13. Lighthouse
14. Ford
15. Cave

← 1 mile →

THE DEAD OF WINTER

Dramatis Personae

The Townspeople:

Ahdiovizun; Ahdiomer Viz; Ahdio—*Proprietor of Sly's Place, a legendary dive within the Maze.*

Lalo the Limner—*Street artist gifted with magic he does not fully understand.*
Gilla—*His indomitable wife.*
Alfi—*Their youngest son.*
Latilla—*Their daughter.*
Vanda—*Their daughter.*
Wedemir—*Their son and eldest child.*

Dubro—*Bazaar blacksmith and husband to Illyra.*
Illyra—*Half-blood S'danzo seeress with True Sight.*
Arton—*Their son, marked by the gods and magic as part of an emerging divinity known as the Storm Children.*

Hakiem—*Storyteller and confidant extraordinaire.*

Harran—*Overworked surgeon for the false Stepsons and one-time priest of the nearly forgotten goddess, Siveni.*

Jubal—*Prematurely aged former gladiator. Once he openly ran Sanctuary's most visible criminal organization, the Hawkmasks. Now he works behind the scenes.*

Kurd—*Vivisectionist slain by Tempus upon whom he had performed some of his viler experiments.*

Lastel; One Thumb—*Proprietor of the Vulgar Unicorn. Betrayed by local magicians, he spent a small eternity in death's embrace. Freed when Cime wreaked havoc on the local Mageguild, he is a shadow of his former self.*

Moruth—*King of the Downwind beggars.*

Myrtis—*Madam of the Aphrodisia House.*

Tamzen—*Young woman, daughter of a tavernkeeper, who loved Niko and was killed by Roxane.*

Zip—*Bitter young terrorist. Leader of the Popular Front for the Liberation of Sanctuary (PFLS).*

The Magicians:

Askelon—*The Entelechy of Dreams, a magician so powerful that the gods have set him apart from men to rule in Meridian, the source of dreams.*

Datan—*Supreme of the Nisibisi wizards; slain by the Stepsons and Randal. His globe of power, which now belongs to Randal, was the foremost of such artifacts manufactured along Wizardwall.*

Enas Yorl—*Quasi-immortal mage cursed with eternal life and constantly changing physical form.*

Ischade—*Necromancer and thief. Her curse is passed to her lovers who die from it.*
  Haught—*Her apprentice. A Nisibisi dancer and freed slave.*
  Mor-am—*Her servant. A Hawkmask she saved from certain death, whose pain and torment she holds at bay in exchange for other services.*
  Moria—*Mor-am's sister, also a Hawkmask but now the somewhat alcoholic chatelaine of Ischade's uptown establishment.*
  Stilcho—*One of the Sanctuary natives chosen to replace the Stepsons when they followed Tempus to Wizardwall. He was tortured and killed by Moruth, then reanimated by Ischade.*

Roxane; Death's Queen—*Nisibisi witch. Heiress to all Nisi power and enemies.*
Snapper Jo—*A fiend summoned and controlled by Roxane.*

Others:

Bashir—*A Free Nisi fighter and ally of the Stepsons during their sojourn at Wizardwall.*

Brachis—*Supreme Archpriest of Vashanka, companion of Theron.*

Mradhon Vis—*Nisibisi mercenary, adventurer and occasional spy.*

Theron—*New military Emperor. An usurper placed on the throne with the aid of Tempus and his allies.*

The Rankans living in Sanctuary:

Chenaya; Daughter of the Sun—*Daughter of Lowan Vigeles, a beautiful and powerful young woman who is fated never to lose a fight.*
Dayrne—*Her companion and trainer.*

Gyskouras—*One of the Storm Children, conceived during an ill-fated Ritual of the Ten-Slaying, a commemoration of Vashanka's vengeance on his brothers.*
Seylalha—*His mother, a temple dancer chosen to be Azyuna in the Ritual of the Ten-Slaying.*

Prince Kadakithis—*Charismatic but somewhat naive half-brother of the recently assassinated Emperor, Abakithis.*
Daphne—*His official wife, missing since the arrival of the Beysib.*

Lowan Vigeles—*Half-brother of Molin Torchholder, father of Chenaya, a wealthy aristocrat self-exiled to Sanctuary in the wake of Abakithis' assassination.*

Molin Torchholder; Torch—*Archpriest and architect of Vashanka; Guardian of the Storm Children.*
Rosanda—*His wife.*

Rankan 3rd Commando—*Mercenary company founded by Tempus Thales and noted for its brutal efficiency.*
  Kama; Jes—*Tempus' barely acknowledged daughter.*
  Sync—*Commander of the 3rd.*

Rashan; the Eye of Savankala—*Priest and Judge of Savankala. Highest-ranking Rankan in Sanctuary prior to the arrival of the Prince.*

Razkuli—*Hell-Hound slain for vengeance by Tempus.*

Stepsons; Sacred Banders—*Members of a mercenary unit founded by Abarsis who willed their allegiance to Tempus Thales after his own death.*
  Critias; Crit—*Leftside leader paired with Straton. Second in command after Tempus.*
  Janni—*Nikodemos' rightside partner; tortured and killed by Roxane.*
  Nikodemos; Niko; Stealth—*Bandaran Adept skilled in mental and martial disciplines. Once a captive of Roxane and Datan.*
  Randal; Witchy-Ears—*The only mage ever trusted by Tempus or admitted into the Sacred Band.*
  Straton; Strat; Ace—*Rightside partner of Critias. Enamored of Ischade and, so far, immune to her curse.*

Tempus Thales; the Riddler—*Nearly immortal mercenary, a partner of Vashanka before that god's demise; commander of the Stepsons; cursed with a fatal inability to give or receive love.*

Walegrin—*Rankan army officer assigned to the Sanctuary garrison where his father had been slain by the S'danzo many years before.*

Zalbar—*Captain of the Hell-Hounds which, since the arrival of the Beysib exiles, have lost most of their influence.*

The Gods:
  Enlil—*Storm God/wargod for the more recently conquered Northern parts of the Rankan Empire.*

Mriga—*Mindless and crippled woman elevated to divinity during Harran's abortive attempt to resurrect Siveni Gray-Eyes.*

Sabellia—*Mother goddess for the Rankan Empire.*

Savankala—*Father god for the Rankan Empire.*

Siveni Gray-Eyes—*Ilsigi goddess of wisdom, medicine and defense.*

Stormbringer—*Primal Storm God/wargod. The pattern for all other such gods, he is not, himself, the object of organized worship.*

Vashanka—*Storm God/wargod of the original Rankan lands; vanquished and exiled beyond the reach of his onetime worshippers.*

The Beysib:

Monkel Setmur—*Young chief of clan Setmur, an extended kinship of fishermen and sailors.*

Shupansea; Shu-sea—*Head of the Beysib exiles in Sanctuary; mortal avatar of the Beysib mother goddess.*

INTRODUCTION

Robert Lynn Asprin

"You may remove your blindfold now, old one."

Even as he fumbled with the knot binding the strip of cloth over his eyes, Hakiem knew much of his surroundings. His nose told him that he was in one of Sanctuary's numerous brothels . . . though exactly which one he was unsure of. At his advanced age he did not frequent the town's houses of ill-repute even though he could now easily have afforded them, and therefore he was unfamiliar with their individual nuances. The memories of his youth, however, still lingered strong enough for him to recognize the generic aroma of a dwelling where women sold sex for a living and the incense used in a vain attempt to disguise that profession.

More important than the room's location was its inhabitant, and Hakiem had good reason to recognize the voice that now instructed him. It was Jubal, once Sanctuary's crimelord . . . now the underground leader of one of the armed factions that fought overtly and covertly for control of the city.

"It takes longer to reach you these days," Hakiem said with a casualness that bordered on insolence as he removed his blindfold.

Jubal was sprawled across a large, throne-like chair which Hakiem recognized from earlier days when the black ex-gladiator/slaver had openly operated out of his

Downwind mansion. He wondered briefly what it had taken to retrieve that piece of furniture; the Stepsons had attacked the dwelling, driven the crimelord into hiding. Of course, the "ersatz" Stepsons had been there for a while, which might have made the recovery easier . . . but that would have to be a story to be purloined on another day.

"These are dangerous times," Jubal said without a trace of apology. "One as observant as yourself must surely have noticed that, even though you have seldom relayed such information to me since your promotion."

Hakiem felt vaguely uncomfortable at this subtle accusation. He knew that he had long enjoyed favored status in Jubal's eyes, and at one time would have tentatively called him a friend. Now, however . . .

"I have brought someone to meet you," he said, striving to shift the conversation away from himself. "Allow me to present . . ."

"You would not have reached me if I hadn't known both that you were accompanied by someone and that person's identity," Jubal interrupted. "All that remains to be discovered is the motive for this visit. You may remove your blindfold as well, Lord Setmur. My earlier instruction was meant for both of you."

Hakiem's companion hastily removed his eye covering and stood squinting nervously.

"I . . . I wasn't sure, and thought it better to err on the side of caution."

"A sentiment we both share," Jubal said with a smile. "Now tell me, why would one of you Beysib interlopers, much less the head of the Setmur clan of fishermen, seek an audience with a lowly Sanctuarite such as myself? I am neither noble nor fisherman, and it's been my impression that the Beysib are interested in little else in our town."

Hakiem felt a moment of sympathy for the little Beysib. Monkel Setmur was unaccustomed to dealing with those who specialized in words, much less those who habitually honed their tongues to razor-sharpness. It was clear that Jubal was in a bad mood and ready to vent his annoyance on his hapless visitor.

"Surely you can't hold Monkel here responsible for . . ."

"Stay out of this, old one," Jubal snapped, stopping Hakiem's attempted defense with a suddenly pointing finger. "Speaking for the Beysib has become a habit with you which would be better broken. I wish to hear Lord Setmur's thoughts directly."

Sketching a bow so formal it reeked of sarcasm, Hakiem lapsed into silence. In truth, he himself was curious about the reason behind Monkel's visit. The Beysib had sought out Hakiem to arrange an audience with Jubal, but had steadfastly refused to reveal his motive.

The Beysib licked his lips nervously, then locked gazes with the ex-crimelord and straightened his back proudly.

"One hears that you have power in the streets of Sanctuary . . . and that of the gang leaders, you are the only one whose favor can be bought."

Hakiem winced inwardly. If Monkel had intended to make an enemy of Jubal, he could not have picked a better opening gambit. The diplomat in him wanted to close his eyes and avoid the sight of Jubal's response to this insult, but the storyteller part of him required that he witness every detail and nuance.

To his surprise, Jubal did not immediately lash out in anger . . . either verbally or physically.

"That is a common misconception," he said instead, nodding slowly. "In truth, I am simply more open about my interest in money than most. There are some causes or chores which even I and my forces will not touch . . . regardless of the fee."

The head of the Setmur clan sagged slightly at this news. His gaze dropped, and as he replied, his voice was lacking the edge of confidence and arrogance it had held earlier.

"If by that you mean you wish to have nothing to do with my people, then I will waste no more of your time. It had been my intention to ask for your protection for the Beysib here in Sanctuary. In return, I was willing to pay handsomely . . . either a flat fee or, if you wished, a percentage of my clan's revenues."

In his head, Hakiem damned Monkel for his secrecy. If only the little fisherman had asked his counsel before they were in Jubal's presence. On the surface the proposal seemed reasonable enough, except. . . . It was common knowledge in town that Jubal had long sought to obtain a foothold on Sanctuary's wharfs, but that to date he had been forestalled by the tight unity of the fishing community. Apparently this common knowledge had escaped the ears of Lord Setmur. Either that or he was unaware of the fragility of the union between his clan and the local fishermen. If the local captains discovered that he was offering Jubal an opening to drive a wedge into the fishing community in exchange for safety . . .

"Your request is not unreasonable, and the price you offer is tempting," Jubal said thoughtfully, the earlier note of mockery in his voice gone now. "Unfortunately I am not in a position to enter into such a negotiation. Please accept my assurance that this is not because I hold a grudge against your people, but rather that I would be unable to fulfill my part of the bargain."

"But I thought . . ." Monkel began, but Jubal waved him to silence.

"Let me explain the current situation to you, Lord Setmur, as I see it. The city is currently a battlefield. Many factions are fighting for control of the streets. Though it may seem that the Beysib are the target of this violence, they are more often than not innocent bystanders caught in the crossfire of the real war."

Jubal was leaning forward in his chair now, his eyes burning with intensity as he warmed to the subject.

"If I were to guarantee the safety of your people, it would mean openly committing my troops to your defense. Anyone who wanted to attack me would soon learn that all that was necessary would be to attack the Beysib, whereupon my forces would emerge from hiding to receive the brunt of the attack. In short, rather than relieving you of your enemies, your proposed deal would simply add my enemies to yours . . . a situation less than favorable to the Beysib. As for me, I cannot afford to have my fighting strength eroded away by becoming predictable. My current activities are more covert in nature, playing each faction off against the others so that they will be weakened as I grow stronger. When I am confident that there is sufficient inequity of power to assure a victory, my forces will sweep the streets and restore order once again. At that time, we will be able to discuss terms of coexistence. Until then, you are best to heed the advice of people such as Hakiem here in regards to which faction holds which neighborhood, and plan your movements accordingly. Such information is readily enough available that there is no need to pay my prices for it."

"I see," Monkel said softly. "In that case, I thank you for your time . . ."

"Not so hasty, Lord Setmur," Jubal interrupted with a

smile. "I occasionally deal in currency other than gold. Now, I have given you some new and honest information. Could I trouble you to respond in kind?"

"But . . ." the little Beysib shot a confused glance at Hakiem in silent appeal for guidance. "What information could I possibly have that would interest you? All I know is fishing."

"I am still learning about the Beysib," Jubal said. "Specifically, about how they think. For example, it occurs to me that the fishing clan of Setmur has suffered few casualties in the street wars when compared to the losses experienced by the royal clan Burek. I am therefore surprised that the request for my protection comes from you rather than a representative of the clan suffering the most from the current civil upheaval. Perhaps you could enlighten me as to this seeming contradiction?"

Monkel was taken aback. Apparently it had never occurred to him that he would have to explain his motives to Jubal.

"Could . . . could it not be that the loss of any country-man concerns me? That clan Setmur stands ready to pay the price for the good of all?"

"It could be," Jubal acknowledged. "Though it would mean that your people are considerably more noble than mine . . . particularly when the poorer stand ready to pay for the protection of the richer. I had thought that the reason might possibly be that you suddenly had reason to be personally interested in the safety of clan Burek . . . say, specifically, the safety of one member of that clan? A guardswoman, perhaps?"

Monkel simply gaped, unable to respond. As a relative newcomer to Sanctuary, he had not expected Jubal's information network to include his own personal activi-ties. As head of one of the two clans of invaders, he should have known better.

"If that were indeed the case," Jubal continued smooth-ly, "we might yet work something out. The safety of one person I could guarantee."

". . . At a reduced rate, of course," Hakiem said, risking Jubal's wrath but unable to hold his silence.

"Of course," Jubal echoed without releasing the Beysib from his gaze. "Well, Lord Setmur?"

"I . . . I would have to think about it," Monkel man-aged at last. "I hadn't considered this possibility."

"Very well," Jubal said briskly. "Take your time. If you wish to discuss the matter further, wear a red neck scarf. One of my agents will identify himself to you with the word *Guardswoman* and lead you to my current headquarters. While Hakiem here is trustworthy enough, there is no need for you to have to contact me through him. The fewer who know when we meet and how often . . . much less what is discussed, the better it will be for both of us."

"I . . . thank you."

"Now then, if you would wait in the next room, my man Saliman will see to your needs. I would like a few words alone with Hakiem."

Hakiem waited until the door had closed behind the little Beysib before speaking.

"Well, it seems I have led yet another fly into your web, Jubal."

Instead of replying to this insolence, Jubal studied the ex-storyteller for several moments in silence.

"What distresses you, old one?" he said finally. "I dealt fairly with your fish-eyed companion, even to the point of admitting my own weaknesses and limitations. Still your words and stance reek of disapproval, as they have since you first entered the room. Have I done or said something to offend you?"

Hakiem started to snap out an answer, then caught himself. Instead, he drew a deep breath and blew it all out slowly in a silent whistle.

"No, Jubal," he sighed at last. "All you have said and done is consistent with who and what you have been since we first met. I guess my time at court has simply taught me to view things on a different scale than I did when I was selling stories on the street for coppers."

"Then tell me how you see things now," Jubal demanded, impatience sharpening his tone. "There was a time when we could speak openly together."

Hakiem pursed his lips and thought for a moment.

"There was a time when I thought as you do, Jubal, that power alone determined right and wrong. If you were strong enough or rich enough, you were right and that was that. At court, however, I see people every day who have power, and that has caused me to change my views. Seeing things on a grander scale, I've learned that power can be used for right or wrong, to create or destroy. While everyone thinks they use their power for the best, narrow-visioned or shortsighted exercise of power can be as destructive as deliberate wrong . . . sometimes even worse, because in the case of deliberate wrong one is aware of what he is doing and moderates it accordingly. Unintended wrong knows no boundaries.''

"This is a strange thing to say to me," Jubal laughed mirthlessly. "I have been accused of being the greatest wrongdoer in Sanctuary's history."

"I've never believed that," Hakiem said. "Frequently your activities have been illegal and often brutal, but you have tried to maintain a degree of honor . . . right and wrong, if you will. That's why you wouldn't sell Monkel protection you couldn't give, even though the price was tempting."

"If that is true, then what distresses you? I haven't changed the way I do business."

"No, and that's the problem. You haven't changed. You still think of what's best for you and yours . . . not what's best for everybody. That's fine for a small-time hoodlum in a dead-end town, but things are changing. I've long suspected what I heard you say openly today . . . that you're playing the other factions off against each other to weaken them."

"And what's wrong with that?" Jubal snapped.

"It weakens the town," Hakiem shot back. "Even if you succeed in gaining control, can you keep it? Open your eyes, Jubal, and see what's going on outside of your own little sphere. The Emperor is dead. The Rankan Empire is facing a crisis, and the rightful heir to the throne is right here in town. What's more, those 'fish-eyed' Beysib you scorn have made us the gateway to a new land . . . and a rich land at that. Sanctuary is becoming a focal point in history, not a forgotten little backwater town, and powerful forces are going to be set in motion to control it, if they haven't been mobilized already. We need to unify what strength we have, not erode it away in petty local squabbles that leave us drained and ripe for the picking."

"You're becoming quite a tactician, old one," Jubal said thoughtfully. "Why haven't you said this to anyone else?"

"Who would listen?" Hakiem snorted. "I'm still the old storyteller who made good. I may have the ear of the Beysa, and through her the Prince, but they don't control the streets. That's your arena, and you're busy using what power you have to stir up trouble."

"I listen to you," the ex-crimelord said firmly. "What you say gives me much food for thought. Perhaps I have been shortsighted."

"At least we're headed into winter. The rainy season should cool things off . . . and maybe give you enough time to reflect on your course of action."

"Don't count on it," Jubal sighed. "I was going to warn you to stay away from my old mansion. I have information that the Stepsons are on their way back into town . . . the original ones, not the mockeries who took their place."

Hakiem closed his eyes as if in pain.

"The Stepsons," he repeated softly. "As if Sanctuary didn't have enough trouble already."

"Who knows?" Jubal shrugged. "Maybe they'll restore that order you long for. If not, I'm afraid there'll be a new meaning for 'the dead of winter'."

HELL TO PAY

Janet Morris

On the first day of winter—a sodden, sullen dawn of the sort only Sanctuary's southern sea-whipped weather could provide—the bona fide Stepsons, elite fighters trained by the immortal Tempus himself, crept round the barracks estate held by pretenders to their unit name and defilers of all the Sacred Banders stood for.

Supported by Sync's Rankan 3rd Commando renegades and less quotidian allies—wraiths of the netherworld lent to the Band by Ischade, the necromant who loved the band's commander, Straton; Randal, the Stepsons' own staff enchanter; and Zip's gutterbred PFLS rebels—they stormed gates once theirs at sunrise, naphtha fireballs and high-torque arrows whizzing from crossbows in their hands.

By midmorning the rout was over, the whitewashed walls once meant to keep in slaves now bright with blood of ersatz Stepsons who'd betrayed their mercenaries' oaths and now would pay the customary, ancient price.

For nonperformance was the greatest sin, the only error unforgivable, among the mercs. And Sacred Banders, the paired fighters who cored the Stepsons unit which had spent eighteen months warring on Wizardwall's high peaks and beyond, could not forgive incompetence, nor cowardice, nor graft nor greed. The affront had brought the ten core pairs to Strat, their line commander and half a

Sacred Band pair himself, with ultimata: either the barracks was reclaimed, and purified, the honor and the glory of their unit restored so that Stepsons could once again hold their heads high in the town, or they were leaving—going up to Tyse to find Tempus and lay before him their grievances.

So it was that Strat walked now among the slaughter within the barracks' outer walls, among corpses burned past recognition and others disemboweled, among women and children gutted for being where they had no right to be and housepets slit from jaws to tails, their entrails already out at Vashanka's field altar of handhewn stones, ready to be offered to the god.

Ischade walked with him, inky eyes agleam within her hood. He'd promised Ischade something, one night last autumn. He wondered if this was it—if the killing had gotten out of hand because Ischade was there, and not because Zip's Popular Front for the Liberation of Sanctuary knew nothing of restraint and Sync's 3rd Commando, not to be outdone, forsook all thoughts of proper measure once it was clear that the ersatz Stepsons had been keeping dogs on grounds consecrated to Vashanka, the Rankan god of rape and pillage.

Rape, of course, was still under way in the stables and in the long low barracks. Strat saw Ischade turn her head away at the piteous cries of women who'd been where women had no right to be and now paid the soldiers' tithe.

Around them, PFLS rebels ran to and fro, heavy sacks or gleaming tack upon their shoulders—pillaging had begun.

Strat didn't move to stop the stealing or the defilement of the luckless few who'd been comely enough to live a little longer than their fellows. He was the ranking officer and his was the burden of command—even when, as now, he didn't like it.

Crit, Strat's absent partner, might have foreseen and forestalled the moment when the 3rd's bloodthirsty nature surfaced and Zip's rabble followed suit, and blood began to spill like Vashanka's rains or a whore's tears.

But he hadn't. Not until it was far too late. And then, knowing that if he tried to stop them he'd lose only his command, he'd had to let the bloodlust work through the assault force like dysentery works through those fool enough to drink from the White Foal River.

Ischade knew his pain; her hand was on his arm. But the necromant was wise—she said not one word to the Stepsons' chief interrogator and line commander as they came upon Randal—the Tysian Hazard who was the only magical ally besides herself the Stepsons tolerated—quartering a dog to roast and bury at the barracks' compass points.

"For luck, Witchy-Ears?" Straton growled to Randal, and Ischade relaxed. "It's hardly lucky for that pup."

He must take his anguish out on someone, vent his spleen. She'd thought while they walked among the corpses askew on training grounds and open-legged in doorways that the "someone" might be her. She'd raised shades to help the siege—even one named Janni who'd been a Stepson before his death. And Strat, who'd known Janni and Stilcho and others among Ischade's part-living cadre when they'd laid a clearer claim to life, had had shadows in his eyes.

The same shadows of disgust scoured his mouth now as the big Stepson spat over his shoulder and demanded, "Randal, give me an answer."

But Randal, the big-eared, freckled mage who was so cautious and yet no man's fool or pawn despite his slight and unassuming person, knew that Straton wanted more than a reason for the sacrifice of a cur. Strat wanted someone to tell him that the massacre he walked through fit somehow into the Stepsons' code of honor.

But it didn't. Not in any way at all. It was war out of hand and blood begetting blood and the only justification or reason for it was the nature of Sanctuary itself—Sanctuary was out of balance, gnawing on its own leg while it frothed at the mouth, beset by enemies from within and without. The town was full of factions among men and among gods and among sorcerers, so full that even Ischade, who had interests here, had to come out into daylight to protect them, and to throw in her lot with Straton's Sacred Band and Sync's amoral 3rd Commando.

When Randal didn't answer, just favored Strat with an eloquent sickened look full of accusation, since Strat was putatively in command, Ischade said to the officer beside her, "Order is its own reward. And reason makes its bed with us, not with the Beysib interlopers who have the Prince enthralled, or with the quasi-mages locked up tight in their guild, or with Roxane's undead death squads."

Then Randal put down his knife and wiped his long

nose with a gory hand. "Maybe it'll bring your god back, Strat. Rouse Vashanka from wheresoever the Pillage Lord is sleeping. The men think so, that's sure enough." The mage rose up and made a pass over the quartered dog and all four parts of it—fore and hind—rose into the air, dripping fluids, and floated away toward the field altar out behind the training ground.

Strat watched the pieces disappear around a corner before he said, "Vashanka? Back? What makes you think the god's gone? He's reverted to His second childhood, is all. He's lost all sense of proportion like a child." Then Strat turned on Ischade, as she'd thought he might, and his eyes were as flat and hard as her nerves told her his heart had become.

"Does this suit you, then, Ischade? All this 'order' that you see here? Will it help us—give us a few nights more for you to lie with me without your 'needs' taking over? Are you sated? Can a necromant ever have enough? Is it safe for you to take me home?"

Home to her embrace, he meant. To her odd and shadowed house, all gleam and velvet by the White Foal's edge. Straton made her soul ache and because of him she'd mixed in where no necromant belonged. And it was true: The death here was partly of her making; she'd be content now, without having to stalk the night for victims, for days.

She saw in his eyes that he knew too much, that all she'd done to give him what he wanted—*her*—for stolen evenings on brocade cushions was about to exact the price she'd always known it must.

Randal, knowing the conversation was getting too intimate for outsiders, hurried off, wiping hands on his winter woolens as he followed his sacrifice out toward the altar and called over his shoulder, "You'll have to say the rites, Ace." Ace was Straton's war name. "I'm not qualified, being an envoy of magic and thus an enemy of gods—even yours."

Strat ignored the Hazard and watched Ischade still. "*Is* it my fault?" he asked simply. "Some consequence of lying with you against all that's natural?"

"No more than Janni's fate, or Stilcho's, can be laid at any other's feet. Men make their own fates—it's personal, not a matter for debate." She reached up, taking a chance, touching his lips gone white as the big Stepson struggled for control, his hand upon his sword hilt. He might well try to kill her there and then, to exorcise his guilt and pain.

Then what would she do? Hurt this one, in whose arms she could be a woman, not a Power too fearful to survive for any other man? Never. Or not unless he forced it.

Her touch on his lips didn't cause him to toss his head or step away. He said, "Ischade, this is more than I bargained for . . ."

"It's more, Strat, than any of us bargained for." Her hand slipped from his lips, down his neck, across the sloping shoulder to rest on his powerful right arm—in a moment she could numb it, if there was need. "It's your god, warring against the Ilsig gods and the Beysib gods—if they have them—turning men's heads and hearts. Not us. We're as close to innocent as your sword, which would as soon stay in its scabbard. Trust me. We all knew there'd be hell to pay, should this day come."

Strat nodded slowly: Ersatz Stepsons had rousted real ones in the town, and even dared to confront the black-souled 3rd Commando rangers. And Zip's indigenous fighters had reason to hate all oppressors—the PFLS would as soon have made the gutters run with blood up to Zip's knees.

"So now what?" said the big man, distress naked in his tone.

The necromant looked up, reached up again, craned her neck so that her hood fell back and only her hair shadowed her face. "Now you remember the promise you made me, that first night—not to blame me for being what I am, not to blame yourself for doing what you have to do. And not to ask too many questions whose answers you won't like."

The soldier closed his eyes, remembering what she'd bade him forget until the time was right. And when he opened them, they'd softened just a bit. "Your place?" he said tiredly. "Or mine?"

That night, down in Sanctuary on a perpetually dank street called Mageway, in a tower of the citadel of magic, Randal the Tysian Hazard woke in his Mageguild bed, strangling in his own sheets.

The slight mage went pale beneath his freckles—pale to his prodigious ears—as the sheets, pure and innocent linen as far as anyone knew, bound him tighter. If he ever got out of this alive, he'd have to have a talk with his treacherous bedclothes—they had no right to treat him this way. Had his mouth not been stoppered by their grasp, he could have shouted counterspells or cursed his inanimate bedclothes, come alive. But Randal's mouth, as well as his hands and feet, was bound tight by hostile magic.

His eyes, alas, were not. Randal stared into a darkness which lightened perceptibly before the bed on which he struggled, helpless, as the Nisibisi witch Roxane coalesced from nimbus, a sensuous smile upon her face.

Roxane, Death's Queen, was Randal's nemesis, a hated enemy, a worrisome foe.

The young mage writhed within the prison of his sheets and wordless exhortations came from his gagged mouth. Roxane, whom he'd fought on Wizardwall, had sworn to kill him—not just for what he'd done to help Tempus's Stepsons and Bashir's guerrilla fighters reclaim their homeland, Wizardwall, from Nisibisi wizards, but because Randal had once been the right-side partner of Stealth, called Nikodemos, a soul the witch Roxane sought to claim.

Sweating freely, Randal tried to wriggle off his Mageguild bed as Roxane's form lost its wraithlike quality and became palpably present. He succeeded only in banging his head against the wall, and cowered there, wishing witches couldn't slit Mageguild wards like butter, wishing he'd never fought with Stepsons or claimed a Nisi warlock's Globe of Power, wishing he'd never heard of Nikodemos or inherited Niko's panoply, armor forged by the entelechy of dream.

"Umn hmn, nnh nohnu, rgorhrrr!" Randal shouted at the witch who now had human form, even down to perfumed flesh whose scent mixed with his own acrid, fearful sweat: *Go away, you horror, evermore!*

Roxane only laughed, a tinkling laugh, not horrid, and minced over to his bedside with exaggerated care: "Say you what, little mageling? Say again?" She leaned close, smiling broadly, her lovely sanguine face no older than a marriageable girl's. Her fearsome faith, behind those eyes which supped on fear and now were feasting on Randal's anguish, was older than the Mageguild in which she stood—stood against reason, against nature, against the best magic Rankan-trained adepts and even Randal, who'd learned Nisi ways to counter the warring warlocks from the high peaks, could field.

"Whhd whd drr whdd? Whr hheh?" Randal said from behind his sopping, choking gag of sheets: *What do you want? Why me?*

And the Nisibisi witch stretched elegantly, leaned close, and answered. "Want? Why, Witchy-Ears, your soul, of course. Now, now, don't thrash around so. Don't waste your strength, such as it is. You've got 'til winter's shortest day to anticipate its loss. Unless, of course . . ." The luminous eyes that had been the last sight of too many great adepts and doomed warriors came close to his, and widened. "Unless you can prevail on Stealth, called Nikodemos, to help you save it. But then, we both know it's not likely he'd put his person in jeopardy for yours. . . . Sacred Band oath or not, Niko's left you, deserted you as he's deserted me. Isn't that so, little maladroit nonadept? Or do you think honor and glory and an abrogated bond could bring your one-time partner down to Sanctuary to save you from a long and painful stint as one of my . . . servants?" Teeth gleamed above Randal in the dark, as all of Roxane's manifestation gleamed with an unholy and inhuman light.

The Tysian Hazard-class adept lay unmoving, listening to his breathing rasp—unwilling to answer, to hope, or to even long for Niko's presence. For that was what the witch wanted, he finally realized. Not his magic Globe of Power, bound with the most deadly protections years of fighting Roxane's kind had taught mages of lesser power to devise; not the Askelonian panoply without which, should he somehow survive this evening, Randal would never sleep again because that panoply was protection against such magics as Roxane's sort could weave about a simple Hazard-class enchanter. Not any of these did the witch crave, but Niko—Niko back in Sanctuary, in the flesh.

And Randal, who loved Niko better than he loved himself, who revered Niko in his heart with all the loyalty a rightman was sworn to give his left-side leader even though Niko had formally dissolved their pairbond long before, would gladly have given up his soul to Roxane right then and there to prevent a call going out on ethereal waves to summon Niko into Roxane's foul embrace.

He would have, if his mind had been able to control his fear. But it could not: Roxane was fear's drover, mistress of terror, the very fount from which the death squads plaguing Sanctuary sprang.

She began to make arcane and convoluted passes with her red-nailed hands over Randal's immobilized body and Randal began to quake. His mouth dried up, his heart beat fast, his pulse sought to rip right through his throat. Panicked, he lost all sense of logic; unable to think, his mind was hers to mold and to command.

As she wove her web of terror, Randal's mage's talent screamed silently for help.

It screamed so well and so loudly, with every atom of his imperiled being, that far away to the west, in his cabin before a pool of gravel neatly raked, high on a cliffside overlooking the misty seascape of the Bandaran Islands' chain, Nikodemos paused in his meditation and rubbed gooseflesh rising suddenly on his arms.

And rose, and sought the cliffside, and stared out to sea awhile before he bent, picked up a fist-sized stone, and cast it into the waves. Then Niko began making preparations to leave—to forsake his mystical retreat once more for the World, and for the World's buttocks, the town called Sanctuary, where of all places in the Rankan Empire Niko, follower of *maat*—the mystery of Balance and Transcendent Perception—and son of the armies, least wanted to go.

Even for Niko's sable stallion, the trek from Bandara to Sanctuary had been long and hard. Not as long or hard as it would have been for Niko on a lesser horse, but long enough and hard enough that when Niko arrived in town, bearded and white with trail dirt, he checked into the mercenaries' guild north of the palace and went immediately to sleep.

When he woke, he washed his face with water from an ice-crusted bedside pot, scratched his two-months growth of beard and decided not to shave it, then went down to the common room to eat and get a brief.

The guild hostel's common room was unchanged— wine-dark even in morning, quiet all and every day. On its sideboard stood steaming bowls of mulled wine and goat's blood and, beside, cheese and barley and nuts for men who needed possets in the morning to brace them for hard work to come.

These days, in Sanctuary, the mercs were eating better

—a function, Niko determined from the talk around him as he filled a bowl, of their new regard and esteem in a town coming apart at its seams, a town where personal protection was a commodity at an all-time high. There was lamb on the sideboard this morning, a whole pig with an apple in its mouth, and fish stuffed with savory. It hadn't been this way when last Niko'd worked here—then the mercs were tolerated, but not sent goodies from the Palace and from the fisherfolk or from the merchants.

It hadn't been this way, before. . . . He ate his fill and got his brief from the dispatching agent, who sketched a map of faction lines which divided up the town.

"Look here, Stealth, I'll only tell you once," the dispatching agent said intently. "The Green Line runs along Palace Park; above it are your patrons—the Palace types, the merchant class, and the Beysibs . . . don't tell me what you think of that. The Maze's surrounded by Jubal's Blue Line; you'll need this pass to get in there." The dispatcher, who'd lost one eye before Niko had ever set foot in Sanctuary, pulled an armband from his hip pocket and handed it to Niko.

The band was sewn from parallel strips of colored cloth: green, red, black, blue, and yellow. Niko fingered it, said, "Fine, just don't call me Stealth in here—or anywhere. I need to sniff around before I make my presence known," and tied it on his upper arm before he looked questioningly at the dispatcher.

The old soldier in patched off-duty gear said, "You're on call to the Green Liners, remember, no matter what name you choose. The red's for the Blood Line: that's Zip's PFLS—Popular Front for the Liberation of Sanctuary. Third Commando's backing that lot, so unless you've friends there, be careful in Ratfall, and in all of Downwind —that's their turf. The Blue Line follows the White Foal—those two witches down there, Ischade and the Nisibisi witch-bitch, have death squads to enforce their will, and Shambles Cross is theirs. The Black Line's round the Mageguild—the quays and harbors, down to the sea; the Yellow Line your own Stepsons threw up out west of Downwind and Shambles. You need any help, son, take my name in vain."

Niko nodded, said, "My thanks, sir. Life to you, and—"

"Your commander? Tempus? Will he follow? Is he here?" The eagerness in the dispatcher's voice gave Niko pause. Stealth's caution must have showed in his face, for the rough-hewn, one-eyed merc continued: "Strat's reclaimed the barracks for the Stepsons, but it was bloodier than a weekend pass to hell. We'd like to see the Riddler—nobody lesser's going to straighten this season's mess out."

"Maybe," Niko said carefully, "after the weather breaks—it's snow to your horse's belly upcountry by now." He wasn't empowered to say more. But he could ask his own question now. "And Randal? The Tysian Hazard who came downcountry with the advance force? Seen him?"

"Randal?" The bristling jaw worked and Niko knew that he wasn't going to like what he was about to hear. "Strat was asking for him, three, four times. Seems he was spirited right out of the Mageguild—or left on his own. You never know with wizards, do ya, son? I mean, maybe he up and left. It was right after the sack of Jubal's old—of the Stepsons' barracks, and it was so bad Strat took to sleeping here with us until they got the place cleaned up."

"Randal wouldn't do that," Niko said under his breath, rising to his feet.

"What's that, soldier?"

"Nothing. Thanks for the work—and the advance." The mercenary, who was older than he looked, even with a beard to point up hard-won scars, patted the purse hanging from his swordbelt. "I'll see you after a while."

Stealth needed to get out of there, ride perimeters, make sense of the worsened chaos in a town which had been as bad, last time he'd been here, as Niko would have thought a town could be.

And that got him to thinking, as he tacked up his horse and led it snorting into the sulky air of a late dawn only a week shy of the year's shortest day, about the last tour he'd done here.

Two winters ago, Stealth, called Nikodemos, had lost his first partner in Sanctuary—the man he'd partnered with according to Sacred Band rules for better than a decade had been killed here. It had hurt like nothing since his childhood servitude on Wizardwall had hurt; it had happened down on Wideway, in a wharfside warehouse. Return to Sanctuary was bringing back too many memories, unlaid ghosts and hidden pain. The following spring, still here as part of Tempus's cohort of Stepsons, he'd lost

his second partner, Janni. He'd lost Janni to the Nisibisi
witch, Death's Queen, and left then, quit Sanctuary for
cleaner wars, he'd thought, up north.

In the north he'd found the wars no cleaner—he'd
fought Datan, lord archmage of Wizardwall, and Roxane
on Tyse's slopes and up on the high peaks where he'd
spent his youth as one of the fierce guerrillas called
Successors, led now by his boyhood friend, Bashir. Then
Niko had fought beside Bashir and Tempus, his commander, against the Mygdonians, venturing beyond Wizardwall
to see what no man should see—Mygdonian might allied
with renegade magic so that all the defenders Tempus
arrayed against them were, by default, pawns in a war of
magic against the gods.

After that campaign, he'd taken part in the change of
emperors that occurred during the Festival of Man and
then, tired to his bones of war and restless in his spirit and
his heart, he'd taken a youth—a refugee child half Mygdonian and half a wizard—far west to the Bandaran isles of
mist and mysticism where Niko himself was raised, where
he'd learned to revere the elder gods and the elder
wisdoms of the secular adepts, who saw gods in men and
men in gods and had no truck with such young and warring
deities as Ilsigi and Rankan alike brought alive with
prayers and sacrifice.

Yet all the blood he'd spilled and honors he'd won and
tears he'd shed, far from Sanctuary, fell away from him as
soon as he'd saddled his sable stallion in the stable behind
the mercenaries' guildhall and gone venturing in the town.
For there was one thread of continuity, one sameness
Niko's *maat* sensed in Sanctuary that had been with him
since last he'd served here as one of Tempus's Stepsons
and—with the exception of his time in far Bandara—had
been with him ever since as it was with him still: Roxane,
the Nisibisi witch.

Sidling through the upscale crowd in the Alekeep to find
the owner, a man Niko had known well enough to court
his daughter when he'd been stationed here before and a
man who had a right to know that the daughter's shade,
long undead under the witch's spell, had finally been put
to rest by Niko's own hand, the fighter called Stealth was
suddenly so aware of Roxane that he fancied he could
smell her musk upon the beerhall's air.

She was here, somewhere. Close at hand. His *maat* told

him so—he could glimpse the cobalt-shining trails of
Roxane's magic out of the corner of his inner eye the way
some lesser man might glimpse a stalker's shadow in his
peripheral vision. Niko's soul had its own peripheral vision
in the discipline of transcendent perception, a skill which
let him track a person or sense a presence or gather the
gist of emotions aimed his way, though he could not
eavesdrop on specific thoughts.

The Alekeep was freshly whitewashed and full of determined revelers, men and women whose position in the
town demanded that they show themselves at business as
usual, undisturbed by PFLS rebels or Beysib interlopers or
Nisibisi wizardry. Here Rankan Mageguild functionaries
in robes that made them look like badly-set tables hob-
nobbed with caravanners and Palace hierophants all intent
on the same end: safety for their business transactions
from the interference of warring factions; safety for their
persons and their kin from undeads and less numinous
terrorists; safety—it was the most sought after commodity
in Sanctuary these days.

Safety, so far as Niko was concerned whenever he came
out of Bandara into the World, was beside the point. In his
cabin on its cliff he could be safe, but then his gifts of *maat*
and his deep perceptions were turned inward, useful only
to the student, not, as they were meant, carried by him
abroad in the World to turn a fate or two or stem a tide
gone too far in any one direction.

Maat forced its bearer out, among its opposite, Chaos,
to set whatever imbalances he could to rights. It always
hurt, it always cost, and he always longed for Bandara
when his strength was spent. But, when he was home, he
always grew restless, strong and able, and so he'd come
out again, even into Sanctuary, where Balance was just an
abstract, where everything was always wrong, and where
nothing any man—or even demigod like Niko's commander Tempus—could do would bring even an intimation of
lasting peace.

But peace, Niko's teacher had said, was death. He
would have it by and by.

The witch, Roxane, was death also. He hoped she
couldn't sense him as clearly as he could her. Though he'd
been at pains to keep his visit here a secret from those
who'd use him if they could, Niko was drawn to Roxane
like a Sanctuary whore to a well-heeled drunk or, if rumor

could be believed, like Prince Kadakithis to the Beysa Shupansea.

Not even Bandara's gravel ponds or deep seaside meditation had cleansed his soul of its longing for the flesh of the witch who loved him.

So he'd come down again to Sanctuary, on the excuse of answering Randal's ephemeral summons. But it was Roxane he'd come to see. And touch. And talk to.

For Niko had to exorcise her, take her talons from his soul, cleanse his heart of her. He'd admitted it to himself this season in Bandara. At least that was a start. The lore of his mystery whispered that any problem, named and known, was soluble. But since the name of Niko's problem was Roxane, Stealth wasn't sure that it was so.

Thus, he must confront her. Here, somewhere. Make her let him go.

But he didn't find her in the Alekeep, just a fat old man with a wispy pate who'd aged too much in the passing seasons, who had a winter in his eyes with more bite to it than any Sanctuary ever blew in off the endless sea.

The old man, when Niko told him of his daughter's fate, simply nodded, chin on fist, and said to Niko, "You did your best, son. As we're all doing now. It seems so long ago, and we've such troubles here. . . ." He paused, and sighed a quavery sigh, and wiped red eyes with his sleeve then, so Niko knew that the father's hurt was still fresh and sharp.

Niko got up from the marble table where he'd found the father, alone with the night's receipts, and looked down. "If there's ever anything I can do, sir—anything at all. I'm at the mercenaries' guildhall, will be for a week or two."

The old barkeep blew his nose on the leather of his chiton's hem, then craned his neck. "Do? Leave my other daughters be, is all."

Niko held the barkeep's feisty gaze until the man relented. "Sorry, son. We all know none's to blame for undeads but their makers. Luck go with you, Stepson. What is it your brothers of the sword say? Ah, I've got it: Life to you, and everlasting glory." There was too much bitterness in the father's voice for Niko to have misunderstood what remained unsaid.

But he had to ask. "Sir, I need a favor—don't call me that here, or anywhere. Tell no one I'm in town. I came to you only because . . . I had to. For Tamzen's sake." That

was the first time either man had used the name of the girl
who'd been daughter to the elder and lover to the
younger, a girl now safe and peacefully dead, who hadn't
been for far too long while Roxane had made use of her,
and other children she'd added to her crew of zombies,
children taken from among the finest homes of Sanctuary
and now buried on the slopes of Wizardwall.

He got out of there as soon as the old man shielded his
eyes with his hand and muttered something like assent. He
shouldn't have come. It had done the Alekeep's owner
harm, not good. But he'd had to do it, for himself.
Because the girl had been used by the witch against him,
because he'd had to kill a child to save a childish soul. He
wondered whether he'd expected the old man to absolve
him, as if anyone could. Then he wondered where he'd go
as he stepped out into the Green Zone streets and saw
torches flaring Mazeward—tiny at this distance, but a
warning that there was trouble in the lower quarter of the
town.

Niko didn't want to mix in any of Sanctuary's interne-
cine disputes, to be recruited by any side—even Strat's—
or even know specifics of who was right and wrong.
Probably everyone was equally culpable and innocent;
wars had a way of blotting out absolutes; and civil wars, or
wars of liberation, were the worst.

He wandered better streets, his hand upon his scabbard,
until he came to an intersection where a corner estate had
an open gate and, beyond, a beggar was crouched. A
beggar this far uptown was unlikely.

Niko was just about to turn away, reminding himself
that he was no longer policing Sanctuary as a Stepson on
covert business, but here on his own recognizance, when
he heard a voice he thought he knew.

"*Seh,*" said a shadow separating itself out from shadows
across from where the beggar sat. The curse was Nisi; the
voice was, too.

He stepped closer and the shadows became two, and
they were arguing as they came abreast of the beggar, who
stood right up and demanded where they'd been so long.

"He's drunk, can't you see?" said the first voice and
Niko's gift gave him a different kind of light to place the
face and find the name he'd known long since.

The first speaker was a Nisi renegade named Vis, a man
who owed Niko at least one favor, and might know the

answer to the question Niko most wanted to ask: the whereabouts of the Nisibisi witch.

The second shadow spoke, as the drunken beggar clawed at its clothes and Niko's sight grew sharper, showing him bluish sparks swirling round the taller of the two shadows solidifying despite the moonless dark. "Mor-am, you idiot! Get up! What's Moria going to say? Fool, and worse! There's death out here. Don't get too cocky. . . ." The rest was a hostile hiss from a lowered voice, but Niko had placed this man easier than the first: The deeply accented voice, the velvet tones, had made him know the other speaker was an ex-slave named Haught.

This Haught was a freedman. The Nisibisi witch had freed him. And Niko had saved him from interrogation, long ago, at Straton's hands. Strat, the Stepsons' chief inquisitor, was no man to cross and one who was so good at what he did that his mere reputation loosened tongues and bowels.

So it was not that these were strangers, or even that they picked the beggar up between them and carried him toward the open gate beyond which lights blazed in skin-covered windows, that gave Niko pause. It was that Haught, who'd been little more than a frightened whelp, the slave's collar bound 'round his very soul, when last Niko had chanced across him, was giving orders with assurance and had, by the way his aura glittered blue, magical attributes to back him up.

There was nothing magical about Vis's aura, just the red and pink of distress and passion held in check—and fear, the spice of it tingling Niko's nerves as he moved to intercept them at the gate, sword drawn and warming as it always did when in proximity to magic.

"Vis, he's got a weap—"

"Remember me, puds?" Niko said, halting all three in a practiced interception. "Don't move; I just want to talk."

Vis's hand was on his hip and a naked blade would surely follow; Niko let his attention dwell on Vis, though Haught ought to have been his first concern.

And yet Haught didn't push the beggar (moaning, "Whaddya mean, Haught, 's nothin' wrong with a little fresh air . . .") at Niko or cast a spell, just said, "Years ago—the northern fighter, isn't it? Oh yes, I remember you. And so does someone else, I'd bet—"

Vis—too taut, planning something—interrupted, "What is it, soldier? Money? We'll give you money. And work for an idle blade if . . . Remember you?" Vis took a step forward and Niko felt, rather than saw, eyes narrow: "Right, that's right. I know who you are. We owe you one, is that it? For saving us from Tempus's covert actors downtown. Well, come on in. We'll talk about it indoors."

"If," Haught put in on that silken tongue that made Niko wonder what he might be walking into, "you'll sheath that blade and treat our invitation as what it is . . . a luxury. If you want to fight, we'll not be using bronze or steel in any case."

Niko looked between the two, still holding up their beggar friend, and sheathed his blade. "I don't want your hospitality, just some information. I'm looking for Roxane —and don't tell me you don't know who I mean."

It was Haught's laughter that made Niko know he'd found more than he'd bargained for: It sent chills screeching up and down his spine, so self-assured it was and so full of taunt and anticipation. "Of course I know—me and *my* mistress both know. But don't you think, fighter, that by now Roxane's looking for you? Come in, don't come, wait here, go your way—whatever choice, she'll find you."

My mistress, Haught had said. Someone else, then, had taught him what Niko saw there—enough magic for it to be an attribute, not an affectation; real magic, not the prestidigitator's tricks that abounded in Sanctuary's third-rate Mageguild.

Niko shook his head and his hand of its own accord found his sword's pommel and rested there as he retreated a pace.

By then Vis was saying, "It's not a thing I'd seek, soldier, were I you. But we'll give you what we can to help you on your way to her. Yes, by all that's unholy, we'll surely give you that."

When Roxane, in her Foalside haunt, an old manor house refurbished from velvet hangings to weeds head-high in her "garden," heard a footstep belonging not to an undead or to one of her snakes—who occasionally took human form—outside her window, she went personally to see who her uninvited guest might be.

It was a Nisi type, a youth she'd never noticed, some local denizen with a trace of Nisibisi blood.

His soul was smooth and unctuous over customary evil; he was some familiar of another power here. He said, far back in the dark with wards springing up between them, "I've brought you something, Madam. You're going to like him. A gift from Haught, in case things go your way in the end."

Then there was a soft "pop" and the presence was gone, if it had ever been there. Haught. She'd remember.

Just as she was turning, a pebble skittered, a soft whicker cut the night. She blinked—twice in one night, her best wards violated, slit like cobwebs? She'd have to make the rounds tomorrow, set up new protections.

And then she concentrated on what was there: a horse, for certain; and a person on it, a person drugged and tied to its saddle.

A present from this Haught. She'd have to thank him. She went out into her garden of thornbush and night-shade, down to where the water mandrake threw poison-ous tubers high along the White Foal's edge.

And there, in the luminous spill from the polluted river's waves, she glimpsed him.

Niko, drugged to a stupor, or drunk—the same.

Her heart wrenched, she ran three steps, then calmed herself. He was here but not of his own will.

Fingers working a soft and silken spell, she half-danced toward him. Niko was her beloved and yet her undoing lay within him. Seeing him was more the proof: She wanted to take him, cut his bonds away, heal him and caress him. Not the proper reaction for a witch. Not the proper motivation for Death's Queen. She'd sent for him, used Randal the mageling to lure him, but she dared not take him now, not use him thus. Not when this Haught was obviously tempting her.

Not when Roxane had a war on her hands, a war of power with a necromant called Ischade, a creature of night who might just have orchestrated this untimely meeting.

So, while Niko, bent over his horse's neck, slept on, she came up to the horse, which flattened its ears but did not move away, cut the bonds that held the fighter to his saddle, and said, before sending him away, "Not now, my love. Not yet. Your partner Janni, your beloved Sacred Band brother, is the thrall of the necromant Ischade—he lies in unpeaceful earth, is rousted out to do her foul bidding and wear her awful collar at night. You must free him from this unnatural servitude, beloved, and then we will be together. Do you understand me, Niko?"

Niko's ashen head raised and he opened his eyes—eyes still asleep, yet registering all they saw. Roxane's heart leaped; she loved the touch of his gaze, the feel of his breath, the smell of his suffering.

Her fingers spelled his fate: He would remember this moment as a true dream—a dream that, his *maat* would understand, bore all he needed to know.

She stepped forward and kissed him, and a moan escaped his lips. It was hardly more than a sigh, but enough of a sign to Roxane, who could read his heart, that Niko had come to her at last—of his own free will, to the extent that free will was possessed by mere men.

"Go to Ischade. Free Janni's spirit. Then get you both here to me, and I shall succor you."

She touched his forehead and he sat up straight. His free hands reined the horse around and he rode away—ensorceled, knowing and yet unknowing, back to his hostel where he could sleep undisturbed.

And tomorrow, he would do evil unto evil for her sake, and then, as he had never truly been, Nikodemos would be hers.

In the meantime, Roxane had preparations to make. She quit the Foalside, went inside, and looked in upon the Hazard Randal. Her prisoner was playing cards with her two snakes—snakes which she'd given human form to guard him. Or sort of human form—their eyes were still ophidian, their mouths lipless, their skin bore an ineradicable cast of green.

The mage, his torso bound to his chair with blue pythons of power, had both hands free and just enough free will left to give her a friendly wave: She had him tranquilized, waiting out the time until his death day—the week's end, come Ilsday, if Niko did not return by then.

A little saddened at the realization that, if Niko did come back, she'd have to free the mage—her word was good; it had to be; she dealt with too many arbiters of souls—Roxane waved a hand to lift the calming spell from Randal.

If she had to free him, she'd not keep him comfy, safe and warm, till then. She'd let him suffer, help him feel as much pain as his slender body could. After all, she was Death's Queen. Perhaps if she scared him long enough and well enough, the Tysian magician would take his own life, trying to escape, or die from terror—a death she'd have the benefit of but not the blame.

And in his chair, Randal's face went white beneath his freckles and his whole frame began to rock while, with every lunge and quaver, the nonmaterial bonds around his chest grew tighter and the snakes (stupid snakes who never understood anything) began querulously to complain that it was Randal's bet and wonder what was wrong as cards fell from his twitching fingers.

Strat was out at Ischade's, where he shouldn't be but mostly was at night, just taking off his clothes when the damned door to her front room opened with a wind behind it that nearly doused the fire in her hearth.

Accursed Haught, her trainee, stood there, arch mischief glowing in his eyes. Strat hitched up his linen loinguard and said, "Won't you ever learn to knock?" feeling a bit abashed among Ischade's silks and scarlet throw pillows and trinkets of gem and noble metal—the woman loved bright colors, but never wore them out of doors.

Woman? Had he thought that, said it to himself? She wasn't exactly that, and he'd better remember it. Haught, once slave-bait, looked at Strat and through him as if he didn't exist as he entered and the door closed behind him of its own accord.

"Best remember that you're mortal, Nisi boy. And that respect is due your betters, be you slave or free," Strat warned, looking at his feet where, somewhere in a confusion of cushions, his service dagger lay buried. Best to teach this witch's familiar some manners before he'd have to do worse.

But behind him he heard a stirring and a soft step as sinuous as any cat's. "Haught, greet Straton civilly," came her voice from behind him and then her hand was on his spine, pouring patience into him where patience had no right to be.

"Damned kid comes and goes like he owns the—"

Haught was abreast of him, then, speaking to the necromant beyond. "You'd want this warning, if you weren't so busy. Want to be ready. Trouble's on the way."

Then something unspeakable happened: Ischade, hushing the Nisi ex-slave, came round Strat and did something to the other man, something that included not quite touching him but circling him, something Strat didn't like because it was intimate and didn't trust because he could tell that information was being exchanged in a way he didn't understand.

Abruptly, the creature called Haught turned in a flare of cloak and arrogance and the door opened wide, then shut again behind him, leaving candles flickering huge shadows upon the wall and a chill in the air Strat was expecting Ischade to dispell with a caress.

But she didn't. She said, "Ace, come here. Before the fire. Sit with me."

He did that and she cuddled by his knee in that way she had, so much a woman then that Strat could barely refrain from pulling her onto his lap. She looked up from under the darkness that veiled her and her eyes clamped on his: "What I am, you know. What I do, you understand better than many. What life Janni has with me, his soul has chosen. Someone is going to come here, and if you don't tell him all of that, the result will not sit well with you. Do you understand?"

"Ischade? Someone? A threat to you? I'll protect you, you know—"

"Hush. Don't promise what you'll not deliver. This one is a friend of yours, a brother. Keep him from my doorway or, despite what I'd like to promise you, he'll become a memory. One that will hang between us in the air forever." She reached up toward his face.

He jerked his head back; she lay her head upon his knee. He couldn't tell if she was crying, but he felt as if he would, so sad was she and so helpless did the big Stepson feel.

An hour later, outside her door, stationed like a sentry, he began to wonder if her creature hadn't lied. Then his big bay, tied at her low gate, let out a challenge and some horse answered from the dark.

Sword drawn, he sidled down to calm the beast, wondering what in hell he was supposed to do about something she hadn't explained, when a darkness separated from the midnight chill and a tiny coal, red-hot, seemed to bobble toward him in midair.

Closer it came, until the soft radiance of Ischade's hedges caught its edges and he made out a mounted man smoking something—pulcis, by the smell of it, laced with krrf and rolled in broadleaf.

"Hold and state your business, stranger," Strat called out.

"Strat?" said a soft voice full of distaste and some measure of disbelief. "Ace, if it's really you, tell me something a man would have had to fight on Wizardwall to know."

"Ha! Bashir can't hold his liquor, is what—not even laced with blood and water," Strat responded, then added, "Stealth? Niko, is that you?"

The little coal of red grew brighter as the smoker inhaled and in its flare Strat could see the face of Nikodemos—bearded, but with scars showing like white tracks among the hair, just where those scars should be.

A surge of joy went through the Stepsons' leader. "Is Crit with you? The Riddler—is Tempus come back?" Then he sobered: Niko was the problem Ischade'd sent him out here to deal with. Now her distress, and her cautions, made good sense.

"No, I'm alone," came Niko's voice soft as a winter gust as sounds and the movement of the smoke's coal let Straton know the Sacred Bander was dismounting.

They had a bond that should have been deeper than Straton's with Ischade—that *had* to be. Straton considered alternatives as Niko tied his Askelonian to the fence on the other side of Ischade's gate from where Strat's bay was tethered, and vaulted over the hedge, then grinned: "Not good form to enter a witch's home through a portal she's chosen. How'd you find out about this? No matter—I'm glad to have your help, Ace. Janni's going to be, too."

So that was it—Janni. All Straton's mixed feelings about Ischade's minions roiled around in him and kept him speechless until he realized that Niko was reaching over the fence to get a bow and bladder of naphtha and rags from his horse's saddle.

"Niko, man, this isn't the time or the place for the talk we've got to have."

Stealth turned and as Strat bore down upon him, the Bandaran fighter said, "Strat, I've got to do this. It's my fault, in a way. I've got to free him."

"No, you don't. From what? For whom? He's fighting a war he still has a stake in—fighting it his way. I've fought beside him. Stealth, things are different here from the way they were upcountry. You can't make any headway without magic on your—"

"Side?" Niko supplied the missing word, his face glowing red from the coal of the smoke between his lips. Then he dropped the smoke and ground it under his heel. "Got a girlfriend, do you, Straton? Crit would beat your ass. Diddling around with magic. Now either help me, as your oath demands, or step aside. Go your way. I owe you too much to make an issue of what's right and wrong between us." Niko's hand went to his belt and Straton stiffened: Niko was an expert with throwing stars and poisoned metal blossoms and every kind of edged weapon Strat knew enough to name. The two were thought to be, by Banders, of nearly equal prowess, though Strat's was fading as he aged, Niko's coming on.

"Whatever I'm doing, Stealth, is worse than what you've done? Don't I remember some fight up at the Festival, one in which you protected the Nisibisi witch from a priestess of Enlil?"

That stopped Niko's hand, about to lever a bolt to ready in his crossbow. "That's not fair, Ace."

"We're not talking fair—we're talking women. Or womanish avatars, or whatever they are. You leave this one alone—she's on our side; she's fought with us, for us . . . saved Sync from Roxane, for one thing." Suspicion leaped into Straton's mind, suspicion enough to chase the memory of Janni's tortured shade. "Roxane didn't put you up to this, did she? *Did* she, Stealth?"

Niko, a flint in one hand, naphtha bladder in the other, paused with the bladder poised above the rags on his arrow's tip. "What difference does that make? What's going on here, anyway? Randal's disappeared and no one's looking for him? You're sleeping with a necromant and no one gives a damn?"

"You stay around, and you'll find out. But I can guarantee you're not going to like it. I don't. Crit wouldn't. Tempus would bust all our butts. But he's not here, is he? It's you and me. And I'm bound to protect this . . . lady, here."

"More bound to her than to me? Sacred—"

Niko stopped and stared, his mouth half open, at something behind Strat, so that the big fighter turned to see what Niko saw.

On Ischade's doorstep, beside the necromant swathed in her black and hooded robe, was Janni—or what remained of Janni. The ex-Stepson, ex-living thing was red and yellow and showing bone; things glittered on him like fireworks or luminescent grubs. He had holes for eyes and too-long hair and the smell of newly-turned earth proceeded him down the steps.

Despite himself, Strat looked over his shoulder at Niko, who slumped against the waist-high fence, his eyes slitted as if against some blinding light, his crossbow pointing at the ground.

Strat heard Ischade murmur, "Go then. Go to your partner, Janni. Stay awhile. Have your reunion." Then, louder, "Strat! Come in. Let them be alone. Let them solve it—I was wrong; it's between these two, not us."

And then, as Niko threw the bow up to his shoulder and took fluid, sudden aim at Ischade—before Straton could put himself between her and Niko's arrow, or even thought to move—Ischade was beside him, facing Niko with a look on her face Strat had never seen before: deep pain, compassion, even acknowledgment of a kindred soul.

"So you're the one. The special one. Nikodemos, over whom even the god Enlil and the entelechy of dreams contend." She nodded as if in her drawing room, sipping tea at some civil table. "I see why. Nikodemos, don't choose your enemies too quickly. The witch who sent you here has Randal—is that not a greater wrong, a deeper evil, than giving the opportunity for vengeance to a soul such as Janni, who craves it?"

Ischade waited, but Niko didn't answer. His gaze was fixed on the thing that shambled toward him, arms outstretched, to embrace its erstwhile partner.

Strat, were he the one faced with love from such a zombie, would have run screaming, or shot the bow, or lopped the head off the undead who sought to hold him.

But Niko took a deep breath that Strat could hear, so shuddering was it, dropped the bow, and held his own arms out, saying, "Janni. How is it with you? Is she right?"

And Strat had to turn away; he couldn't watch Niko, full of life, embrace that thing who'd once ridden at his side.

And when he did, Ischade was waiting there to take Strat's hand and cool his brow and usher him inside.

But no matter the depth of her eyes or the quality of her

ministrations, this time Straton knew he had no chance of
forgetting what he saw when a Sacred Band pair was
reunited, the living and the dead.

Niko was drinking off his chill in the Alekeep, which
opened with the rising sun, when he realized that somebody was drawing his picture.

A little fellow with a pot belly and black circles under
his eyes, who was sitting in the beamed common hall's far
corner, was looking at him too often, then looking down
at a board he held on his lap.

Just the day barman was present, so Niko didn't try to
ignore a problem in the making. He'd had too rough a
night, at any rate, to have patience with anyone—let alone
a limner who didn't ask permission.

But when he was halfway to the other man, his intention
clear enough, the day barman reached out a hand to stay
him. "I'd not, were I you, sir. That's Lalo the Limner,
who drew the Black Unicorn that came alive in the Maze
and killed so many. Just let the scribbler be."

"As far as I know, I'm alive already, man," Niko said,
knowing that his accursed temper had already slipped its
bonds and that things would doubtless get worse before he
got it in check again. "And I don't like having my picture
scrawled on anything—walls, doors, hearts. Maybe I'll
turn the tables and draw my sign on that fat, soft
belly. . . ."

By then, the little, rat-faced limner was scrabbling up,
running for the door, his sketching board under his arm.
Niko didn't chase him.

He went back to his table and sat there, digging in the
wood with the point of his blade the way Janni used to do,
thinking of the meeting he'd had and wanted to forget
with a dead thing happy to fight beyond mortal battles at
the bidding of the necromant, wondering if he should—or
could—find a way to put Janni's soul to rest despite its
assurance that it was content enough as it was. Did it
know? Was it really Janni? Did the oath they'd sworn still
obtain when one respondent wasn't a man any longer?

Niko didn't know. He couldn't decide. He tried not to
drink too much, but drink dulled the picture in his mind's
eye, and at nightfall he was still sitting there, trying
unsuccessfully to get thoroughly drunk, when the priest
known as Torchholder happened to come in with others of

his perfumed breed, all with their curl-toed winter shoes and their gaudy jewelry.

Torchholder knew him, but Niko didn't have the sense to leave before the High Priest of Vashanka recognized the fighter who'd been with Tempus at the Mageguild's Fête two winters past.

So when the priest sat down opposite him, Niko raised his head from the palm on which he'd been propping it and stared owlishly at the priest. "Yeah? Can I help you, citizen?"

"Perhaps, fighter, I can help you."

"Not if you can't lay the undead, not a chance of it."

"Pardon?" Torchholder was watching the half drunk Sacred Bander closely, looking for some sign. "We can do whatever the god demands, and we know you are pious and well disposed to—"

"Enlil," Niko interrupted firmly. "Gotta have a god around here, so I'm making it plain: Mine's Enlil, when I need one. Which is as infrequently as possible." Stealth's hand went to his belt and Torchholder froze in place.

But Niko only patted his weaponbelt and brought the hand back to the table, where he propped his chin on it. "Weapons'll do me, mosttimes. Other times . . ." The Sacred Bander leaned forward. "You any good at fighting witches? I've got a friend I'd like to get out of one's clutches . . ."

Torchholder made a warding sign with practiced fluency before his face. "We'd like to show you something, Nikodemos called—"

"Ssh!" Niko said with exaggerated care, and looked around, right and left, before leaning forward to whisper. "Don't call me that. Not here. Not ever. I'm just visiting. I can't stay. Too much magic. Hurts, you know. Dead partners that aren't dead. Ex-partners that aren't ex. . . . Very confusing—"

"We know, we know," soothed the priest with wicked eyes. "We're here to help you sort it out. Come with us and—"

"Who's we?" Niko wanted to know, but two of Molin's cohort already had him by the armpits. They lifted the only mildly protesting fighter up and eased him out the door to where a carriage with ivory screens was waiting and, after some little difficulty, boosted him inside and closed the door.

Niko, who'd been abducted more than once in his life,
expected the carriage to jerk and horses to lunge and to be
carried off into the night. He also expected to fight being
bound hand and foot. And he expected to be alone in
there, after that, or at least alone but for the company of
guards.

None of his expectations came to pass. Before him, on
the other side of the carriage, were two children, one on
either side of a harried looking woman who might once
have been beautiful and whom Niko, who liked women,
vaguely recalled: a temple dancer. The two children were
hardly more than babes, but one of them, the fair-haired,
sat right up and clapped his little hands.

And the sound of those hands clapping rang in Niko's
ears like the thunder of the god Vashanka, like the Storm
God's own lightning that seemed to issue from the childish
mouth as the boy began to giggle in joy.

Niko sat back, slouched against the opposite corner of
the wagon, and said, "What the . . . ?"

And though the child was now just a child again,
another, deeper voice, rang in the Stepson's head, saying,
*Look on Me, favorite of the Riddler, and take word back to
your leader that I am come again. And that I would take
advantage of all you have to give before the little world that
is thine suffers unto perishing.* The boy from whose mouth
the words could not have issued was saying, "Sowdier?
Hewo? Make fwiends? Fwiends? Take big ride? Water
pwace? Soon? Me want go soon!"

Niko, stone sober, sat up, looked at the woman sharply
and then nodded politely, as he hadn't before. "You're
that one's mother? *That* temple dancer—Seylalha, the
First Consort who bore Vashanka's child." It wasn't really
a question; the woman didn't bother to answer.

Niko leaned forward, toward the two children, the
darker of whom had his thumb in his mouth and regarded
Niko with round black eyes. The fair child smiled beatifi-
cally. "Soon?" the boy said, though it was too young a
child to be discussing anything as sensitive as Niko knew it
was.

He said, "Soon, if you're worthy, boy. Pure in heart.
Honorable. Loving of life—*all* life. It won't be easy. I'll
have to get permission. And you've got to control—what's
inside you. Or they won't have you in Bandara, no matter
how they care for me."

"Good," said the fair child, or maybe just "Goo"; Niko wasn't sure.

These were toddlers, the both. Too young and, if Niko's *maat* was right and a god had chosen one as His repository, too dangerous. Niko said to the woman, "Tell the priests I'll do what I can. But he must be taught restraint. No child can control his temper at that age. Both of them, then, must be prepared."

And he pushed on the wagon's door, which opened and let the sobered fighter out into the blessedly cold and normal Sanctuary night.

Normal, except for the presence of Molin Torchholder and the little scribbler, whom the priest held by the collar. "Nikodemos, look at this," said the priest without preamble as if Niko were now his ally—which, so far as Stealth was concerned, he indubitably was not.

Still, the picture that the scribbler, who was protesting that he had a right to do as he willed, had scribed was odd: It was of Niko, but with Tempus looking over his shoulder and both of them seemed to be enfolded in the wings of a dark angel who looked altogether too much like Roxane.

"Leave the picture, artist, and go your way." It was Niko's order, but Torchholder let go of the bandy-legged limner, who hurried off without asking when or if he'd get his artwork back.

"That's my problem . . . that picture. Forget you've seen it. Yours, if you want what the god wants, is to get those children schooled where they can be disciplined—by Bandaran adepts."

"What makes you assume I want any such—"

"Torchholder, don't you know what you've got there? More trouble than Sanctuary can handle. Infants—one infant, anyhow—with a god in him. With the power of a god. A Storm God. Can you reason out the rest?"

Torchholder muttered something about things having gone too far.

Niko retorted, "They're not going any further unless and until my partner Randal—who's being held by Roxane, I hear tell—is returned to me unharmed. Then I'll ride up and ask Tempus what he wants to do—if anything—about the matter of the godchild you so cavalierly visited upon a town that had troubles enough without one. But one way or the other, the resolution isn't going to help you one whit. Get my meaning?"

The architect-priest winced and his face screwed up as if he'd tasted something sour. "We can't help you with the witch, fighter—not unless you want simple manpower."

"Good enough. As long as it's priest-power." And Niko began giving orders that Torchholder had no alternative but to obey.

On the dawn of the shortest day of the year, Niko had still not come back to Roxane.

It was time to make an end to Randal, whom she despised enough—almost—to make the slight dealt her by the mortal whom she'd consented to love less stinging.

Almost, but not quite. If witches could cry, Roxane would have shed tears of humiliation and of unrequited love. But a witch shouldn't be crying over mortals, and Roxane was reconstituted from the weakness that had beset her during the Wizard Wars. If Niko wouldn't come to her, she'd make him notorious in hell for all the lonely souls his faithless, feckless self-interest had sent there.

She was just getting the snakes to put aside the card game and fetch the mage when hoofbeats sounded upon her cart-track drive.

Wroth and no longer hopeful, she snatched aside the curtain, though the day was bright and clear as winter days can be, with a sky of powder blue and horsetail clouds. And there, amazingly, was Niko, on a big sable horse of the sort that only Askelon bred in Meridian, his panoply agleam as it came within orb of all her magic.

So she had to shut down her wards and go outside to greet him, leaving Randal half unbound with only the snakes to guard him.

Still, it was sweeter than she'd thought it could be, when anger had consumed her—ecstasy just to see him.

He'd shaved. His boyish face was smiling. He rode up to her and slipped off his horse, cavalry style, and slapped its rump. "Go home, horse, to your stable," he told it, then told her, "I won't need him here, I'm sure."

Here. Then he was staying. He understood. But he'd not done anything she'd asked.

So she said, "And Janni? What of the soul of your poor partner? How can you leave him with Ischade—that whore of darkness? How can you—"

"How can you torture Randal?" Niko said levelly, taking a step closer to Roxane, hands empty and outstretched. "It makes it so hard for me to do this. Can't you—for my sake, won't you let him go? Unharmed. Unensorceled. Free of even the taint of hostile magic."

As he spoke, he pulled her against him gently until she pushed back, fearful of the burns his armor could inflict. "If you'll get rid of that—gear," she bargained, trying to keep her hackles from rising. He should know better than to come to her armored with protections forged by the entelechy of dream. Stupid boy. He was beautiful but dumb, pure, but too innocent to be as canny as his smile portended.

She waved a hand behind her. "Done." And as she spoke, a howl of rage and triumph issued from inside and something, with a crash, came bursting out the window.

Niko gazed after Randal as the mage ran, full-tilt, into the bushes. He nodded. "Now it's just the two of us, is that it?"

"Well . . ." she temporized, "there are my snakes, of course." She was primping up her beauty in a way he couldn't see, letting her young and girlish simulacrum come forward, easing the evil and the danger in her face and form. By all she revered, did she love this boy with his hazel eyes so clear and his quiet soul. By all she held sacred, the feel of his hand on her back as he ushered her into her own house in gentlemanly fashion was unlike the touch of any man or mage she'd ever known.

She wanted only to keep him. She sent away the snakes, having to discorporate one who objected that she would then be defenseless, open to attack by man or god.

"Take that silly armor off, beloved, and we'll have a bath together," she murmured, preparing to spell water, hot and steaming, in her gold-footed tub.

And when she turned again, he'd done that and stood before her, hands out to strip her clothes away, and his body announced its intention to make her welcome.

Welcome her he did, in hot water and hot passion, until, amid the moment of her joy and just before she was about to begin a rune to claim his soul forever, a commotion began outside her door.

First it was lightning that rocked her to her foundations, then thunder, then the sound of many running feet and chanting priests as all Vashanka's priesthood came tramping up her cart-track, battle-streamers on their standards and horns to blow the eardrums out of evil to their lips.

He was as nonplussed as she. He held her in his arms and pressed her close, telling her, "Don't worry, I'll take care of them. You stay here, and call back all your minions—not that I don't think I can protect you, but just in case."

She watched him dress hurriedly, strapping on his armor over wet skin, and run outside, his weapons at hand and ready.

No mortal had ever come to her defense before. So when, snakes by her side and undeads rising, she saw them wrestle him to the ground, disarm him, put him in a cage (no doubt the cage they'd meant for her) and drive away with him, she wept for Niko, who loved her but had been taken from her by the hated priesthood.

And she planned revenge—not only upon the priesthood, but upon Ischade, the trickster necromant, and Randal, who should never have been allowed to get away, and on all of Sanctuary—all but Niko, who was innocent of all and who, if only he could have stayed a little longer, would have proclaimed in his own words his love for her and thus become hers forevermore.

As for the rest—now there *would* be hell to pay.

THE VEILED LADY
OR
A LOOK AT THE NORMAL FOLK

Andrew Offutt

The veiled lady traveled to Sanctuary with the caravan
that originated in Suma and had grown at Aurvesh. She
was faceless behind the deeply slate blue arras or veil that
backed the white one. It covered her head like a miniature
tent, held in place by a cloth chaplet of interwoven white
and slate. In her Sumese drover's robe of grayish, off-
white woolen homespun, the veiled lady was not quite
shapeless; she appeared to be either fat or with child.
True, others often scarf-muffled their lower faces against
the cold, but the point was that the veiled woman never,
never showed her face above the eyebrows and below her
large medium-hued eyes.

Naturally the caravanseers and her fellow pilgrims
wondered, and speculated, and opined and discussed. An
innocent child and a rude adult-or-nearly were actually so
crude as to ask her why she was hiding behind a veil and
all that loose robe.

"Oh my cute little dear," the veiled lady told the child,
cupping its plump dark cheek with a nice and quite
pretty hand, "it's the sun. It makes me break out all
in green warts. Wouldn't that be awful to have to look
at?"

No such touch accompanied the veiled lady's response
to the rude almost-woman who breached the bounds of
gentility and mannered decency by asking the same question.

"Pox," the veiled lady said tersely. The questioner,
while bereft of the sensitivity to blush or even apologize,
said no more. Eyes widening, she abruptly remembered
that her presence was required elsewhere.

(The first "explanation" was pooh-poohed, though not
directly to the veiled one; if that were so, a fellow pilgrim
wisely observed, then why were her hands not gloved, and
why were they so pretty—a lady's hands? The second
explanation was considerably more troubling. It was suspect, but who wanted to take a chance on catching some
pox or other? People began to keep their distance, just in
case.)

The big good-looking guard from Mrsevada was rude,
too, but in a different way. He knew what flashing those
good big teeth in that handsome face would get him. It
had got him plenty, and would again. Having assured his
comrades that he would soon bring them the answer, he
addressed her with cocky confidence.

"Whatcha hiding under all them robes and veil,
sweets?"

"A syphilitic face and a pregnant belly," the faceless
woman told him. "Want to visit me in my tent tonight?"

"Uh—I uh, no, I was just—"

"And what are *you* hiding behind that totally phony
smile, swordsman?"

He blinked and the dazzling smile faded away in
patches, like the dissipating of those fluffy white clouds
that signify nothing.

"You have a sharp tongue, pregnant and syphilitic."

"That," she told him, "is true. You can understand that
I don't like men with winning smiles . . ."

The handsome guardsman went away.

After that, no one asked her questions. Furthermore,
the guardsmen, her fellow travelers, and the caravanseers
not only left her alone, but indeed shunned the veiled
woman—who after all could surely be no lady . . . !

She had paid her way—the full charge, too—without
argument or complaint and with only the modicum of
dickering that showed her to be human, though not
arrogant. (Most nobles showed their arrogance either by

stating their own price and paying it—usually less than
what could be considered fair. Others at once paid what
was asked, so as to show that they were far too well off and
noble to dicker with mere clerks and caravan masters or
booking stewards.) She had brought her own water and
foodstuffs. She stayed to herself and caused no trouble,
while giving others something to talk about. She was no
trouble at all.

The tall caravan master, his gray-shot beard and easy
confidence reminders of his experience, did not believe
that she was syphilitic, or pocked, or sun-cursed, or
pregnant either. Nor did he view her as sinister merely
because she refused to show her face. Thus Caravan
Master Eliab was not pleasant to the little delegation
of three women and the prideless husband of one of
them, when they came to demand that the veiled *person*
reveal and identify herself on the grounds that she
was mysterious and therefore sinister and Frightening
The Children.

Master Eliab looked down upon them, literally and
figuratively. "Point out to me those children who are
affrighted of the Lady Saphtherabah," he said, making up
an impressive name for in truth she had signed on with
him simply as "Cleya," a name common in Suma, "and I
shall make them forget her by giving them something else
to be fearful of."

"Hmp. And what might that be, Caravan Master?"

"ME!" he bellowed, and he transformed his bushily
bearded face into a fearful scowl. At the same time he
swept out the curved sword from his worn paisley-
patterned sash. Curling his other hand into a claw, he
pounced at them.

He took only the one big lunging step, but the members
of the delegation took many. Squealing and worse, four
disunited individuals fled his company.

When Eliab arose next morning—with the sun, of
course—it was to find that the veiled lady had prepared
breakfast for him from her own stores and was calmly
sharpening her dagger.

"Thank you, Lady," the big caravan master said, with a
bow almost courtly.

"Thank *you,* Caravan Master."

"And will you join me in breaking the night's fasting
with this wonderful repast, Lady?"

"No, Caravan Master," she said, rising. "For I could not eat without showing you my face."

"I understand, Lady. And thank you again."

He made a respectful sign and watched her glide away, robe's hem on the ground and cloak whipping in the wind that blew worse than chilly, to her own tent. After that he assigned a man to pitch and strike that tent for her. Thus the delegation obtained some result, at that.

At last the cavalcade of humans, beasts, and trade goods reached the tired town called Sanctuary, and the veiled lady detached her three horses and went her way into the dusty old "city." The others saw her no more and soon she was completely out of their thoughts. Neither the big good-looking guard from Mrsevada nor Master Eliab ever forgot her, really, but she slipped easily from their minds, too. The former began flashing his smile and cutting a swath through the girls of Sanctuary, if not the women. As a matter of fact none of them had seen her and so never saw her again or knew if they did, for the veiled lady soon unveiled herself.

In this moribund town of thieves now ruled by weird starey-eyed people or "people" from oversea and un-succored by "protecting" and "Imperial" Ranke, it was easy for the veiled lady to employ a lackey for a few coins and a promise or two. Next she startled and nearly whelmed the poor wight by having him take her to his own home. Within that poorly heated hovel and amid much buzzing curiosity among the neighbors, she effected a change of clothing. That involved removal of all headgear and thus both veils. And that, when she emerged, elicited more buzz, even unto awe.

They were the first outside Suma to see the face and figure of her whose name was not Cleya or Saphtherabah, but Kaybe Jodeera.

She was blessed with beauty, true beauty. It was at once a blessing and a curse. Jodeera knew herself for a beauty. She admitted and understood and accepted the fact. She had learned that it was not a blessing, but a curse. She had lived long with it, and paid the price; several prices. One was that it was not wise for a woman so staggeringly well-favored to travel unaccompanied. Even with a protector and amid the whistling winds of winter, she might well have proven invitation to and source for trouble within the caravan. Jodeera knew this; she had long been beautiful and admitted and accepted it—as curse. Therefore she had chosen to conceal herself utterly. Better to be a source of speculation and gossip than of trouble! (She was neither pregnant nor obese, nor even "overweight," that delicate phrase for people of sedentary habits who were without restraint in the matter of food and drink.)

Furthermore, Jodeera and the sun were not enemies. She was not syphilitic. She was not even pocked.

She stepped forth from the house of her new lackey unveiled and clasping a long amethystine cloak over the azure-and-emerald gown of a lady, and she was breathtaking. She was radiance to challenge the sun; she was Beauty to challenge the goddess Eshi Herself.

And she was looking for a man. A particular man.

She and her lackey—his name was Wintsenay and he was best described as an overage street urchin—returned through town, saw a killing and pretended not to, two blocks farther along stepped carefully around another murder victim not yet cold, satisfactorily answered the questions of a Beysib who looked worse than nervous and ready to draw the sword on its or her back, and came at last to a fine inn. There they installed her.

Oh, but Jodeera turned heads in the White Swan! Nevertheless, she caused herself to be conducted at once to an available chamber, one with a good bed and a good lock on the door. Though many waited and watched and some of them entertained dreams and pleasant fantasies, she did not return to the common room. She remained in her own rented chamber. Her hireling Wintsenay slept before the door, armed, but nothing untoward befell her at the White Swan.

Word of her arrival in Sanctuary was abroad before she rose next day. Beautiful women did not come at all often to Sanctuary. Not even Hakiem could remember when last one had arrived here alone. Yet this time a *true* beauty had arrived, and alone, and she was a mystery. Having taken on a low and baseborn servant who was about ten minutes out of the downwind area of Downwind, she had given her name at the White Swan as Ahdioma of Aurvesh, and she was nigh incredible.

As for the lady herself . . . "See you this ring?" she asked of the White Swan's day-man, who was trying hard to gather up his lower lip so as to close his mouth while

staring at her. He remembered to nod and she said,
"When next you see it, it will be sent you, and you will
honor it, and my wishes."

He assured her that he would, indeed.

Taking no breakfast and seeming uninterested in the
chatter of last night's bloody PFLS activities, she went
forth into ratty Thieves' World of the creaking commerce
and cracking, peeled stucco and stones leaking their
mortar onto the streets and "streets." Its powder freighted
the wind that whistled along those streets, disarranging
cloaks and scarves while bearing the scent of death.

She was noticed wherever she went in damnèd Sanctuary. Hair of a dark red, the shining maroon of a rich old
wine. Large eyes that were perhaps hazel and perhaps
green—it depended upon the viewer, and where she was
standing with relation to the sun. A face in which the
bones were prominent and the mouth generous. (Some
few marked the absence of what passed for dimples and
later for creases and were truly smile-lines, and pounced
to the conclusion that, incredibly for one of her looks, she
had had no happy life.) A figure to turn dry the mouths of
men and never mind their ages. A lackey called Wints
whose face was washed and who strove to look mean while
keeping his hand on one of those dauntingly long Ilbarsi
"knives" thrust through a red-and-yellow sash worn over
his old brown cloak.

In the Bazaar she crossed a brown, clutching palm with
a small silver coin, and was allowed to adjourn to a
rearward chamber. She emerged with her hair caught in a
plain snood of dull old green. A veil of medium green
concealed her lower face. Displayed were ears pierced but
not bejeweled, which she knew was unattractive.

She tarried there, in that booth of a seer blindingly
dressed in multicolor, while the S'danzo's daughter and
the lackey Wints bore the ring back to the White Swan.
No, she did not care to be read by the S'danzo. Was the
kind S'danzo discreet?—*Yes.* Then did she perhaps know
of a certain man . . . And the newcomer, veiled again,
mentioned a name and then a description.

No, the S'danzo did not know him; perhaps a reading
might help?—*No, no reading;* there would be no Seeing
into the affairs of the veiled lady.

The S'danzo wisely said no more. She assumed that this
stranger either was so cautious as to want not even a

close-mouthed seer to know aught of her—or wished not to know more of herself and her future's possibilities and probabilities than she already did.

Wintsenay and the nine-year-old returned anon with the veiled lady's three horses. She dispatched them to arrange lodgings for her at the inn suggested by her new S'danzo friend.

She did not see him she sought, that day. Twice she must stop and show her face to members of the occupying force, but apparently she did not resemble whomever they sought. Two of their number had been slain last night. The word was murder, but Sanctuarites did not use it in connection with the deaths of the Beysa's minions.

She kept Wintsenay with her, calling him Wints, that he might not talk o'ermuch to his acquaintances and, if he had any, his friends. Obviously he was enjoying his rôle as well as the pay. Wints was quite willing to remain with her and comply with any of her wishes.

On the day following she wore a still different guise, and changed her lodgings yet again. Again, the inn was a good one. Having gained some knowledge of bankers, she left money and jewels with a man she felt she could trust. He also stabled her horses. She left with a receipt and a more secure feeling. That day, again, she looked more for him she sought.

In mid-afternoon on the fringe of the Bazaar, she saw him.

"Oh my," she said, from behind her lower-face veil of scarlet (and above her garish S'danzo garb, skirts and apron and blouse in seven colors and six hues), "whoever is that big man who just ordered crockery from your neighbor, there?"

"Ah, m'girl, that's Ahdio—Ahdiovizun, but it's Ahdio he's callt. Runs that hole, back in the Maze—Sly's Place, it's callt. You know. Big, ain't he!"

"Indeed," the veiled lady said softly, and went away.

"Well, I can't help that," the very big man said to the dealer. "You just tell Goatfoot what I said: When even *my* customers complain about his beer, it's *bad!* Thin as . . . well, if I find out he has a lot of cats over there, I'll be mighty suspicious about what he puts into his so-called prime ale!"

"That ain't nice, Ahdio. You want good stuff, whyn't you buy it then?"

"As you damned well know, Ak, I do. But not from Goatfoot! However, not all my patrons can afford the premium brew, and not all of them know the difference, anyhow. I serve maybe twenty to one of the stuff made by Goatfoot and Maeder. And based on the quality, I ought to be charging more for Maeder's Red Gold!"

"Or maybe less for Goatfoot's True Brew," Akarlain said, tilting his head to one side and doing his best to look clever. It was a strain.

"I'm willing to do that," Ahdio told him, "just as soon as you and Goatfoot get the keg price down to what it should be." He sighed and raised a silencing hand as the much smaller man started to reply. "That's all right, that's all right. I'll need thirteen more kegs tomorrow, and don't forget what I told you to tell Goatfoot. And that I'm looking for another brewer. My customers may be scum, but they've got rights!"

Ahdio, his face open and showing no menace, held eye contact with Akarlain for a long moment before he turned away. He moved on to another merchant's kiosk in the ever-noisy open market. Face working, Ak watched him. How was it that such a genuinely bigger than big man moved so easily in a gait that no one could ever describe as "lumbering"? He was almost graceful! And so lucky, Ak mused with a shiver; Ahdio seemed not to notice the cold although he was not wearing nearly as much clothing as most others. *Like to have me a wife that generated that much heat,* Akarlain thought, and with a sigh he turned to enter Ahdio's order on the slate headed **G-Foot.**

Ahdio stopped at a fold-down counter under a sheltering awning of bright green and faded yellow. After doubling his order for the sausages in brine he had tried out on consignment, he complimented their creator.

"They loved them, Ivalia. Helped sell more beer, too! My customers loved those special sausages of yours—and so did I!" Abruptly the big man laughed a big man's laugh. "Not my cat, though. Should've seen him wrinkle his nose and shake his head when he started to settle into a nice sausage meal and smelled that brine! Could've heard his ears rattle two buildings away!"

"Ohh, poor pussy cat," Ivalia said, interrupting her delighted marking down of his order to look up with a

sympathetic expression. "What a mean shock for a cat
. . . well, here! You take this to that poor disappointed
kitty of yours, Ahdio, with my compliments."

"Mighty nice of you, Ivalia," Ahdio said, accepting the
brown-wrapped package she hurriedly prepared and prof-
fered. It looked strangely smaller, once it was transferred
from her hand to his huge one.

Someone passing behind Ahdio bumped him. Ahdio
showed no hint of taking offense as his size would have
allowed; he merely dropped a hand to the wallet at his
belt. It was still there. The bump must have been a
genuine one, then—not that it would have mattered
much. He kept only three coppers, two sharply jagged bits
of rusty steel, and a few pebbles in that leathern bag. His
money was in a pocket-purse sewn inside the down-filled
vest he wore in lieu of coat or winter cloak. Still, he was
not anxious to lose what he thought of as the Fool's Purse
at his belt; he'd just have to raise a great fuss and try to
chase down the thief . . . and of course replace the thing
with another cheap bag of goatskin.

"Mighty nice order you just gave me, Ahdio," Ivalia
was saying with a smile. "Mighty nice doing business with
you—and gracious, I had no idea you were a cat person,
too! That makes it all the better."

The disposition of an angel, Ivalia had—a red-faced
angel—and arms like a cooper's. Everything about her
was round and healthy and on the large side, positively
brimming and glowing ruddy with health. Everything
except her nose and her chest, he thought, a little wistfully; both were as flat as a fallen pie. Still . . . a man did get
lonely and thought now and again of a real woman, a
companion rather than merely some one-night wench.
And in this gods-forsaken town to which he had exiled
himself. . . . Ahdio smiled at her. That showed as a
crinkling of his eyes and a writhing of his winter beard; he
stopped shaving every year in autumn and removed the
whole growth again a few months later when real heat
started to set in. Just now the beard was not long, but
already obscured most of his face.

"What's your kittycat's name, Ahdio?" she asked,
practically burbling, beaming at him.

Ahdio looked a bit embarrassed, pushed a finger up into
his brown-pepper-and-salt beard, and scratched. "I, ah,
named him Sweetboy," he admitted.

The round-faced sausagemaker clapped her hands. "How sweet! My kittycats are named Cinnamon, and Topaz, and Micklety, and Kadakithis, wasn't that naughty of me?—and Chase (that's short for Chase-mouser) and Pan-pie, and Hakiem, and Babyface, and—oh, pardon me; yes, what would you like?"

That to the new customer who had come to the unwitting rescue of Ahdio, whose expression of shock had increased with each new cat Ivalia listed—and without showing signs of running out of either names or cats anytime soon.

"Try one of her pickled sausages," Ahdio said to the newcomer. "And remember it was Ahdio who told you. Stop in at my tavern—Sly's Place near Wrong Way Park. First beer's on me."

He waved a hand in friendly farewell to Ivalia and departed. Thus he did not see the look her prospective customer gave her, or hear him mutter, *Sly's Place!* Theba's eyeballs . . . I'd as soon slit my throat as go near that dive!"

Ivalia leaned on her counter, face in hands, and gave him a nice smile. "Why don't you, then?"

Bulkily visible with his broad back emphasized by the vest of tired red, Ahdio wended his way out of the Bazaar, returning greetings, stopping to say a few words to this or that merchant and a couple of Stepsons with ever-wary eyes. His words to the beautifully-dressed noble Shafralain went unanswered and Ahdio grinned. He just managed not to wink at an armed but not particularly mean-looking Bey, and headed for home.

Home was upstairs over the dive called Sly's Place, well back in that most unsavory and unsafe district of Sanctuary called the Maze. Today he had gone to the street called Path of Money early, to put away some of last night's income. He never visited his banker at the same time on two days within any week, so as not to be predictable. Sanctuary was that kind of town. It was a goodly walk, too. When he bore money out of Sly's, he got out of the Maze as fast as he could, and to hell with shortcuts. He stepped directly out onto the Street of Odors—also called Stink Street and Perfume Boulevard, with the tanners and charnel houses right there—and walked north to Straight Street. Once it crossed the Processional, it jogged a little and became the Path of Money. There bankers and lenders and changers lurked, and some were even honest. It was Ahdio's belief and hope that his was.

Then it was back to the Bazaar and/or Farmer's Market, by some route or other; he was a known walker who attracted little attention from the divviers and "guardians" of this or that section of town. Stepsons competent and in-, or 3rd Commando members, or the dangerous usually-youths of the PFLS—"Piffles," some were pronouncing it—or sword-backed Beysibs, forced by the weather to cloak the bare breasts they apparently loved to flaunt, painted. He gave them little attention in return, speaking when they were obviously not supposed to be concealed, and pretending not to see them when they were.

Ahdio assumed that he was one of the very few in the Maze who had made a deal with the 3rd Commando Unit of Ranke. After all, it was in his back room that Kama of the 3rd C. and Zip of PFLS had met with Hanse, for the purpose of persuading that thief called Shadowspawn to break into the Palace. Oh, Ahdio knew that, now; Kama had been back and they were friends—make that "on friendly terms."

Not infrequently he stopped at a better inn just to take note of it and its clientele and enjoy a measure or two served by someone else. Then it was back to his residence and place of business, which was sort of sphinctered in the improbable three-way intersection where the Serpentine sort of extruded Tanner Lane as it slithered by, at the place where Odd Birt's Cross became Odd Birt's Dodge.

The lowest dive in the lowest of towns, some called Sly's Place.

Ahdiovizun called it home. He also called it never dull and always fascinating, even inspiring. (Sly was a man dead these three years, but who wanted to change the name and take credit for the skungiest and most fight-prone watering-hole in all Thieves' World? In consequence, no one was sure just who did own it. True, Sly's widow seemed not to be hurting any for finances, but certainly she never came near the place, and no one ever reported having seen Ahdio or his helper Throde go to her home.)

Since today he had settled a few bills with last night's

receipts, he had not gone over to the Path of Money at all. Thus he extended his walk by taking the longer way around from the Bazaar. When he entered the Maze from the north, onto the Serpentine, nature had been calling for several minutes. With a little smile he decided to avail himself of the little cul-de-sac variously called Tick's Vomitorium, or Safehaven, or more descriptively: The Outhouse. Even in the ever-present shadows, the lower walls of all three buildings abutting on Safehaven were stained dark. The area, a squared horseshoe, reeked of urine and worse. The Vulgar Unicorn was just around the corner and many a patron had come hurrying into just this odd little shelter to relieve his bladder or his stomach or both. (This was the reason Ahdio had been known to refer jocularly to the place as the Vulgar Unicorn Annex.)

He was just contentedly spraying the eastward wall when a slight sound behind him was followed quickly by a swift, jerky pressure at his side, a shade forward of the kidney. The pressure-point was tiny, and Ahdio recognized the touch of a knife's tip.

"Uh," he said, and splashed his thick-soled walking buskin. "Damn."

"All right," a voice snarled in an obvious attempt both to sound dangerous and to disguise itself, "let's have yer purse, bigun." The pressure remained at Ahdio's side.

"I'll give you this," Ahdio said without turning, "you're light on your feet and may amount to a real thief someday. But I think you have me confused with someone else—I'm Ahdio."

"Ah—*Ahdi*—"

"Probably couldn't recognize me in the dark, here. You know: Ahdiovizun, the great big mean and cantankerous proprietor of Sly's Place, who always wears . . ."

"A mailcoat!" the snarler snarled loudly, and the pressure of his knifepoint instantly left Ahdiovizun's person. The would-be thief was not nearly as quiet departing in haste as he had been at stalking.

Ahdio let go a goodly sigh and restored his clothing. Having deliberately given the thief opportunity to escape unseen, he turned slowly and paced out of the Maze's public convenience. He felt around at his rearward side with a big hand that had gone a bit sweaty.

Good. The little idiot didn't prick my vest. Hate to start leaking goose feathers. Glad he was too scared and stupid to run a test by leaning on that sticker . . . what sort of glutton for punishment would I have to be to wear my mailcoat all day, just walkin' around town?

Still, he would not claim even to himself not to be unnerved. *With the whole town gettin' to be as dangerous as the Maze, maybe I should!*

He wiped wet hands on his leggings, and considered dropping in at the Vulg for a short one. No, he'd just stay away from that place; it was no trick to spot the two Beysibs, so very casually hanging about across the "street," keeping an eye on a dive to which Ahdio felt Sly's was eminently superior. Doubtless a PFLSer or two would be about, too, keeping an eye or four on the Stare-Eyes. He'd just head on home and drink his own, with Sweetboy for company.

He followed the Serpentine on down and around onto Tanner. With a casual wave at the enormous (and teetotaling) bodyguard of Alamanthis, the physician located conveniently across the street from Sly's and prospering accordingly, Ahdio went around back. He whacked the door a couple of times while he whistled a few notes, to avoid a misunderstanding with Sweetboy, and slipped the first of two keys into the smaller lock. Then the other one, and he entered. He dropped the big bar across the door behind him.

"Hey, you mangy furbag, daddy's home!"

"Mrarr," Sweetboy said in what was almost a travesty of a cat's customary sound, and meandered over. Ahdio stood still long enough to let the black, mange-free animal sinuously whack its left flank against his buskin and pace back and forth a few times, rubbing, getting rid of some excess fur while saying Hello Good To See You My Bowl's Empty.

"Just had a bit of a scare, Sweetboy. Let's have a drink."

Sweetboy made a profoundly enthusiastic remark and lost all dignity in industriously rubbing both Ahdio's legs while the big man lighted an oil-lamp. Moving to a table on which rested a small keg, he twisted out the bung: This was good Maeder's brew he had re-bunged last night after close of business. He had done a good job of it, too, he saw when he poured: Head foamed up high and rich.

Ahdio bent and gave himself a white mustache to keep it from flowing over, then set it aside while he drew another cup.

Watching, Sweetboy reared up to clap both paws to the table-leg and stretch, meanwhile purring loud enough to vibrate the table.

"Uh-huh. Soon's the head settles down. True beer-lovers know you need to raise the foam and wait for it to lapse, Sweetboy ole Tige. Remember that."

The cat, jet with an odd strawberry- or heart-shaped white patch on its face and one white paw, made an urgent remark.

Picking up the first cup, Ahdio squatted to the floor beside a cut-down mug of wide diameter, with a handle. "Wait," he said, in a particular voice, and poured Red Gold into the cat's bowl. Sweetboy waited, staring, saying nothing but expressing his impatience with a lashing of the stub of his tail.

That sight was disconcerting to everyone but Ahdio. Any cat expressed itself or at least acknowledged noises or its name with movements of its tail, often merely the tip. A tailless cat, if not a cripple, was at least the equivalent of a human with a severe lisp. Sweetboy, however, seemed unaware of his lack and expressively moved what he had. He even managed to make it obvious when he was not just moving the thumb-length stub, but lashing it. Now he peered at his bowl under a thigh the thickness of a trim man's waist. It moved, straightened.

"Drink up, Tige," Ahdio said, and turned to his own mug. By the time he lifted it to his lips, his beer-loving cat was sounding more canine than feline in its enthusiastic lapping. Hip against the table and one elbow on the keg, Ahdio quaffed his beer while watching Sweetboy put away his. The big man's face wore an indulgent smile. It faded, and he sighed.

The hard part was the disappearance of Sweetboy's former companion and fellow watch-cat, Notable. Both Ahdio and Sweetboy missed the big red cat. First Hanse had popped in late one afternoon and just *had* to borrow him; then, even while Ahdio was trying to explain that Notable was a one-man cat, the damned traitor had come in all high-tailed and started in rubbing Shadowspawn as if the cocky thief were his favoritest person in the whole world. So off went large watch-cat with smallish thief, and into the governor's palace and out. And Hanse had brought Notable back, too, bragging on his loyalty and valor—and loud voice. That was right before Hanse had left town, in a hurry. Apparently he had taken with him the eldest daughter of the murdered S'danzo, Moonflower.

Next morning, Notable was gone, too. Just short of frantic, Ahdio searched and asked; put out the word. Notable was gone without a trace. At least it was hard to imagine such a fighter's having been snatched and used to fill someone's hungry belly. Ahdio swallowed hard, then turned up his mug.

"I hope he's with Hanse," he muttered, lowering the emptied cup, and Sweetboy gave his abbreviated tail a twitch in acknowledgment. "But if he is and they ever come back to Sanctuary, I'm going to pin back all four of their ears!"

With another sigh, Ahdio decided to have another before he fixed himself something to eat and joined Throde in preparing to open up for tonight's business in the lowest dive in Sanctuary. He had no idea that it would be one of the very most eventful nights ever.

He was just finishing his early dinner—he'd snack while he worked and enjoy a late supper while counting tonight's take—when he heard Throde at the door. He hurried to lift the bar and let in his lean and wiry assistant. The youth entered, thump-*clump* thump-*clump*. Neither ugly nor handsome, he was known to some as Throde the Gimp, and now and again a customer tried calling "Hey Gimp!" or "Gimpy—over here" when he wanted service. Throde, with more encouragement from Ahdio than mere approval, did not respond in any way. (He did respond to calls of "Boy" or "Waiter" or "Hey you!") If a newcomer chose to take offense and become surly despite being advised by a fellow patron of Throde's name and humanity, Ahdio was always ready to prevent any violence on his assistant. Sometimes they even came back, those he graphically warned and cooled by throwing out.

Enveloped in big brown cloak from crown to instep, the youth leaned his staff against the wall; a shade under an inch and a half in diameter, the inflexible rod was six feet long, five inches longer than its owner.

"'Lo, Ahdio. Hey, Sweetboy."

He unclasped and twisted out of the hairy cloak that looked nigh big enough for Ahdio, except in length. As usual, Throde's brown hair came out of the cloak's hood mussed in six or nine directions. He carried the garment over to hook it on one of the pegs just inside the door, on the wall opposite the eight or so untapped tuns of beer. He turned back to Ahdio, left hand pushing his hair up off his forehead above the left eye in a gesture Ahdio had seen a thousand times or more. His smooth face was long and bony, and his lean body gave that appearance. Ahdio knew that was a bit deceptive; wiry and rangy, Throde had good musculature. Even his bad leg looked strong, though Ahdio had seen his helper only once without leggings, even back in high summer. He introduced Throde as his cousin's son, from Twand. Ahdiovizun was not from Twand. Neither was Throde.

"Ah. New tunic?"

Throde blinked and little twitches in his face hinted at a smile. He looked down at the garment, which was medium green with a wave-imitating border at neck and hem, in dark brown. Ahdio recognized that gesture, too; Throde wasn't studying the tunic, he was ducking his head. The lad was shy, and just a shade more gregarious than his walking stick.

He nodded. "Yes."

"Good for you. Good-looking tunic, too. Going to have to think about a new belt for that one, to do it justice. Buy it in the Bazaar?"

Throde shook his head. "Country Market. Bought it off a woman who made it for her son."

"Oh," Ahdio said, and as usual tried to force his helper into something approaching conversation. "Didn't he like it? Sure doesn't look worn."

"Was a present for him. Never been worn." Throde was looking at the cat, which had assumed a ridiculous sitting position with one hind leg straight up while it licked its genitals. "You'll go blind, Sweetboy."

"Lucky you," Ahdio said, and kept trying: "Bet you got a good price on it. Her boy didn't like it?"

"Never saw it. Took a fever on the first cold night. He died."

"Oh. Listen, I was a little nervous about you when you left last night. No trouble going home?"

Throde shook his head. "I better get set up."

"No trouble at all? Didn't see those three meanheads?"

Shaking his head, Throde went through the door into the taproom—the inn proper. Ahdio sighed.

"Sure nice to have company," he muttered, and Sweetboy looked up and belched. Ahdio gave him a look. "Here! Cats do *not* belch, Tige. Maybe you should consider giving up strong drink."

The final word brought the cat to attention, and to its mug. It peered within as if myopic, looked pointedly up at its human, twitched its stub and said "Mraw?"

"No," Ahdio said, and Sweetboy showed him an affronted look before it slithered in between a couple of barrels to sulk.

Accommodatingly, Ahdio let those tuns sit and picked up another to carry into the other room. He handled it as if it weighed about half what it weighed. Throde was arranging benches and stools, squatting to rearrange the sliver of wood that for three months had "temporarily" steadied the table with the bad leg.

"Maybe tonight we ought to turn that damned table up and slap a nail up through that hunk of wood into the leg," Ahdio said, his voice only a little strained. He set the barrel down behind the bar, without banging it.

"Not thisun," Throde said. "The wood'd split out."

"Uh," Ahdio said, thinking about last night's trouble.

The arising of trouble in Sly's Place was hardly noteworthy. Patrons who came to push and shove or worse either settled down, or helped clean up and pay for damage, or were told not to come back. Now and again Ahdio relented. But when sharp steel flashed he moved in fast with a glove and a club. Both were armored. Such things happened, and usually he stopped it without a blow and before someone got stuck. Not always. What he would not tolerate was yellers and plain bullies. That big one last night had been both. Ahdio warned him. Others warned him. Eventually Ahdio had felt compelled to pick up the big drunken troublemaker by the nape, just the way he'd have picked up a kitten. In sudden silence from patrons once again impressed by his strength, he carried the loosely wriggling fellow over to the door and deposited him outside, without roughness. He returned to applause and upraised mugs, smiling a little and never glancing back; he knew that if the ejected one came back in behind him, other patrons would call a warning.

Two men, however, stood staring in manner unfriendly. Ahdio stopped and returned the gaze.

"You boys his buddies?"

"Right."

"Yes. Narvy didn't mean no harm."

"Probably not," Ahdio said equably. "Just drank too much, too fast and wouldn't take anything to eat. You boys want a sausage and a beer, or you think you ought to help him . . . Narvy . . . home?"

The two of them stared at him in silence, mean-faced, and the taverner stared back with his usual open, large-eyed expression. After a time they looked at each other. The handsome one shrugged. The balding one shrugged. They sat down again.

"Couple of sausages and beers coming up," Ahdio said, and that was that.

Still, he had worried that they or perhaps all three might decide to take out their mad on Throde, and Ahdio warned the youth, who walked home every night alone. They had made it well known that he carried no money but did bear a big stick. On the other hand, he *needed* that staff because he had a gimped leg. Now his employer was more than glad that his apprehension had been for nothing.

He was heading back to the storeroom when he heard the banging sound back there. Sweetboy didn't make banging sounds, particularly when he was napping.

That was when it hit Ahdio that he and Throde had both forgotten to replace the bar across the outer door. Some godless motherless meanhead had just walked in for sure, he thought, already racing that way. He was bulling through the door when he heard the screams: two. A man's, and a cat's. Not just any cat's. It was Sweetboy's war-cry. He had never achieved the volume of Notable, but he could sure raise hell, nape-hair and heartbeats. The pair of yowling sounds were followed by a much louder banging than the first. And a yell that was positively a shriek.

From the doorway Ahdio glimpsed it all at once. The balding man and his big ejected pal Narvy, from last night, were in the act of removing a barrel marked with the hoofprint of a goat branded in black; the scream-trailing black streak was a watch-cat earning its keep. The cat landed acrouch on the barrel between them, having in passing opened the balding man's sleeve without even trying. It hissed, whipping its stub back and forth, and uncoiled to hit Narvy's big chest. Narvy's friend yelled when he felt his arm hit; when he saw the demonic apparition appear as if by ghastly sorcery right on the barrel he was so happily stealing, he let go his end.

It was his friend Narvy who let out the high-voiced shriek; the impact of the hurtling cat was bad enough, but the feel of all those claws puncturing his chest through two layers of blue linsey-woolsey was a lot worse. Besides, Sweetboy wasn't just *there;* he was climbing, and that evilly fanged face was terribly close to Narvy's own. Naturally he too let go the tun of beer, to get both arms in front of his face. Since his friend had already let go, the barrel swung in as it dropped, and got Narvy's shin and one foot. He positively bellowed. Besides, the carefully misnamed Sweetboy, intent on reaching his face, was busily trying to chew his way through Narvy's sleeved arm. Narvy's throat erupted more noise.

His friend caught a glimpse of the big taverner coming through the doorway he absolutely filled, and the balding man whirled to exit by the outer door at a speed that would have brought him in at least second in a seven-horse race. Narvy kept on screaming.

"Damn," Ahdio said. "I told you last night you were a noisy beerhead, and damned if you aren't even noisier by day and sober-I-guess. Now look what you've done! You've disturbed that poor pussy's nap and got him all angry."

Narvy was flailing both arms, to one of which clung a chomping cat anchored by twenty or so claws and an unknown number of needly teeth.

"Get him offf meee!" poor Narvy shrieked.

"Are you daft or jesting, man? I'm not wearing mailed gloves!"

Screaming enough for six, Narvy wheeled and limp-dashed out the open doorway in the wake of his friend— who was already out of sight.

"Sweetboy! Let's have a *drink!*"

Sweetboy opened his mouth, retracted all claws, hit the

ground facing the rear door of Sly's Place (drooling a
shred of red-smeared blue fabric), and became a blur
again until he was standing at his bowl. Finding it empty,
he glanced accusingly around and up. He was also licking
at the blood on his mouth.

"Goo-ood boy, goo-ood kitty," Ahdio crooned, using
his foot to roll the barrel aside. It was intact and pleasantly
sloshy.

He drew two cups of beer and unwrapped the brineless
sausage Ivalia had given him. Sweetboy watched as if
entranced, ears on the move. Ahdio had treacherously
saved back the six-inch length of sausage about the
thickness of Throde's staff. Now the big man gave it to
Sweetboy all at once, as reward. Along with a full
mug-bowl.

Sweetboy immediately proved that he was a cat who
loved beer, not an alcoholic. He flicked his ears at the
bowl, made a small appreciative remark, and went for the
meat.

"What happened?" That from Throde, in the doorway
with broom in hand. He held it in the manner of a
spearman awaiting the command to charge.

"You and I both left the door unbarred and let two
cess-heads disturb this nice li'l kittycat's nap, that's what!"

"Oh, gredge," Throde muttered, staring downward.
"'m sorry, Ahdio."

"No harm done. If those two don't talk about it, let's be
sure the story gets around." Eyes twinkling, Ahdio
hoisted his mug.

"Uh . . . what if they spread it that you keep a *demon*
back here?"

"So? In Sanctuary? Who'd care?" his grinning employer
rhetorically asked. "Demons and vampires and dead gods
and living goddesses involved in street-fights . . . a demon
in the back room of Sly's Place seems perfectly normal to
me! What do you think, Sweetboy?"

Sweetboy thought the sausage was just lovely and that it
was time for a swig or three of beer.

• • •

When the veiled lady came into Sly's Place, it was
three-quarters full and altogether noisy. Also, predictably, male. Nor did any of their attire reflect wealth,
nobility, or the military. Oh, of course they wore daggers,

that standard utensil for eating, among other uses. She
saw three other females, all of whom looked as if they
belonged here. The one in her teens wore a sort of skirt
the color of new gold that was slit on both sides to the belt,
and a black singlet that looked as if it had been stitched
onto her. Her hair matched the skirt, despite her black
eyes and brows, and three bangles chimed on each wrist.
The oldest of the three sat against the wall with a bald and
white-bearded man. He was presumably her husband,
since they were saying nothing to each other. The third
was a blowze of perhaps thirty who wore a low-necked
white blouse that displayed a great deal of her pair of
highly mobile head-sized breasts. Her skirt was heel-
length, unslit, and wildly striped. Her voice was just as
loud.

Among the tables and stools moved a thin young man in
a nice green tunic and waist-apron over fawn-colored
leggings. He had a tray, a towel, a shock of unruly brown
hair, and a limp.

The advent of the veiled lady through the curtain of
colored Syrese rope attracted attention, naturally; there
was, after all, the veil, in addition to her hooded emerald
cloak of obviously good cloth and weave. She was,
however, escorted. Someone recognized him and called
out with a wave. Wintsenay, self-consciously *with* Jodeera,
barely nodded acknowledgment. The newcomers stood
where they were, on the entry platform a step above the
room.

The veiled lady paid no mind to any of them. Her eyes,
as invisible below the hood's shadow as her face behind
the quietly colored paisley veil, followed only the movements of the big man in the coat of scintillant, softly
jingling chain mail. He set down a double handful of mugs
and slipped some coins into his apron before following the
gazes of those he served. His brows rose at the sight of the
two. He glanced around, raised a hand, and both looked
and pointed to his left. He saw the man and the hooded
and veiled woman look at the table he indicated, at the
wall; saw the man look questioningly at her. The hood
nodded. Perhaps she said something. Without uncloaking,
they descended the step and moved to the table Ahdio
indicated.

She was in charge, Ahdio noted immediately. The man

was her servant or bodyguard, then. He caught Throde's eye, indicated a table of empty cups, and headed for the new arrivals.

"Welcome to Sly's Place, my lady; sir. I am Ahdio and, yes, this is a real chain-coat. What would you like?"

"Your best wine for milady; your better beer for me," Wints said.

Ahdio knew that she had told her escort what to order; he was not to be privileged to hear her voice in addition to seeing no glimpse of her face, then. The point was, what in the name of the Shadowy One was she doing here? While her retention of her hooded cloak along with the veil attracted attention just because others wondered what she was hiding, he hoped she kept both in place. Just the presence of a woman of quality here in Sly's was enough to touch off trouble from some of these jackasses. If she happened to be well-favored behind the veil, and shapely within her doubtless expensive and fashionable attire, he might well need Sweetboy's aid!

Ouleh jiggled over while he poured qualis into a nice cup and was about to turn to Maeder's Better True Brew, which Maeder identified with a blue **MB** on the barrel. She leaned across the bar to give Ahdio a high-eyebrowed look.

"Hai, Ahdio ole handsome . . . who's the one in the veil and hood, hmmm?"

"Get your things off the bar," he said, grinning, and she chuckled dutifully at their old joke. Instead she ground herself down on it, wagging her shoulders, so that the things he mentioned were pushed above her low blouse in great outrounding moonshapes to her collarbones. He leaned toward her conspiratorially, keeping his gaze on her face.

"My cousin from Twand," he said quietly. "For all the gods' sakes and mine, don't ask her about her face or twit her either."

"That ugly, huh?"

"I can't answer that, Ouleh. Just be good and tell your friends, all right?"

"Me? Be good? Oh, *Ahdio!* Qualis and Red Gold 'stead of True Blue Brew for them, hmmm? Didn't know you had moneyed relatives, bigun, in Twand or anyplace else." She flashed him a teasing smile; Ouleh was good at that. "I've got me an idea that we're being treated to a visit by the mysterious Veiled Lady just everybody's talking about! Your *cousin,* Ahdio?''

Ahdio gazed at her, blinking. *The mysterious veiled lady everyone was talking about?* In that case, why hadn't he heard about her? True, it seemed not the sort of gossip that interested his patrons. They tended to talk about their work, to damn anyone with authority or wealth, to talk about who was doing what with and to whom, and who was going to get into whom, how and when, and who was going to get into Ouleh next. He glanced past her at the two newcomers over there, waiting for him to bring their order. His patrons' favorite breasty blowze had just described her, all right: a mysterious veiled lady. On the other hand, within and under cloak and hood and veil she might as well be Ouleh or any other easygirl.

No; not with the aura he felt about her; she even moved—even *sat* with class.

"Just be good, Man-killer. Or be bad as usual, but leave her alone; physically and with that mouth of yours." Hearing how harsh that sounded, he smiled and added, "Please. Tell you what. Anyone who gives her or her escort trouble is out of here on his tailbone."

It was Ouleh's turn to blink, in surprise. "*Es*-cort! That's *Wints,* bigun. He's no escort—not for the likes of *her.* Bodyguard, maybe. Lackey. Someone she found to guide her in what she's doing—slumming. I'll spread your word, bigun—for you," she said, glancing back at many men at many tables. "But others're going to think she's slumming, and that Wints is putting on airs, and there's likely to be trouble."

"Anyone starts any trouble tonight, Ouleh, it's going to be me who ends it."

She gave him a lazy grin, again leaning forward onto the bar to show him a pair of pale mountains and the deep dark canyon dividing them. "Isn't it always, big boy? All I'm sayin' is that it may happen anyhow."

He sighed. Not sure why, he said, "Ouleh—keep a secret?"

"Me? Betray a confidence? Cross my treasure chest and hope to die!" Her finger slid down one mountain and into the valley, up the other slope, and back in a necessarily large X. Ahdio immediately looked ceilingward. "What's the matter, Ah-dio? Can't look? Want me to start wearing loose robes to the chin?"

I'd have fewer fights and shouting matches if you did, he
mused, but said, "Just looking for the thunderbolt, after
that oath of yours. Anyhow. First, here. You take this cup
of qualis, on ole Ahdio. Second: Spread the word as I
said. Third, and this is the secret now, Man-killer: The
reason is that's my . . . lady. She just came here to see
me. You can understand that I have to watch out for her.
Here's your wine, dear. Start helping me out, all right?''

"Ohh, Ahdio! Reeeeally? Your la—oh, Ahdio, you
devil! And here I've had my cap set on you for years!"

*Why am I doing this for some slumming stranger who
may well be a Bey, come to spy on us with an Ilsigi sell-out,*
he demanded of himself, and said, "Sure, sure you have.
You don't even have a cap."

She gripped the nice goblet with one hand and the rim
of her bodice with the other. "No? What d'you call this?"
She whipped the blouse down below the salient of her
leftward mountain, held it there for two or three beats,
and flipped it up over her nipple again. Then she swung
away, laughing.

Briefly closing his eyes while he shook his head, Ahdio
filled another goblet with that best of wines and topped off
the mug for Wints, the head having subsided. He headed
for the table against the wall, his scintillant coat jingling
softly. Just as he passed a regular named or rather called
Weasel, Ahdio heard his loud conversation topper: "In a
pig's ass!"

"Someone call for my special sausage?" Ahdio called *en
passant,* and went on, ahead of a wake of laughter.

He set wine and beer before the strange couple, and
noted the coins on the table. He smiled at the invisible
face that, judging from the angle of the hood, seemed to
be looking up at him. "In this place, those who put coins
on the table are running a tab. Unless you think you're
just going to have one and run." There. That would get a
few words from the woman who had eased coin onto the
table while no one was looking.

Wrong. Wints looked at his companion/employer a
moment, then up at the huge man looming over their table
and occluding an immoderate number of tables. "Thanks,
taverner. We'll be here awhile. My lady would like to
know why you wear that chain-coat."

Ahdio shook his arm to emphasize the jing-jing of the
mail that covered him from collarbone to wristbone and to

a point just below his loins. "For effect," he said with an easy smile. "Ambience? A conversation piece. A little added color in a place I can't afford to fancy up much."

Wints glanced at the veiled lady and gave the taverner a knowing grin. "With the price of a coat of good butted chainmail being what it is? You sure that's the reason?"

Ahdio shrugged, jing-jing. "Maybe I wear it for the same reason a soldier does in battle. This is a tough dive with me as proprietor, bartender and bouncer. Maybe I'd be dead or full of scars by now if I didn't wear these forty-seven pounds of linked steel."

Wints's grin broadened and just as he started to laugh, Ahdio heard the first sound from the man's companion: a nascent chuckle swiftly drowned by his full laugh.

"Hey, Ahdio, you still sellin' ale around here?"

Ahdio swung away from the strangers. "Ale! In this place? Glayph, you wouldn't know ale if I poured some in your ear! Want another mug of junk beer?"

"Junk beer's right," another man said, as Ahdio moved that way. "Is it true you've got that beer-drinkin' demon-cat you keep back there trained to take his leaks in the kegs?"

"No," Ahdio said with an easy grin, "just in the qualis." When the laughter subsided, he made his face serious and added, "But I'll tell you this. I accused my brewer of that, just this afternoon. I also put him on notice that I'm lookin' around for another supplier. I am. All right, how many?"

"Two for me; I just got here. Is it true that's your girl over there, Ahdio, all bundled up?"

"My cousin Phlegmy brews good brew, Ahdy!"

"Girl! I'm too old for girls, two-beers. You think I put this gray in my beard with chalk? Now who's been blabbing that I have a secret lady who dropped in tonight to watch me work?" *It worked,* he thought. *Good old Ouleh—all you have to do is ask her to keep a secret and it's the same as hiring thirty boys to shout the news!*

Laughter and shouts followed him to the bar, and he made sure that he gave Ouleh a scowl. She bit her lip in the manner of a chastised child. While sitting on Tervy's knee with her hand inside the shirt of Frax, *former* palace guardsman. Someone reached out and yanked at the hem of Throde's tunic, in back. Throde reeled and his tray tipped. A mug dropped off into someone's lap. That

someone cursed and came up fast, drawing back a fist.
One moment he was looking at Throde's whimpery face
saying "Oh, oh, I'm sorry" while his peripheral hearing
reported the steel-jingle sound of a battlefield; the next he
was staring at Ahdio's chest and it was too late to arrest his
swing.

His fist slammed into quintuply-linked chain that
seemed to be backed by a wall of stone.

"Yaaowww!"

"You don't want to go hittin' my cousin's boy Throde,
friend," the chainmailed stone wall said, while the subject
of his pleasant-voiced address danced and clutched his
wounded fist. Tears welled out of his eyes. "It wasn't his
fault—somebody grabbed his tunic from behind and don't
ask who. Besides, that mug didn't hurt your jewels or
you'd never uv got up so fast. Sit down now and I'll bring
you a full one."

"You big—that really *is* chain! I'm *hurt!*"

Ahdio lifted his hand between them and doubled it into
a fist the size of an infant's head. "What hurts?"

"My . . . f . . ." The fellow trailed off. Staring at the
fist and glancing at his considerably smaller one, he sank
slowly down into his chair.

"That'll teach ya, Tarkle," one of the injured man's
tablemates said.

Having hurt his knuckles and arm and been backed
down, Tarkle was happy to snarl and reach for that
man—with his uninjured hand. That fast, an enormous fist
came down onto the table between them with a bang.
Unable to stop his movement, Tarkle rammed his outstretched hand into the knuckles and stove up three
fingers. He repeated his previous yaow.

Ahdio said only, "Now damn it—"

Lots of eyes watched while the table's complement sat
in silence, with Ahdio bending over it and his fist resting in
place. Slowly he straightened.

"Easy now, Tarkle, that beer's coming right up," he
said, and turned to continue barward.

"Ahdio!" a female voice screamed. *"Look out!"*

At the same time as he reacted by hunching his shoulders and pushing his chin into his chest, Ahdio glanced in
the direction of the cry. He saw the veiled lady, on her feet
and pointing. Meanwhile he was pivoting, spinning, one
tree-branch arm straight out from his body.

Fortunately only one man was on his feet behind him: Ahdio's forearm whacked into the side of Tarkle's neck. Tarkle went sideways over his own chair and onto his table. Its other occupants vacated their chairs with admirable speed even while Tarkle's wrist banged down on the table's edge. His knife vacated his fist. Throde's foot was on it before Tarkle's head whacked the table and bounced. While he was still disconcerted and seeing bright lights before his eyes, a huge hand closed on the back of his neck and hoisted him onto his feet. Never mind his watery legs; Ahdio walked him to the door. Along the way his other hand dropped to come up with another man.

"Gawk! Here! I didn't do nothin'!"

"Sure you did," Ahdio advised him in an equable voice. "You started this hothead off by yanking the hem of my cousin's boy's brand-new tunic. And a lovely good night to you both," he said, thrusting them out the door back-to-back with a twist and thrust of his arms. "Sorry, boys. Don't even think of coming back in tonight, mind."

"You—you sumbitch—"

"Yes, yes," Ahdio said, turning back into the doorway; "I never thought much of her myself."

Having demonstrated why he wore the mailcoat, he closed the wooden winter door against the cold, and with both hands swept back the thirty-one strands of dangling colored rope that for most of the year were the inn's only door. He was right in assuming that no one in Sly's Place was looking anywhere but at him. Standing there on the one-step entry platform he had installed to make it easy for comers-in to spot friends or empty tables, he gave them the full benefit of his lungs.

"Now that is enough trouble for one night! Settle damn it down! Throde: one round of Red Gold for everyone at True Brew prices. That includes you and me."

To the sound of applause, Ahdio returned to the bar. His customers made plenty of room. To Throde he spoke quietly:

"Take care of our mysterious patron and her *escort* for the rest of the night, Throde."

The youth nodded. Anyone else might have said "You're not going to thank her?" but not Throde. Looking at the floor, he said, "I'm sorry, Ahdio. Thanks."

"Going to have to get you a club to wear in your belt, or brass knuckles. But forget the apology—I saw it all. Not your fault at all. Here. First one's for you. Next one's for me. Going to be an edgy night, Throde. Who the blazes is that woman?''

Throde had no answer. He served the veiled lady's table. She had two glasses of wine only, without ever showing her face; her companion put away several beers. There was no further trouble. Nevertheless, Ahdio was right: it was an edgy night. Avenestra, the teenaged girl in the skintight top and slit skirt, left with Frax and came back an hour or so later, alone. By then, about half of the patrons had departed Sly's Place, in various stages of inebriation. Avenestra went to the bar for a beer, specifying lots of foam, and approached that table by the wall.

"You a Bey behind that veil?" she asked, licking at the foam boiling above her blue-glazed mug.

"No," the blue-green veil said. "I'm Ahdio's girl. Just came in tonight to watch him work. Sure knows how to settle fights, doesn't he?"

"Uh-huh." Avenestra licked foam. "You sure better treat him right, Ahdio's gurl. He sure does have friends." And she moved off. Less than three-quarters of an hour later, she left with another man.

"I'd say she's about fourteen," the veiled Jodeera quietly murmured to Wints.

"About," Wints said.

"One more round before closing!" Ahdio called. "One, I say one more round and that's it. How about savin' wear and tear on our legs and puttin' hands in the air, dear friends?"

Wintsenay's hand went up, with many others. Ahdio and Throde went to work moving fast. No, Throde told his employer, he had not heard the veiled lady's voice.

"Just drink this one right down, Wints," his hooded and veiled employer said. "When the last of these scum is leaving, you leave too. I'm staying."

"Milady . . ."

"Just get up and amble out with the last of them, Wintsenay."

"Yes'm."

The last round was served, and quaffed. More men left. Ouleh was long gone. The veiled lady had long since become the only woman in the place. Keeping an eye on her without seeming to, Ahdio announced closing. Throde went into the back room and returned with his broom, a reminder that could not be overlooked. Sweetboy meandered into the main room, yawning, glancing hopefully at the bar. More people straggled out. Ahdio helped one. Throde helped one. The last two, companions, rose. They hoisted their mugs to Ahdio and then to the woman whose face or even hair they had never seen, and drained their cups. With considerable pride, both departed without support.

"Not right out in front now, boys!" Ahdio called after them.

Looking a little nervous, teeth worrying his lip, Throde watched both men all the way out the door.

Ahdiovizun stared at the veiled lady. Throde looked at her, at Ahdio. Who knew where she was looking, under hood and behind veil?

"My lady . . ." Ahdio began, and broke off as she rose to her feet.

He and Throde stared as she tossed back her hood, then unclasped the cloak, and with one hand pulled her veil straight out until it dropped free. Her hand fell to her side, carrying the veil. She said nothing. Neither did Ahdio. He stared, mouth open. He dropped one big hand to the back of a chair as if he needed support.

"Not," he said in a very low voice, "possible!"

"Oh," Throde said, with feeling, as he looked upon the most beautiful woman he had ever beheld.

The unveiled lady gazed at him while he and Throde stared at her. She said nothing.

"Throde," Ahdio said, and his voice sounded funny to his helper, "let's leave the tables and sweeping up till tomorrow. Go ahead home, and don't forget to be careful out there tonight."

Swallowing hard, looking at him, Throde stood blinking. He had never seen Ahdio look this way before. The big man looked . . . stupid.

Also impatient. "Throde!"

Throde jerked as if awakening, and headed for the back room with his unused broom. The whole night had been truly unique, a succession of new experiences adding new knowledge to Throde's store. It had not ceased. No woman had ever stayed behind this way, not both sober and clothed. And saying absolutely nothing; she was merely . . . being here. Nor had Ahdio ever behaved in such a way. Throde had often thought that his huge, tough and yet kind employer should have a woman; even women, in the plural. Yet he had never envisioned such a woman as this; never dreamed that she might be such a beauty as this veiled—as this now *un*veiled lady.

He set the broom in its place and made sure the back door was locked as well as barred. Then he swung his big hairy cloak about himself, pausing only long enough to lift the hood and close the clasp. Taking his staff, he headed for the front door. He walked between the man and the woman without looking at either, but noticed nevertheless that they remained as if frozen in place, gazing at each other in silence. As he reached the hanging before the door, a new thought struck him and he turned back.

"Ahdio? You're . . . all right?"

"Of course. And you be careful, Throde." Ahdio spoke without looking at him. He stood as if in shock, thunderstruck.

"Uh." And, still nervous and going motherly, the youth said, "uh, don't—don't, uh, forget to lock the door after me, Ahdio."

"Good *night,* Throde."

Throde departed, pulling the door securely shut behind him.

The moment he was gone, the unveiled lady spoke. "I'm sorry I called that warning—you handled everything so well, and purely physically, too, without a sign of your Ability."

Her voice was soft and she seemed to lean toward him, but he stood stiffly, a dozen paces away. Glaring at her. Still he appeared to be in shock, and she saw pain in his face.

"What in four hells are you doing here, Jo?" He could not have made his displeasure more obvious, but the catch in his voice bespoke pain, too.

"I'm sorry I felt I had to come here, in disguise. It's all right, Ahdio, it's all right now. Ezucar died over four weeks ago. I left just days later. I had no care for what 'looked right,' Ahdio. I am a widow. I am free. I may even be able to smile again. I came straight here, with a caravan. I came looking for Ahdiomer Viz . . . and I find one Ahdiovizun, wearing mail in a rough, low place peopled by rough, low patrons; tending bar and handling trouble with—with hands and strength alone?!"

He glanced away. "Yes, well . . . this isn't Suma, and I had to leave. You know that." He took up a wet cloth and began rubbing the bar's counter-top.

"I know that you are a superlative wizard among wizards, and were surely on your way to being Chief Wizard and Advisor," she said, with a note almost of pleading in her voice. "And then you simply vanished." She looked around, gestured. "And I find you . . . in this."

"I didn't vanish, Jodeera. I left because of a woman—she was the wife of a mighty well-off and powerful noble, and I loved her. I couldn't stand being so close to her; couldn't stand being in Suma anymore."

Perhaps he noticed her sudden pained look when he put the word "love" in the past tense; perhaps he did not. She was worse than uncomfortable; she felt positively wretched. Knowing that he was uncomfortable and worse did not help.

"I gave up my magickal practice," he said, staring at the bar, rubbing and rubbing it with his wet cloth. "Completely. I came here and became who and what I am. This is my life. And now—gods, Jo, gods . . . why have you come here?"

She straightened up, lifted her chin, put back her shoulders. "Why don't you look at me, Ahdio, and I will tell you." She waited until he did so. She saw the torture in his large dark eyes and knew it showed in hers. First she swallowed hard, and then she told him: "Because that woman you loved; she loved you too and still does, and shamefully soon after Ezucar died, I came after you. Now I am not going to leave, my love; you might try throwing me out but I will *not* go back to Suma . . . or anyplace else, except where you are."

With one huge hand on the bar as if he needed its support to keep his knees from buckling, he stared at her. The look of pain had not left his face. She could not imagine why until he said, "I am not about to take up Practice again, Jo. That is behind me. The wizard Ahdiomer Viz is no more."

"Oh?" she said, putting her head a little to one side. "What about the cats? And that assistant of yours—Throde?"

Again he looked away from her stricken eyes and her beauty. He heard the rustle and the quiet footsteps as she

moved toward him, but would not look; could not. Could
this be? Didn't she love what he had been, that brilliant
and prospering Sumese wizard-on-the-rise? She was a
woman of beauty and she had been married to wealth and
power; Ezucar of Suma. This was . . . this was Sly's Place.

And I am Ahdiovizun, not Ahdiomer Viz. Not anymore.

"That's different. That's all there is, and all there will be
of my power and my Practice, Jodeera. I'm so out of
practice that one of the cats left me and I can't even locate
him. That's all buried. Ahdiovizun is the man who runs
Sly's Place in the Maze in Sanctuary, and serves drinks
wearing a coat of chain."

He partly turned and bent then, to wriggle his shoulders
and let the mailcoat rustle clinkingly down over his head
and arms. It became a smallish package, which he placed
on the bar as if it were not at all heavy.

"Let it be buried with Ezucar then," she said softly,
right beside him behind the bar, "and the rest of the past.
The present is that I love you, Ahdio. What about the
future? Can't we start it right now?"

He looked at her, and the tears he saw on her cheeks
caused those in his eyes to well over. Then he was
embracing her and being embraced, both of them striving
to meld their bodies into one. The embrace lasted a long,
long while, and surely no one who knew or thought he
knew Ahdiovizun could imagine him weeping, as he wept
now. Some of their murmuring was incoherent but most of
it was the repeating of the other's name, over and over.

"Home is where Ahdio is," she murmured, in a moment of coherence, "and the rest of his name doesn't
matter. I've come home."

At last she reminded him that he hadn't locked the front
door. He did that, and they went upstairs.

The following night she was there, very much there and
enough to bring gasps from every patron, men and women
alike, and Ahdio stood and bellowed to gain their attention and silence while he made an announcement. What
he made clear was that this was his woman. She had better
not be touched or called out at or spoken to with disre-
spect. And Jodeera remained behind the counter, pouring, helping him and Throde.

Of course it did not work. Men who had never bothered

to get themselves up and go to the bar kept doing so, rather than calling or signaling to Ahdio and Throde. They fetched and carried their own brew just to be able to approach the counter and have a look at her. Predictably, the looks became more intense and more lustful as the night wore on and the beer and wine flowed. Inevitably someone made a remark. Then someone else did. Someone else, whether from a sense of honor and rightness or in order to curry Ahdio's favor, conked that man with his fired clay cup. It broke on a hard head. The collapsing man's brother went after the mug-wielder. Ahdio came after them both and Throde went after his staff. Jodeera stood looking on, feeling pained and wretched again and showing it.

Her very presence here had caused trouble. Perhaps both she and Ahdio had known it would happen, but both hoped it would work, her beauty in this place. They had told themselves it would be all right, that it would work out, because they wanted it so.

So there was trouble. Ahdio ended it, and Ahdio closed early.

"Oh darling," she quavered through her weeping, "I'm so sorry!"

"It wasn't your fault and we both know it. And we also know that now you're here, after last night and today, I am not about to let you go. Nothing is going to interfere. Nothing!"

Holding her so fiercely that his hands hurt her upper arms, he stared at her. His Jodeera, who had always been his Jodeera, but they had had to wait so long, so long. He knew what had to be done; what he had to do. He hated it, but he knew that he was going to do it. Tonight, Ahdiomer Viz had to be reborn. Just for tonight.

The hit on Throde came as he limped and tap-tapped homeward, leaning on his long staff. Since everyone knew he carried no money and was harmless, the motive of the three men was vengeance, not robbery. They could not get at Ahdio; they would have their fun with Throde. He recognized the ejected Tarkle and the two who had sat with him, and remained after.

They stood in a line across his path in the alley, smiling. To Throde, Tarkle loomed about as big as an outhouse.

He made a show of looking all around. "Don't see Ahdio
nowheres. Reckon he won't appear 'tween you and my fist
this time, Gimp!"

Throde said nothing, and Tarkle made his move.

Then Throde did. The cripple's staff practically leaped
across him into both his hands, becoming the quarterstaff
it was. Right end went low to whack Tarkle's left leg just
below the knee, hard; Throde reversed the push and pull
of his arms and the staff's other end rapped the man's right
arm, between shoulder and elbow. The swiftness of
Throde's assuming the stance and delivering those blows
was not believable, but Tarkle's pain was. He cried out at
the first impact and moaned at the second. His better arm
dropped to hang useless and he was staggering. Throde
was still moving: third stroke high to catch the left side of
Tarkle's neck with a meaty *thup* sound. The bully's only
sound was a throaty noise. He went down. One of his
astonished cronies had already started moving in; the third
underwent a sudden attack of intelligence and paused to
draw his dagger. Throde feinted to the right and drove the
end of the stave straight into the stomach of his second
attacker. He made a truly ugly noise and bent right over
and Throde whacked him right on the top and back of his
head. The fellow fell onto Tarkle. Tarkle was moving and
groaning; his crony wasn't.

And the third man was coming in from the side, his
knife out and held low in the manner of a man who knew
how to use it on other men and had done so before.

His mouth dropped open. The cripple had shown that
he could move, and move fast; now he moved even faster,
and in a way and direction not at all believable. The knife
glittered as it rushed in, its wielder partly crouched and
extending his arm, and Throde wasn't there. He ran
several steps right up the wall on his attacker's left with all
the speed and facility of a frightened cat. Five steps up he
wheeled and came dropping like a stone, his right shoulder
hunched above the stave he held in both hands. The
knife-wielder, going into shock or something like at the
absolutely incredible, knew real fear. He made the wrong
move. That cost him his eye, which his dodging put into
the path of the down-rushing quarterstaff. His cry was a
shriek as he went down and Throde landed in a crouch.
He had to yank his staff out of the man's eye socket and
brain. The last three or four inches were dripping as he

turned, crouching, to meet whatever had to be faced and braced next.

That was nothing; mumbling and whimpering, Tarkle was crawling away. Throde's arms quivered under the impetus of adrenaline and excitation, but he stopped himself.

"Guess Throde and me fooled you bastards," he snarled in the best fakey voice he could find.

Tarkle didn't look back. Tarkle kept right on crawling up the alley toward the light. Throde looked down at his two victims. They lay sprawled ugly, messily. So what? This was an alley in the Maze: Who cared?

Throde did. Shaking all over and leaning on his staff, he limped back to the house of Alamanthis, and awoke the physician. Then the youth went on home, limping, his staff clacking the street. Throde lived alone.

The following night, Ahdio and Throde worked alone. Once again Ahdio made an announcement, sadly: his woman was gone. That brought groans and embarrassed, chastened faces and expressions of sympathy. It was the first quiet night at Sly's Place in anyone's memory.

On the night following, however, Ahdio and Throde had help. Mostly she stayed behind the bar, pouring, slapping bread and sausage onto wooden plates. She was not attractive and furthermore was specifically unattractive, this new helper in Sly's. Her big chaincoated employer called her Cleya. Remarks were not made to her. No one bothered to approach the counter to get a look at her, in her long and nigh-shapeless gray dress. Ouleh announced that she liked this Cleya. The reason was simple, and it was Frax who put it best:

"Whew. Got a face her mother couldn't love and I've saw better figures on brooms."

The woman now publicly called Cleya did not mind. To be with Ahdio at last, she accepted the price, even this. All her life her beauty had after all been more a curse than a blessing. One man, among all men, had treated her as other than an object, a bauble, and he was the only man she had ever loved. Her father and the powerful noble of wealth, Ezucar, had arranged and forced her marriage to the latter, who wanted an object and a bright and beautiful bauble to wear in public and at his parties. Meanwhile the man she loved had left Suma. Now, years later, she

had followed and they were together. The two rooms
above the tavern were eminently superior to the servant-
staffed mansion of Ezucar. She was sorry that because of
her Ahdio had felt that he must take up his Practice again.
Yet it was only this once; it was enough and more than
enough that at night in their apartment above Sly's Place
in the Maze, his spell was off her so that the veil of ugliness
was lifted, and she was again his beautiful Jodeera.

THE GOD-CHOSEN

Lynn Abbey

He might have been a stonemason by the way he swung the long-handled hammer save that no solitary stonemason would be working before dawn in the unfinished temple. He might have been a soldier since, when a younger man appeared, he exchanged the hammer for a sword and held his own in a practice session that went on until the sun edged through the leaning stone columns. He was, in fact, a priest—a priest of the Storm God Vashanka, and therefore a soldier and stonemason before all else.

He was a Rankan aristocrat: distant nephew to the late, unlamented Emperor; equidistant to the new one as well—though none would have recognized him with sweat making dirty tracks down his back and his black hair hanging in damp, tangled hanks. Indeed, because of the hair and the sweat his peers from the capital would have picked his tall, blond companion as the aristocrat and labelled the priest a Wrigglie or some other conquered mongrel. But there were no observers and none who knew Molin Torchholder mentioned his ancestry.

He'd been born in the gilt nursery of Vashanka's Temple in Ranke—the well-omened offspring of a carefully arranged rape. His father maimed or killed ten men of impeccable lineage before claiming Vashanka's sister,

Azyuna, in the seldom-enacted Ritual of the Ten-Slaying. It did not matter that Azyuna had been a slave or that she'd died giving birth to him. Molin had been raised with the best his mortal father and Vashanka's cult could offer.

His rise was steady, if not meteoric: An acolyte at age five, he traveled with the army before he was ten. He was fourteen when he engineered the siege at Valtostin, breaching the walls at four places in a single night. Some said he'd become Supreme Hierophant, but his accomplishments in war, destruction and intrigue were not accompanied by the proper deference to his superiors. He'd disappeared, apparently in disgrace, into the inner sanctums of the Imperial Temple, re-emerging in his early thirties to accompany the inconvenient Kadakithis into exile in Sanctuary.

"You'd send half the men on the barricades to an early death," Walegrin, commander of the regular army's garrison in Sanctuary, complimented the priest as they set aside their swords. "Pity the fool who thinks Vashanka's priests are soft."

Molin immersed his face in a bowl of icy water rather than acknowledge Walegrin's admiration. Vashanka's priests were soft, due in no small part to the irremediable absence of the god himself. Vashanka had died in Sanctuary—*died* because when a god is separated from his worshipers, the worshipers go on living—not the god. And the priests, intermediaries between worshipers and gods, what of them when a god had simply vanished? It was not a question Molin enjoyed pondering.

He settled the tunic of a successful tradesman around his shoulders and hid the hammer in a crack between two man-high blocks of stone. "Did the barricades hold last night?" he asked, tucking the sword into a saddle-sheath.

"Our lines held," Walegrin replied with a grimace as they left the enclosure of Vashanka's last, incomplete temple. "There was trouble Downwind between the Stepsons and the rabble—again. And something dead or deadly moving along the White Foal. But nothing to disturb our fish-eyed masters."

It was Ilsday for the Ilsigi, Savankhday for the Rankans and Belly's-day for the Beysin (who demonstrated their barbarism by giving days to their bodies rather than to the gods); but, most important, it was Market-day. Civil war would abate for one day while partisans and rivals rubbed shoulders in disorder of another kind. The Path of Money, like every other thoroughfare in town, was filled with the intense activity of commerce—legal and otherwise. The pair was separated near the Processional when a food stall erupted in flames. Walegrin, the soldier and representative of such order as the town possessed, went to the merchant's aid and Molin, in the disguise of a merchant himself, found his journey redirected into a tangle of streets.

Here, where a rainbow of painted symbols proclaimed which gangs and factions had been paid off by each household, there was no amnesty and a well-fed man on a well-fed horse was only a moving target. Torchholder shed his merchant's demeanor: straightening his back, holding the reins in one hand while the other rested on his thigh ready to wield whatever weapon his cloak might conceal. Ragged children gauged his ability to defend himself by shouting epithets combining anatomy and ancestry with an originality a soldier could admire—never guessing that they cursed Vashanka's Hierarch in Sanctuary. He ignored them all as he turned down a sunnier alley.

Then the sunlight vanished. The heavy black clouds which had foretold countless perversions of weather since the Storm God's demise condensed overhead. A blast of ice-laced wind roared down the alley making the horse rear in panic. The children and beggars struck the moment Molin's attention was on the horse instead of Sanctuary, and the priest found himself in the midst of a deadly little alley-fight even as needle-like pellets of sleet began their own assault from the sky.

He dropped the reins, a signal to his army-trained horse that it was free to attack, and drew the sword from its saddle-sheath. The odds swung back in his favor once he got a firm grip on the hand pressing a knife into his kidney and tossed that urchin back into the street. Whatever his attackers had expected it wasn't a merchant who fought like one of the thrice-damned Stepsons and, though they would have dearly loved to drag this anomaly back to their leader for a closer interrogation, they cowered back under the eaves. Molin gathered the reins, pounded his heels against the gelding's flanks and made a dash for the Palace.

"Send for a groom to take this horse to the stables and see that he's well-cared for," Torchholder demanded

when he reached the guardhouse at the West Gate of the
Palace, forgetting his torn and dripping tradesman's
clothes.

"Forgettin' your place, scum? I don't take orders from
stinkin' Downwind scum . . ."

"Send for a groom—and hope that I forget your face."

The soldier froze—tribute to the instant recognition the
Storm Priest's oratory could claim and to the unconcealed
rage that accompanied Molin's crisp movements as he
wrapped the reins around the guard's trembling hand. The
terrified young man hauled away on the stable-gong rope
as if his life depended on it.

The storm intensified once the Hierarch stepped into
the vast, empty parade-ground before the Palace. Lightning grounded in the mud, releasing steam and stench.
Those who remembered the terrible storms of the summer
had already taken cover in the deepest, driest rooms.
Molin glanced at the annex which housed the two children
who were, somehow, avatars of both Vashanka and a new,
unconsecrated Storm God, just as lightning caressed it
with blue-and-silver. His instinct was to run across the
courtyard but his belief that he would survive such brav-
ery was not strong enough; he ducked into one of the
stair-niches built into the West Gate.

"My Lord Molin," the bald courtier in rose-and-purple
silk said, catching his arm as he strode down the corridors.
A mere clothing disguise would never fool a Beysib
courtier, accustomed as the Beysibs were to dressing like
flowers and dyeing their skin to match. "My Lord Molin, a
word with you—"

The Beysibs only called him "Lord" when they were
frightened. They had a snake-loving bitch for their only
goddess and knew nothing of the temper of Storm Gods.
Molin plucked his dripping sleeve from the courtier's
hands with all the disdain his anger and frustration could
muster. "Tell Shupansea I'll come to the audience chamber when this is over—not before," he said in perfect
Rankene rather than in the bastard argot that passed for
communication between the cultures.

Lightning reflected off the courtier's scalp as he ran to
inform his mistress. Molin slid behind a dirty tapestry into
the honeycomb of narrow passages the Ilsigi builders had
put in the Palace and which the Beysibs had not yet
unraveled. Barely the height and width of an armed man,

the passages were foul-smelling and treacherous, but they kept the remnants of the Rankan Presence in Sanctuary united, to the consternation of their fish-eyed conquerors.

Molin emerged in an alcove where the sounds of the storm were inconsequential in comparison to the fury emanating from a nearby room. An unnatural brilliance filled the corridor before him. His skin tingled when he crossed the sharp line from shadow to light. Thirty-odd years of habit told him to fall to his knees and pray to Vashanka for deliverance—but if Vashanka could have heard him there would have been no need for prayer. He told himself it was no worse than walking on the deck of a sailing ship, and entered the nursery.

The blond, blue-eyed demon he'd named Gyskouras, on the advice of a S'danzo seeress, was the focus of the brilliance. He was shouting as he swung his red-glowing toy sword, but the words were lost in the light. The other child, the peaceful child of that S'danzo seeress, had a hold of Gyskouras's leg, trying to pull him away from the motionless body he was battering. Arton, though, was no match for his foster-brother while the god's rage was in him.

Molin forced himself deeper into the blazing aureole until he could grab the child and lift him from the floor.

"Gyskouras," he bellowed countless times.

The boy fought with the determination of a street urchin: biting, kicking, flailing with the straw-sword until Molin's damp clothes began to steam. But Molin persisted, imprisoning the child's legs first, then trapping his arms beneath his own.

"Gyskouras," he said more gently, as the radiance flickered and the sword fell from the child's hand.

"'Kouras?" the other child echoed, clinging now to both of them.

The light flared once and was gone. Gyskouras became only a frightened child wracked with sobs. Molin stroked the boy's hair, patted him between the shoulders, and glanced down where one of his priests lay in a crumpled heap. With a gesture and a nod of his head, Torchholder commanded the others to do what had to be done. When he and the children were alone he sat down on a low stool and stood the child in front of him.

"What happened, Gyskouras?"

"He brought porridge," the boy said between sobs and

sniffles. "Arton said he had candy but he gave me porridge."

"You are growing very fast, Gyskouras. When you don't eat you don't feel good." Since they'd brought Arton into the nursery some four months earlier, both children had grown the length of a man's hand from wrist to fingertips. Growing pains were a living nightmare for all concerned. "If you had eaten the porridge I'm sure Aldwist would have given you the candy."

"I wished him dead," Gyskouras said evenly, though when the words were safely out of his mouth he fell forward against Molin. "I didn't mean it. I didn't *mean* it. I told him to get up an' he wouldn't. He wouldn't get up."

It was only Molin's experience with the children that let him make sense out of Gyskouras's garbled syllables—that and the fact that he'd known, in his heart, what had happened as soon as the storm began.

"You didn't know," he repeated softly to convince himself, if not the child.

Gyskouras fell asleep once his sobs subsided; the Storm God rages always exhausted the small body of their perpetrator. Molin carried an ordinary child to a small bed where, with any luck, he would sleep for two or three days.

"'Kouras can't stay here any longer," Arton said, tugging at the hem of the priest's much-abused tunic.

The S'danzo boy rarely spoke to anyone but his foster-brother. Torchholder let Arton take his hand and lead him to a corner away from the others who were beginning to return to the now-quiet nursery.

"You have to find a place for us, Stepfather."

"I know, I'm looking. When I hear from Gyskouras's father—"

"You cannot wait for Tempus. You must pray, Stepfather Molin."

Talking with Arton was not talking to a milk-toothed child. The seeress had warned him that her son might have the legendary S'danzo ability to foretell the future. At first Molin had refused to believe in the child's pronouncements, until Arton had utterly rejected Kadakithis and the Prince had finally owned up to Gyskouras' true paternity. Now he trusted the child completely.

"I have no gods to pray to, Arton," he explained as he

walked toward the door. "I have only myself and you—remember that."

He pulled the curtain shut. The two acolytes who had been arranging Aldwist's corpse on a simple pallet moved aside to let the Hierarch speak the necessary rites of passage. A war-priest, Molin had sanctified the deaths of so many unrecognizable chunks of mortal flesh that nothing could bring a tremor to his voice or gestures. He had come to believe himself truly immune to death's outrages, but the imploded face of the gentle old priest brought twisting pangs of despair to his gut.

"We do not have enough bitterwood for the pyre. Rashan took what we had with him," Isambard, the elder of the two acolytes, informed him.

Molin pressed his fingertips between his eyes, the traditional priestly gesture of respect for the departed and one which, coincidentally, dammed his tears.

Rashan: that conniving, provincial priest whose sole purpose in life, even before Vashanka's death, had been to thwart every reform Molin instituted. A cloud of rage worthy of Vashanka swirled up invisibly around Molin Torchholder. He wanted to confront Rashan, the so-called Eye of Savankala, shove every splintered log of bitterwood down the whey-faced priest's gullet and use that nonentity to light Aldwist's pyre. He wanted to take his ceremonial dagger and thrust it so deep in Gyskouras's chest that it would pop out the other side. He wanted to take Isambard's tear-stained face between his hands. . . .

Molin looked at Isambard again, little more than a child himself and unable to hide his grief. He swallowed his rage along with his tears and rested comforting hands on the acolyte's shoulders.

"The Storm God will welcome Aldwist no matter what wood we use for his pyre. Come, we three will carry him back to his rooms and you will be his chorus."

They bore their burden in silence. Molin chanted the first chorus with them, then departed for his quarters hoping that the sincerity of the young men's grief would compensate not merely for the missing bitterwood but for Vashanka, Himself, and for his own heart's silence. The priest used another set of passageways to reach a curtained vestry behind his priest's sanctum. A robe of fine white wool was waiting for him and Hoxa, his scrivener, could be heard prodding the brazier on the other side of the tapestry—though just barely. His wife, and whatever gaggle of disaffected Rankan women she'd gathered since dawn, were clambering in the antechamber that separated his sanctum from their conjugal quarters.

He pulled the tunic over his shoulders and winced as the cloth reopened a wound he didn't remember taking. Fumbling in the darkness he found a strip of linen, then emerged into his sanctum clad in boots and loincloth; his robe draped over one shoulder; blood running from his left forearm and a strip of linen between his teeth. Hoxa, to his credit, did not drop the goblet of mulled wine.

"My Lord Torchholder—My Lord, you're injured."

Molin nodded as he dropped his robe on top of Hoxa's carefully arranged scrolls and studied the pair of bloody horseshoes on his arm. The street urchins, possibly, but more likely Gyskouras. With his good arm and teeth he ripped the linen in two. He pulled a knife from his belt and handed it to Hoxa.

"Hold it above the coals. No sense taking chances—I'd rather have the bite of a sword than the bite of a child any day."

The priest didn't wince when the cautery singed his skin, but after the wound was bandaged he used both trembling hands to carry the goblet to his work-table.

"So tell me Hoxa, what sort of a morning has it been for you?"

"The ladies, Lord Torchholder—," the scrivener began, jerking a shoulder toward the door, beyond which a chorus of feminine voices was raised in unintelligible argument. "Your brother, Lowan Vigeles, has been here looking for his daughter—and complaining," Hoxa paused, took a deep breath and continued with a credible imitation of Vigeles's nasal twang, "about the lowness of the Rankan estate in Sanctuary, which is still part of the Empire although you have seen fit to conceal the arrival of a coterie of Beysib exiles, and their poorly defended gold, from the Empire, which could put all that gold to good use in its campaigns rather than see it squandered by Wrigglie scum and fish-eyed barbarians."

He took another gasping breath. "And the storm shook the windows loose from the walls. Your Lady Wife's glass from Ranke is ruined and she is in high wrath, I fear—"

Molin rested his head in his hands and imagined

Lowan's aristocratic, somewhat vapid face. *My brother,* he thought to the memory, *my dear, blind brother. An assassin sits on the Imperial Throne, an assassin who sent you running to Sanctuary for your life. In one breath you tell me how desperate, how depraved the Empire has become, and in the next you chide me for abandoning it. You cannot have it both ways, dear brother.*

I've told you about Vashanka. It will take many years, generations, before the Empire disappears, but it is dead already, and it will be replaced by the people of the new Vashanka. I've already made my choice.

But the priest had said all this, and more, to his brother and would not say it again. "Hoxa," he said, shaking Lowan from his thoughts, "I've been attacked in the streets; I've been to the nursery where the child has killed one of my oldest friends; my arm is on fire, and you talk to me about my wife! Is there anything worthy of my attention in this forsaken pile of parchment before I go fawn at the feet of Shupansea and tell her everything is under control again?"

"The Mageguild complains that we've not done enough to locate the Tysian Hazard, Randal."

"Not done enough! I've poured twenty soldats into our informers. *I'd* like to know where the little weasel's vanished to! Damn Mageguild: Wait till Randal's here; Randal can do that; Randal fought on Wizardwall—he can control the weather. I could control the weather better than that damned pack of incanting fools! Gyskouras is making the ground move. He's three years old and his tantrums are shaking the stones. We'll have to go to the witch-bitch herself if this keeps up—tell them that, Hoxa, with flourishes!"

"Yes, my Lord." He shuffled the scrolls, dropping half of them. "There's the bill from the metal-master Balustrus for mending the temple doors. The Third Commando asks for a list of warrants against their enemies; Jubal's proxy asks for warrants against Downwinders and merchants; citizens from the jewelers' quarter demand warrants against Jubal's lot and half the Commando; everyone wants warrants on the Stepsons—"

"Any word from the Stepsons' Commander?"

"Straton presented his warrant—"

"Hoxa!" Molin looked up from his writing table without moving his head.

"No, Lord Torchholder. There's no reply from Tempus."

The enmity between the priest and the not-quite-immortal commander of the Stepsons had never been expressed in words. It was instinctive and mutual on both sides but now, because Kadakithis had admitted that Tempus was the real father of the tantrum-throwing godlet in the nursery, Molin needed Tempus and Tempus was incommunicado somewhere along Wizardwall.

Torchholder was not, however, allowed the luxury of contemplating the myriad disappointments around him. The door from the antechamber burst open to admit the unhappy figure of his wife, Rosanda.

"I knew you were in here—sneaking around like vermin —avoiding me."

A wife had never been part of Molin's dreams for the future—and certainly not a wife like Brachis had foisted off on him. It was not that the priests of Vashanka were celibate; they had problems enough without such unnatural strictures. Simply put, it was the custom of Vashanka's priests—priests, after all, of the Divine Rapist—to choose rather more casual liaisons among the many Azyunas the temple housed in their cloisters. No Vashankan ever voluntarily plowed the fields with a Celebrant (Hereditary Harridan, in the vernacular) of Sabellia.

"I have affairs in the city which require my presence, Milady Wife," he answered her, not bothering to be polite. "I cannot stand idle each morning while you diddle through your wardrobe."

"You have more important affairs right here. Danlis informs me that *no* preparations have been made for our Mid-Winter Festival—which, need I remind you, is a mere ten days from now. None of the bitterwood I sent to Ranke for has arrived. Sabellia's sacred hearth will be unpurified and there won't be enough embers for the women to take back to their home-hearths. Now, I know it's too much to think that snake-smitten puppy of a Prince would take *his* position as Savankala's Flamen seriously enough to attend to these matters, but I would think that *you,* the ranking Hierarch in Sanctuary, would see that *our* gods receive proper respect.

"The Flamens of Ils have set *their* altars up, the Snake-Chanters have theirs. Rashan struggles to honor all the gods without any aid—"

Molin spun the empty goblet between his fingers. "I have no god, Milady Wife, and precious little interest whether anyone scatters scented ashes this winter. Did you feel the ground quiver during the storm—"

"The glass in our bedroom, which you choose to ignore, is on the floor instead of in the windows. You'll have to get that horrid little metal-worker to fix it—I won't spend a night with the sea air ruining my complexion."

He paused, thought better of commenting on her complexion, then continued in a softly modulated tone that signaled the end of his patience. "I'll send Hoxa. Now—I have more important matters—"

"Impotent coward. You have no god because you let Tempus Thales and his catamites usurp you. 'Torchholder's a True Son of Vashanka,' they told my father. True son of the Wrigglie whore that whelped you—"

The rage Molin had repressed when he looked at Isambard's face burst out. The goblet stem broke with a tiny snap; the only sound or movement in the room. He forced himself to move slowly, knowing he would kill her if she did not get out of his sight and knowing, in a still-sane corner of his mind, that he would regret it if he did. Rosanda edged backward toward the door as her husband pushed himself up from the table on whitened knuckles. She was through the antechamber and barricaded in the bedroom before he said a word.

"Gather my possessions, Hoxa. Move them downstairs while I speak with Shupansea."

Mid-Winter drew closer in a series of dreary days remarkable only for their raw unpleasantness. Gyskouras, still chastened by the death of Aldwist, was almost as reserved as his foster-brother, giving Molin the opportunity to realize that, even without supernatural meddling, the weather of Sanctuary left much to be desired. Not even a blizzard along Wizardwall was as bone-numbing cold as the harbor mists, and no amount of perfume could disguise the fact that the city was filling its braziers with offal and dung.

There were still too many residents in the Palace, Beysib and otherwise, despite reclamation of a dozen or more estates beyond the city walls. Molin, having refused any reconciliation with his wife, lived in a barren room not far from the dungeon cells it resembled. He'd delegated all responsibility for the Rankan state cults to Rashan who, it seemed, was eager to insinuate himself in Lowan Vigeles's good graces. The Eye of Savankala promptly moved his entire disaffected coterie out to his estate at Land's End in hopes that not only could the Rankan upper class maintain itself there, untainted by the Beysib presence, but that they could somehow promulgate the ultimate miracle and propel Prince Kadakithis successfully back to the Imperial Throne.

Molin, in turn, spent all his time studying the reports his underlings and informants brought him, searching for the clues that would tell him which of Sanctuary's numerous factions was most powerful or most volatile. He ceased to care about anything Rankan and thought only of the fate of Sanctuary as it revealed itself through his informants. He left his room only to visit the children and practice with Walegrin each morning before dawn.

"Supper, My Lord Torchholder?" Hoxa inquired.

"Later, Hoxa."

"It *is* later, Lord Torchholder. Only you and the torturers are still awake. Your old quarters are empty now. I've taken the liberty of scrounging a new mattress. Lord Torchholder, whatever you're looking for, you won't find it if you don't get some sleep."

He felt his tiredness; the cramps in his legs and shoulders from too little movement and too much dampness; and remembered, with a flicker of shame, that he hadn't bathed in days and stank like a common workman. Limping, he followed his scrivener up to the sanctum where Hoxa had laid out fresh linen, a basin of faintly warm water and the somewhat soggy remnants of dinner. His glass windows, he noted, had been replaced with dirty parchment; his gilt goblets with wooden mugs and his Mygdonian carpet was gone. But she hadn't dared to touch his work-table.

"Drink wine with me, Hoxa, and tell me how it feels to work with a disgraced priest."

Hoxa was a Sanctuary merchant's son, without pedigree or pretensions. He accepted the beaker, sniffing it cautiously. "The ladies and the other priests—they were the ones to leave the Palace. It seems to me that you're not the one in disgrace—"

He would have said more, but there was a screeching outside the window. His mug bounced across the floor as the black bird sliced through the parchment with a beak and steel-shod talons that were more than equal to the task. "It's back," the young man gasped.

The raven—Molin felt it had begun its life as a raven, at least—carried messages between the Palace and a ramshackle dwelling by the White Foal. It had made its first journey long before the Beysib fleet set sail, offering the priest a precious artifact: the Necklace of Harmony hot off the god Ils's neck. Since then he had trained other ravens, but none was like this bird with its malevolent eyes and a glowing band around one leg to make it proof against all kinds of meddling and magic.

"Get the wine," Molin told Hoxa. "It has a message it would just as soon be rid of."

The scrivener retrieved his mug and refilled it for the bird, but he would go no closer to it than the far side of the work-table and shrank back to the corner while Molin lured the beast onto his arm. Unlike his other winged messengers who carried tiny caskets, this one spoke its message in a language only the proper receiver could understand: another property of the spelled ring. Molin whispered a reply and let it take flight again.

"The Lady of the White Foal wishes to see me, Hoxa."

"The Nisi witch?"

"No—the Other One."

"Will you go?"

"Yes. Find me the best cloak *she* left behind."

"Now? I'll send for Walegrin—"

"No, Hoxa. The invitation was clearly for one. I hadn't expected this—but I'm not surprised, all the same. If anything happens, you can tell Walegrin when he comes looking for me in the morning. Not before."

He shook out the cloak Hoxa offered him. It was black, lined with crimson-dyed fur, and appropriate for visiting Ischade.

Winter's night in Sanctuary belonged to the warring partisans, the forces of magic and, especially, the dead—none of which challenged Molin as he rode by. He felt eerie sensations as he neared her home: the eyes of her minions, their silent movements around him, her dark-woven wards lifting when he touched the flimsy iron gate.

"Leave the horse here. They don't like it closer."

Molin looked down into the ruined face of a man he had once known—a man long dead and yet very much alert and waiting. He hid his revulsion behind a benign, priestly demeanor, dismounted and let what remained of Stilcho lead the gelding away. When he looked back to the house the door was open.

"I have often wished to meet you," he greeted her, lifting her tiny hand to his lips after the custom of Rankan gentlemen.

"That is a lie."

"I have wished for many things I never truly wanted to have, My Lady."

She laughed, a rich sound that surrounded and enlarged her, and led him into her home.

Molin had prepared himself for many things since clasping the cloak around his shoulders. He had met Stilcho's one eye without flinching, but he swallowed when he entered her seraglio. In candlelight the cacophony of color and texture was shocking. Sunlight, if it ever reached this forsaken chamber, would have blinded a fish-eyed Beysib. Ischade shoved aside a ransom's worth of velvet, silk and embroidery to reveal an unremarkable chair.

"You had something to tell me, in person?" Molin began, sitting uneasily.

"Perhaps I wished to meet you, as well?" she teased. Then, seeing that he did not share her light-heartedness, spoke more seriously: "You have been seeking the Stepson Mage, Randal."

"He vanished more than a month ago. Stolen out of the Mageguild—as I suspect you know."

"Roxane holds him in thrall until he delivers her lover to her. He will die at Mid-Winter if he fails."

"What else—if he fails? One mage, or lover, more or less, could hardly matter to you."

"Let us say that regardless of who might fail—it is not to my interest that Roxane succeed. Let us say that it is not to my interest that *you* should fail, and fail you would if Roxane has her way."

"And it is certainly not to your interest that you, yourself, fail. So you think that we should, together, protect the mage, the lover and our own interests from the Nisibisi witch?" Molin said, striving to match her tone.

Ischade spun down to sit among her pillows. The hood of her cloak fell back to reveal a face that was beautiful, and human, in the candlelight. "Not together, no. In our separate ways—so none of us fail and Roxane does not succeed. You can understand the dangers of the preternatural around us, the danger to the children you shelter? The ways of magicians do not mix well with the ways of the god-choosers. Sanctuary grows bloated with *power*."

"And the *power*ful? If I am to protect those children, I'd be best without any magicians. You, Randal, *or* Roxane."

She laughed again. Molin saw that it was her eyes that laughed with death-madness. "It is not *my* power that we're talking about. My power is born in Sanctuary itself—in life and death."

"Especially death."

"Priests! God-chooser, you think that because you have a ready buyer for your soul you are somehow better than those who must sell theirs piecemeal."

She was angry and her inky eyes threatened to engulf him. Molin rose unsteadily from the chair but faced her without blinking.

"Madame, I am not any persuasion of soul-selling magician: witch, necromancer, or whatever. You speak of interests and failures as if you knew mine. I served Vashanka and the Rankan Empire; now I serve His sons . . ." He hesitated, unwilling to speak aloud the concluding phrase that had formed in his head.

Ischade softened. "And Sanctuary?" she concluded. "You see, we are not so different after all: I did not choose Sanctuary; my self-interest chose it for me. My life is complicated by enemies and allies alike. Every step my self-interest dictates forces me further down a path I would not willingly travel."

"Then you will help me bring order to Sanctuary?"

"Order brings light into all the corners and shadows. No, Torchholder, Bearer of Light, I will not help bring your order to Sanctuary. I find that snakes, be they Roxane's or Shupansea's, are not to my interests."

"My Lady, we both use black birds. Does this make you a priest or me a wizard? Does it mean we are like Roxane, who favors a black eagle, or like the Beysib, who revere a white bird almost as much as they revere their snakes? Has not our shared, unwilling, concern for this cesspool of a town made us allies?"

"We could be more than allies," she smiled, moving closer to him until he could smell the sweet musk that surrounded her. Molin's dread mastered him. He bolted from the otherworldly house, her laughter and parting words ringing in his ears: "When you meet Randal, ask him about Shamshi and witch-blood."

Stilcho was gone. The gelding's eyes were ringed with white; flickering witch-fire clung to its saddle. Molin had scarcely set his feet into the stirrups before it bounded away from the misty clearing. The gelding wanted the warmth and familiarity of its stall within the Palace walls; Molin fought it the length of the Wideway, past the curious fishermen waiting for the tide and the enticements of the few whores not yet taken for the night. They approached Vashanka's abandoned temple, passing behind the arrays of wood and stone which were now being appropriated for the reconstruction of the old Ilsig villas ringing Sanctuary.

One stone, a vast black boulder set deep into the soil and fractured by Vashanka's annihilation, would never be moved again. Molin approached it on foot. He could not make himself form the words to the Vashankan invocations he'd known from childhood, nor could he bring himself to pray, like an ordinary worshiper, to another god. His anxiety, despair and helplessness fled naked toward whatever power might be disposed to hear them.

"OPEN YOUR EYES, MORTAL. GAZE UPON STORMBRINGER AND BOW DOWN!"

Whatever Ischade believed, priests did not often look upon their gods. Molin had seen Vashanka only once: in the chaotic moments before the god's destruction. Vashanka had been swollen with rage and defeat, but his visage had been that of a man. The apparition which flickered above the stone had erupted from the bowels of hell. Molin's quivering knees guided him quickly to the ground.

"Vashanka?"

"DEPARTED. *I* HAVE HEARD YOUR PRAYERS. I HAVE BEEN WAITING FOR YOU."

Priests shaped the prayers of the faithful to a form acceptable to the god. Each priesthood evolved a liturgy to keep god and worshiper at a proper distance, one from the other. Private prayer was universally discouraged lest it disrupt that delicate balance. Molin had been caught in prayer so private that his conscious mind did not know what longings had drawn the swirling entity from its esoteric plane. Nor did he have any idea how to dispel or appease it if, indeed, either could be accomplished.

"I am troubled, O Stormbringer. I seek guidance to restore Vashanka's power to its proper place."

"VASHANKA WAS, IS, AND WILL BE NO MORE. *HE* DOES NOT TROUBLE YOU. YOUR TROUBLES ARE BOTH GREATER AND LESSER."

"I have but one need, O Stormbringer: to serve Vashanka's avatars."

"USE STEALTH, PRIEST, TO SERVE YOUR AVATARS. THAT IS *YOUR* LESSER TROUBLE. I WILL NOT HELP YOU WITH THE GREATER." The seething cloud that called itself Stormbringer, the ultimate Storm God, inhaled itself. "THAT THORN AND ITS BALM LIE WITHIN YOUR PAST," it whispered as it blended into the first red streamers of dawn light.

Molin remained on his knees thinking he was surely doomed. He had not begun to recover from Ischade's suggestions and insinuations, and now the gods were speaking in riddles: Use stealth; lesser troubles and greater troubles; thorns and balms. He was still on his knees when Walegrin clapped him on the shoulder.

"I had not thought to find you praying here."

The soldier flinched when Molin turned.

"Have I changed so much in one night?" the priest asked.

"Have you been here all night? The sea air is dangerous for those not born to it."

"And lying is dangerous for those not born to it." He took Walegrin's arm and rose to his feet. "No, I went first to the house of Ischade, by the White Foal. She told me that our wayward mage, Randal, has been caught in the Nisi witch-bitch's web to serve, our necromancer says, as bait for Roxane's lover." He looked at the swords Walegrin carried. "I think we will only talk this morning and walk a little—until I can feel my feet. Hoxa will blame himself if I return limping. It was not a good night—"

Walegrin held up his hand for silence. "To walk away from her is cause for prayer."

Molin shrugged the sympathy aside. The need to confess and confide had become all-consuming and Walegrin, however inappropriate, had become its object. "I came here because I did not know what to do next and my thoughts, not prayers, summoned something—a god called Stormbringer. I don't know—maybe it was only a dream. It said I must use stealth to serve Gyskouras and

Arton—but that's the lesser of my problems, it says. The
greater one is inside me. God or dream, I make no sense
from it."

Walegrin stopped as if struck. "Stealth? Randal is bait
for Roxane's lover—eh?"

"According to Ischade."

"It fits. It fits, Molin," the blond soldier exalted, using
his superior's given name for the first time in their
acquaintance. "Niko's been seen at the Merc's Guild."

"Niko—Nikodemos the Stepson? I met him once—with
Tempus. Has Tempus returned, then?" Molin brightened.

"Not that anyone's seen. But Niko—he'd be the lover,
if rumor's true. More important: He's Stealth."

Torchholder leaned against the gelding. The habit of
taking war names was not limited to the Stepsons. He'd
become Torchholder one night on the ramparts at Valtostin, though unlike most, he'd made his war name a part
of his known name.

"Find him. Arrange a meeting. Offer him whatever he
wants, if necessary." He swung into the saddle, shedding
his aches and tiredness.

"Whoa." Walegrin caught the gelding's reins and
looked Molin square in the eye. "It said that was your
lesser problem. Hoxa says you don't eat enough to feed
one of your damn ravens and you sleep on the dirt under
your table. You're the only one in the Palace my men
respect—the only one *I* respect—and it's not right for you
to be off with 'greater problems.'"

Molin sighed and accepted the conspiracy between the
officer and his scrivener. "My greater problems, I was
told, lie within my past. You'll have to let me struggle with
them on my own."

They rode away from the temple in silence, Walegrin
keeping his mare a good distance behind the gelding. He
bit his lip, scratched himself and gave every indication of
reaching an unpleasant decision before trotting the mare
to Molin's side.

"You should go to Illyra," he stated sullenly.

"Heaven's forfend—why?"

"She's good at finding things."

"Even if she were, and I admit she is, I've taken her son
from her. She's got no cause to do me a favor. I'd sooner
ask Arton directly," Molin said, thinking it might not be a
bad idea.

"Illyra'd be better. And she'd do it—because you have Arton."

"That smith-husband of hers would use me for kindling. Even if she's forgiven me, he hasn't."

"I'll crush a few wheels and send Thrush with a message that he's needed at the barracks to mend some iron. You'll have the time."

The priest had no desire to talk to the seeress. He had no desire to go rooting around his own best-forgotten memories. Since his estrangement from Rosanda thoughts about his origins, never before a subject of consideration, haunted him. He hoped they'd vanish now that he had a fertile connection between Nikodemos, Randal, Roxane, and the avatars to pursue. "We'll see," he temporized, not wanting to offend his only efficient lieutenant. "Maybe after Mid-Winter. Right now, look for Niko. And strengthen the barricades around the Beysib cantonment. Ischade was honest and playing games of her own at the same time."

Walegrin grunted.

Two days, and the miserable nightmare-filled night between them, were sufficient to make Molin reconsider a visit to the seeress. He watched Walegrin mangle some stable implements, then headed for the Bazaar along a route which would not likely bring him into contact with Illyra's husband, Dubro.

He was recognized by the smith's apprentice and admitted into Illyra's scrying room.

"What brings you to my home?" she asked, shuffling her cards and, unbeknown to the priest, loosening the catch on the dagger fastened beneath her table. "Arton is well, isn't he?"

"Yes, very well—growing fast. Has your husband forgiven you?"

"Yes—he blames it all on you. You were wise to see that he was not here. You will be wiser to be gone when he gets back."

"Walegrin said you could help me."

"I should have guessed when that soldier came to fetch Dubro. I have had no visions of gyskourem since Arton went to the Palace. I won't look into your future, Priest."

"There is work for him to do at the Palace and a fair price for his labor. Your brother says you can find that which has been lost."

She set the cards aside and brought the candlestick to the center of the table. "If you can describe what it was that you lost. Sit down."

"It's not a 'something,'" Molin explained as he sat on a stool opposite her. "I've had . . . visions . . . myself: warnings that there is something within my past which is—or could cause—great trouble. Illyra, you said once that the S'danzo saw the past as well as the future. Can you find my—" He hesitated at the ridiculousness of the request. "Can you show me my mother?"

"She is dead, then?"

"In my birth."

"Children bring about such longings," she said sympathetically, then stared into the void, waiting for inspiration. "Give me your hand."

Illyra sprinkled powders and oils of various colors on his palm, tracing simple symbols through each layer. His palms began to sweat; she had to hold his fingers tightly to stop him from pulling his hand back in embarrassment.

"This will not hurt," she assured him as, with a movement so unexpected he could not resist it, she twisted his wrist and held his palm in the candle flame.

It didn't. The powders released a narcotic incense that not only prevented injury but banished all worry from the priest's mind. When she released his hand and extinguished the candle, most of the morning had passed. Illyra's expression was unreadable.

"Did you see anything?"

"I do not understand what I saw. What we do not understand we do not reveal, but I have revealed so many things to you. Still, I do not think I *want* to understand this, so I will answer no other questions about it.

"Your mother was a slave of your temple. I did not 'see' her before she had been enslaved. I could see her only because she was kept drugged and they had cut out her tongue; your hierarchy feared her. She was raped by your father and did not bear you with joy. She willed her own death."

Torchholder ran his fingers through his beard. The S'danzo was disturbed by what she had seen: slavery, mutilation, rape and birth-death. He was concerned by what it had to mean.

"Did you see her? See her as mortal eyes would have seen her?" he asked, holding his breath.

Illyra let hers out slowly. "She was not like other women, Lord Hierarch. She had no hair—but a crown of black feathers covering her head and arms, like wings, instead."

The vision came clear to him: a Nisi witch. His elders had dared much more than he had imagined possible; Stormbringer's warning and Ischade's whispers made chilling sense to him now. Vashanka's priests had dared to bring witch-blood to the god. His mouth hung open.

"I will hear no other questions, priest," Illyra warned.

He fished out a fresh-minted gold coin from his purse and laid it on her table. "I do not want any more answers, My Lady," he told her as he entered the sunlight again.

The difference between priests and practitioners of all other forms of magecraft was more than philosophical. Yet both sides agreed the mortal shell of mankind could not safely contain an aptitude for communicative—that is, priestly—power, along with an aptitude for more traditional, manipulative magic. If the combination did not, of itself, destroy the unfortunate's soul, then mage-kind and priest-kind would unite until that destruction was accomplished.

Yet Molin knew that Illyra had seen the truth. Pieces of memory fell into place: childhood-times when he had been subtly set apart from his peers; youth-times when he had relied on his own instincts and not Vashanka's guidance to complete his audacious strategies; adult-times when his superiors had conspired to send him to this truly god-forsaken place; and now-times when he consorted with mages and gods and felt the fate of Sanctuary on his shoulders.

No amount of retrospective relief, however, could compensate for the anxiety Illyra had planted within him. He had relied on his intuition, had come to trust it completely, but what he called his intuition was his mother's witch-blood legacy. He did not merely sense the distinctions between probable and improbable—he shaped them. Worse, now that he was conscious of his heritage, it could erupt, destroying him and everything that depended on him, at any moment.

He walked through the cold sunlight looking for salvation—knowing that his impulsive searches were an exercise of the power he feared. Still, his mind did not betray him; his priest-self could accept the path intuition revealed: Randal, the Hazard-mage become Stepson. The magician's freedom would be the byproduct of Molin's other strategies, and for that freedom a priest might reasonably expect the instructions a disowned mage could provide.

It took Walegrin less than three days to corner Nikodemos. Regular sources denied the Stepson was in town. An alert ear in the proper taverns and alleys always heard rumors: Niko had exchanged his soul for Randal's—the mage did not reappear; he had joined Ischade's decaying household—but Strat denied this with a vigor that had the ring of honesty; he was drinking himself to oblivion at the Alekeep—and this proved true.

"He's shaking drunk. He looks like a man who's dealing with witches," Walegrin informed Molin when they met to plot their strategies.

The priest wondered what he, himself, must look like; the knowledge that witch-blood dwelt in his heart had done nothing for his peace of mind. "Perhaps we can offer him service for service. When can you bring him to me?"

"Niko's strange—even for a Whoreson. I don't think he'd agree to a meeting and he's Bandaran-trained. Dead drunk he could lay a hand on you and you'd be in your grave two nights later."

"Then we'll have to surprise him. I'll prepare a carriage with the children in it. We'll bring it outside the Alekeep. I trust Stormbringer. Once Stealth sees those children he'll solve that problem for us."

Walegrin shook his head. "You and the children, perhaps. Bribes aside, the Alekeep is not a place for my regulars. You'd best go with your priests."

"My priests?" Molin erupted into laughter. "My priests, Walegrin? I have the service of a handful of acolytes and ancients—the only ones who didn't go out to Land's End with Rashan. I have greater standing with the Beysib Empire than with my own."

"Then take Beysib soldiers—it's time they started earning their keep in this town. We sweat bricks to protect them."

"I'll arrange something. You let me know when he's there."

So Molin moved among the men of Clan Burek, selecting six whose taste for adventure was, perhaps, greater than their sense. He was still outlining his plans when Hoxa announced that the borrowed carriage was ready. They roused both children, and the dancer, Seylalha, from their beds. The Beysib bravos had not exchanged their gaudy silks for the austere robes of Vashanka's priests before it was time to leave the Palace.

As predicted, Niko was drunk. Too drunk, Molin feared, to be of any use to anyone, much less Gyskouras and Arton. The priest tested him with the sort of pious cant guaranteed to get a rise out of any conscious Stepson. Wine had thickened Niko's tongue; he babbled about magic and death in a language far less intelligible than Arton's. There were rumors that Roxane had stolen Niko's manhood and bound the Stepson to her with webs of morbid sensuality. Molin, watching and listening, knew the Nisi witch had stolen something far more vital: maturity. With a nod of his head the Beysibs dragged the unprotesting Nikodemos to the carriage.

He left them alone, trusting Stormbringer's riddles and turning his attention to the frightened little man the Beysibs were interrogating with a shade too much vigor.

"What has he done?" the priest interceded.

"He's painted a picture."

"It's not a crime, Jennek, even if it doesn't reach your aesthetic standards." He took a step closer and recognized the painter who had unmasked an assassination conspiracy a few years back. "You're Lalo, aren't you?"

"It's not a crime—like you said, My Lord Hierarch—it's not a crime. I'm an artist, a painter of portraits. I paint the faces of the people I see to keep in practice—like a soldier in the arena."

Yet the Ilsigi painter was plainly afraid that he *had* committed a crime.

"Let me see your picture," Molin ordered.

Lalo broke free of the Beysibs, but not quickly enough. Molin's fingers latched onto the painter's neck. The three of them: Molin, Lalo and the portrait moved back into the carriage lantern-light just as a shaken, sober Niko emerged.

"Nikodemos," Molin said as he studied the unfinished, frayed canvas tacked onto a battered plank, "look at this."

The limner had painted Niko, but not as a drunken mercenary in a whitewashed tavern. No, the central figure of the painting wore an archaic style of armor and looked

out with more life and will than Niko, himself, possessed.
And yet that was not the strangest aspect of the painting.

Lalo had included two other figures, neither of which
had set foot in the Alekeep. The first, staring down over
Niko's shoulder, was a man with glowing blue eyes and
dark-gold hair: a figure Molin remembered as Vashanka
moments before the god vanished into the void between
the planes. The second was a woman whose half-drawn
presence, emerging from the dark background, overshad-
owed both man and god. Lalo had been interrupted but
Molin recognized a Nisibisi witch like his mother had
been, or as Roxane still was.

He was still staring when Niko dismissed the Ilsigi
limner. The Stepson began to speak of Arton and Gyskouras as if he alone understood their nature. The children,
Niko announced, needed to be educated in Bandara—an
island a month's sailing from Sanctuary. When Molin
inquired how, exactly, they were supposed to transport
two Storm Children, whose moods were already moving
stones, across an expanse of changeable ocean, the Stepson became irrational.

"All right, they're not going any further unless and until
my partner Randal—who's being held by Roxane, I hear
tell—is returned to me unharmed. Then I'll ride up and
ask Tempus what he wants to do—if anything—about the
matter of the godchild you so cavalierly visited upon a
town that had enough troubles without one. But one way
or the other, the resolution isn't going to help you one
whit. Get my meaning?"

Molin did. He also felt a tingling at the base of his spine.
Witch-blood rushed to his eyes and fingertips. He saw
Nikodemos as Roxane saw him: his *maat,* his strength and
his emotions displayed like the Emperor's banquet table—
and the priest knew witch-kind's hunger.

Niko, oblivious to Molin's turmoil, continued with his
demands. He expected Molin to get Askelon's armor out
of the Mageguild and to storm Roxane's abode with a
company of warrior-priests.

"Are you sure that will be enough?" Molin inquired, his
voice turned sweetly sarcastic by the witch-blood appe-
tites.

"No. I will free Randal, but your priests will free me. I
will be Roxane's champion—facing your priests—one man

against many. You will arrange to capture me unharmed, but you'll make it look good. *She* must never suspect my allegiance. *She* must think it's all your doing: priest-power against witchery."

"We are ever eager to serve," the priest agreed.

"And the timing. It must be Mid-Winter's Eve at midnight—exactly. Timing is everything, Hierarch. You know that. When you're dealing with Death's Queen, timing is everything."

Molin nodded, his face a rigid mask of obedience lest his laughter emerge.

"And I'll need a place to stay afterwards. Wherever you've been keeping those children and their mother will do. It's time they had the proper influences around them."

It was all Molin could do to keep silent. Whatever *maat* gave a man, it wasn't a sense of irony. Stormbringer and the rest of his Storm-kind were leaning hard on this drunk mercenary. His picayune demands became prophecy the moment they slurred out of his mouth. His babble trapped Stormbringer in Sanctuary like a fly in a spider's web. Already Molin could feel the necessary strategies and tactics crowding into his thoughts. Success was inevitable —with one, unfortunate, shortcoming: Molin would become Roxane's personal enemy, and what she would do when she found out who had been his mother was beyond even a Storm God's guess.

Niko was still drunk. He bumped into the carriage as he headed back inside the Alekeep, still muttering orders. The Beysibs moved to haul him back.

"No, Jennek, let him go. He'll be ready when we need him again; his kind always is."

"But, Torchholder," Jennek objected. "He asks for the sun, the moon, and the stars and offers you nothing in return. That's not the bargain you described back at the Palace."

"And it's not the bargain he thinks it is, either."

The witch-hungers vanished as quickly as the Stepson. Molin grabbed the carriage door to keep himself from collapsing. The door swung open, Jennek lurched forward and Molin barely had the presence of mind to haul himself onto the bench opposite the children.

"To the Palace," he commanded.

Molin closed his eyes as the carriage rattled forward

along the uneven streets. He was weak-kneed and exhilarated enough that he held his breath to stifle a fit of hysterical laughter. He had felt the naked power of his witch-blood heritage and, much as it had horrified him, he had mastered it. He was revelling in the wonder and simplicity of the strategies unfolding in his mind when Lalo's picture shifted under his arm. With a shiver, the priest reopened his eyes and pulled it away from Gyskouras's candy-coated grasp. The child's eyes glowed more brightly than the lanterns.

"Want it."

"No," Molin said faintly, realizing that not even Stormbringer could anticipate the influence and desires of a Storm Child.

"I want it."

Seylalha, Gyskouras's mother, tried to distract him, but he pushed her back into the corner with a man's strength. Her eyes were as fearful as the child's were angry. Torchholder heard the rumble of thunder and did not think it was his imagination.

"'Kouras—no," Arton interceded, taking his brother's hand. The children stared at each other and the light ebbed gradually from Gyskouras's eyes. Molin sighed and relaxed until he realized that the light had moved to Arton's eyes instead. "He is ours already, Stepfather. We do not need to take him," the dark-eyed child said in a tone that was both consoling and threatening.

They made the rest of the journey in silence: Seylalha huddled in the corner; the children sharing their thoughts and Molin staring at the triple portrait.

There were two hectic days until Mid-Winter's Eve. Molin had the satisfaction of knowing his plans could not be thwarted and the irritation of knowing the events already in motion were of such magnitude that he had no more power than anyone else to alter them.

By the time the sun set, Torchholder had become hardened to the cascade of coincidence surrounding his every move. He went out of his way to stop the Mageguild from donating Askelon's, and Randal's, enchanted armor to Shupansea in gratitude for her permission to meddle with the weather at their Fête. He even considered refusing it when she suddenly turned around and offered it to him "as we have no Storm Gods nor warrior-priests worthy to wear it." But, in the end, he accepted all her gifts gratefully—including the authority to name Jennek and his rowdy friends as his personal honor guard.

He retired to his sanctum to await the unfolding of fate alone—except for Lalo's portrait. There would be no surprises until Randal walked through the door at midnight—then there would be surprises enough for gods, priests, witches, soldiers and mages alike.

KEEPING PROMISES

Robin W. Bailey

A horse careered insanely along the Governor's Walk, heedless of the cold, drizzling mist that treacherously slicked the paving stones. Its breath came in great steaming clouds. It made the corner onto the Avenue of Temples at a speed that threatened to unseat the two cloaked riders on its back.

From the shadowed steps of the Temple of Ils a small, lithe figure leaped into the road. There was the glint of metal in its clenched fist. With a wild shout the figure flung out its arms. The horse whinnied in terror, reared, and crashed to a stop.

The rider in the saddle answered with a curse, swung downward with a sword, and made a swift end of the attacker on the ground.

"More behind and coming fast!" the second rider warned, wrapping arms even more tightly about the first rider. "Go, damn it!"

Again, the horse raced onward, past the park called the Promise of Heaven where half-starved women sold their bodies for the price of a lean meal. The beast wheeled to the right and down a street between two dark and immense edifices. A set of massive iron gates loomed.

The first rider jerked sharply on the reins, threw a leg over the mount's head, and jumped to the ground. The second rider slid backward over the damp, lathered rump, stumbled, then sagged to the pavement.

A hood was flung back; a pommel smashed against the unyielding barriers. A voice called out full of desperation and anger. "Father! Let us in! Dayrne—anyone—awake!"

"Chenaya!" The second rider rose to a timid crouch and drew a small dagger. "They're coming!"

Four men ran down the street, weapons drawn. Even as they came on, three more emerged from the shadows to join them. Chenaya whirled to face them, cursing. Gods knew what the hell they wanted! This was too much trouble for a common robbery. Perhaps it was vengeance for the two she'd already slain that drove them.

"Get behind me," she ordered, dragging her companion by the arm. Then she put a pair of fingers to her lips, gave a sharp whistle, and called, "Reyk!"

The lead runner gave a choked scream, then a long gurgling cry of frightened pain. He dropped his sword, fell to his knees, beat at his face. But he was much too slow. The falcon, Reyk, climbed back into the sky, leaving the man's eyes in bloody ruin. He winged a tight circle, then settled on his mistress's arm. She sent him aloft once more. "Can't carry you and fight," she whispered tersely. Without turning away she banged her pommel on the gate again. "Father!"

One runner stopped to help his fallen comrade. The rest rushed on. She couldn't make out their features or identify their dress, but she could feel their hatred.

Her companion beat on the gates with a dagger. "Open! For pity's sake, let your daughter in!"

Chenaya ripped off her cloak and drew a second sword. With the two blades she stepped forward to meet her attackers. "All right, you miserable dung-balls!" She twirled the weapons in dazzling double arcs. "I don't know what you want, but I'll play your game. Try to entertain me, you sons of whores!"

Before the first blow could be struck the gates swung wide. Six giants, in various stages of arming themselves, spilled into the street, steel gleaming in their fists. Chenaya's pursuers caught themselves up short, then ran in the other direction, dragging their blinded friend with them. They were quickly swallowed by the damp gloom.

Chenaya spun to face the tallest of the giants. "Dayrne,

what the hell's going on around here? We've barely arrived in Sanctuary, but we've been attacked twice. Some group hit us in Caravan Square at the end of General's Road. Then these attacked as we came along Governor's Walk. Nobody's on the streets but madmen!"

Dayrne's gaze lingered on her face a bit longer than was proper, and he gave a distinct sigh of relief even as he chewed his lip. "Politics later, Mistress," he said finally as he ushered Chenaya and her hooded companion inside the estate grounds. He paused to make sure the gates were sealed then continued. "Things have gone to hell in the city since you've been gone. We can talk more of it later, but first you must see your father. Lowan Vigeles has been nearly ill worrying about you." His brows knit in consternation. "You promised to return before the onset of winter."

"Something important came up," she answered defensively, avoiding his eyes. She extended her arm again. In the light of the few torches that illumined the interior courtyard the metal rings of her manica glimmered. Again, she whistled. It was impossible to see the bird in the dark, but she heard the soft beat of its pinions, felt the rush of air by her cheek as he took a familiar place on her wrist. Chenaya slipped a jess from her belt and fitted it over Reyk's leg. From another small pocket she extracted a hood to cover his eyes. Only then did she pass him into Dayrne's care. "Have one of the men clean his talons immediately." She stroked her pet. "He scored one of them. Don't let the blood crust. And have someone take care of that poor horse. He's carried the two of us a long way."

Chenaya took her traveling companion by the elbow then and led her across the court. Dayrne gave quick orders to the other men and fell into step behind. As they crossed the grounds she noted how well the restoration of the old estate was progressing. Land's End, the locals called the place, though she was damned if she knew why.

Light streamed through an open doorway. She stepped inside a grand entrance hall and gazed up the wide staircase that curved along the east wall. Lowan Vigeles stood at the top. His face was full of relief at the sight of her, but he couldn't hide his anger.

Two of her gladiators, the former thieves Dismas and Gestus, flanked him according to standing instructions.

Lowan was not to be left unguarded during a disturbance. But there was someone else at the top of the stair who she could barely see. The woman seemed to hang back.

Lowan descended the stairs and stopped halfway down. "You've been gone far longer than your three months, Daughter." There was a hard edge to his voice, but it couldn't mask the deeper joy he felt. "You broke your promise. You're long overdue." Then he relented and extended his arms. "Welcome home."

Chenaya unfastened her weapon belt and dropped it at the foot of the stair. She ran up to her father, threw her arms about him, and pressed her head against his shoulder. Lowan Vigeles was a tall man, but the past months had made him appear haggard. He had lost weight and there was little color left in his cheeks. "You worried too much!" she admonished with a whisper only he could hear.

"How much is too much?" he said, letting a hint of his anger show once more. "Things are changing, Chenaya. Law has broken down all over the city. Hell, all over the Empire. You could have been dead and rotting for all I knew."

"I'm sorry, Father," she said honestly. "It couldn't be helped. You know I'd have come home if I could've." And that was enough of that, her tone conveyed without her needing to say more. She regretted having caused him pain, and she *knew* he had worried, but she wasn't a child. She wouldn't be treated as one, even by her father. She started to remind him of that, then caught a clearer look at the woman above.

It took her by complete surprise. Then, abruptly, a broad grin spread over her face. Chenaya had become immune to shock long ago. Still, she found considerable amusement in the idea that her father might cuckold his own brother.

"Good evening, Lady Rosanda," she said grandly. "How's Uncle Molin these days?"

Rosanda's shy, delicate smile turned to a look of infinite perplexity. Then the older woman blushed hotly and fled from Chenaya's view.

Daughter winked at father. "A chunky little tidbit to ease your worried mind, eh?"

Lowan rapped her lightly on the brow with his fingers. "Don't be impudent, child. She and Molin have separated, and your aunt is quite upset. She's staying here a few days until she gets herself together."

"By the Bright Light!" Chenaya exclaimed, clapping a hand melodramatically to her heart. "She must be giving Dayrne fits about the housekeeping."

"Not at all, Mistress," Dayrne said from the foot of the stair.

"She's actually been quite helpful," Lowan Vigeles insisted. "She's taken a firm hand in the restorations." He laid a hand on his daughter's shoulder and compelled her to meet his gaze. "And you must be kind to her. Whatever you think of Molin, Rosanda is a lady and a guest in our house. Her head may be full of sky, but her heart is full of love." He smiled suddenly and ran a hand over her blonde curls. "And she's inordinately fond of you. She thinks you're the only true Rankan woman left in the city . . . beside herself, of course." He reached for her hand. "Now, come sit by the hearth in my room and tell me of your journey."

Chenaya hesitated. "I'm afraid we're going to have more company than Rosanda." She indicated her companion who had remained patiently near the entrance. "I've brought someone home, too."

Still clutching the unsheathed dagger, her companion pushed back the concealing hood and glared sullenly up at her hosts. A spray of wild, black hair tumbled forward, partially obscuring classic features turned hard and thin.

Lowan Vigeles turned pale. Then he bowed his head respectfully to the small, silent woman. "Please, come up!" he urged, holding out his hand. "Come up and get warm."

But Chenaya intervened. "Not now, Father. She's tired and needs a bath. Dayrne will prepare the room next to mine for her." She glanced down at her companion, and an unspoken message passed between them. "Then, tomorrow she starts a new life."

Dayrne touched the woman's elbow to guide her up the staircase and to her quarters. Adder-quick, she slapped his hand away, spun, and spat at him. The dagger flashed.

"Daphne!" Chenaya's harsh shout was enough. The tiny weapon froze in mid-plunge. Chenaya and Dayrne exchanged hasty glances. Of course, he'd never been in danger. The giant was one of the best gladiators Ranke had ever produced, more than able to defend himself from such a feeble attack. But it wouldn't do to have Daphne's little wrist broken, either.

"He doesn't touch me!" Daphne screamed. "No man touches me again." Then she drew herself proudly erect. A malicious smirk creased her mouth. "Unless I want him to." She drew the dagger's edge meaningfully along her thumb, then without another look at Dayrne, she marched up the stair, around Lowan Vigeles, and disappeared the way Rosanda had gone. Dayrne followed at a safe distance.

"She's half-mad," Chenaya said softly with a shake of her head.

Lowan Vigeles raised an eyebrow. "Which half?"

An hour later Lowan greeted his daughter again with another hug and a goblet of hearth-warmed wine. She accepted both gratefully, sipped the drink, and took one of the two massive wooden chairs before the fireplace. She had hastily bathed and changed into a gown of soft blue linen. The traveling leathers she had lived in for months were even now being buried by one of her men.

"I really tried to keep my promise, Father." She set her wine on the chair arm and stretched wearily. "I tried to get back." She gazed into the fire, finding a measure of tranquility in the dancing flames, and she took another drink. The liquor warmed her thoroughly.

"It's all right, child," Lowan soothed. "So long as you're safe. I just worry too much." He sipped his own wine and regarded her. "Where did you find Daphne? Did you learn of anyone else?"

Chenaya shook her head slowly. Memories of her journey flooded her head, overpowering her emotions. "No one else," she said at last. "Either the rest of the Royal Family is dead, or they're hidden too damn well in fear of Theron." She looked up at him. "In fact, I was on my way home when I happened through Azehur. That's just the other side of the Gray Wastes."

She told him of the tavern she had stopped at. There had been a high-stakes game of dice. She wasn't playing for once, just watching with interest, especially when one of the players pulled a ring from a pouch on his belt.

"It was a Royal Sigil," she said, holding up one hand to

show the ring she wore, "just like you and I and Molin and Kadakithis and all the Royal Family own. It wasn't a fake. It was real."

She had waited until the player lost even that, then she had followed him from the tavern. There was no need to bore her father with the details of how she had lured the man into an alley or how she had convinced him to talk. Lowan wouldn't have approved.

Chenaya tossed back the last of her wine and held out the cup for more. Lowan rose, fetched the bottle from the mantel above the fire, and poured for her. "The son of a bitch was a part-time sell-sword. Nearly a year before, he'd helped attack and destroy a caravan leaving Sanctuary for Ranke as it crossed the Wastes."

"Daphne and the Prince's concubines," Lowan interrupted as he filled his own vessel, "fleeing the Beysib invasion."

Chenaya nodded. "They were supposed to kill the women. Instead, they saw a chance to make a little more profit and sold them outside the Empire."

Lowan turned sharply, splashing his sleeve with the red liquor. "Sold . . . ?"

She fully approved of the anger she read in his expression. She shared it in fullest measure. Daphne had always been a whiner and a constant complainer. Chenaya hadn't liked her much. Still, she hadn't deserved such a fate. "Those men were hired," Chenaya continued, "by someone right here in Sanctuary."

Lowan leaned on the mantel and chewed his lip. He turned the goblet absently in his hands. "Did your man tell you who?"

"I don't think he knew," she answered with a frown. "Or if he did, he preferred to expire with his secret." She drank again and licked the corners of her mouth. "But he did tell me where the women were sold. That's why I was late coming home, Father. I made a side-trip to Scavengers' Island."

Lowan squeezed his eyes shut and muttered a quick oath.

"I can take care of myself!" she snapped before he could say anything. She didn't need his lecture on what a hell-hole Scavengers' Island was reputed to be. She'd seen for herself, had walked among the scum of humanity that dwelled there. "I hired a boat to take Reyk and me across. For anyone who asked I claimed to be a fugitive from one of Theron's purges. That wasn't hard. After a couple of fights most of the rowdies left us alone." She winked. You know how mean that falcon looks.

"It took days to find her," she continued after another swallow. "Turned out she was a special attraction at a particularly nasty brothel that catered to, shall we say, deviated tastes." She paused and smiled a malicious little smile, remembering. "Tempus Thales would've loved it." She shook her head and let the smile fade, wondering vaguely what had happened to that butcher. She looked up at her father and handed him her empty cup to set on the mantel. "You've known men, I'm sure, who could only get excited by violent rape. Well, the proprietor sent those to Daphne." Chenaya wrapped her arms about herself. Despite the fire's warmth, lingering memories of Scavengers' Island sent a chill through her. "They kept her locked in a room. Father, she was a mass of bruises and scratches. She still is. Every time she fought tooth and nail. All it got her was a reputation on the island and a lot more customers with ideas of taming her." She shuddered.

Lowan Vigeles refilled her vessel a third time and urged it upon her. Then he asked quite calmly, "Did you kill the proprietor?"

"I didn't get the chance." She took one more drink, then set the wine aside. She hadn't come here to get drunk with her father, and there were things she had to do come daylight. She didn't need a fuzzy head. "There was plenty of blood-letting, though, when I broke her out. Some customers tried to get in the way. But as soon as Daphne spied her keeper she grabbed one of my daggers and leaped at him with a screech that, I swear, made my flesh crawl! The man didn't even get a chance to fling up his arms. I tell you, she carved him like a mince pie. I had to drag her off and hustle her down to the quays before the entire island came after us. Good thing I had a boat waiting."

"Where is she right now?" Lowan asked softly.

"Rosanda volunteered to bathe her. It's probably the first bath she's had since her capture. Speaking of Aunt Rosanda, can you keep her busy out here for a few days?

Very busy? I don't want her spreading word of Daphne's return. I want that pleasure for myself, and I want it to be very special."

Lowan frowned. "Now I see. Daphne's just a tool for you, isn't she? Another thorn to stick in Shupansea's side?"

Sometimes, Lowan Vigeles could be irritating, particularly in the accuracy with which he saw her motives. Chenaya had to admit she intended to relish the moment when Shupansea learned about Daphne, but her own father shouldn't be so snide about it.

"You're partly right," she admitted sheepishly. "That Beysib bitch is going to squirm like a hooked fish." Chenaya hooked her little finger in the corner of her lip and stretched it upward to illustrate her words. "But my motives run a little deeper than that, as you'll learn in time." She changed her mind and took one more sip of wine. "I'm glad I rescued Daphne. No woman should suffer what she did. I've promised to find out who in Sanctuary was responsible for the caravan attack."

Lowan sat back down in his chair and met her gaze over the rim of his winecup. The firelight glimmered on the burnished metal and reflected strangely in his eyes. "Promised who?" he said cautiously.

"Daphne," she answered evenly, "and myself."

He closed his eyes. After a while she wondered if he'd fallen asleep. Then she saw him move to speak. "How will you even begin? It's been a year."

There had been weeks on the road to ponder that. It would do no good to ask the Hell-Hounds to investigate. Even before she left those bumblers seemed to have locked themselves in the garrison and hidden there. Nor could she rule out that one of their rank might be the guilty one. Certainly, they would have known of the caravan's departure. For that matter, it could have been anyone in the palace. Or, she had to admit, anyone who just kept a watchful eye on the city gates. That meant anybody in Sanctuary. No, she needed help to find her answers, and she had someone special in mind for that.

Of course, Lowan Vigeles wouldn't have approved, so all she told him was, "I have a plan, Father."

● ● ●

She awoke at sunrise after only a couple hours' sleep. She could have used more, but there was a lot to do. She had promised Daphne a new life. It began today.

But before she could stretch and climb out of bed Rosanda knocked quietly and entered with a breakfast tray. Chenaya pushed herself up against the headboard and gawked in utter surprise as the noblewoman spread a soft white cloth over her lap and set the tray upon it. It contained several slices of cold roast meat, fresh bread, and a rare Enlibar orange. There was a vessel of water to wash it down.

"Aunt Rosanda," Chenaya protested, "this wasn't necessary. The men take care of everything, or we see to our own needs."

Rosanda shushed her. "I don't mind, really. It's been far too long since I lifted my hand in a kitchen. I baked the bread myself early this morning." She blushed and looked away. "I thought I'd forgotten how. It used to be the duty of every Rankan woman to bake bread, you know, but we've all become so spoiled. No wonder there are stories that the Empire is crumbling."

Rosanda turned to leave, but Chenaya caught her hand. "Rosanda," she said in confidential tones, "what happened between you and Uncle Molin?"

Sadness was reflected in the older woman's features, but then she drew herself erect. "Chenaya, no matter how long I live in this city of thieves and vipers," her eyes narrowed to angry slits, "I am still a Rankan. I can't turn my back on my heritage." Rosanda began to rub at some invisible spot on her palm. "Molin has forsaken it all. Ranke means nothing to him. He schemes with the Beysib fish-folk. He turns away from our gods and our customs." She threw up her hands suddenly in frustration, and there was a moistness in her eye. "I just couldn't stay with him anymore. I still retain my lands and my titles. But I needed to get away from the Palace and all its intrigues for awhile. You and Lowan Vigeles are the only relatives I have in this city, so I came here." She leaned down and placed a gentle hand on Chenaya's hair, smoothing it on the pillows. "You and your father are the best of Rankan society, of all that we hold ideal. I needed a little of what you have to remind me who I am."

It was Chenaya's turn to flush. Perhaps she should

have taken time long ago to get to know her aunt. The old woman might seem air-headed, but there was a kindness in her that was endearing. "Thank you, Lady," Chenaya said simply. Then, she decided to trust Rosanda. "I asked Father to find a way to keep you here a while . . ."

Rosanda put on a faint, patient smile. "So I wouldn't talk about Daphne?"

That startled Chenaya. Her aunt was perceptive, too. More and more about Rosanda surprised her.

"You needn't worry about that," her aunt promised. "But the palace walls are going to shake when word gets out. Are you planning to take her to the Festival of the Winter Bey?"

Chenaya picked up the orange, peeled it, and took a juicy bite. "Festival?" she said with barely contained interest. An amusing idea began to form in her head. She hadn't yet decided how or when to reveal Daphne to an unsuspecting Sanctuary.

"The Beysa is hosting a lavish celebration to honor the seasonal aspect of their fish-goddess." Rosanda smiled again and winked. "They tie Mid-Winter to the moon rather than the sun. Our festivals will be long done with. Literally everyone who's anyone will be there."

Chenaya hid a grin behind her water goblet as she sipped. "Thank you again, Aunt Rosanda. I'm in your debt."

Rosanda nodded with mock sobriety, but she struggled to repress a giggle. As her aunt left, Chenaya noticed there was decidedly more bounce in her old step. When the door closed and Chenaya was finally alone, she sprang out of bed. She loved parties, and this festival came at just the perfect time. Gods, how she would enjoy it! She went to the window, drew a deep breath of fresh air, and gazed up at the sun that rose in the east. *Thank you, Bright Father,* she prayed, *Savankala, thank you!*

She dressed hurriedly in a short red fighting kilt. Around her waist she fastened a broad, gold-studded leather belt. She added a white tunic, then sandals, and tied back her long hair. Lastly, she set on her brow a golden circlet inset with the sunburst symbol of her god.

On the grounds of the estate, midway between the house and the Red Foal River, Chenaya and her gladiators had constructed a workout arena. It was crude by capital standards. There was no seating for spectators, but there was a complete series of training machines, iron weights for strength development, wooden and metal weapons of all types, and even a huge sandpit for wrestling or small matches. Of all the household, only Lowan Vigeles was exempt from the vigorous daily training sessions.

Her eight warriors and Daphne were already hard at work. On the sand, Gestas and Dismas slashed at each other with real weapons, testing each other, each secure in the other's skill and control. To the inexperienced eye it looked like the final climax of a long and bitter blood-feud. She nodded approvingly.

These eight were the best the Rankan arenas had produced. There were no longer crowds to fight for, no games, no purses, but she was damned if she'd let that fine training fade.

Daphne stood attentively beside Dayrne before a rack of weights. She was dressed much like Chenaya, but without the leather belt. That honor was reserved for one who'd triumphed in an arena death match. Daphne had never fought. But looking at the scratches and bruises on the young woman's legs, recalling how she'd disposed of the brothel keeper, Chenaya wondered just how long it would be before she too wore the band of an accomplished warrior. Daphne hung on Dayrne's instruction as he explained a particular curling movement, and she took the heavy weight without complaint when he told her to. Her face twisted in a grimace as she strained, but she executed the motion perfectly.

"Are you sure this is what you want?" Chenaya said as she joined them. "Up at dawn every day, working until your body aches all over, bleeding or bruising in places you never knew you had? It's no life for a Rankan lady."

Daphne performed one more perfect exercise, then she set the weight aside. She met Chenaya's gaze unflinchingly. The sun shone brilliantly in those dark eyes, shimmered in the thick, black luster of her hair. She pointed to the mottling on her legs. "There's no place I haven't bruised or bled already." She crossed to another rack, took down an old sword. The hilt was too big for her grip and the blade too long, but that didn't matter to Daphne. "And you're a lady, Chenaya." She said the words as if they were an accusation. "Yet you slaughtered half a dozen men to break me out of that hell on Scavengers' Island and another six at the quay before we got away. On top of that you saved us from those men last night. You ask if I want this?" She raised the sword between them and shook it so the sunlight rippled on the keen edge. "Cousin, this is *freedom* I hold in my hand! With this, you go anywhere, do anything you wish. No man dares touch you unless you want him to. No one orders you. Nothing frightens you. Well, I want that same freedom, Chenaya. I want it, and I'll have it!"

Chenaya regarded Daphne for a long, cool moment, wondering what door she was about to open for the younger woman. Daphne was but a few years her junior, but an age of experience separated them. Still, there was a fire in Daphne's eyes that had never been there before. She glanced once more at those scratches and bruises, then made up her mind.

"Then I'll train you as I'd train any slave or thief sent to the arena. When you stand on this field in those garments you're no more than the least of my men. You'll do exactly what I or Dayrne or any of them tell you. If you don't you'll be beaten until you do. It will break your spirit, or it will make you tougher than ever before. I pray for the latter. If you agree, then you'll learn every trick and skill a gladiator could want, and you'll learn from the best teachers." Chenaya walked a tight circle around her new pupil. "Whether that will make you free or not . . ." She faced Daphne again and shrugged. There were many kinds of freedom and many kinds of fear. But Daphne would have to learn that for herself. "Now, say that you agree to my terms. Swear it before the Bright Father, Savankala, himself."

Daphne hugged the sword to her breast. The sunlight that reflected from the blade made an amber blaze across her features as she swore. "By Savankala," she answered fervently. "But you won't beat me, Chenaya. No one will. I'll work twice as hard as your best man."

Chenaya hid a knowing grin. It was easy to say such a thing now. But when her muscles began to crack, when the training machines knocked her to the ground, after the first broken bone or the first slice of steel through skin— would she still prove so eager?

"Then pay attention to Dayrne. He'll be responsible for

your daily regimen. Of all the men I ever fought in the games only he gave me a dangerous cut." She showed the pale scar that ran the length of her left forearm. "Couldn't bend or use it for nearly a month. Some physicians even thought I would lose it. Fortunately, the gods favored me."

Daphne put on a smirk. "But I've heard rumors that you never lose."

Chenaya frowned. She had fostered the rumors herself to frighten opponents. Nor were the rumors untrue, though only she and Molin Torchholder knew the details of her relationship with Savankala the Thunderer. In truth, she couldn't lose at anything.

But here was a chance to teach Daphne an important first lesson. "It may be true that I cannot lose, Daphne," she said sternly, "but not losing is not the same as always winning. And remember, even winning can cost a very dear price. Be sure you're willing to pay it."

She turned away, but Daphne stopped her. "I've taken your vow, and on this ground as I train I'll call you Mistress as the others do." Something flared in the young woman's eyes, and her hand closed around Chenaya's wrist. "But you swear now, too, to remember your promise to me."

Calmly, but quite firmly, Chenaya freed herself from Daphne's grip. "I've already given you my promise. This afternoon I'll begin to search."

"I want a name, Mistress," Daphne hissed, giving special emphasis to the title, "and I want a throat between my hands. Soon."

Chenaya reached out casually, seized Daphne's tunic, easily lifted the smaller woman up onto the tips of her toes. She pulled Daphne's face very close to her own. She could smell Daphne's breath. "Don't dictate to me; don't threaten, even with subtlety," Chenaya warned. "And don't ever play games with me." She set Daphne back on her feet and motioned for Dayrne to resume the training. "Now work hard. And make up your mind to let Dayrne touch you. Each day he'll massage the soreness from your muscles." Then she winked. "And in four days you and I are going to a party."

"Where?" Daphne asked suspiciously.

"The Governor's Palace," she answered lightly. "Where else in this city?" She left Daphne then, chose a manica, a buckler, and a sword from the weapon stores and went to engage both Gestas and Dismas at once.

She had changed to leathers again to move through the afternoon streets. One sword hung from her weapon belt, and two daggers were thrust through straps on her thighs. She wore a heavy, hooded cloak to conceal her face and to keep out the chilly cold that seemed to bite right through to her bones.

In daylight, more people braved the streets. Apparently, the different factions that tried to carve up the city restricted their activities to nighttime. That suited her. She had plenty to attend to without the minor distractions of wild-eyed fanatics.

The doors to the Temple of the Rankan Gods stood open. She mounted the marble steps one at a time and went inside. At the entrance she paused, pushed back her hood, gazed around. The structure was magnificent, yet it had an odd, unfinished feel to it. The interior was lit by hundreds of lamps and braziers and by a huge skylight that illumined the prime altar with Savankala's own glory. Above the altar an immense sunburst of polished gold burned and shimmered and cast reflections around the huge chamber.

On either side of Savankala's altar were smaller altars to Sabellia and Vashanka. They were of equal beauty and craftsmanship, but they were illumined only by the fires of men. Marvelously carved figures of the goddess and her son rose behind their altars. Such a representation of Savankala was not allowed, however. A man could look upon the moon and stars; a man could see the lightning. But who could see the Thunder or bear to look upon the blazing face of the Bright Father Himself?

As she approached the sunlit altar a young, white-robed novice came forth to greet her. Chenaya made the proper obeisance to her god and ignited the stick of incense the young priest offered. She spoke a soft prayer and watched the smoke waft toward the open skylight.

When the incense was consumed she spoke to the novice. "Will you tell Rashan that I am here?"

He bowed gracefully. "He has been expecting you, Lady Chenaya." He left her, disappearing into the maze of corridors that honeycombed the temple.

Rashan, called the Eye of Savankala, appeared moments later. He was a grizzled old man. There was a toughness to his features that suggested he had not always been a priest. Or perhaps it was that difficult, she thought, to rise through the priestly hierarchy. It had taken him years to achieve his position and title. Indeed, before the coming of Molin Torchholder, Rashan had been the High Priest of the Rankan faith in this part of the Empire.

He smoothed his gray beard, and his eyes showed a rare sparkle as he came forward. "Lady," he said, taking her hand. He dropped to one knee and lightly kissed her fingertips. "I was told to expect you."

She pulled him to his feet. "Oh, and who told you?"

He raised a finger toward the skylight. "He sends the signs and the portents. You make no move He does not know about."

She laughed. "Rashan, you are too devout. The Bright Father has more to do than watch constantly over me."

But Rashan shook his head. "You must accept his plan for you, child," he urged. "You are the Daughter of the Sun, the salvation and guardian of the Rankan faith."

She laughed again. "Are you still insisting on that? Look at me, Priest. I'm flesh and blood. I'm no priestess, and certainly no goddess. No matter how many dreams come to you, that will not change. I'm the daughter of Lowan Vigeles, nothing more."

Rashan bowed politely. "In time you will learn otherwise. It isn't for me to argue with Savankala's daughter. You will accept your heritage or reject it as fate decrees." He went to stand before the altar of Vashanka, and his shoulders slumped. "But there is a void in the pantheon. Vashanka has fallen silent and will not answer prayer." He turned and leveled a finger at her. "I tell you, Chenaya, if something has happened to the Son of Savankala, then the time will come for the Daughter to accept Her responsibilities."

"No more of this talk!" Chenaya snapped. "I tell *you*, Rashan, it borders on blasphemy. No more, I say!" She paused to collect herself. The first time Rashan had suggested such a thing it had frightened her beyond words. She herself had received dreams from the Bright Father, and she knew their power. In such a dream Savankala had granted her beauty, promised she would never lose at

anything, and revealed the ultimate manner of her death.
All in a single dream. *Now it was Rashan who dreamed!*
And if his dream was not false—if it was a true sending
from the Bright Father. . . . She shut her eyes and refused
to think about it further. Of course, the dream was false.
No more than the wishful fantasy of an old priest who saw
his empire fading.

"Have you thought more about what I asked when last
we met?" she said, changing the subject. "It is more
important now when the streets are so dangerous. You
know I've come before only to find these doors closed."

Rashan held up a hand. "I'll build your small temple,"
he told her. "You can ask nothing that Rashan will not
grant."

"What about Uncle Molin?" she said in a conspiratorial
tone.

Rashan looked as if he would spit, then remembered
where he was and hastily made the sign of his gods.
"Molin Torchholder has no power in this House any
longer. Your uncle has turned his back on the Rankan
gods. He reeks of dark allegiances with alien deities. The
other priests and I have agreed to this silent mutiny." He
spoke with impressive anger, as if he were pronouncing
sentence on a criminal. "I will build your temple, and I
will consecrate it. Molin won't even be consulted."

It was all she could do to keep from throwing her arms
around the old priest. It thrilled her to see others defy her
uncle. For too long his schemes and plots had gone
unopposed. Now, perhaps there was divine justice after
all.

"Build it on the shore of the Red Foal at the very edge
of our land," she instructed. "Keep it small, just a private
family altar."

Rashan nodded again. "But you must design it."

"What?" She gave a startled look. "I'm no architect!"

"I'll handle the mechanics and the geometries," he
assured her. "But you are the Daughter of the Sun. The
core design must spring from your own heart and soul."

She sighed, then remembered her other errand. It was
getting late, and the gods knew she didn't want to worry
her father. She clasped the priest's hand gratefully. "I *will*
design it," she said, relishing the idea of a new challenge.
"We'll begin immediately. The cold mustn't stop us. My
thanks, Rashan." She pulled up the hood to conceal her

face and started to leave. But at the door she stopped and called back, "And no more dreams!"

Outside again, her breath made little clouds in the air. She hadn't meant to spend so long with Rashan. The daylight was weakening; a gray shroud had closed over the city. She hurried down the Avenue of Temples and turned onto Governor's Walk, passing with a wary eye the same corner where she and Daphne had been attacked the night before. It was quiet now; the shadows and crannies appeared empty of threat. She turned down Weaver's Way and crossed the Path of Money. At last, she reached Prytanis Street and her destination.

The air seemed suddenly colder, unnaturally cold as she pushed back an unlocked gate and approached a massive set of wooden doors. She knocked. There was no answer, nor any sound from within. She gazed around at the strange stone statues that loomed on either side of the door. There was a curious atmosphere of menace about them. They cast huge shadows over the place where she waited, completely blocking the sun. But she wasn't frightened. She embraced Savankala in her heart and felt safe.

The second time she knocked the door eased open.

There was no one to greet her, so she stepped inside. Eerily, the door closed, leaving her in a foyer lit by soft lamps. "Enas Yorl?" she called. The words echoed hollowly before fading. Chewing her lip, she wandered deeper into the house. Everything looked so old, covered with the dust of centuries. Brilliant pieces of art and sculpture were half-hidden by cobwebs. The air smelled of must and mold. She wrinkled her nose and went through an interior door.

Halfway across that chamber she stopped. A shiver crept up her spine. *It was the same room she had just left behind.*

"Enas Yorl!" she shouted angrily. "Don't play your wizard's games with me. I want to talk." She hesitated, waited for some kind of answer. "I thought you had a servant," she continued impatiently. "Send him to guide me to you, or come yourself. I'll wait here." She crossed her arms stubbornly, but on the far side of the room another door opened. She thought about it, then sighed. "Oh, all right. Whatever amuses you."

Once again she passed through the door, and once again

found herself in the same room. "I've heard a lot about you, Enas Yorl," she muttered, "but not that you were boring."

Again the far door opened. To her relief it was a different room. The smell of mold was gone, replaced by a heady incense. Instead of soft lamps, braziers glowed redly, providing the light. This new room was much larger, full of shelves with books and old furniture. Thick carpets covered the floor. In a corner an odoriferous vapor steamed from a large samovar.

At the opposite end of the room was a huge chair on a low dais. Someone, completely obscured by a voluminous cloak, sprawled upon it.

"Pardon me if I'm mistaken," the figure addressed her, "but most people tremble in my presence. You're not trembling."

She batted her eyes innocently. "Sorry to disappoint you."

He held up a hand to silence her, and he pulled himself more erect. "You have the mark of a god upon you." Two red eyes gleamed at her from beneath a hood as spacious as her own. "You are Chenaya, called by some the Daughter of the Sun."

She was beginning to hate that title. "I came to bargain with you, Wizard. I've heard of your power. If there's anything to know in this hell-hole, you know it. It's information I want."

His laughter fairly shook the walls. "Have I changed so drastically? Do I look like Hakiem the Storyteller, or Blind Jakob? Seek those for your information, woman. I'm no peddler of gossip. More important things occupy my time."

"Indeed? Well, occupy yourself with these!" She flung back her cloak and brazenly cupped her breasts. "Nearly a year ago a caravan bearing the Prince's wife and concubines was attacked in the Gray Wastes. The conspirators organized the attack from right here in Sanctuary. You have power, Enas Yorl, and you can find things out. You give me their names, and I'll give you the time of your life!"

The red eyes shone like twin coals. The wizard leaned forward to regard her with interest. "Why on earth, woman, would you offer such a bargain? Do you not know what I am, what my body is? Yes, I can give you what you seek, but do you truly know the price?"

Chenaya barked a short laugh. "You've seen my god's mark upon me, but do you know what it means? It means I can't lose—at anything. And that would get boring if I didn't find new and exciting ways to amuse myself." She unlaced her cloak and let it slide to the floor. "You're the most feared wizard in the Empire, and I decided when I first came to this city that it might be fun to crawl around in your bed. But the price of my flesh is the information I seek."

"But my body, Rankan," the wizard interrupted. "Do you know how it changes?"

"Of course," she answered with another laugh. "And I'll be very disappointed if you don't undergo some transformation while we're making love." She winked. "I told you, I'm always after a new thrill."

His voice took on a deeper, more lusty quality as he rose from his chair. "I have no control over the changes. I can't promise such a thing."

But he changed, even as he whispered in her ear.

Chenaya frowned in irritation as she hugged the cloak tighter about her shoulders and crept from shadow to shadow. It wasn't her normal way of travel. She preferred to stride the center of the streets and damn anyone stupid enough to block her path. But tonight was different. She had business, and there was no time for pointless altercations with any of the factions that governed the night.

The animal pens of Corlas, the camel merchant, were on the shore of the White Foal River just outside the Bazaar. According to rumor, it was one of the places to avoid these days. The war between the two witches, Ischade and Roxane, had made an unpredictable hell of the area, and half the residents had apparently chosen sides.

Games, games, she sighed. *Everybody plays.* And who could tell—if things got dull maybe she'd take a closer interest in the players. On the other hand, things were looking anything but dull. Enas Yorl had surprised her in more ways than one.

Unexpectedly, she heard voices behind her. She ducked into the nearest cranny and crouched behind a barrel.

Slops, to judge by the odor. She held her nose and waited.
A ragtag squad of men passed without noticing her. Most
appeared to wear swords, though a few carried only clubs.
There was nothing disciplined about them. They talked
too loudly and swaggered as if they owned the night. She
suspected they'd all been drinking.

When they were past she resumed her journey. Quickly,
she reached the bank of the White Foal. The swiftly
flowing surface caught her attention. Starlight sparkled on
the waves. The gentle lapping had an almost mesmerizing
quality. A strange emotion stole upon her, a mixture of
fear and fascination, the same sensation that had overcome her when she set foot upon her first boat and sailed
to Scavengers' Island. Again, she remembered the voice
of Savankala and the promise that sealed her fate. *Not by
sword or by any hand of man,* the Thunderer told her
those many years ago. *By water. . . .*

She shivered and forced herself to move on. So it had
been when she sailed to the island. On the way back there
had been too much to do, plans to make. And there was
much to do now. She felt the water calling, calling. But
she denied it.

A new odor permeated the air, almost as bad as the
barrel's contents. She had spent enough time with Rankan
bestiarii to know a camel when she smelled one. The odor
was quite distinct. She moved silently and came, at last, to
the pens themselves.

Daxus—that was the first name Enas Yorl had whispered in her ear. For several years the man had made his
living standing night watch over Corlas's beasts. According to the wizard, however, he also made a little selling
information about caravan cargoes to various raider
groups such as the desert-dwelling Raggah. It was he,
Enas Yorl claimed, who had arranged the attack on
Daphne's caravan.

Chenaya fingered a folded length of gold chain that
hung on her belt, and she licked her lips. Now Daxus
would pay as she had promised Daphne.

The pens were built of wooden posts set close together
and planted deep in the earth. The outer wall was a small
fortification designed to foil would-be thieves. It would
require a grapple to climb it. There was only one gate, and
it would be barred from the inside. Because of the street

disturbances, Daxus had taken to sealing himself inside with the camels.

Noiselessly, she crept around the walls, peeking through the frequent tiny gaps. The interior was sectioned into smaller pens. She listened for sounds. Even the camels seemed at rest. But . . . was that the glow of a small fire?

She stole up to the gate and laid a hand against the rough wood. Only guile would open it without attracting half the rowdies in the city. And guile wasn't one of her more reliable talents. Daxus was a man, though, and if she'd learned nothing else, she knew she could count on his basest instincts.

She removed her cloak, then shed her tunic, careful not to mislay a thin metal probe secreted up her right sleeve. She hugged herself, wondering about her trousers and boots. Damn, it was cold! Already, she was covered with gooseflesh. Still, if Daxus was suspicious he might want a better look. Cursing silently, she gazed up and down the street and slipped off the rest of her garments. Lastly, she propped her sword against the wall close at hand.

Then she pounded frantically on the gate. "Help!" she cried in a tight whisper. "Please let me in! My husband will kill me! Help!" She beat the wood with the flat of her hand, shooting glances around, hoping no one else would hear.

A narrow portal slid open a bare fraction. No face appeared, but a voice whispered back. "Who's that? I don't want no trouble. Go away."

The portal started to slide shut, but Chenaya shoved her finger into the aperture. "Wait!" she begged. "You're Daxus. I've seen you before. Please, let me in before my husband finds me. He beats me, but this time I ran away. He chased me across Caravan Square, but I lost him. He'll catch up, though. Please, it's so cold!" That much was certainly true. "Hide me, I beg you!"

The portal opened wider; one eye peered through. "Is this a trick?" Daxus grumbled. "Stand back so I can get a look at you. Say, you haven't got a stitch on!"

She thanked the gods for her foresight. But it was freezing! It might be a good touch, she decided, if she sank to her knees, so she did. "I had a dress, but he ripped it off. Tried to rape me, the drunken oaf!" She hoped she was whining convincingly. Was Daphne really worth this kind of humiliation?

The portal slid all the way open, and the watchman poked his face out, glanced from side to side as far as the opening allowed, and licked his lips. Decision gleamed in his eyes as he grinned at her. "Well, I've got a fire that'll warm you, sweet. Warm you through and through."

The portal scraped shut. Chenaya heard the heavy bar lift on the inside of the gate. It started to swing back.

She rose swiftly and grabbed her sword. She remembered that lustful look on his face and how it repulsed her; she loathed the role she had assumed to trick him; on top of that she was chilled to the bone. For those reasons, she hit him a lot harder than was needed. Fortunately for Daxus she only used the pommel of her weapon.

Moving quickly, she dragged him back inside, then retrieved her garments. She pushed the gate closed, took a moment to throw the cloak around her shoulders, then bent over his unmoving form. The length of chain came free from her belt, and she fumbled for the wire-thin probe in her tunic sleeve.

She worked by the light of his fire. At one end of the chain two small, blunt prongs were clasped together with a piece of wrapped string as long as the chain itself. This she inserted in the watchman's right nostril. With the probe she guided the chain up his nose and into the nasal passage that led deep into his throat. Chenaya knew when the prongs were positioned. Carefully, she separated the lengths of chain and string and began slowly to pull. The probe insured that the chain remained in place, but it twisted as she tugged on the string. Moments later, the wrapping came free, and the prongs snapped open. She gave a light tug on the chain. It was firmly anchored.

It was the method used to handle recalcitrant slaves and criminals in Ranke. Awake, the process was quite painful. Daxus was lucky she'd hit him so hard. He wasn't, however, going to like it at all.

She didn't like the smell of the camels. It was time to go. All she had to do was sneak him back to Land's End. She wrapped the free end of the chain around her hand and started to heave him over her shoulder.

The gate pushed open. It was Dayrne.

"What are you doing here?" she whispered angrily,

heart pounding. With her hands full of Daxus she hadn't been able to reach her sword.

"Watching your back," he answered calmly. "Pull on the rest of your clothes. I'll carry him."

She blushed hotly. No doubt he'd seen a lot more than her back. And she'd been in such a rush to get away with Daxus she'd forgotten to pull on more than the cloak. She released the chain and hurriedly dressed. But it irritated her that she hadn't noticed Dayrne, and she mentioned it.

"Mistress," he grinned, "I was sneaking through streets and back alleys when you were still playing with dolls."

"But you got caught," she reminded haughtily.

He nodded. "Everyone gets caught sometime."

She stamped into her boots and pointed to Daxus who showed signs of stirring. "Well, let's not get caught tonight. This package is for Daphne."

Dayrne's fist sent the watchman back to sleep.

"Lady Chenaya, daughter of Lowan Vigeles, cousin to His Highness Prince Kadakithis."

Lu-Broca, the Palace's major-domo, smiled graciously as he announced her arrival to the festival guests. He made a curt bow of personal greeting which she acknowledged with a nod.

Five steps descended from the entrance to the floor of the Grand Hall. She took them slowly, noting the tables piled with food and drink, the musicians and dancers, the faces that turned in her direction.

It was a good mix of the city's upper class; Rankan rubbed shoulders with Ilsig and Beysib in stark contrast to the intense street rivalries. On the far side of the hall Hakiem the storyteller-turned-Beysib-advisor stood in conversation with several guests. Nearby, listening discreetly, was the man called Lastel; Chenaya knew little of him save that he was apparently quite rich. There were others: Gonfred the Goldsmith, Dr. Nadeesha, Master Melilot the Scribe. There were also lots of Beysibs she didn't recognize; they all looked alike to her.

Then she spied Kadakithis. Shupansea, the Beysib ruler, hung on his arm. It amused her to note that even the Beysa had adopted local fashion, covering her breasts instead of brazenly painting them. Of course, Molin Torchholder was with them.

The Prince hurried forward, all smiles and warmth, glad to see her. Neither Shupansea nor Molin appeared to share his enthusiasm.

"Cousin!" the Prince exclaimed over the noise of the celebration. "I'd heard you'd returned to us. Why didn't you come visit?" He wrapped his arms around her and gave his favorite relative a gentle hug.

"Business, my Little Prince," she answered, rumpling his hair in a manner that made Shupansea frown. "There were things I had to do." She glanced back at the entrance, then hugged her cousin again. "Can we speak alone?" she whispered in his ear.

Even as children they had shared confidences. The Prince didn't hesitate. He turned to Shupansea. "Excuse me a moment, my love, while I lead Chenaya to refreshment. I'm sure Molin will see to your entertainment." He gave the Beysa no chance to voice disapproval, but caught his cousin's arm and steered her into the crowd.

"Now, what's so important that it makes you wrinkle your face that way?" he said when they were safely on the far side of the hall.

Chenaya swallowed. Until last night she hadn't thought about her cousin, only about scoring another point on Shupansea—an important point. "You know I love you, Kadakithis," she started, searching for the right words. "But you know I love Ranke more." It didn't sound right; she was stalling and he could tell.

Lu-Broca's voice boomed from the entrance. She caught her breath.

"Lowan Vigeles and the Lady Rosanda," the major-domo announced to her relief. There was still time before all hell broke loose.

She squeezed her cousin's arm fiercely, not wanting to hurt him, knowing it was too late to avoid it. "Cousin, do you have it in mind to marry that Beysib bitch?"

Kadakithis pulled away in irritation. "Chenaya," he said, "I regret that the two of you have taken such a dislike to each other—"

She cut him off. "No games, Cousin. I've seen how you two look at each other, and I know how she feels. But I can't—"

It was his turn to interrupt. "Are you disappointed because I haven't amassed some kind of army and ridden north to reclaim the throne from Theron?" She had never heard him sneer before, and it startled her. "Do you think I'm a coward because I've sequestered myself here in Sanctuary—"

She put a hand over his mouth to stop the ugly accusations. "Of course not!" she snapped. "I know better than you the extent of Theron's power and the length of his reach. You'd be raw meat for Theron; he'd chew you up if you rode against him." She swallowed hard and cast another glance at the entrance. "But no matter who sits on the throne, Ranke must still be preserved. And Sanctuary is part of Ranke, no matter how many Beysib ships sit in the harbor or how many of Shupansea's fish-eyed relatives move into the Palace."

She pressed his face between her hands, hoping in her heart of hearts that he would someday forgive her. "But you can't marry her, Kadakithis. I can't let you marry her. Shupansea must never gain any legitimate claim to this city. A guest she may be, but never your wife, never a princess of Ranke."

Kadakithis bristled. "And how would you stop it, Cousin. *If we had even talked marriage,* how would you stop it?"

Anger made him a stranger to her. He pushed her hands away, and that hurt more than she could say. They had been playmates and friends, confidantes. Now she had driven in a wedge that might never be removed.

Still, it was for Ranke. Shupansea was an invader as evil as any of the forces seeking to fragment the Empire. The fish-faced temptress was more subtle, more patient, but it was still Rankan land she desired, even if it was only the slimepit called Sanctuary.

Chenaya drew a deep breath and ignored the stinging in her eyes. "I have stopped it, my Little Prince. I have stopped it."

Kadakithis backed a step. His gaze bored into her with a menace she had never seen in him. As if on cue, Lu-Broca's voice filled the Grand Hall announcing the newest arrivals. Chenaya spun around. The major-domo was pale, a frightened expression on his face. She located Shupansea and Molin Torchholder. She had wanted to be close, wanted to see their faces. Now it didn't seem so important.

"Her Royal Highness, Daphne, Princess of Ranke, wife to Kadakithis." Lu-Broca swallowed. "And escort."

All color fled from Kadakithis's face as he pushed
through the suddenly silent throng. Chenaya followed him
to the foot of the stair. The Beysa and Molin were quickly
with them. The Beysib met her with a look of purest
hatred. Chenaya had thought about how she would respond: smile, stick out her tongue, bat her eyelashes
innocently, anything to mock the woman, to drive home
another victory. She found instead that she could do
nothing but look away.

Daphne glided down the steps with supreme grace. Her
right hand rested imperiously on Dayrne's massive bare
arm. Her left hand held the end of Daxus's chain, and she
led him like an exotic pet.

Rosanda had done a wonderful job preparing the
princess. Daphne was radiant. Clouds of sky-blue silk
swathed her form, hiding the bruises and scratches. Her
hair was bound in curls about her head. Her eyes were
lightly kohled and her cheeks rouged to perfection.
Chenaya could smell the gentle perfumes. Most pleasing
of all was the sun-burst circlet, one of her own, that
gleamed on Daphne's brow.

"I promise you'll pay for this insult," Shupansea whispered tightly.

"Pay attention, fish-face," Chenaya suggested evenly.
"You don't yet appreciate the full extent of my insult."
She looked down on the shorter woman and forced a
smile. "I *do* want you to appreciate it."

Daphne reached the bottom step. She and Kadakithis
regarded each other for a long moment. The Prince
reached out to take her hand. Daphne clung to Dayrne's
arm instead. "Hello, my husband." She spoke gently, yet
loudly enough for all to hear. "Are you surprised?"

"Yes, yes!" Kadakithis stumbled on his words. "Very!"

"You should be." She didn't snap, but formed her
remarks politely, coolly. "Did you even bother to conduct
a search? Did you look for me or wonder about my fate?"

Chenaya, too, had been puzzled about her cousin's lack
of concern for his wife's disappearance. How, she wondered, could Shupansea have so bewitched him? Still, she
ached for her Little Prince when he hung his head in
shame.

Daphne released Dayrne's arm, dismissed him with a
nod. He moved a few steps back to stand beside Daxus.

Daphne floated past her prince-husband. She stopped directly before Shupansea.

"You do look like a carp, as I've been told," Daphne said with some amusement. Shupansea shot another hateful glance at Chenaya. "Perhaps you're descended from fishes." Daphne paused to survey the faces of those around her. Nobody made a sound, but all pressed closer to hear the exchange. She turned back to the Beysa. "But whatever you are," she continued, "I'll tell you what you are *not and never will be*. You are not Kadakithis's wife. That title will never be yours. Divorce is forbidden among the noble families of Ranke."

Shupansea regarded the younger woman coldly, unmoving, unspeaking.

Daphne went on mercilessly. "Oh, I don't plan to stay here, so I won't be in your way. I've made quarters at Land's End with Lowan Vigeles and the Lady Chenaya whom the gods allowed to find and rescue me." She put on a false smile and looked on Shupansea as she might have looked on a worm. "You can have Kadakithis if you want him. But you'll never be more than his concubine. Number eight if I recall, though the others are dead or wish they were." Daphne's smile vanished. "If you love him, though, the role of whore may be enough."

Kadakithis made a foolish attempt to change the subject. "Who is this poor fellow?" he said, indicating Daxus.

"Perhaps Uncle Molin knows him?" Chenaya interjected.

The priest glared at her from the corner of his eye and shook his head. He was uncharacteristically silent, watching, and, Chenaya knew, scheming how he might turn the situation to his advantage.

"My pretty-boy?" Daphne jiggled the chain, causing Daxus to wrinkle his face in pain. He couldn't catch the chain, for his hands were bound securely behind his back. When he tried to protest all that came out was a harsh, raspy sound that set him to gagging. Maliciously, Daphne shook the chain harder. Tears sprang from her prisoner's eyes, and he sank to his knees. So it had been for Daxus the past three days.

Daphne reeled in the length of chain, making Daxus crawl to her. "Haven't I done him up nicely?" She fingered the fine silk tunic she had put on him and ran her hand over his head. "Fine garments for a piece of dung. He arranged the attack on my caravan and hired the men that sold me into a year of hell. He's only the first to be discovered. I assure you, there will be others." She ran her gaze meaningfully around the hall. "I promise." She jerked on the chain again, and a trickle of blood oozed from Daxus's nose. "And they'll all end up like this!"

With a flick of her wrist she looped the chain around Daxus's throat. Her hands clenched around the chain and she strained, forearms bulging. Her face turned into an insane mask of fury; her lips curled back in a snarl. Daxus emitted a scraping howl as the links bit sharply into his flesh. His cheeks purpled; a vein throbbed in his temple, and his eyes snapped wide with death-fear.

It was over with startling swiftness. Daxus slumped forward, his head making a loud crack as it hit the floor. "So they will all end," she promised again, recovering her composure, patting a loose curl back into place. She stepped away from the body. "But for the moment this business is done." She took Kadakithis's arm in a firm grip. "Many of you were my friends before I left, and I'm eager to speak and laugh with all of you. This is a celebration, so let's celebrate!" Without giving Shupansea another look, Daphne led her husband into the thick of the crowd.

Chenaya motioned to Dayrne that he should take Daxus away. She didn't miss the shocked expression he wore. Neither of them had considered that Daphne would kill Daxus there. She had taken too much pleasure in tormenting her plaything.

Lowan Vigeles appeared at her elbow. His features were stony. "This was not well done, Daughter," was all he said before he left her to rejoin Rosanda.

Shupansea whirled on her. For an instant Chenaya thought the Beysa would spit. The woman seemed barely in control of herself, unable to find words. Instead, she mounted the stairs and stormed from the hall.

Molin was next in line. "You foolish child!" he started. "You've made her a whore in the eyes of the entire city. Do you know what you've done?"

Chenaya glared at him, recalling with disgust how once she had trusted this man. He alone knew of the gifts Savankala had granted her. With that knowledge, of course, he had made a small fortune by betting on her

battles in the arena. She peered at her uncle and felt
nothing but anger.

"If you want to talk, Old Weasel," she said low-voiced,
"we'd better do it on the terrace away from other ears."

Molin looked as if he'd swallowed bitter wine, then he
turned and shoved a path through the guests to the
terrace. Chenaya leaned far over the balcony, tempting
him to push her. On the docks in the distance she could
see the glimmering fires of the poorer Beysib sailors.
They, too, celebrated the Winter Bey in their own less
lavish way.

". . . Stupid, thoughtless action!" Molin Torchholder
raged, shaking his fist. "If Shupansea is angry enough to
take action where will we be? She has a thousand warriors!"

Chenaya's waist was encircled by numerous chains. She
unfastened one of them and draped it around Molin's
neck. One end was pronged.

"You ordered the attack on Daphne's caravan, Uncle
Molin." She held up a hand before he could protest.
"Don't deny it. I *know*. I saw everything, including your
face, in a scrying crystal."

Molin didn't bother to hide his laughter. "You accuse
me because of something you saw in a fortune-teller's
ball? You're as insane as Daphne!"

"No, Uncle," she answered. "What I saw was real. It
was no mere fortune-teller. I promised Daphne the names
of her tormentors, and I did what I had to do to get those
names. Gods know every one of them *deserves* to die.
Scavengers' Island is filthier and more vile even than
Sanctuary." She clasped both ends of the chain around his
neck, slid her hands toward his throat. "But when I left
here over three months ago it was to find and save any
remaining members of the Royal Family. And for better
or worse, you're Family. I won't turn you over to Daphne.
If we ever do get the chance to strike back against Theron
we may need someone with your ability to scheme and
plot." She released the chain, smoothed a wrinkle from
his tunic. "And if we never get the chance," she smiled
darkly, "then, in time, I'll take care of you myself."

Molin drew himself proudly erect. "Don't threaten me,
Niece. The gods have made you powerful, but you forget I
know your secrets. I know how you can die!"

Chenaya grabbed Molin by the front of his robe, ripped

the hem of her own gown as she lifted and bent him
backward over the balcony, twisted him so he could see
the ground far below.

"You know how," she growled, "but not when. Would
you drown me, Uncle, throw me in the river? You foolish
old man! After I discovered what a snake you are the *first*
thing I learned to do was swim. You have my secrets, but
see what good they do you." She set him back on his feet,
pleased by the fine, sudden sweat sheen on his brow.

Molin rubbed his back where the stone had bitten into
it. "Damn you! Don't you ever get tired of games? Don't
you weary of always winning?"

Amazed, she threw back her head and laughed. "Uncle,
you're such a delight! The joy isn't in the winning, but in
seeing the effect of winning on the loser."

She left him, then. Inside the hall, the noise of conversation had reached a new height. Shupansea had not
returned, nor was Kadakithis anywhere in sight. Daphne
moved through the crowd, smiling and tinkling with
laughter with Dayrne as her escort. Lowan and Rosanda
stood alone in a corner in private dialogue.

"Is it true you were undefeated in the Rankan Games?"

Chenaya looked disdainfully at the little man who had
dared to brush her elbow. He offered her a goblet of wine
which she refused, and he repeated his question.

"Your name is Terryle, isn't it?" she asked innocently.
"The tax collector?"

His face lit up, and he made a slight bow. "My fame
precedes me!"

Chenaya wrinkled her nose and imitated his tone. "Is it
true you're the most detested man in Sanctuary?" His
brows shot up. She walked away before any more could
come of the conversation. She saw the man Lastel coming
her way.

Strange, she thought. *None of this is as I thought it
would be.* She'd won, but there was a bitter taste in her
mouth. She recalled something she'd said to Daphne:
Even winning can cost a dear price.

Without a word to anyone she mounted the steps,
nodded goodnight to Lu-Broca and left the Palace. A few
guests mingled in Vashanka's Square on the Palace
grounds, but she avoided them. Just outside the Processional Gate four of her gladiators waited with her palanquin. Too late, she realized she'd left a fine cloak inside.

No matter, she would send for it tomorrow. Right now, she wanted to get home, change into leathers and take a walk with Reyk. The falcon was the only company she wanted.

The palanquin began to move. Chenaya sighed, pulled the curtains closed and hugged herself against the cold.

ARMIES OF THE NIGHT

C. J. Cherryh

I

It was an uncommon meeting of Stepsons, recent and previous. It took place one night at winter's edge, outside the weed-grown garden of a smallish house on the riverside, a house in which the outer dimensions and the inner ones did not well agree. Ischade was its owner. And this meeting was on a midnight when She was occupied with another visitor in the inside of this outwardly-small house and a bay horse waited sleepily at the front.

"Stilcho," the Stepson-ghost whispered; and Stilcho, fugitive from his bed within the house (rejected lately, solitary within the witch's abode) stirred in his dejected posture and lifted his head from his cloaked arms and opened his eyes, only one of which existed.

Janni hovered by the back step, in one of his less palatable manifestations, adrip with gore, rib-bone showing through shreds of skin. Stilcho gathered himself to his feet, wrapped his cloak about him and put a little distance between them—he was no ghost, himself, but he was dead: so he understood ghosts all too well and knew an agitated one when he saw it, both in this world and the next.

"I want to talk with you," Janni said. "I've got to talk."

"Go away." Stilcho was acutely conscious of the living presence in the small house, of wards and watches that existed all about the yard. He spoke in his mind, because

Janni was in his head as much as he was standing on the walk—and just as definitely as Janni was there in his mind, he *was* standing on that walk. Stilcho knew. He had raised this ghost. *Revenge,* Stilcho had whispered simply, and this ghost, wandering aimless on the far shores of nowhere among other lost souls, had turned and lifted its bloody face and licked its bloody lips. *Revenge and Roxane.* That had been enough to bring Janni back to the living.

But there were penalties for revenants such as Janni. Memory was one. Attachments were another sort. Hell was not the *other* side alone. Such dead brought it with them and made it where they walked, even with the best intentions. And this one had been too long out of hell, ignoring orders, going where it pleased in the town.

The aspect grew worse. Blood dropped onto the steps. There was a reek in the air. It would not be denied, would not go away; and Stilcho walked away down the tangled path to the iron gate, where the brush and the trees and the earth itself gave way to dark air, to the black river that gnawed and muttered at the shore on which the house sat. He looked back, never having hoped the ghost would retreat. "For godssakes, man—"

"He's in trouble," Janni said. "My partner's in trouble, dammit—"

"*Not* your partner. No longer your partner. You're *dead,* have you got it yet?" Stilcho blinked and ran a hand through his hair, grimaced as the ghost achieved his worst aspect. Stilcho had a real body, however scarred and maimed; and Janni had none; or had whatever his mood of the moment gave him, which was the way with ghosts of Janni's sort. "If *She* finds you off patrol again—"

"She'll do what? Kill me? Look, friend—"

"*Not* your friend. There're new ghosts in hell. You know them. You know who made them—"

"It was overdue." Janni's face acquired eyes, glaring through a red film in the moonlight. "Long overdue, that housecleaning. What were they to you? Half-Rankene, nothings—They had their chance."

Stilcho turned and glared, his back to the river. "*My* dead—you sanctimonious prig. *My* dead—" Stepsons murdered by Stepsons, *his* barracksmates slaughtered, and several-score bewildered, betrayed ghosts were clamoring tonight at the gates of Hell. It was Ischade's doing, *and* Straton's; but Stilcho did not carry that complaint

where it was due. "No wonder you don't want to go back
down there—Is that it, Janni-butcher? Partner to butch-
ers? Hell got too large a welcoming-committee waiting for
you?" Janni reached for him in anger and Stilcho retreated
against the low gate. It gave backward unexpectedly,
above the abyss, and Stilcho's heart jumped. He feared
wards broken. He feared the steep slope that the path
took along the riverside, and remembered that he could
die of other things than Ischade's inattention. He stood in
the gateway and held his ground with bluff. "Don't you lay
a hand on me. Or I'll take you *back* where I got you. Now.
And you'll find the witch-bitch Roxane was pleasant
company. What's in hell is forever, Janni-ghost. And
they'll love to have you with them, damned, like them.
They'll wait at the gates for you. Real patient. Or shall I
call their names? I know their names, Janni-prig. I don't
think you ever bothered to learn them."

Janni stopped at least. Stood there on the path, silent,
solid- and live-looking, give or take the blood that
smeared his face. Janni wanted badly to be back among
the living, for reasons not all of which were savory. Love
was one. And it was never a savory kind of love, the dead
for the living. Janni had not learned that.

Stilcho had. In that improbably small house he knew
himself supplanted by the living—perhaps fatally.

"You're Rankene," Janni said. "You somehow forget
that, boy?"

"I don't forget a thing. Look at me and tell me what I
can forget. Look what happened to us for your sake, while
you were off a-heroing and left us this sinkhole. And you
come home with thanks, do you? Straton slaughters my
barracksmates for failing your precious purity and your
Niko, that paragon of virtue, falls straight into bed with
the Nisi witch—"

"Lie."

"The witch who killed you, man. Where's his virtue?
Sent to hell with the likes of me and you? I don't bloody
care!"

Ischade half-heard the whisperings of her ghosts outside
the house, the true and the half-dead; and ignored them
for the living inside—for the warm and living and far more
attractive person of the third Stepson, whose name was

Straton. He gazed at her, his head on her silken pillow, in her silk-strewn bed—chief interrogator, chief torturer, when the Stepsons had to apply that art—soldier by preference. He was a big man, a moodish man of wry humors and the most delicate skills with a body (one could guess where acquired), and he would survive this night too—she was determined he should, and she gazed back at him in the dim light of golden candles, in the eclectic clutter of her private alcove—strewn spiderlike with bright silks, with the spoils of other men, other victims of her peculiar curse.

"Why," he asked (Straton was always full of questions), "why can't you get rid of this—curse of yours?"

"Because—" She laid a cautioning finger on his chin, and planted a kiss after it, *"because.* If I told you that you'd not rest; you'd be a great fool all for my sake. And that would be the end of you."

"Ranke's ending. What have I got? Maybe I'd rather be a fool. Maybe I can't help but be one." A tiny frown-line knit his brow. He stared into her eyes. "How many men are this lucky this long?"

"None," she whispered, low as the rustle of wind in the brush, as the ghost-voices outside. "None for long. So far. Hush. Would you love me if there were no danger? If I were safe you'd leave me. The same way you left Ranke. The same way you've stayed in Sanctuary. The same way you ride the streets on that great bay horse of yours that too many know—it's death you court, Strat. Indeed it is. I'm only a symptom."

"You mean to add me to your collection, dammit; like Stilcho, like Janni—"

"I mean to keep you alive, dammit, for my reasons." The dammit was mockery. Her curses were real, and deadly. She touched his temple, where a small scar was, where the hair was growing thin. "You're no boy, no fool, I won't have you become one at this stage of your life. Listen to me and I'll tell you things—"

Stilcho shivered there in the dark against the gate, his back to the river—he still could shiver, though his flesh was less warm than formerly. And having been rash with Janni he passed further bounds of good sense. He stared at the ghost and saw that Janni was not his usual furious self.

There was something *diminished* about the ghost. And desperate. As if his arguments had told. "So you want my help," he said to Janni, "to get *Niko* back. You and he can go to hell together for what I care. Ask *Her*, why don't you?"

"I'm asking you." The ghost wavered and resumed solid shape. "You were one of the best of the ones we recruited. You were one—who'd have been one of us, after. After the war. Where were those precious lads when you wanted help out on that bridge, in that sty Downwind while the Ilsigi took you apart? Who helped you? The Ilsigi-loving dogs Strat cleaned out? You're Rankan."

"*Half.* Half, you bloody prig, and not good enough for you till you were short of help. No, there's a damn lot I don't forget. You left us as bloody meat—Ran out on us, left us to hold this hell-hole, dammit, you *knew* the Nisi would hit at your underbelly, come in here where Ranke's hold's weakest. Not with swords, no; with witchery and money, the sort of thing the Nisibisi are long on and this gods-forsaken pit of a town is apt for—"

"*And* corruption inside, inside the corps. Dammit, how quick did you forget? You love the Wrigglie bastards that did *that* to you? You defend your Wrigglie-loving barracksmates? Stilcho," Janni's face wavered in and out of solidity. "Stilcho—your barracksmates damn well left you on that bridge. They left you to die slow. *I* know about dying slow, Stilcho; believe me that I know. And you're right about the Nisibisi outflanking us—everlasting right. But what else could we do? Lose it up north? The Band did what they could. Men coming back from that—maybe —maybe they had to save what of their honor they could here in Sanctuary. And you *know* what your barracksmates were into, you know what the Band found when they walked in—It was only the dregs survived. Some on the take from the Wrigglies; some, dammit, from the Nisibisi themselves; the rest who dodged every duty they could—you know 'em, doing their patrols in the wineshops and the whorehouses—while you stood out on that bridge while the damn rabble cut you to—"

"Let it go," Stilcho hissed; and in the little house beyond Janni's insubstantial body—gods, the lights dimmed, Stilcho imagined the harsh breathing, bodies twined, knew another of them was in the toils and

irretrievable; and was in a hell of jealousy. "We left all of
that. You've left it further than I have. You ought to learn
that—"

"—it's in my interest," Ischade whispered against Straton's ear. "Whatever else you trust in this world, believe
in self-interest; and my self-interest is this city; and against
my self-interest is Roxane of Nisibis. Hostilities were her
choice—far from mine. I never like noise. I never like
attention—"

"Don't you."

She laughed without mirth, ignored his moving hands,
took his face between hers and stared until his eyes grew
quiet and deep and hazy. *"Listen* to me, Strat."

"Spells, you damned witch."

"Not while you can still curse me. I'm telling you a
truth."

"Half our nights are dreams." He blinked, shook his
head, blinked again. "Dammit—"

"There's no street in Sanctuary I don't walk, there's no
door and no gate I can't pass, no secret I can't hear. I
gather things. I bundle them together and put them in
your hands. I have no luck of my own. I give it away. I've
left nobleborn dead in the gutter—oh, yes, and gathered
up a slave and made him a lord—" She bent and kissed,
lightly, gently, teased the thinning hair at his temple.
"You feel a rumbling of change in the world and you rush
to court your death. But change isn't death. Change is
chance. In chance a man can rise as well as fall. Name me
your enemies. Name me your dreams, Straton-Stepson,
and I'll show you the way to them."

He said nothing, but stared at her in that dim lost way.

"No ambition?" Ischade asked. "I think you have—
more ambition than I. You belong in the sun; and I can't
bear that kind of light—Oh, not factually—" She laid a
finger on his lips. He was always quick with his questions
on that score, always mistook her. "It's *questions* I can't
bear. It's notice. I find my associates in the dark places:
the unmissable; the directly violent. I scour the streets.
But you belong in the sunlight. You were made for leading
men. Listen to me and think of this—are you a greater
fool than Kadakithis?"

"Not fool enough to be Kadakithis."

"A *man* could take this town and make it the wall behind which Ranke could survive. Kadakithis will lose you your Empire and you could save it. Don't you understand this? Ranke is in retreat already. Forces are gathering here in Sanctuary, in the last stronghold Ranke has. And this wispy-minded prince of yours will lie abed with his snake-queen till the venom corrodes the rest of his wits: *Do you not see this?* Do you see only chance in this Beysib invasion?"

He blinked again, blinked twice. "What are you talking about?"

"Do you believe all the Beysib have told about their coming here? What monstrous coincidence—their arrival here among us just as Nisibis exerts pressure from the north and Ranke begins to totter. I don't believe in coincidence. I don't trust *coincidence* where wizards are concerned. Kadakithis in his folly has let a foreign fleet in among us at our south door . . . while Roxane from the north pours foreign gold into the hands of Ilsigi death squads and promises the fools self-rule. *Self-rule!* Listen to me. I can take care of Roxane. But I can't come into the daylight. *You* can. You're a man who understands hard choices. A better man than any in Sanctuary right now, a far better man than Kadakithis—"

"I have my duty—"

"To what? To the Stepsons? Lead them."

"We have a leader. I have a partner—"

"Critias. *He* follows Tempus. And Tempus—Do you understand him, half? He could take a world. *One* of his men could take a city, shore up an empire. You, Straton. And hand it to him. Tempus has a chance here—but you're the one that can take it for him; you're the only one who's in position. Ranke has a chance. Behind Sanctuary's walls. What if Tempus is coming? He might well be too late. What good anything if they come too late? Listen to me. Listen to what I have to tell you and test whether my advice is good."

"You," Janni said, and Stilcho, his back to the black air and the river, felt a tenuous grip on both his arms, gazed into a face all but solid, and Janni's best aspect—Janni as he had been—before. Before Roxane. "You're the only one I can go to. The only one I can reach. I've been through the town—" Gods knew what *that* compassed, the nightbound wandering down the winds: Stilcho guessed. "Stilcho, before the gods, we've got precious little left. The dead of this pesthole patrol her streets; they watch her bridges. Half of them are Roxane's. Some of them—some of them aren't anyone's. Man, you are still a man, they left you that much—are you that afraid of Ischade? Is it that? You slip her cord and she—takes away whatever she gave you? Is that what you march to now, man? You took an oath. You meant it once. *You* kept it and those dogs fouled it; and I'm asking now, I'm asking you get my partner out of this. He's *necessary,* don't you see that? He's—what he is. And they'll use him. Roxane's wrung the sense out of him and the priests will get the rest—"

"You're the worst kind of ghost, Janni. The worst kind. The walking kind. You won't go back. Will you? Not till someone settles you."

"No," Janni said, and the tendrils of something very cold wove their way around Stilcho, between him and his body. Stilcho opened his mouth to cry out; but he had made the mistake, he had let Janni into his mind. And the spot that was Janni got wider. His dead-alive heart lurched against his ribs as the river-wind skirled up at him. "No," Janni said. "You want to know the difference in what you are and what I was? *I was better* than you. I was stronger. I still am. You want me to show you, Stilcho?"

Stilcho's legs trembled. His left foot scraped backward, against Stilcho's every effort to stand firm on the brink.

"A step—a small step, Stilcho," Janni said. "I'll only grow stronger. If the witch does send me back I'll be in hell every time she sends you down after souls—and some night you won't come out of hell, Stilcho-lad. And not all your dead dog-lovers will save you. Or you listen to me now, you *get him out*—"

"Bluff."

The foot dragged backward, knees shook beneath him.

"Try me. How much have I got to lose?"

"Stop—stop it."

The foot stayed. A feeling of oily cold settled into Stilcho's gut. "There are advantages to being wholly dead. But few." Janni's voice faded. "I see the dead walking patrol in hell and in the streets. No way out. I see the past and the future and I can't sort them out—I see Niko—I see two ways from here—and I can't sort them out. Two ways for Ranke—for the corps—for *him*—Niko's got to be free, no priest's pawn—free—Has to be—the god—the god—"

"Shut up!"

The feeling went, just—went. Stilcho stood shivering and leaned on the fence, staring out over the gulf. He had no illusions that the ghost was gone. It was revenge-bound and bound to the living and bound to hang about.

In truth he had nothing left of loyalty himself—not to comrades, not to anything so much as the thin thread that each time hauled him up out of hell when Ischade sent him down.

That thin thread grew strongest when he looked closest into her eyes, when he shared her bed and each morning died for it and came back from hell again, because the thread was always there. It was all he had of pleasure. It was all he had of life. He knew what hell was, being too frequently a visitor; and when he went down again the souls of his dead would cling to him and clamor at him and beg him for rescue—and he would strike at them and leave them in the dark, clawing his own way to the light like a drowning man, back to the next breath that he could win in the world and back to the bed of the woman who killed them.

So much for loyalties. This constant passage back and forth left him no illusions such as Janni had—of ties to anything. There was only fear. And sometime pleasure. But more of fear.

Ischade—had a new amusement. Ischade had herself a man she had not yet killed; one useful to her in this world, and Stilcho was starkly terrified that when Strat died—she might find Strat still useful, in place of a scarred and maimed husk that had never been the man Straton had been.

Stilcho was, at the depth of his attentuated life— terrified; and Janni had put the name to it.

Brush moved, ever so quietly. It might have been the wind. But a touch brushed his arm, a touch where no sound had been; and Stilcho gasped and spun, and all but took that fatal fall—except for the hand that closed on his arm and kept him from headlong flight.

"Does the river draw you?" Haught asked. "The place

of one's death—has a hold on a soul. I'd avoid the water,
Stilcho."

Straton's eyes glazed, the pupils slid aside in slitted lids,
as he lost awareness for the dreams he dreamed, that were
a drug more potent than any apothecary's.

And Ischade shivered, letting the spell wind and build
till the candles fluttered—she was lost a moment, self-
indulgence. But only a moment.

She bent and whispered more things in Strat's ear and
he stirred and gazed up at her with pupils wide and black
and drinking down all she might give him.

"There are actions you have to take," she whispered,
"for Ranke's sake, for Crit's—for Tempus. I'll tell them to
you, to save this city, save the Empire, save what you've
always fought for. You stand in the light, Strat, Ace, in the
clean sunlight—and never look into the dark; never try to
see the shadows. They're far too dark for you—"

"Who was here just now?" Haught asked; and Stilcho
twisted away, wishing to go back from the river-edge. But
the ex-slave, Ischade's Nisi apprentice—had more
strength in his fine hands than seemed likely.

"Janni," Stilcho said. "It was Janni."

"*That* wants fixing," Haught said.

Time was that Stilcho would have spat on the man;
when he was alive and Haught was no more than a slave.
But Haught served Her now. And Haught had talent that
Her talent fed; and the stripping of a soul from a body was
likely a negligible thing for Haught these days. Stilcho felt
the chill that came when Haught's substance passed
between him and Ischade. "Don't—I tried to reason with
him. I tried to tell him he's dead. He's not listening. His
partner's in trouble."

"I know," Haught said. His hand was viselike on
Stilcho's cloaked arm, numbing. "And you very much
don't want to go after him, do you, Stepson?"

"He's—crazy."

Haught's eyes met his, deceptively gentle, woman-
gentle. The fingers loosened. "Difficult times, Stepson.
She has company and you wander the dark." The fingers
wandered gently down his arm and took his bare hand.
"You have such simple loyalties now. Like life. Like those
who can hold you to it. *Ask* me—how you can help me?"

"How can I help you?" The words poured out without a thought of resistance. The same way they did for Ischade. It was only afterward that the shame got to him. Afterward when he had time to think; but that was not now, with Haught this close, death gaping and lapping below the drop from the garden fence.

"You can go to hell," Haught said.

It was not a curse. It was an order. "For *her*—" Stilcho said, lips stammering. "I go for her, that's all."

"Oh, it's in her service. Believe me."

2

Strat blinked in the sunlight and rode past the Blue line checkpoint in the morning—the bay's shod hooves ringing hollow on the cobbles beside the bridge. The misnamed White Foal flowed murkily by, with its scarce traffic on dark-brown water; a skiff or two; a scruffy little barge.

The scarred end-posts stood innocent in the sun. The reeking, rotten streets of Downwind on the other side lost their mystery by daylight and became the ugly thing they were. The poor shuffled about their eternal business of staying alive, whatever the business of the night. It was a peaceful day in Sanctuary and the other-side. The invisible lines still existed; but they weakened by day, descending to amiable formality, expecting no assault. The iron discipline of the gangs and the death squads gave way to pragmatic spot-searches, Ilsigi poor taking their little chances with the lines they could cross, beggars begging their usual territories. Death squads operated nightly; bodies turned up by daylight to impress the populace.

But a Stepson still rode through, down the invisible no-man's line of the riverside. Strat saw the blue graffiti on one wall; saw red on another, where rival gangs blazoned their claims at riverside.

He knew hate surrounded him. He felt it in the city, felt it when he rode up the daylit streets in Jubal's territory— toward the Black line where members of the Band and the 3rd Commando held their own, keeping the bridge and one long street open from the Stepson Yellow line in the west, through Red through Blue and into the Black of the Mageguild's territory, commerce maintained against every attempt of the individual militias and factions to shut it down. It was a demonstration Ranke was not yet done; and some wanted to demonstrate otherwise.

His eyes scanned the way that he rode, his skin absorbed the temperature of the glances that fell on him.

The mongrel crowds of Sanctuary were out by daylight. The workmen and the merchants—the few shops, graffiti scarred, marked with the Permissions of Jubal's gangs that ruled the sector—spread few goods. Merchants *had* few goods. Took few chances. Many doors stayed shut; shop-shutters were boarded over. Uptown did not see this danger-signal; there the shops hired more guards; there the rich doubled the locks on their doors. Walegrin of the Garrison knew: the mercs the prince hired knew, and both prepared as best they could—to hold the other long street open, hill to harbor.

Straton lifted his eyes, blinking in the day. He let the horse carry him in that lassitude his mornings-after had; let his mind carry him in crazed thoughts that darted this way and that, through the streets, to the detail of a graffiti'd wall that informed him of some death squad active in the night—to the beggar on the curb that withdrew from his horse's skittish hooves. A cart of empty jars passed him. A handbarrow groaned past under a load of rags and junk. A sewer-opening afflicted his nostrils with its sweet-ugly stench. And a blue sky shone down on Ranke's slow death.

He blinked again, looked uptown through the haze of morning-smokes from Sanctuary's thousand fires, up the winding of one of the long streets.

And it seemed there was a line drawn in the world, with fools on one side and the other of it, and himself one of the few who could see himself as a fool. The high shining fine houses where Ranke frittered away its last hours barriered themselves in vain against the tide that was about to come uptown. Walegrin could not hold forever. Neither could they, below.

Sanctuary, with its backside to the sea.

With its mongrel gods and its mongrel merchants and the last lost rim of secure land in the Empire. Nisibis would sweep down to the shores; and the Beysib up from the south like a rolling wave; and for an intelligent man who had soldiered all his life away for the fools who wore the gold and the purple—there was in the end, riot and murder and death by stoning in city streets.

Fool, he thought, hating Kadakithis for what he was not. And had a vision of dark eyes and felt the feathery touch of soft lips and the dizzying descent into dark.

He took up on the reins. Looked uphill with thoughts moiling in him: And snapped the reins and sent the bay clattering along the Maze, through increasingly tangled streets. Red PFLS graffiti sprawled across a wall, once, twice, obscuring the usual obscenity, Jubal's blue hawk splashed over that. The bay spurned broken pottery, sent a girl shrieking for the curb. A rock pelted back and rebounded off the cobbles. The young were always the rebels.

The uptown house echoed to soft steps and the closing of doors and Moria came downstairs, wrapped in her robe. She cursed the servants, let out a gutter oath, and stopped dead on the steps, staring wide-eyed at what had gotten in. She clutched the robe about her, wiped at a frowsy tangle of hair and blinked in the dim light. Ex-thief, ex-hawkmask, she *knew* the elegant shape standing in the polished foyer by the Caronnese vase: the elegant, cloaked man who looked up at her and smiled.

Her heart thudded. "Haught." She came pelting down off the steps and remembered all at the same time that she was no longer the street-wiry sylph, no longer the tough woman who knew the ways Haught did not; he was all elegance and she was—she was still Moria of the streets, gone a little fat and altogether terrified.

"Moria." Haught's voice was cool, but a sexual roughness ran through it, and shivered on her nerves. She stopped in her dismay and he took her by the shoulders, in this fine house that was Ischade's, as they all were Ischade's. No one had let him in. He passed whatever doors he liked.

"My brother's missing," she said. "He's—gone."

"No," Haught said. *"She* knows where he is. Vis and I found him. He's doing a little job. Now you have to."

Her mouth began to tremble. First it was outright terror for Mor-am, for her brother, who was half-crazy and bound to Ischade as she was; and second it was for herself, because she knew that she was in a trap and there was no way out. Ischade gave them this fine house and came and collected little pieces of their souls whenever she wanted favors done.

"What?" she asked; and Haught put his hands up to her face and brushed the tangled hair back, gently, like a lover. "What?" Her lips trembled.

He bent and kissed them, softly, and the touch was both gentle and chilling. He gazed closely into her eyes.

Was it possible—Moria stood quite transfixed—*possible* that Haught still loved her? It was a fool's thought. She only had to remember what she was and look at what he had become and know the answer to that. She recovered her wits and stepped back with a small push of her hands. The robe gaped and she cared nothing for that, small and dumpy and wine-sotted woman who had given away all advantage.

"Where *is* he? Where's my brother?"

"Oh, about the streets. Going those places he can go." He reached into his shirt and drew out a thing that never could have come from the lower town. "Here." The red rose showed a little rumpling. It glistened and glowed then, dewed with the illusion of freshness. "I gathered it for you."

"From *Her* garden?"

"The bushes can bloom—even in winter. With a little urging. She doesn't care. She cares for very little. *You* might bloom too, Moria. You only want a little tending."

"Gods—" Her teeth chattered. She shook sense back into her head and looked up at him. At the man she had once known and no longer did, with his fine (foreign) speech. She held the rose in her hand and a thorn brought blood. "Get me *out* of here. Haught, get me out."

"No. That's not the game, Moria." His hands held her face, straightened her hair, smoothed her cheeks. "There, now, you *can* be beautiful." And there was a softer feel to her face and to his hands, cool, like the winter rose. "You can. You can be anything you want to be. Your brother has his uses. But he's weak. You never were. He's a fool. You were never that either."

"If I'm so smart why am I here? Why am I locked in this place with gold I can't even steal? Why do I take orders from a—"

His finger touched her lips but the silence was hers, sudden and prudent. She caught the shadow in his eyes, that perpetually evaded, darted, shifted in a slave's no-where privacy—he had turned that apparent shyness to furtive purpose. Or had always had it.

"She's calling in the debt," she said, "isn't She?"

"Trust me," Haught said. His finger wandered down her cheek to her throat. "There are few women who attract me. Certainly I don't share her bed. Calling in the debt, yes. And when the world changes, you'll wear satins and eat on gold—"

"Gods, Shalpa and Ils de—"

Her voice changed in her throat, lost its harshness and became Rankene-smooth, betraying her. She stopped and spat. "My *gods!*" (But it came out pure and clear.)

"My rose has hurt your hand." Haught gathered her fingers to his lips and kissed the thorn-sting, and Moria, who had faced street gangs dagger in hand and sliced respect into more than one Downwind bully, stood and trembled at that touch.

Trembled more when he turned her toward the mirror and she saw the touseled, dark-haired woman who blinked back at her in shock. Rage flooded through her. He *made* her this. Witchery like the rose. She turned on him with fury in her eyes. "I'm not your toy, dammit!"

(But the voice would not roughen and the accent was not Ilsigi.)

"You're the way I always saw you."

"Damn you!"

"And the way She wants you. Leave Mor-am to the streets. He has his uses. Yours are uptown. Haven't you understood what you're for?"

"I'm not your damn whore!"

He flinched. "Have I ever asked that? No. I'll tell you what you're to do. But I wouldn't use that word. I truly wouldn't, Moria, in *Her* hearing."

More messengers sped during the day. One great one lifted on black wings and scattered a flock of lesser on his way from the river-house roof. The little ones went a dozen ways.

And Ischade (she *did* sleep, now and again, but rarely of late) wrapped herself in a dusky blue cloak unlike her nighttime black and gathered up certain other things she wanted.

"Stilcho," she said; and having no answer, thrust aside the curtains that hid the Stepson's small room.

There was no one there. "Stilcho!" She sent her mind

out in a light scouring of the immediate vicinity; and raised a thin, wan response.

She opened the door and took a look out back: and found him there, a shivering knot of cloak by the rose-bush.

"Stilcho!"

There was refuge of a sort in the house, one of half a dozen hidey-holes they maintained within the black zone for operations this far from base. And Strat paid listless attention to the bay and saw it strawed and fed and watered in the shanty-stable; and climbed the dirty stairs of the deserted place and pulled the vent-chain that let a little light through the shutters.

There was a little food here. A little wine. A waterpot and a few other odds and ends. He stumped about in the dusty silence and knew that he was safe from hearing: below was only the stable, and to either side were warehouses and the owners of them well-heeled and Rankene, uptown.

He had his breakfast. He washed. He found himself trapped in one of those days that had gotten common enough lately, with horror on either end and sheer boredom in the middle. Nowhere presently to go. Nothing presently to do, because it was all waiting, waiting, waiting. Something would break and the 3rd's scattered vigilance would turn up something, but in the meanwhile commerce went on and down by the harbor hammering went on, sound echoing off distant walls.

Building going on while the world ended.

He sat there and chewed a tasteless bit of yesterday's bread and drank a cup of wine and most of what his mind wanted to go to was Her, and the river and the dark. Maybe he could have found something to do with himself, found some use for himself or some plan to pursue—but he had a deep and abiding conviction that there was nothing, presently, worth the doing. And that soon all hell would break.

He grew prophetic since he had shared the witch's bed. Niko had gone down in such a trap and even that failed to alarm him, because he knew why, and accepted. He sat listlessly and heard his heart beat, thump, thump, like the hammer-blows and the thud of cartwheels on cobbles and the whole pulse of the city.

My city. Walls behind which the Empire could last if there were adjustments here.

More than one emperor of Ranke had risen (aye, and come to grief) at the will of the soldiery.

He could snatch up the sword Kadakithis left untouched. Be ready when Tempus returned.

Shock Crit to hell, he would. Hello, Crit. Meet the new emperor. Me.

He shivered. It was crazy. He tried to think back to the night and it was full of dark gaps. Memory of things he had done with Ischade that had all the improbability of efreets and krrf-dreams.

They came and went. Her face did. Her mouth hovered close and spoke words and he could read lips, but he could not read that, as if she spoke some language he knew and did not know when he was awake, or his brain would not let him put the sounds together.

And no man had nights like that, no one could, and have another and another and pay no penalties.

There were sore places; there were marks—(witch-marks?) bites and scratches that confirmed part of what he remembered; could a man's soul leak out through such little wounds?

A spider had spun an elaborate web over by the light-vent, across the slats. He found it uncomfortably ominous. He went and flung it down and crushed the spider under his heel; and felt a chill greater than the killing in the barracks had given him.

"Stilcho." It took an expenditure of energy to bring him back. Ischade put her hands on the Stepson and searched deep down the long threads that led where he had gone; and pulled, and rewove, and brought him up again, there on the cold ground beneath the scraggly roses and the brush. "Stilcho. Fool. Come up and let go."

He wept—tears from one eye and a thin, reddish fluid from the missing one. And he did come back—came rushing back all at once and into the world with a scream that would have drawn attention in any town but Sanctuary and in any neighborhood but this one.

"Well," she said, sitting there with her arms about her knees and regarding this least willing of her servants. "And where were you?"

He knew her then and scrambled back till he hit the rosebushes and impaled himself on the thorns. He began to shiver; and she caught a little remnant of magics about the place.

"That very fool!" she said, knowing of a sudden that signature and that willful pride. At times Haught amused her with his hunger for knowledge and his self-convinced keenness to serve. This was not one of those times. "Where did you go last night?"

"H-h-here."

"Vanity. Vanity. What prodigy did you perform? What did he ask?"

"I—I—" Stilcho's teeth chattered. "Ask—a-ask me—go down—find—f-find—a-answer—"

She drew in a deep breath and slitted her eyes. Stilcho gazed into her face and pressed himself as far in retreat as he could, heedless of the thorns. He flinched when she reached and caught him by the arm. "Stepson. No, I shan't hurt you. I'll not hurt you. What did Haught want to know?"

"N-n-nik-o." Stilcho went into a new paroxysm of shivering. "T-temple—. Said—said tell—you—Janni— Janni is out hunting Niko."

She was very still for a moment. A thread of blood ran down Stilcho's cheek from the thorns. "What side is he playing, Stilcho?"

"Says—says—you spend—" Stilcho trembled and a second runnel joined the first down his cheek. "Too much time on Straton. Says think of Janni. Think—"

It all died away very quickly, very quietly. She stared at him a moment, and he stayed still as a bird in front of a snake. And then she smiled, which made him flinch the more. She reached out and straightened a lock of hair above his ruined face. "You have a good heart, Stilcho. A loyal heart. An honest one. Proof against corruption. Of all sorts. Even though you hate what I did. Haught is Nisi. Does that suggest caution to you?"

"He—hates the Nisi witch."

"Oh, yes. Nisi enemies sold him into slavery. But Stepsons bought him. I tell you, Stilcho, I will not have quarrels in my house. There, you're bleeding. Go in and wash. And wait—" She bent and pressed a kiss against his scarred mouth, another against his wounded cheek. He took in his breath at the second, because she had sent a little prickling spell lancing into his soul. "If Haught tries you again I'll know. Get inside."

He scrambled out of his predicament with the rosebush, gathered himself to his feet and went up the steps into the house. In haste. With what of grace a dead man could manage taking his leave of a sovereign lady who crouched thus in the dust and meditated a few tattered, fresh leaves onto the rosebush.

The door slammed. The rosebush struggled into one further untimely surge, thrust out a wan limegreen shoot and budded. She stood and it unfurled, blood-red and perfect.

She plucked it and sucked her finger, sent out a silent summons and a dozen birds flapped aloft above where they had clung like ill-omened leaves to the skeletal winter trees.

She tucked the rose into the doorlatch. So much for Haught, who thought that his mistress had grown soft-witted. Who thought that she needed counsel; and who took first a bit of latitude with his orders and then a bit more.

This rose likewise had thorns.

It was noon, and Straton headed to the streets again—quietly, or at least with enough attempt at disguise that those who recognized him would know better than to hail him. He left the bay stabled and went afoot; and wore ordinary clothes. First he paid a visit to the backside of a tavern where messages tended to turn up, if there was a chalkmark on a certain wall there. There was nothing. So one informant failed, which meant two others had, down the line from that one.

But Sanctuary stayed uncommonly quiet—considering the carnage that had happened over by the barracks Downwind-side. Or because of it.

He fretted, and bought a hot drink at a counter, and stood there watching Sanctuary urchins batting something objectionable about the gutter. And took a further walk up the street, past an easy checkpoint into Blue, dodging round a fuller-wagon immediately after. A donkey had died in the street. That was the morning's excitement. The tanners from the Shambles were loading it into a cart with more help from local brats than they wanted. A sly wag spooked the tanner's horse and it shied off and dumped the corpse flat, to howls from watchers curbside.

Strat evaded the entire process, felt a jostle and spun, reaching after a retreating arm—his heart lurched; his legs hurled him into action before he thought, but that was temper, and he gave up the chase two steps into it. The thief had failed, his purse was intact, and the only thought left to him was how easily it could have been a knife. The Rankan hitting the pavements right along with the donkey and the Ilsigi rabble howling with laughter.

Or absenting themselves in prudent speed.

He felt cold of a sudden, standing there, his thief in rout, the passers-by giving him curious stares as they jostled about him, perhaps seeing a stranger a little tall and a little fair to be standing on this particular streetcorner, this low in the town. A battlefield had its terror: noise and dust and craziness; but this day by day walking through streets full of knives, full of sly stares and calculations where he stood out like a whore at an uptown party—

—he was in the minority down here, that was what. He was thunderously *alone*. Uptown was where a Rankan belonged.

—in the sunlight—

—at the head of armies—

"Hsst."

He turned with a start, caught the sudden dart of an eye from a curly-headed brat, the inviting jerk of head toward alley, down beyond the donkey-crowd. *Come along*, the gesture insisted.

He froze, there on the street. It was not one of the regular contacts. It was someone who knew him. Or who knew him only as Rankan and a target and *any* target would do to raise the prestige of some damned death squad crazy who wanted a little claim to glory—

Any Rankan would do, any Beysib, any uptowner.

He walked on down the street, slipping his shoulders through the crowd, ignoring the invitation. It was not a situation he liked—crowds, bodies pressing close against him, pushing and shoving; but there was one way away from that alley.

Another tug at his belt; he reached and turned and lost momentum in the crowd as his hand protected his purse.

Another hand was there, on his wrist. He looked up and

it was a dark face, a couple of days unshaven, haggard-eyed, under a dark fringe of hair and a cap that had seen better years.

Vis.

Mradhon Vis pulled at him, edged sideways through the crowd and alleyward, and Straton followed, cursing himself for a twice-over fool. This was a Nisi agent. A hawkmask; and a man with more than one grudge against him. And also a man more than once in his pay.

Vis wanted him in the alley. And of a sudden there was a second man who seemed less interested in the dead donkey than in him.

Fool, Straton thought again, but there were two choices now—the alley with Vis or taking out running, in full flight, and attracting the mob.

3

Moria waited in the antechamber in an agony of uncertainty—cloak close about her and enough muscle waiting out in the street to guarantee her passage through Downwind with jewels on. This foyer of one of uptown's most elegant mansions was no less perilous territory, for other reasons. It was the lady Nuphtantei's mansion, where Ischade had sent her: Haught said so. Haught gave her an escort of some of Downwind's best, bathed and dressed up like a proper set of servants; Haught gave her a paper to hand the servants, a tiny object, and a set of words to say, and Moria, born to Downwind's gutters, stood in this place which was one of the oldest of all Sanctuary mansions (but not the oldest of Sanctuary occupants) and knotted her hands and professionally estimated the wealth that she saw about her, in gold and silver.

A movement caught her eye. She looked down, gulped and skipped four feet backward from the gliding course of a viper.

So she looked up again, still in retreat, an object lost from her hand and rolling somewhere across the carpet, as a set of skirts swayed into her view, covering the serpent: skirts and small bare feet and (Moria's shocked vision traveled up to wasp waist and bare breasts) a plethora of jewelry and blonde curls and a face painted to a fare-thee-well: *(Migods, it's a doll!)*

The doll acquired a more stately companion, taller, with straight blonde hair and a shawl of flounces; blonde hair, unblinking eyes and a very sober face of some few more years.

The doll chittered and chattered in the Beysib tongue. "Oh," lisped the tall one. "A messenger? From *whom?*"

Never you mind, bitch. That was what Moria meant to say; but it came out: "Of no moment to you or me." Pure and Rankene. Her voice rushed, breathless. "Your gold has bought you trouble, your friends have bought you enemies, your enemies multiply daily. I have connections. I came to offer them."

"Connections?" The tall Beysib stared with her strange eyes and fingered a small knife at the edge of her shawl of flounces. One of her necklaces moved, a thing that had seemed cloisonné, and was not. "Connections? To whom?"

"Say that this someone can save you when the walls fall."

"What walls?"

"Say that you serve the Beysa. Say that I serve someone else. And tell the Beysa that the wind is changing. Gold will not buy walls."

"Who are you?"

"Tell the Beysa. Tell the Beysa mine is the house with the red door, downhill from here. My name is Moria. Say to the Beysa that there are ways to safeguard her people. And ways to pass any door." It came out in a rush and was done. She did not know what she had said, except that the two Beysib stared at her and the tall woman's necklace had risen up to stare too, quite unpleasantly.

The doll spoke, rapidly. Started forward and looked mad enough to spit, but the other restrained her. There were men about now, elegant, quiet men, half a dozen of them.

"I'm done," Moria said, and waved a hand toward the door. Backed a step, thought of snakes and decided to turn and look. It was not a comfortable retreat. She turned her face to the Beysib again. "I'd say," she said, and her voice was more her own, "that you better lock your doors and stay behind them. You've been fools to walk about so rich. There's a lot fewer of you than there were. Bread's dearer, gold's cheaper, and two blocks

downhill from my house even the Guard won't walk.
Think about that."

"Come here," the Beysib said.

"Not with those snakes," Moria declared, and snatched
the door open and slammed it after.

Her guard was not precisely apparent outside; it materialized when she came down off the steps, a man slouching
along here, another joining them from an alley. Only one
walked with her openly, one of her own servants, a
nine-fingered man very quick with a knife. He wore
brocade and a gold chain and had a sword at his hip which
he had not the least idea how to use, but she knew that of
brigands on the street she was walking with the very worst,
and they took her orders.

She was scared beyond clear thought. She scanned the
street and walked down it with the flounced swish that had
(since the Beysib) become fashionable; and all the while
knew that she had just delivered something deadly to that
house. She had let fall a small silver ball, and it had rolled
away from her feet and lost itself. Perhaps a Beysib snake
would investigate it. It was too small for anything else to
notice.

It did not at all shake her confidence that even Ischade's
sorceries needed physical objects to anchor them. It shook
her more to know how tiny those objects could be, hardly
more than a bead, a droplet of silver, undetectable
without magic to use in turn—and perhaps not then. If
that was not a witch who had met her, then she was no
judge.

A lifelong resident of Sanctuary learned to judge such
things.

Strat balked at the alley-mouth: he had half-thought of a
fast move and a quick break; but so, obviously, had Vis.
Vis was not alone. Three men were in the alley; waiting.
One more behind. So it was either revenge or a serious
talk; and it was easy to get bad hurt trying to get out of this
now.

He went on in and stopped as close to the street as he
could; or tried to. One caught his arm and dragged and he
found the sharp point of a knife in his back from Vis's
side.

He stopped struggling then. Kidney-hit was a bad way

to go, not that there were good ones. He was a profession-
al himself, and this was not one of the times to turn hero.
He let them push and haul him along to a bending of the
alley and push him up against a wall—the push was their
idea, the wall was his, to get something besides the knife
at his vulnerable back; but they followed up close and
personal and Vis and the knife followed up against his gut,
where it was utterly disconcerting.

"This is a talk," Vis said.

"Fine," Straton said, back to the bricks. "Talk."

"No, this is you to us."

"Uhhn. Who's *us?*"

Strat had his stomach tight. He waited for the blow to
the gut; it failed to come. That puzzled him; and unnerved
him more than violence. They wanted more than he had
thought.

"Us is the same source you're used to," Vis said. "Us is
a man you know. This is all business. Word is something's
on the move."

"You and I've talked," Strat said. "You want to get me
a little breathing room and we can trade—" He stopped.
The knife indicated stop. He was in no disposition to
argue. He was careful about breathing for a moment. The
dark look of the men about him might have been Ilsigi. It
wasn't—quite. He suddenly knew what he had fallen in
among. Nisi death squad. In Jubal's pay—maybe.

"You and I have talked," Vis said. "Now I want you to
tell me a few things. Like who's giving you your orders. I
hear you're in her bed. True?"

He sucked in his breath; mistake: the knife gave him
no room to take another. "*Soght-ohon,*" he said, Nisi obscenity. And waited for the knife. Vis grinned. It
was a wolf-grin. Mountain-lunatic grin. Men smiled
like that who hurled themselves off walls, disdaining
surrender.

"She's got you," Vis said. "You're sweating, man. You
know that?"

He said nothing. Stood still and breathed in what little
space he had, starting to add where he could move and
how fast before he might die. Or whether it was time to try
it.

*—The sun and the armor and the walls of Ranke,
Sanctuary become true to its name, the wall behind which—*

"She's got something moving," Vis said, and hooked a finger under Straton's jaw, compelling attention. "Word's flying. That mess over Downwind—the barracks—that wasn't any of *our* doing."

No answers. No answer was the wisest answer and hope to the gods Vis was in control of the other four. Vis had a brain and a grudge the limit of which he knew. The others might be plain crazy. "Let's," Strat said thoughtfully, "not complicate this, Vis. I'm not on your payroll. You're on mine. And let's keep it that way. It's been the same side so far. If something's coming down I'm as interested as you are and I haven't heard—Uhhh."

"You think you still run things, do you?"

"You can kill me. There's those will pay it."

He had meant the Band. Crit. He saw a flicker of something else in Vis's face; and remembered who else would pay it, and whom Vis feared more than he feared Ranke—considerably.

"You got your own hell," Vis said. "I want a straight answer. Is it her? Is it her pulling the cords right now? Where's the rest of your lot?"

Quick mental addition. The slaughter at the barracks: dead giveaway of a new wave of Rankan activity among those in a position to know *they* hadn't done it. And Vis was at least marginally on *Rankan* funds, not Nisibisi. Vis and his lot hated Roxane and her lot. *That* they had in common. "A few of the Band's here," Straton said. "Say that—we've funded this and that in the streets. Same as you. And we want that street to stay open. You want any more funds, Vis, you better think again. I *don't know* what She's up to; and I sure as hell won't hand it out if I find out. But my lads have steered yours clean so far and none of mine have cut your throats. This Jubal's doing? That who's behind this? Is he running your lot? Or is it Walegrin?"

"Oh, we're still bought," Vis said, and the knife eased off. "On all the usual sides. If I was a fool I'd pay you a personal debt right now; but you aren't marked and I'm not a fool." Another of Vis's wolf-grins. "You don't promise and you don't make threats. You just want out of here with as little said as possible. On my side I've been helpful. In spite of some things. I'm telling you now— won't charge you a thing. Something's coming. Debts are being called in. In the Downwind. Moruth's lot. You understand me."

Moruth. Beggar-king. The hawkmasks' old nemesis. Straton looked at Vis and his pseudo-Ilsigi company and added it up again—Vis willing to risk his Rankan income and Vis running information against Moruth and his beggars. It added up to Jubal. For certain it did. Straton let go a slow breath. "Tell Jubal I'm on it. I'll find out. But I don't run his errands."

"You're too smart, Whoreson."

"You're too rash, bastard. So's Jubal if he thinks he's bought out you and these dogs of yours. How many others in the town? Coming in with the trade, are you?"

"Like you. Here. There. A lot of us. But we don't die like the Whoresons in barracks. You're dealing with something else now."

"There's Nisi want your guts for ribbons. My spies tell me that." Strat grinned deliberately into Vis's dark face. *"Us* is a damn small number. *Us* doesn't include most of the mountaineer-Nisi. I know what they want you for, Vis. But don't let's discuss that. You may find Jubal can't hide you singlehanded. You may find Ilsigi money runs thin. Say you and your fine friends just back off now and thank your peculiar gods you and I've kept our tempers. And we won't remind each other of old times."

"So it's not Ranke on the move."

"No, it's not Ranke. It's not us. It's not you. Whatever's moving, it's not either one of us. Or Jubal."

"Ilsigi," Vis said.

"Ilsigi." Freed, Straton spat in sheer amazement. "Wrigglies." He stared at the Nisi outlaw, recalling the peculiar silence of the streets.

"It's Ilsigi," Vis said. "What's either of our lives worth when that breaks loose, huh? That's a lot of knives."

More messengers flew. Most were black, and feathered. One landed in the Maze, bearing a certain amulet. One landed on the wall of the palace and with characteristic perverseness, ran its designated recipient to panting hysteria trying to overtake it and retrieve the small cylinder affixed to its leg. It took off, landed, took off again, and finally, coyly surrendered and bit the hand of the priest who retrieved it.

One landed on a small bush and hopped onto a sill in the Street of Red Lanterns.

And Haught, returning home after delivering one message in person—discovered a rose thrust through the doorhandle, and blanched.

He gathered it up; and thrust it into his bosom as unwillingly as if it had been a snake.

"I do trust," Ischade said when he had come inside, "you'll be more kind in future. Stilcho's not yours."

"Yes," Haught said fervently.

"You think I'm indolent."

"No, Mistress."

"How Nisi, to be in a hurry. How Nisi to be so punctiliously, superciliously careful of my affairs. Sometimes I'd forgotten that. But you do justly chide me for my nature."

"I only tried to care for things—"

"Haught, Haught, Haught. Spare me. You think you've become indispensable. Or rather—you hope to become so." Ischade kicked aside a cloak of fine rose silk. "Few things are."

"Mistress—"

"You fear I don't care for details. Well, you may be right, Haught. I accept your judgment. And your warning. And I want you to take care of a matter for me. Yourself. Since you've become so skilled."

"What—matter?"

She smiled and came and touched the rose he wore. "Take care of Roxane. Keep her out of my way."

Haught's eyes went white, all round.

"Oh, you'll have Stilcho's help," Ischade said. "And Roxane's hardly what she was. Niko's seen to that. She might well make a try for him, but then, you have Janni. And Stilcho. Don't you? I'm sure I can trust you with it."

Another bird fluttered into the open window, and took its perch on a chair back. *This* one came from uptown. It had a spelled ring about its inky leg, and it whetted a chisel-keen beak against steelshod claws. Regarded them both with a mad gold eye.

"Oh, indeed," she said. And to Haught: "Be useful. *Feed* it. Mind your fingers."

"That's the high priest," Haught said, meaning where it had come from. Its message, shrilled in a high thin voice, was not within his understanding.

Query, query, query. "Molin wants answers," Ischade said, and smiled, because those answers were forthcoming, but not in the way the high priest wanted. "Tell Janni he's welcome to *take* Niko if he can. When you see him."

"Where have *you* been?" Black Lysias of the 3rd Commando asked questions when Strat came up into the stables, back inside the Black line. "We've been scouring—"

"Say I had an urgent meeting." Strat caught the man by the sleeve. Fastidious Lysias looked like a ratsnest; smelled like fish. That was the way the 3rd traveled these days. Strat propelled him through into the slant-walled tackroom, where a little daylight got through the cracks of the leaky roof. The bay snorted and stamped and kicked a board nearby, having had enough of this den. Second kick, like half the building was falling. "Damn. *Cut it*, horse."

Sulky silence then. A snort and switch of tail.

"We've got something moving," Straton said. "You hear it?" And in the absence of confirmations: "What have you heard?"

"We got a line on Niko. Got rumors where he is. Uptown. Priests. We got areas we can't get into. Randal sent—says Roxane's stirring about last night; *she*'s looking too. Fast. We still haven't got where. Kama's got her piff connection sniffing round; haven't found *her* yet. Melant's down harborside; Kali's trying that Setmur contact; we've got—"

A shiver went up his back. He gripped Lysias's shoulder, hard. "Listen. I'm going out again. Get the word out, get the Third to positions, full alert."

"You going—"

"Get out of here. Get it moving."

"Right," Lysias said, and dived round the corner: no further questions.

But Strat lingered there in the dim light, with the sinking feeling that panic had impelled that. He wanted the daylight; wanted—

—easy answers.

Kadakithis will lose the Empire—

Niko in trouble. Plots went through Sanctuary like worms through old meat. Tempus delaying and Randal discomfited. Straton considered himself no fool, not ordinarily; upstairs in that nasty little room, men and women had tried to make him one and he had unerringly stripped souls down to little secrets, most of which he was not interested in, a few of which he was, and they spilled them all before they went their way either loose (for effect) or into the Foal (for neatness). He was not particularly proud of this skill, only of a keen wit that did not take lies for an answer. *That* was what made him the Stepsons' interrogator; a certain dogged patience and a sure instinct for unraveling the mazy works of human minds.

That skill turned inward, explored blanks, explored tracks he had no wish for it to follow.

She, she, she, it kept saying, and when it did it traveled round the edges of a darkness more than dark to the eyes; womb-dark, unknowable-dark, warm dark and comfortable and full of too many gaps. Far too many gaps. He had found a certain peace. Courted it. Congratulated himself that he escaped. That perpetual escape had become meat and drink to him; the stuff of his self-esteem.

Think, Stepson. Why can't you think about it?

—Horse wandering in the morning, pilfering apples, rider infant-helpless by dawn—

(He winced at the image. *Is this a sane man?*)

—Kadakithis dying, conveniently dead on the marble floor, the tread of military boots brisk in the halls of the palace—

Good, Tempus would say, finding one of his men had anticipated him; the shadow-play came into sunlight, himself a hero, not the creature of the little room upstairs, but a man who did the wide thing, the right thing, took the chance—

He shivered, there in the dark. There was the taste of blood in his mouth. He leaned there against the wall, jolted as the bay took another kick to let him know its opinion of this dark stable.

He suspected. He suspected himself—*is this a sane man?*

He had to go—there. To the river. To find out. Not by

dark, not during her hour—but by his; by the daylight, when he might have his wits about him.

The river house huddled small and unlikely-looking in the tangle of brush that ran the White Foal's edge on town-side. If you asked a dozen people were there trees in Sanctuary's lower end they would say no, forgetting these. If you asked were there houses hereabouts, they would say no, forgetting such small places as this one with its iron fence and its obscuring hedge. This one was, well, abandoned. There were often lights. Once or twice there had been fire—conspicuous disturbance. But the prudent did not notice such things. The prudent kept to their own districts, and Strat, having ridden past the several checkpoints down mostly deserted streets, rode not oblivious to signs now; thinking, and taking mental notes as he tethered the bay horse out in front of this house that few saw.

He shoved the rusty gate aside and walked up the overgrown flags to the little porch. The door opened before he knocked (and before anyone on the other side could have reached it), which failed to surprise him. Musky perfume wafted out. He walked in, in the dim light that shone through a milky window—Ischade was *not* tidy except in her person.

"*Ischade?*" he called out.

That she would not be at home—that had occurred to him; but he had, in his haste and his urgency, shoved that possibility aside. There was not that much of day left. The sun was headed down over the White Foal, over the sprawl of Downwind buildings.

"Ischade?"

There were unpleasant things to meet hereabouts. She had enemies. She had allies who were not his friends.

A curtain whispered. He blinked at the black-clad figure who walked forward to meet him. She was always so much smaller than he remembered. She towered in his memory. But the eyes, always the eyes—

He evaded them, walked deliberately aside and poured him and her a drink from the pitcher that sat on the low table. Candles brightened. He was accustomed to this. Accustomed too, to the light step that stole up behind him—*no* one walked up behind him; it was a tic he had. But Ischade did it and he let her; and she knew. Knew that no one touched him from behind, that it was one of their little games, that he let her do that. It made a little frisson of horror. Like other games they played. Soft hands came up his back, rested on his shoulders.

He turned round with both wine cups and she took hers and a kiss, lingering-slow.

They did not always go straight to bed. Tonight he took the chair in front of the fire; she settled half beside him and half into his lap, a comfortable armful, all whisper of cloth and yielding curves and smell of rich musk and good wine. She sipped her wine and set it down on the sidetable. Sometimes at such moments she smiled. This time she gazed at him in a way he knew was dangerous. He had not come tonight to look into those dark eyes and forget his own name. He felt a cold the wine could not reach, and felt for the first time that life or death might be equally balanced in her desires.

Ischade treading the aisles of the barracks, surveying murder—satisfied. Sated. It was not death that appealed to her. It was *these* deaths.

"You all right?" he asked of the woman staring so close into his eyes. "Ischade, are you all right tonight?"

Blink. He heard his pulse. Hers. The world hung suspended and day or night made no difference. He cleared his throat or tried to.

"You think I better get out of here?"

She shifted her position and rested her arms on his shoulders, joined her hands behind his head. Still silent.

"I want to ask you," he said, trying, in the near gaze of her eyes, the soft weight of her against his side. "—want to ask you—" That wasn't working. He blinked, breaking the spell, and took his life in his hands, grinned in the face of her darkness and sobered up and kissed her. His best style. He could get things out of a body one way; he had, now and again, used pleasanter persuasions. He was not particularly proud of it, no more than the other. It was all part of his skill—knowing a lie from a scrap of truth, and following a lead. He had one. Truth was in her silence tonight.

"You want something," he said, "you've always wanted something—"

She laughed, and he caught her hands down. Hard.

"What can I do," he asked, "what is it you want me to do?" No one held onto Ischade. He sensed that in the darkening of her eyes, in the sudden dimming of the room.

He let go. "Ischade. Ischade." Trying to keep his focus. And hers. Right now he ought to get up and head for the door and he knew it; but it was infinitely easier to sit where he was; and very hard to think of what he had been trying to think of, like the memory gaps, like the things they did/he thought they did in that bed sprawled with silks. "You've got Stilcho, got Janni, got me—is it coincidence, Ischade? Maybe I could help you more if I was awake when you talked to me—" *Or is it information you go for?* "Maybe—our aims and yours aren't that far apart. Self-interest. Weren't you talking about self-interest? What's yours, really? And I'll tell you mine."

Arms tightened behind his head. She shifted forward and now there was nothing in all the room but her eyes, nothing in all the world but the pulse in his veins. "You think hard," she said. "You go on thinking, thinking's a counterspell, you've come here all armed with thinking, and yet it's such a heavy load—aren't you tired, Strat, don't you get tired, bearing all the weight for fools, being always in the shadow, isn't it worth it, once, to be what you are? Let's go to bed."

"What's going on in town?" He got the question out. It wandered out, slurred and half-crazed and half-independent of his wits. "What have you got your hand into, Ischade? What game are you using us for—"

"Bed," she whispered. "You afraid, Strat? You never run from what scares you. You don't know how."

4

"I don't know," Stilcho said, limping along through the streets in Haught's company. Haught took long strides and the dead Stepson made what speed he could, panting. A waterskin sloshed in time to his steps. "I don't *know* how to make contact with him—he's *here*, that's all—"

"If he's dead," Haught said, "I'd think you had an edge. I don't think you're trying."

"I can't," Stilcho gasped. Twilight showed Haught's elegance, his supercilious gaze, and Stilcho, about to clutch at him, held back his hand. "I—"

"She says that you will. She says that you'll be quite adequate. I really wouldn't want to prove less than that, would you?"

The thought ran through Stilcho like icewater. They

were near the bridge, near the running-water barrier, and while it did not stop him (he was truly alive in some senses) it made him weak in the knees. There was a checkpoint the other side of the bridgehead, that was a line of no color; and few meddled with *that* one, which had some living warders, but not all that patrolled the streets beyond were alive, and the Shambles suffered horrors and the malicious whimsy of Roxane's creatures. "Listen," Stilcho said, "listen, you don't understand. He's not like the dead when he's like this. Dead are everywhere. Janni's tied to one thing, he's got an attachment, and he's like the living in that regard. No good news for what he's attached to—But you can't find him like the rest of the dead. He's got *place, where* applies to him same as you and me—"

"Don't lump me in your category." Haught brushed imaginary dust from his cloak. "I've no intention of joining you. And whatever you told the mistress about that business with the rosebush—"

"Nothing, I told her nothing."

"Liar. You'd tell anything you were asked, you'd hand her your mother if she asked—"

"Leave my mother out of this."

"She down in hell?" Haught wondered, with a sudden wolfish sharpness that sent another icy chill through Stilcho's gut. "Maybe *she* could help."

Stilcho said nothing. The hate Haught had toward Stepsons was palpable, a joke most of the time, but not when they were alone. Not when there was something Haught could hold over him. But Stilcho glared back. He had been a marsh-brat and a Sanctuary drayman before the Stepsons recruited him, neither occupation lending itself to bright, sharp acts of courage. He was slow to anger as his lumbering team had been. But there was a point past which not, the same as there had been with his plodding horses. The beggar-king who tortured him had found it; Haught had just located it. And Haught perhaps sensed it. There was a sudden quiet in the Nisibisi wizardling. No further jibes. Not a further word for a moment.

"Let's just get it done," Stilcho said, anxious less for Haught than for Her orders. And he gathered his black cloak about him and walked on past the bridge. A bird swooped overhead—a touch of familiarity, perhaps, avian inquisitiveness. But it was not the sort to be interested in riverside unless there was a bit of carrion left. It flapped away to the Downwind side of the bridge, heedless of barriers and checkpoints, as other birds winged their way here and there.

That one was bound for the barracks, Stilcho reckoned. Across the bridge he saw, with his half-sight—(the missing eye was efficacious too, and *had* vision in the shadow-world, whether or not it was patched: it was, lately, since he had recovered a little bit of his vanity, under the sting of Haught's taunts.) He saw the PFLS bridgewarder, but he saw several Dead gathered there too, about the post where they had died; and Haught was with him, but not exactly in the lead as they walked down the street and cut off toward the Shambles.

"Gone back to the witch, that's where." Zip dropped down on the wooden stairs of a building in the Maze, there on the street, and the beggar-looking woman who slouched in her rags nearby was listening, although she did not look at him. Zip was panting. He pulled out one of his knives and attacked the wood of the step between his legs. "He's one damn fool, you know that."

"Mind your mouth," Kama said. It was a slim woman and a lot of weaponry under all that cloak and cloth, and her face was smeared with dirt enough and her mouth crusted with her last meal, part of the disguise. She would even fool the nose. "You want to make yourself useful, get the hell to the *Unicorn* and pick up Windy. Tell him move and leave the rest to him."

"I'm not your damn errand-boy."

"Get!"

He got. Kama got up and waddled down the darkening street in her best old-woman way, toward another contact.

Moruth heard the dull flap of wings before the bird alit in the window of Mama Becho's. The beggar-king clenched his hands and listened, and when it appeared, a dark flutter outside the shutters, he resisted going to that window at the tavern's backside. But a hard, chisel beak tapped and scrabbled insistently. Wanting *in*.

He went and shoved the window open. The bird took off and lit again, glaring at him with shadowy eyes in the almost-night. It lifted then with a clap of wings and flapped away, mission accomplished.

Moruth had not the least desire in the world to go out tonight; he lived in constant terror, since the massacre over by Jubal's old estate, in the Stepson barracks. There were a lot of souls out on patrol in Sanctuary, round Shambles Cross. Old blind Mebbat said so; and Moruth, who had carried on warfare in the streets with Stepsons and hawkmasks, had no particular desire to meet what walked about on such nights.

But he went to the door and sent a messenger who sent others, and one ran up to a rooftop and waved a torch.

"Snakes," Ischade whispered, in bed with her lover. She kissed him gently and disengaged his fingers from her hair. "You ever put it together, Strat, that both Nisibis *and* the Beysib are fond of snakes?"

He recalled a serpentine body rolling under his heel, a frantic moment the other side of Roxane's window.

"Coincidences," Ischade said. "That's possible of course. True coincidences are a rare thing, though. You know that. You don't believe in them any more than I do, being no fool at all."

Stilcho stopped, moving carefully now. Haught's hand sought his arm. "They're here," Haught said.

"They've been here for some time," Stilcho said of the shadows that shifted and twisted, blacker than other shadows. "We've crossed the line. You want to do the talking?"

"Don't try me. Don't try me, Stilcho."

"You think you're powerful enough to walk through the Shambles now and deal with all the ghosts at once. Do it, why don't you? Or why'd you bring me?"

Haught's fingers bit painfully into his arm. "You talk to them, I say."

No more remarks about his mother. Stilcho turned his head with deliberate slowness and looked at the gathering menace. No one alive was on the street but Haught. And himself. And many of these were Roxane's. Many were not—just lost souls left unattended and lately, in the lamentable condition of Sanctuary, without compulsion to go back to rest.

"I'm Stilcho," he said to them. And he took what he carried, a waterskin, and poured some of the contents on the road. But it was not water that pooled and glistened there. He stepped back. There was a dry rustling, a pushing and shoving, and something very like a living black blanket of many pieces settled above the glistening puddle on the cobbles. He backed away and spilled more. "There'll *be* more," he said. "All you have to do is follow."

Some ghosts turned away in horror. Most followed, a slow drifting. He dribbled more of the blood. He had not asked where it came from. These days it was easy come by.

For Ischade—more than most.

Strat struggled to open his eyes, and when he did there was a whisper in the air like bees in summer, there was a darkness above him like uncreation. "You suspect me," a voice said, like the bees, like the wind out of the dark, "of all manner of things. I told you: self-interest. Mine is this town. This town is where I hunt. This wicked, tangled town, this sink into which all wickedness pours—suits me as it is. I lend my strength to this side and to that. Right now I lend it to the Ilsigis. But you'll forget that by morning. You'll forget that and remember other things."

He got his eyes open again. It took all the strength he had. He saw her face in a way he had never seen it, looked her in the eyes and looked into hell, and wanted now to shut them, but he had lost that volition.

"I've told you what to do," she said. "Go. *Leave,* while you can. *Get out of here!*"

High on the hill a horn blew, brazen and pealing alarm. The alarm outside the *Unicorn* was more mundane and less elegant: a series of old pots battered with all the strength in a watcher's arm.

Help, ha! Invasion, incursion, mayhem!

There was fire in Downwind. And uptown.

In a dozen intersections barricades started going up, torches flared, horses' hooves clattered wildly through the night.

"Get 'em," Lysias the Black instructed his small band, and arrows rained down on one of Jubal's bands that planned to barricade the Blue line. "Rouse our wizard-help up here, move it! That road stays open!"

From his vantage on a rooftop, bright fire sprang up on the hill.

More horns and clatterings and brayings of alarms in the night. Militias hit the streets.

And a rider on a bay horse pelted down the riverside with reckless abandon right through the Blue, headed for Black lines and comrades.

All hell was loose in the streets. Shutters broke (thieves in Sanctuary were no laggards, and had had their eyes set on this and that target from *long* before: when the riot broke, they smashed and grabbed and ran like all the devils and the Rankan pantheon was at their heels.)

Uptown, one of the horns braying and one of the alarms ringing was the merc barracks and the Guard; but Walegrin, who had not been slow to pick up the rumors, already had *his* snipers posted, and the first surge of looters uptown met a flight of arrows and a series of professionally organized barricades. This was standard operation. It deterred the more dilatory of invaders.

It did not deter all of them.

Down on riverside, Ischade sat wrapped only in her black robe, in the tumbled fiery silks of her bed, and grinned while her eyes rolled back in her head.

Shadows poured down the riverside, shadows marched from the ravaged barracks in Downwind, and ignored the barriers the Beggar-king and his kind had erected. Ignored the PFLS and its flung stones and its naphtha-bottles and the fires: that demi-legion had seen the fires of hell and were not impressed. They had already passed the Yellow line, and they swaggered along Red territory, the winding streets of Downwind, with a swiftness no ordinary band could achieve, faster and faster.

"They're coming," Stilcho said to Haught, and the Nisi magus hardly liked the satisfaction in Stilcho's face. Haught snatched the skin of blood and shook out a few more drops to keep the Shambles-ghosts on the track— glanced a second time at Stilcho, thinking uncomfortably of treachery.

"Janni. Where's Janni? Have you located him?"

"Oh, I can guess where he'll go," Stilcho said.

"Roxane."

Stilcho laughed and grinned. He had a patched eye and was missing one tooth on the side, but in the dark when the scars showed less there was a ruined handsomeness about him. An elegance. He snatched the skin from

Haught and hurled it, spattering the cobbles. *"Run!"* he yelled at Haught, and laughed aloud.

"Stilcho, damn you!"

"Try!" Stilcho yelled. Ghosts streamed and gibbered about them, swirled and whirled like bats, and Haught assessed the situation in an eyeblink and whipped his cloak about his arm and ran as if the fiends of hell were on his track.

Stilcho howled. Slapped his knees. *"Run,* you friggin' bastard! Run, Nisi, run!"

He would pay for it in the morning. Haught would see to that. But he had Her orders, direct.

He jogged off in the direction of the bridge, where a shadowy troop needed help passing running water. His old partner was in the lead and the company insignia was intact.

Behind him the ghosts did what everyone else in Sanctuary was busy doing: They chose sides and took cover and had at one another.

Stilcho turned his own troop up the riverside and through the streets—slower now, because they had a half-living man for a guide. But he would take them only so far. *They* would have no trouble with Walegrin's uptown barricades or the Stepsons' eastward; and they were not in a negotiating mood, having their murders recently in mind. Teach the uptowners their vulnerability —show the bastards who gave the orders that there were those who remembered their *last* orders and their *last* official mistakes—

He jogged along, panting, limping—Ischade's repair work was thorough, but a long run still sent pain jolting through him.

Ghosts passed them, headed where they wished to be. They were polyglot and headed for old haunts, former domiciles, old feuds. Sanctuary might get pragmatic about its haunts, but the ghosts grew bolder and nervier in these declining days of the Empire; and these were not the reasoning kind. *These* had been walking patrol in Ischade's service, or Roxane's; and a few luckless ones tried to go complain to Roxane about the matter.

Roxane cursed a blue streak (literally) and in a paroxysm of rage conjured a dozen snakes and a demon, an orange-haired, grayskinned being named Snapper Jo which ran rampaging up the riverside till it forgot quite

what it was about and got to rampaging through a
warehouse full of beer. It was not, all in all, one of
Roxane's better nights: the attack was desultory, Ischade
was definitely aiming at something else, and Roxane was
willing to use the diversion while *she* took wing
crosstown—

"Damn!" Haught yelled. His sight picked that up, a
pale blue arc headed across Sanctuary with only one target
in mind. He was earthbound. He ran for the river and
Ischade with all his might, and came pelting past the wards
to find Ischade sitting on the bed wrapped in orange silk
and the skirts of her black cloak and laughing like a
lunatic.

Uptown the Lady Nuphtantei's door went wide open
and the elegant Lady Nuphtantei, Harka Bey and *not*
easily affrighted, went pelting down the street naked as
she was born, for the drunken demon that had materialized in her house breaking porcelains and crunching silver
underfoot was not a thing the servants or her daughter had
stayed to deal with, not for a moment.

She ran straight into a company of Walegrin's guard and
kept going, so fast the guard hardly had time to turn and
stare.

Then what was behind her showed up, and the troops
scattered.

Arrows flew. A barricade was afire over by the Maze
edge where Jubal's gangs tried to hold against rooftop
archers, mage-illusions, and a handful of paired riders
who had the style and manner of the old Stepsons. And
the fire spread to buildings, which doubled the chaos. Men
threw water and ducked arrows. A frantic family scurried
out with possessions and arrows pelted indiscriminate.

The physician Harran wrung his hands (one was a
woman's) and paced his upstairs room and took another
look out the window, in the little garret where he had
hidden his affliction—fortuitously hidden, considering
what had befallen everyone else in the barracks. But he
had no practice now, no home, no direction. Mriga gone.
There was the little dog, which paced about after him
panting and whuffing in mimic concern.

He was (whatever his affliction) still a doctor. The pain
he spied on worried at him and gnawed his gut. "Oh,
damn," he muttered to himself, when a boy darted from

cover, limned red in the firelight, and flung a torch. Tried to fling it. An arrow took him. The boy fell, writhing, skewered through the leg, right near the great artery. *"Damn."*

Herran slammed the shutter, shut his eyes and suddenly turned and ran down the stairs, thundering down the hollow boards, into the smell of smoke and the glare outside. He heard shouting, wiped his eyes. Heard the boy screaming above the roar of the burning barricade, above the shouts of men in combat. Horses screamed. He heard the thunder of hooves and dashed out to reach the boy as the riders streaked past. "Lie still," he yelled at the screaming, thrashing youth. *"Shut up!"* He grabbed him about the arm and hauled it over his shoulders, heard a frantic barking and another great shout as he stumbled to his feet, the oncoming thunder of riders on the return, a solid wall of horsemen.

"Goddess—"

Strat met the shockwave of his own forces that had kept the way open: a moment of confusion while they swept about and followed him in a clatter on the pavings. The burning barricade was ahead, a sleet of stones. An uneven pair of figures blocked his path, dark against the light—

Strat swept his sword in an arc that ended in the skull of the taller and took a good part of it away: he rode through. The rider behind him faltered as his horse hit the bodies and recovered; then the rest of the troop went over them, crushing bone under steel-shod hooves, and swords swung as they met Jubal's men at the barricade, on their way back through.

There was a decided interest on the childrens' part. One boy kept climbing up to the window and gazing out, less talkative than his wont. The other never left it, and stared when Niko came and took both in his arms.

He saw the circling of something sorcerous that could not get in. Saw something dark stream up to fight it off, and that something was torn ragged and streamed on the winds. But what it had turned was dimmer fire now. He heard a forlorn cry, like a great hunting bird. Like a damned soul. A lost lover.

The wards about the place glowed blinding bright. And held.

Sanctuary was beset with fires, barricades, looting. The armed priests of the Storm God were no inconsiderable barrier themselves.

But they were ineffectual finally against a torn, bloody thing that haunted the halls and that tried the partnership that had been between them. He *knew* what had come streaking in to find him; he knew what faithful, vengeful wraith had held the line again. It pleaded with him in his dreams, forgetting that it was dead. He wept at such times, because he could not explain to it and it was not interested in listening.

"Get me out of here," he yelled down the hall, startling the children. A priest showed up in the hallway, spear in hand, eyes wide. "Dammit, get me *out* of this city!"

The priest kept staring. Niko kicked the door shut and sank down against it, child in either arm.

They crawled into his lap, hugged him round the neck. One wiped his face, and he stared past, longing for the dawn and the boat they promised would come.

A barge went down the White Foal, an uncommonly sturdy one by Sanctuary standards. Ischade watched it, arms about her, the hood of her black cloak back. Her faithful were there: chastened Haught, smug Stilcho. The usual birds sat in the tree. Breath frosted on the wind—a cold morning, but that hardly stopped the looting and the sniping. There was a smoky taint to the air.

"They want war," Ischade said, "let them have war. Let them have it till they're full of it. Till this town's so confounded no force can hold it. Have you heard the fable of Shipri's ring? The goddess was set on by three demons who plainly had rape in mind; she had a golden armlet, and she flung it to the first if he would fight off the other two and let her go. But the second snatched at it and so did the third; the goddess walked away and there they stand to this day. No one devil can get it; and the other two won't let go till the world ends." She turned a dazzling smile on them both, in a merry humor quite unlike herself.

The barge passed beneath the White Foal bridge. A black bird flew after it, sending forlorn cries down the wind.

The bay horse was dead. Strat limped when he walked, and persisted in walking, pacing the floor in the temporary headquarters the Band had set up deep within the mage quarter. A clutter of maps lay on the table. Plans that the ever-changing character of the streets changed hourly. He wanted sleep. He wanted a bath. He reeked of smoke and sweat and blood, and he gave orders and drew lines and listened to the reports that began to come in.

He had not wanted this. He had no wish to be in command. He was, somehow. Somehow it had fallen on him. The Band fought phantoms, confounded them with the living and mage-illusions. Sync was missing. Lyncaeos was dead. Kama had not been heard from. The bay horse had damn near broken his leg when an arrow found it. He had had to kill it. Stepsons and commandos killed with terrible efficiency and the Ilsigi guerrillas who thought they knew what side they were on and thought they knew all about war might see things differently this morning. And change alliances again. In a situation like this alliances might change twice in a morning.

And Kadakithis sat in his palace and the Guard and the mercs held it. Strat limped to the window and entertained treasonous thoughts, hating thoughts, staring up toward the palace through the pall of smoke.

DOWN BY THE RIVERSIDE

Diane Duane

> . . . But who could ever tell of all the daring
> in the stubborn hearts of women, the hard will,
> how the female force crams its resisted way
> through night, through death, taking no "no" for answer?
> Yet still Right's anvil stands staunch on the ground,
> and there smith Destiny hammers out the sword.
> Should that force, that fierce gift, be used for ill,
> delayed in glory, pensive through the murk,
> Vengeance comes home. Yet odd the way of life,
> for if the power's used for good, then still
> She comes; though in far other form, and strange . . .

In Sanctuary that day the smoke rose up to heaven, a sooty sideways-blowing banner against the blue of early winter. Some of that smoke rose up from altars to attract the attention of one god or another, and failed. Most of the immortals were too busy looking on in horror or delight or divine remoteness as their votaries went to war against one another, tearing the town into pieces and setting the pieces afire. A god or two even left town. Many non-gods tried to: some few succeeded. Of those who remained, many non-immortals died, slaughtered in the riots or burned in the firestorms that swept through the city. No one tried or bothered to count them all, not even the gods.

One died in Sanctuary that day who was not mortal (quite), and not a god (quite). His death was unusual in that it was *noticed*—not just once but three times.

He noticed it himself, of course. Harran had worked close to death much of his life, both as apprentice healer-priest of Siveni Gray-Eyes and as the barber and leech to the ersatz Stepsons. He knew the inevitable results of the kind of swordcut that the great dark shape a-horseback swung at him. *No hope,* he thought clinically, while he ducked staggering away with a boy's weight slung over his shoulder. *That's an expert handling that sword, that is.* Past that mere thought, and a flash of pained concern for the arrow-shot boy he'd been trying to save, there was no time for anything but confusion.

The confusion had been a fixture in his mind lately. For one thing, the real Stepsons had come back, and Harran was not finding their return as funny as he'd once thought he would. He hadn't reckoned on being counted a traitor for supporting the false Stepsons in the true ones' absence. But he also hadn't reckoned on having so much trouble with his lost goddess Siveni when he summoned her up. Her manifestation, and her attempt to level Sanctuary—foiled by the clubfooted beggar-girl he'd been using as idiot labor and "mattress"—had left him confused to a standstill. Now Mriga the idiot was Mriga the goddess, made so by the same spell that had brought Siveni into the streets of Sanctuary. And, involved in the spell himself, Harran had briefly become a god too.

But his short bout of divinity had made the world no plainer to him. Suddenly bereft of Mriga, who had taken Siveni and gone wherever gods go—stricken by the loss of a hand during the spell, and by its abrupt replacement (with one of Mriga's)—Harran had retreated to the fake Stepsons' barracks. He had taken to wearing gloves and drinking a great deal while he tried to think out what to do next with his life. Somehow he never seemed to get much thinking done.

And then the real Stepsons stormed their old barracks, slaughtering in Vashanka's name the "traitors" who had impersonated them with such partial success. They were evidently particularly enraged about dogs being kept in the barracks. Harran didn't understand it. What was Vashanka's problem with dogs? Had one bit Him once? In any case, when Harran fled to a Maze-side garret to escape the sack of the barracks, he made sure to take little brown Tyr with him.

She was yipping and howling unseen behind him now, as that sword descended, and there was nothing he could do. It hit him hard in the temple, and there was surprisingly little pain. He *was* faintly horrified to feel the top of his head crumple and slide sideways; and out of the corner of his left eye he saw half his skull and its contents come away clean on the edge of the sword. Harran fell—he *knew* he fell, from feeling his face and chest smash into the bloody dirt—but his vision, until it darkened, was frozen on that sidewise look. He became bemused; brains were usually darker. Evidently the typical color of the other ones he had examined was due to clotting of blood in the tissues. His had not yet had time, that was all. The next time he . . . the next time . . . but this was wrong. Where was Siveni? Where was Mriga? They always said that when . . . you died, your god or goddess . . . met you. . . .

. . . and night descended upon Harran, and his spirit fled far away.

Tyr didn't know she was a dog. She didn't know anything in the way people do. Her consciousness was all adjectives, hardly any nouns—affect without association. Things *happened*, but she didn't think of them that way; she hardly thought at all. She just *was*.

There was also something else. Not a person—Tyr had no idea what persons were—but a presence, with which the world was as it should be, and without which her surroundings ceased to be a world. A human looking through Tyr's mind would have perceived such a place as hell—all certainties gone, all loves abolished, nothing left but an emotional void through which one fell sickeningly, forever. It had been that way long ago. In Tyr's vague way she dreaded that hell's return. But since the Presence came into the world, knitting everything together, hell had stayed far away.

There were also familiar shapes that moved about in her life. One was thin and gangly with a lot of curly straggly fur on top, and shared one or another of Tyr's sleeping spots with her. The other was a tall, blond-bearded shape

that had been with her longer and had acquired more
importance. Tyr dimly understood that the presence of
this second shape had something to do with her well-being
or lack of it, but she wasn't capable of working out just
what, or of caring that she couldn't. When the tall shape
held her, when in its presence food manifested itself, or
sticks flew and she ran and brought them back, Tyr was
ecstatically happy. Even when the skinny shape subtracted
itself from her universe, she wasn't upset for long. Both
the Presence and the tall shape, though surprised, seemed
to approve; so it must have been all right. And the shape
that *counted* hadn't gone away. It was when *that* shape was
missing, or she smelled trouble about it, that Tyr's world
went to pieces.

It was in pieces now. It had been since the time she had
been cheerfully rooting in the barracks' kitchen-midden,
and suddenly a lot of horses came, and some of the
buildings around got very bright. Tyr didn't identify as fire
the light that sprang up among them, since fire as she
understood it was something that stayed in a little stone
place in the center of the world, and didn't bother you
unless you got too close. So, unconcerned, she had gone
on rooting in the midden until the tall thing came rushing
to her and snatched her up. This annoyed Tyr; and she
became more annoyed yet when her nose told her that
there had begun to be *meat* lying all over. Tyr never got
enough meat. But the tall one wouldn't let her at it. He
took her to some dark place that wasn't the center of the
world, and once there he wouldn't be still, and wouldn't
hold her, and wouldn't let her out. This went on for some
time. Tyr became distressed. The world was coming
undone.

Then the tall one began to smell of fear—more so than
usual. He ran out and left her, and the fraying of the world
completed itself. Tyr cried out without knowing that she
did, and danced and scrabbled at the hard thing that was
sometimes a hole in the wall. But no matter what she did,
it wouldn't be a hole. Then it occurred to her that there
was another hole, up high. The tall one had been by it,
and with some frantic thought of getting close to him by
being where he had been, Tyr jumped up on things she did
not know were tables and chairs, clambered her way onto
the windowsill to perch there wobbling, and nosed the
shutter aside.

She saw the tall shape lurching across the street, with
something slung over its shoulder. Tyr's nose was full of
the smell of burning and blood from below her. She added
everything swiftly together—the tallness and the scorch
and the meat down there—and realized that he was
bringing her dinner after all. Wildly excited, she began to
yip.

Then horses came running at the tall one. Tyr's feelings
about this were mixed. Horses kicked. But once one horse
had stopped kicking, and the tall one had given her some,
and it had been very good. *More food?* Tyr thought, as
much as she ever thought anything. But the horses didn't
stop when they got to the tall one and the meat. For a
moment she couldn't see where the tall one was. Then the
horses separated, and Tyr whimpered and sniffed the air.
She caught the tall one's scent. But to her horror, the
scent did something she had never smelled it do before: it
cooled. It thinned, and vanished, and turned to meat. And
the Presence, the something that made the world alive,
the Presence went away. . . .

When the universe is destroyed before one's eyes, one
may well mourn. Tyr had no idea of what mourning was,
but she did it. Standing and shaking there on the windowsill, anguished, she howled and howled. And when the
horses got too close and the tall things on them pointed at
her, she panicked altogether and fell out of the window,
rolled bumping down the roof-gable and off it. The pain
meant nothing to her: at the end of the world, who counts
bruises? Tyr scrambled to her feet, in a pile of trash,
limping, not noticing the limp. She fled down the dirty
street, shied past the flaming barricade, ran past even the
crushed meat that had been the tall thing. She ran,
howling her terror and loss, for a long time. Eventually
she found at least one familiar smell—a midden. Desperate for the familiar, she half buried herself in the garbage,
but it was no relief. Footsore, too miserable even to
nose through the promising bones and rinds she lay in,
Tyr cowered and whimpered in restless anguish for
hours. Finally weariness forced her, still crying, into a
wretched sleep. Soon enough the sun would be up. But it
would rise black, as far as Tyr was concerned. Joy was
over forever. The tall thing was meat, and the Presence
was gone.

As sleep took her, Tyr came her closest ever to having a genuine thought. Moaning, she wished she were meat too.

Sanctuary's gods, like most others, resided by choice in the timelessness which both contains all mortal time and space, and lies within them. That timelessness is impossible to understand—even the patron gods of the sciences shake their heads at its physics—and difficult to describe, especially to mortals, whose descriptions necessarily involve time, in the telling if nowhere else.

Light, overwhelming, is what most mortals remember who pass through those realms in dream or vision. The fortunate dead who come there, having given up time, see things differently. So do the gods. In that place where the absence of time makes space infinitely malleable, they rear their bright dwellings and demesnes with no tool but thought, and alter them at whim—changing, too, their own forms as mortals change clothes, for similar reasons: hygiene, courtesy, boredom, special occasions. Like mortals, too, they have their pet issues and favorite causes. There are collaborations and feuds, amours with mortals or other divinities, arguments between pantheons or within them. Some of the gods find this likeness to mortal behavior distressing. Most profess not to care, just as most profess to ignore the deeper light that often broods beyond and within the Bright Dwellings, watching what gods and mortals do.

Recently the neighborhood had seen the advent of one Dwelling that wasn't always bright. It tended to be either a high, chaste, white-columned temple of the kind aesthetically promising mortals built, or a low thatched hut of stone crouching defiantly in a rammed dirt yard. But either way, it always had a positively mortal look about it that passing deities variously found tasteless, deliciously primitive, or avant-garde. The dwelling's changes sometimes came several to the minute, then several to the second; and after such spasms lightningbolts tended to spray out the windows or doors, and thumps and shouting could be heard from inside. The neighbors soon discovered that the division of this house against itself was symptomatic. The goddess(es) living there were in the middle of a personality crisis.

"Do you ever think about anything but clothes?!"

"At least I do think about them now and then. You're a goddess, you can't go out in those—those *rags!*"

"I beg your pardon! This shift is just well broken in. It's comfortable. And it covers me . . . instead of leaving half of me hanging out, like that old tunic of Ils's that you never take off. Or that raggy goatskin cape with the ugly face on it."

"I'll have you know that when my Father shakes 'that raggy goatskin' over the armies of men, they scatter in terror—"

"The way it smells, no wonder. And that's *our* Father. Oh, do put the vase down, Siveni! I'll just make another. Besides, when has Ils scattered an army lately? Better give him that thing back: He could probably use it just now."

"Why, you—"

Lightnings whipped the temple's marble, scarring it black. Screeching, a silver raven flapped out from between a pair of columns and perched complaining in the topmost branches of a golden-appled tree a safe distance away. The lightning made a lot of noise as it lashed about, but even a casual observer would have noticed that it did little harm. Shortly it sizzled away to nothing, and the stagy thunder that had accompanied it faded to echoes and whispers, and died. The temple convulsed, squatted down, and got brown and gray, a beast of fieldstone and thatch. Then it went away altogether.

Two women were left standing there on the plain, which still flickered uncertainly between radiance and dirt. One of them stood divinely tall in shimmering robes, crested and helmed, holding a spear around which the restrained lightnings sulkily strained and hissed—a form coolly fair and bright, all godhead and maidenhead, seemingly unassailable. Just out of arms' reach of her stood someone not so tall, hardly so fair, dressed in grime and worn plain cloth with patches, crowned with nothing but much dark curly hair, somewhat snarled, and armed only with a kitchen knife. They stared at each other for a moment, Siveni and Mriga, warrior-queen of wisdom and idiot wench. It was the idiot who had the thoughtful, regretful look, and the Lady of Battles who had the black eye.

"It's got to stop," Mriga said, dropping the knife in the shining dust and turning away from her otherself. "We tear each other up for nothing. Our town is going to pieces, and our priest is all alone in the middle of it, and we don't dare try to help him until our own business is handled . . ."

"You don't dare," Siveni said scornfully. But she didn't move.

Mriga sighed. While she had been insane just before she became a goddess, her madness had not involved multiple personalities—so that when she suddenly discovered that she was one with Siveni Gray-Eyes, there was trouble. Siveni was Ils's daughter, mistress of both war and the arts and sciences, the Ilsig gods' two-edged blade Herself: both Queen of cool wisdom, and hellion God-daughter who could take any god in the Ilsig pantheon, save her father, for best two falls out of three. Siveni had not taken kindly to losing parts of herself into time, or to seeing the Rankan pantheon raised to preeminence in Sanctuary, or to coming off a poor second in a street brawl with a mortal. But all of those had happened; and the first, though now mending in timelessness, irked her most.

When gods become snared in time and its usages—as had many of Sanctuary's gods—their attributes tend to leach across the barrier, into time, and embed themselves in the most compatible mortal personality. In Siveni's case, that had been Mriga. Even as a starving idiot-beggar she had loved the edge on good steel. Sharpening swords and spears was the work to which Harran had most often put her, after he found her in the Bazaar, dully whetting a broken bit of metal on a rock. Clubfooted and feeble-witted as she was, she had somehow "managed" to be found by the last of Siveni's priests in Sanctuary, "managed" to be taken in by him as the poor and mad had always been taken into her temple before. And when Harran went out one night to work the spell that would set Siveni free of time and bring her back into the world, to the ruin of the Rankan gods, Mriga was drawn after him like steel to the magnet.

The spell he had used would infallibly bring back the lost. It did, not only bringing back Siveni to her temple, but also retrieving Harran's lost divinity and Mriga's lost wits. Harran, blindly in love with his goddess in her whole and balanced form, had been shocked to find himself dealing not with the gracious maiden mistress of the arts of peace, but with a cold fierce power made testy and irrational by the loss of vital attributes. Siveni had been quite willing to pull all Sanctuary down around all the gods' ears if the deities of Ranke would not meet her right in battle. Harran tried to stop her—for vile sink though it was, Sanctuary was his home—and Siveni nearly killed him out of pique.

Mriga, though, had stopped her. She had recovered the conscious godhead every mortal temporarily surrenders at birth, and was therefore in full control of the attributes of wise compassion and cool judgment that Siveni had lost into time. She and her otherself fought, and after Mriga won the fight, both saw swiftly that they were one, though crippled and divided. They needed union, and timelessness in which to achieve it. Neither was available in the world of mortals. With that knowledge they had turned, as one, to Harran. They took their leave of him, healing the hand maiming that Siveni had inflicted on him, and then departed for those fields mortals do not know. Of course they planned to come back to him—or for him—as soon as they were consolidated.

But even in timelessness, union was taking longer than either had expected. Siveni was arrogant in her recovered wisdom, angry about having lost it, and bitter that it had found nowhere better to lodge than an ignorant cinder-sitting house-slut. Mriga was annoyed at Siveni's snobbery, bored with her constant anecdotes about her divine lineage—she told the same ones again and again—and most of all tired of fighting. Unfortunately she too was Siveni: when challenged she had to fight. And being mortal and formerly mad, she knew something Siveni had never learned: how to fight dirty. Mriga always won, and that made things worse.

"If you just wouldn't—"

"Oh stop," Mriga said, waving her hand and sitting down on the crude bench that appeared behind her. In front of her appeared a rough table loaded down with meat and bread and watered wine of the kind Harran used to smuggle for them from the Stepsons' store. Now that she was a goddess, and not mad, Mriga could have had better; but old habits were hard to break, and the sour wine reminded her of home. "Want some?"

"Goddesses," Siveni said, looking askance at the table, "don't eat mortal food. They eat only—"

" '—the gods' food and drink only foaming nectar.' Yes, that's what I hear. So then how am I sitting here eating butcher's beef and drinking wine? Who could be here but us goddesses? Have some of this nice chine."

"No."

Mriga poured out a libation to Father Ils, then applied herself to a rack of back ribs. "The world of mortal men," she said presently, while wiping grease off one cheek, "mirrors ours, have you noticed? Or maybe ours mirrors theirs. Either way, have you noticed how preoccupied both of them are just now with cat-fighting? The Beysa. Kama. Roxane. Ischade. If all that stopped—would ours stop too? Or if *we* stopped—"

"As if anything mortals do could matter to the gods," Siveni said, annoyed. She thumped the ground with her spear and an elegant marble bench appeared. She seated herself on it; a moment later a small altar appeared, on which the thigh bones of fat steers, wrapped attractively in fat and with wine poured over, were being burned in a brazier. She inhaled the savor and pointedly touched none of the meat.

"What a waste," Mriga said. ". . . That's just what Harran said, though. The gods became convinced that time could bind them—and so it did. They became convinced that other gods could drive them out—and so it happened. If we could convince men that the pantheons were willing to get along together, and that they should stop killing each other in gods' names . . . then maybe the fighting would stop up here. Mirrors. . . ."

Mriga was becoming better at omniscience—another attribute Siveni had lost to her—and so heard Siveni thinking that idiocy was one of those conditions that transcended even immortality. Mriga sighed. It was harder than she'd thought, this becoming one. Siveni didn't really want to share her attributes . . . and Mriga didn't really want to give them up. Hopeless. . . . Then she caught herself staring at the rib bone in her hand, and by way of it became aware of an emptiness in the universe. "I miss my dog," Mriga said.

Siveni shrugged coolly. Most of her affections and alliances lay with the winged tribes, birds of prey or oracular ravens. But as the silence stretched out, she looked over at Mriga, and her face softened a bit.

"Goddess!"—

Mriga looked up at Siveni in surprise. The voice caught

at both their hearts as if hooks had set deep there.
Startled, the two of them looked around them and saw no
one; then looked out of timelessness into time. . . .

. . . and saw Harran go down under the hooves of
Stepsons' horses, with half his head missing.

"My master," Mriga said, stricken. "My priest, my
love—"

"*Our* priest," Siveni said, and sounded as if she could
have said something else, but would not. She got up so
quickly that the marble bench fell one way and the elegant
brazier the other. Her spear leapt into her hand, sizzling.
"I'll—"

"*We'll*," Mriga said, on her feet now. It was odd how
eyes so icy with anger could still manage tears that flowed.
"Come on."

Thunder cracked about them like sky ripping open. The
neighbors all around turned in their direction and stared.
Uncaring, two goddesses, or one, shot earthward from the
bright floor of heaven, which, behind them, hesitated,
then furtively turned to dirt.

The fire by the Maze-side street barricade had died
down, and the street was empty except for the slain and
the scavengers. Now and then someone passed by—a
Stepson on one of their fierce horses, or a random
member of some Nisi death squad, or one of Jubal's
people just slipped out of the blue on business. No one
noticed the grimy street idiot, sitting blank-eyed beside a
trampled corpse; much less the sooty raven perched on a
charred wagon and eyeing the same corpse, and the
younger, arrow-shot one it lay on, with a cold and
interested eye. Black birds were no unusual sight in
Sanctuary these days.

"His soul's gone," Mriga whispered to the bird. "Long
gone, and the poor body's cold. *How?* We came straight
away—"

"Time here and there run differently," said the raven,
voice hoarse and soft. "We might have done something
while the tie between soul and body was still stretching
thin. But it's too late now—"

"No," Mriga said.

"I should have leveled this place the last time I was
here. This would never have happened!"

"Siveni, be still." Mriga sat by Harran's crushed remains, one hand stretched out to the awful ruin of his head; a purposeful gesture, for without actually touching the cold stiff flesh, she found herself unable to believe in death. That was one of the problems with being a god. Immortal, they often found it hard to take death seriously. But Mriga was taking it very seriously indeed.

She strained for omniscience; it obliged her a little. "We could get him back," she said. "There are ways. . . ."

"And put him where? Back in *this?*" In her raven form, Siveni flapped down to the cold stiff mess of shattered bones and pulped muscle, and poked it scornfully with her beak. It didn't even bleed. "And if not here, where?"

"Another body? . . ."

"Whose?"

Mriga's omniscience declined an answer. This didn't matter: she was getting an idea of her own . . . one that scared her, but might work. "Let's not worry about it right now," she said. "We'll think of something."

"And even if we do . . . who's to say his soul's survived what happened to him? Mortal souls are fragile. Sometimes death shatters them completely. Or for a long time . . . long enough that by the time they've put themselves back together, it's no good putting them in a body; they've forgotten how to stay in one."

"He was a god for a little while," Mriga said. "That should count for something. And I don't think Harran was that fragile. Come on, Siveni, we have to try!"

"I'd sooner just burn the city down," the raven said, hopping and flapping up onto Mriga's shoulder as she stood up.

"A bit late for that, I fear." Mriga looked around her at the smoldering barricade, the scorched and soot-blackened faces of the surrounding buildings. "The cats have been busy setting one another's tails on fire, and not much caring what else catches and goes up as they run around screeching."

"Cats . . ." Siveni said, sounding thoughtful.

"Yes: my thought exactly. We'll deal with one or two of them before we're done. But first things first. Where's my puppy?"

Tyr woke up with the upset feeling that usually meant she'd had a dream of the bad old days before the Presence came. But by the time she was fully awake, she had already realized that this time the feeling had nothing to do with any dream. For a few minutes that part of Sanctuary slammed its windows shut against the bitter howling that emanated from the garbage heap behind the Vulgar Unicorn. Tyr's throat was sore, though, with smoke and her long crying the day before, so that she coughed and retched and had to stop.

She lay there panting, deep in grief's apathy, not knowing it, not caring. The garbage all around her smelled wonderful, and she had no appetite for it. Inside the Unicorn there was the sound of people moving around, and from upstairs a cat wailed an enraged challenge, and Tyr couldn't even summon up the energy to get up and run away. She made a sound half whimper, half moan, and behind it a feeling that a human looking through her mind would instantly have recognized as a hopeless prayer. Oh, whatever there is that listens, please, please, *make it didn't happen!*. . . .

. . . and suddenly there was someone there beside her, and old reflex took over. Tyr struggled to her feet, ready to run. But her nose countermanded her legs, and Tyr froze—then leaped up, whining madly, bouncing in a frenzy of relief, licking at the skinny figure that was crouched down next to her. The skinny one tasted better than usual. There was something else with her—a black bird of the kind Tyr usually liked to chase—but somehow the bird also smelled like the skinny one, so she let it be. She crowded into the skinny shape's arms, whimpering incredulous welcome, terror, reawakened hunger, sorrow and loss, the news of the world turned upside down . . .

"I know, I know," Mriga said, and though the words meant nothing to Tyr, the dog was comforted. Mriga knew exactly how she felt, without omniscience being involved. Her own retarded mind, before the onslaught of divinity, had been the same nounless void, full of inexplicable presences and influences. Now the dog nosed at her, both vastly relieved and freshly wounded by the reminder of what was wrong with the world. She whimpered, and her stomach growled.

"Oh, poor child," Mriga said, and reached sideways into timelessness for the rib bones she'd been working on. Tyr leaped at the half-rack of ribs almost before they were entirely into time, and fell to gnawing on them.

"She thinks she's in hell," Mriga said to Siveni.

The raven laughed, one harsh bitter caw. "Would that she were, for *he's* certainly there. She could lead us to him. . . ."

Mriga looked at the raven in swift admiration. "That lost wisdom's coming back to you, sister. So she might. Of course, we would have to find a way to get into hell ourselves."

"Then think of one," Siveni said, sounding both pleased and annoyed.

Mriga thought. Her omniscience stirred, though not precisely in the direction required. "I don't know how just yet," she said. "But there are experts in this town . . . people who know the way. They've sent so many others down that road. And they bring them back again."

Tyr looked up and yipped. She had been bolting the meat and already looked somewhat better—not just from having eaten after a long fast. The food and drink of the gods work strangely in mortals. Tyr's eyes were already brighter and deeper than Mriga ever remembered having seen them; and the dog had abruptly stopped smelling like a garbage-heap.

"Yes," Mriga said. "It might just work. Finish that, little one. Then we'll go down by the White Foal . . . and go to hell."

Tyr yipped again and went at the ribs with dispatch. The raven looked sidewise at Mriga. "What if she won't help us?" she said.

Omniscience spoke up again, and Mriga frowned, for it was no comfort. "She will," she said. "Always assuming that between here and there, we can figure out the right things to say. . . ."

Even necromants need to sleep occasionally, and in the last few days Ischade had gotten less sleep than usual. Now, in this bright chill winter afternoon she had evidently counted Sanctuary deep enough in shock at its troubles that she might rest a little while. The shutters of the house by the White Foal were all closed. What black birds sat in the trees did so with heads under wing, mirroring their mistress. There was no sound there but the rattling of dry leaves and withered rose-hips in the thorny hedge.

"This place smells like death," said the raven perched on the shoulder of the skinny, ragged girl who stood by the little wicket gate.

"It should," said Mriga, and reached out sorrowfully to something that wasn't wholly there. At least her mortal senses refused to acknowledge it. Her godsight clearly showed her a big bay steed, still saddled, its reins hanging loose, standing forlornly by the gate and gazing at the rundown house. As Mriga reached out to it the bay rolled eye-whites at her and put its ears back, but the gesture was half-hearted. After a second it relented, whuffling, and put its nose in her hand, then swung its great head around to breathe of her breath by way of greeting.

"Poor, poor . . ." Mriga said, stroking the shivering place just under the bay's jaw. Tyr looked on suspiciously, eyeing the horse's hooves. Siveni in her raven-shape cocked a bright black eye. She was fond of horses: she had after all invented them, thereby winning a contest.

"One more ghost," she said. "And recent. The woman breeds them."

"Recently, yes." And the door at the top of the steps opened, and there was another ghost, more or less. At least the man was dead. Outwardly he merely looked scarred. One eye was covered with a patch and his face was a wealed ruin in which an old handsomeness lurked as sad and near-unseen as the ghost-bay. His carriage had ruin about it too. Mriga saw the ghost of it, straight and tall, under the present reality—a hunched posture, the stance of someone cowering under the lash of a fear that never went away.

The man stared at them, more with the patched eye than with the whole one, Mriga thought. "Stilcho," she said, "where's your mistress? Bring us to her."

He stared harder, then laughed. "Who shall I say is calling? Some guttersnipe, and her mangy cur, and . . ." He noticed the black bird and grew more reserved. "Look . . . get out of here," he said. "Who are you? Some Nisi witchling, one she missed last night? Get out. You're crazy to come here. You're just a kid, you're no match for *her,* whoever you think you are!"

"Not Nisi, at least," Mriga said, mildly nettled.

Siveni looked up at Stilcho from Mriga's shoulder and said, "Man, we are the goddess Siveni. And if you don't bring us to your mistress, and that speedily, you'll be spoiled meat in a minute. Now get out of our way, or show us in to *her*." The scorn was very audible.

Tyr growled.

"Stilcho you fool, shut that, the wind's like knives," said another voice from beyond the door. And there came a smaller, slimmer man, who wore a cold composure exactly the opposite of Stilcho's desolation; but under it, ghost to its solidity, dwelt the same impression of unrelenting fear. The man looked out and down at them, and his face went from surprise to amused contempt to uncertainty to shocked realization in the time it took him to take a breath and let it out in cloud.

"You at least have some idea what you're looking at, Haught," Mriga said, waving the wicket gate out of existence and walking through where it had been. Haught stared, as well he might have, for the deadly wards laid inside that gate unravelled themselves and died without so much as a whimper. "If I were you, I'd announce us."

With some difficulty Haught reassumed his look of threat and contempt. "My mistress is unavailable," he said.

Mriga looked at the raven. "Slugging abed again."

The raven snapped its beak in annoyance and flapped away from Mriga's shoulder. Abruptly a helmeted woman in an oversized tunic stood there, a spear in her hand, and rapped with its butt on the ground. With a roar, the dry hedge and the barren trees all burst forth in foliage of green fire. Screeching, the black birds went whirling up out of the tree like scorched papers on the wind, leaving little trails of smoke and a smell of burnt feathers behind them.

"She's up now," said Siveni.

One last man came hurriedly to the door, swearing, a tall, fair, and broad man—and Tyr launched herself at him, stiff-legged, snarling. "No, Tyr!" Mriga said hurriedly, and grabbed at the dog, just catching her by the scruff of the neck . . . a good thing, for a knife had appeared as if by magic in the man's hand, and was a fraction of a second from being first airborne and then in Tyr's throat. Tyr stood on her hind legs and growled and fought to get loose, but Mriga held on to her tight. "This is no time to indulge in personalities," she hissed. "We've got business." The dog quieted: Mriga let her stand, but watched her carefully. "Straton, is the lady decent?"

He stared at them, as dumbfounded by the outrageous question as by the simple sight of them—the armed and radiant woman, fierce-eyed and divinely tall: the ragged skinny beggar girl who somehow shone through her grime: and the delicate, deer-slim, bitter-eyed brown dog wearing a look such as he had seen on Stepsons about to avenge a lost partner. "Haught," he said, "go inquire."

"No need," said a fourth voice behind him in the doorway's darkness: a voice soft and sleepy and dangerous. "Haught, Stilcho, where are your manners? Let the ladies in. Then be off for a while. Straton, perhaps you'll excuse us. They're only goddesses, I can handle them."

The men cleared out of the doorway one by one as the three climbed the stair. First came the dog with her lip curled, showing a fang or two; then the gray-eyed spear-bearer, looking around her with the cool unnoticing scorn of a great lady preparing to do some weighty business in a sty. Last came the beggar, at whom Straton looked with relaxed contempt. "Curb that," he said, glancing at Tyr, then back at Mriga, in calmest threat.

Mriga eyed him. "The bay misses you," she said, low-voiced, and went on past, into the dark.

She ignored the hating look he threw into her back like a knife as he turned away. If her plan worked, vengeance would not be necessary. And she was generally not going to be a vengeful goddess. But in Straton's case, just this once, she would make an exception.

Ischade's downstairs living room was much bigger than it should have been, considering the outside dimensions of the house. It was a mad scattering of rich stuffs in a hundred colors, silks and furs thrown carelessly over furniture, piled in corners. Here were man's clothes, a worn campaigning cloak, muddy boots, sitting on ivory silk to keep them off the hardwood floor; over there was a sumptuous cloak of night-red velvet scorching gently where it lay half in the hearth, half out of it, wholly unnoticed by the hostess.

Ischade was courteous. She poured wine for her guests, and set down a bowl of water and another of neatly chopped meat for Tyr. Once they were settled, she looked at them out of those dark eyes of hers and waited. To mortal eyes she would have seemed deadly enough, even without the flush of interrupted lovemaking in her face.

But Mriga looked at her and simply said, "We need your help."

"Destroying my property, and my wards, and upsetting my servants," said Ischade, "strikes me as a poor way to go about getting it."

Siveni laid her spear aside. "Your wards and your gate are back," she said, "and as for your servants . . . they're a bit slow. One would think that a person of your . . . talents . . . might be better served."

Ischade smiled, that look that Mriga knew was dreaded upwind and down, in high houses and alleys and gutters. "Flattery?" she said. "Do goddesses stoop to such? Then you need me indeed. Well enough." She sipped from her own goblet, regarding them over the edge; a long look of dark eyes with a glint of firelight in them, and a glint of something else: mockery, interest, calculation. Siveni scowled and began to reach for her spear again. Mriga stopped her with a glance.

"Now is it goddess*es*, truly?" Ischade said, lowering the cup. "Or 'goddess' in the singular? Gray-Eyes, if I remember rightly, was never a twofold deity."

"Until now," Mriga said. "Madam, you had some small part in what happened. May I remind you? A night not too long ago, about midnight, you came across a man digging mandrake—"

"Harran the barber. Indeed."

"I got caught in the spelling. It bound all three of us together in divinity for a while. But one of the three is missing. Harran is dead."

Those dark eyes looked over the edge of the cup again. "I had thought he escaped the . . . unpleasantness . . . at the barracks. At least there was no sign of him among the slain."

"Last night," Siveni said, and the look she turned on Ischade was cruel. "Your lover did it."

Tyr growled.

"My apologies," said Ischade. "But how cross fate is . . . that your business, whatever it is, brings you to deal with me . . . and precludes your vengeance against anyone under my roof." She sipped her wine for a moment. "Frustration is such a mortal sort of problem, though. I must say you're handling it well."

Mriga frowned. The woman was unbearable . . . but had to be borne, and knew it. There was no way to force her to help them. "I have some experience with mortality," Mriga said. "Let's to business, madam. I want to see what kind of payment you would require for a certain service."

One of those dark brows lifted in gentle scorn. "The highest possible, always. But the service has to be one I wish to render . . . and the coin of payment must be such as will please me. I have my own priorities, you see. But you haven't told me clearly what the service is."

"We want to go to hell," Siveni said.

Ischade smiled, tastefully restraining herself from the several obvious replies. "It's easily enough done," she said. "Those gates stand open night and day, to one who knows their secrets. But retracing your steps, finding your way to the light again . . . there's work, there's a job indeed. And more of a job than usual for you two." She looked over at Siveni. "You've never been mortal at all; you can't die. And though *you've* had experience at being mortal, you apparently haven't died yet. And only the dead walk in hell."

Mriga's omniscience spoke in her mind's ear. "Gods have gone there before," she said. "It's not as if it's never been done."

"Some gods," Siveni said, "have gone and not come back." She looked at Mriga in warning, silently reminding her of the daughter of Dene Blackrobe, merry Sostreia: once maiden goddess of the spring, and now the queen and bride of hell, awful and nameless.

"Yes," Ischade said, "there is always some uncertainty about the travels of gods in those regions." Yet her eyes were inward-turned, musing; and a tick of time later, when they focused on Mriga again, the goddess knew she had won. There was interest there, and the hope that something would happen to relieve the terrible tedium that assails the powerful. The interest hid behind Ischade's languid pose the way Stilcho's old handsomeness haunted his scars.

"A pretty problem," she said, musing out loud now. "Mortal souls I could simply send there—a knife would be sorcery enough for that—and then recall. Though the bodies would still be dead. But that won't work for you two; your structure's the problem. Gods' souls enclose and include the body, instead of the other way around. Killing the bodies won't work. Killing a soul . . . is a contradiction in terms: impossible." She sighed a little. "A pity, sometimes; this place has been getting crowded of late."

Then firelight stirred and glittered in Ischade's eyes as for a moment they became wider. "Yet I might reduce that crowding, at least temporarily . . ."

Siveni's eyes glittered too. "You're going to use the ghosts," she said. "You're going to borrow their mortality."

"Why, you're a quick pupil indeed," Ischade said, all velvet mockery. "Not their mortality exactly. But their fatality . . . their deadness. One need not *die* to go to hell. One need only *have* died. I can think of ways to borrow that. And then hell will have two more inmates for the night."

"Three," said Mriga.

"Four," said Siveni.

They looked at each other, then at Ischade.

Ischade raised her eyebrows. "What, the dog too?"

Tyr yipped.

"And who else, then?"

"Madam," Siveni said, "the best way to be sure we come back from this venture is to have with us the guide who opens the way. Especially if the way back is as difficult as you claim."

Ischade held quite still for a moment, then began to laugh, and laughed long and loud. A terrible sound it was. "These are hard times," she said, "when even gods are so suspicious."

"Treachery is everywhere," said Mriga, wondering swiftly how the thought had escaped her before.

"Oh indeed," Ischade said, and laughed again, softly, until she lost her breath. "Very well. But what coin do you plan to use to pay the ones below? Even I only borrow souls, then send them back; and believe me, there's a price. To get your barber back in the flesh and living, the payment to those below will have to be considerable. And there's the problem of where you'll put him—"

"That will be handled," Mriga said, "by the time the deed's done. Meanwhile we shouldn't waste time, madam. Even in hell time flows, and souls forget how to stay in bodies."

Ischade looked lazily at Mriga, and once again there was interest behind the look, and calculation. "You haven't yet told me what you'll *do* with your barber once you've got him," she said. "Besides the predictable divine swiving."

"You haven't yet told us what payment you'll require," said Mriga. "But I'll say this. Last time you met my lord, you told him that if he brought Siveni back among the living, you'd find the proceedings merry to watch. And did you not?"

Ischade smiled, small and secret. "I watched them take away the temple doors that she smashed down into the street," she said softly, "and I saw the look on Molin Torchholder's face while they carted them off. He was most distressed at the sudden activity of Ilsig gods. So he began to pull what strings he could to deal with that problem . . . and one of the strings he pulled was attached to Tempus and his Stepsons, and the Third Commando."

"And to you," Mriga said. "So that the barracks burned, and then the city burned, and Harran and a thousand others died. All so that the town will keep on being too divided against itself to care that you go about in it, manipulating the living and doing your pleasure on the dead . . . to alleviate your boredom."

"The gods are wise," Ischade said, quietly.

"Sometimes not very. But I don't care. My business is to see what I love brought somewhere safe. After that— this town needs its own gods. Not Rankan, or Beysib, or even Ilsigi. I'm one of the new ones. There are others, as you know. Once the 'divine swiving' is out of the way. I intend to see those new young gods settled, for this place's good, and its people's good. That may take mortal years, but while it's going on, there'll be 'merry times' enough for even you—without you having to engineer them. There'll be war in heaven . . . which is always mirrored on earth."

"Or the other way around," Ischade said.

"Either way, you'll find it very interesting. Which is what you desire. Isn't it?"

Ischade looked at Mriga. "Very well. This business is apparently in my interests. We'll discuss payment after- ward; it will be high. And I shall go with you . . . to watch the 'merry times' begin." She smiled. Mriga smiled too. Ischade's velvet, matter-of-fact malice was wide awake, hoping disaster would strike and make things even more 'interesting,' perhaps even considering how to help it strike. The woman was shameless, insufferable—and so much *herself* that Mriga suddenly found herself liking Ischade intensely.

"Excellent," Mriga said. "What needs to be done?"

"If you haven't buried him already," Ischade said, "do so. Otherwise we would find him on the wrong side of the frontier . . . and matters would become even more complicated than they are at the moment."

"Very well. When will we be leaving?"

"Midnight, of course: from a place where three roads meet. Ideally, there should be dogs howling—"

Tyr gave Ischade an ironic look, tilted up her head and let out a single long note, wavering down through half-tones into silence.

"So that's handled," Siveni said, reaching for her spear. "And as for three roads meeting, what about the north side of that park by the Governor's Walk and the Avenue of Temples? The 'Promise of Heaven,' I think it's called."

Ischade chuckled, and they all rose. "How apt. Till midnight, then. I will provide the equipment."

"That's gracious of you, madam. Till midnight, or a touch before."

"That will do very well. Mind the second step. And the hedge: it has thorns."

Mriga walked through the open gate with satisfaction, patted the bay's neck, and stepped sidewise toward midnight. Siveni came after her, her spear shouldered and sizzling merrily, and went the same way. Only Tyr delayed for a moment, staring at the bay—then nipped it neatly in the left rear fetlock, scrambled sideways to avoid the kick, and dove past Mriga into night.

Ischade also looked at the bay; then, more wryly, at her yard's trees and bushes, still full of green fire that burned but did not consume. She waved the godfire out of existence and shut the door, thinking of old stories about hell.

"Haught," she called toward one of the back rooms. "Stilcho."

They were there in a hurry: It never did to keep Ischade waiting. "Jobs for you both," she said, shutting the door. "Stilcho, I need a message taken to the uptown house. And on your way back, pick me up a corpse."

Dead as he was, Stilcho blanched. Haught watched him out of the corner of his eye, looking slightly amused.

"And for you," she said to Haught, watching amused in turn as he stiffened slightly, "something to exercise those talents you've been so busy improving to please me. Fetch me a spare ghost. A soldier, I think, and one without any alliances. Be off, now."

She watched them go, both of them hurrying, both of them trying to look as if they weren't. Ischade smiled and went off to look for Straton.

All it took was the sight of a slender woman-shape, cloaked in black and strolling sedately down the Avenue of Temples, to clear the midnight street to a windscoured pavement desert. Behind her followed a bizarre little parade. First came a dead man, hauling a bleating black ram and black ewe along behind him on ropes: then a live man, small and scared-looking, leading a cowed donkey with a long awkward bundle strapped across its back. He stank of wine, Mor-am did: anyone but the donkey would have been revolted. Behind him and the beast came a slight-built man whose Nisi heritage showed in his face, a man bearing a small narrow silk-wrapped package and another bulkier one, and looking as if he would rather have been elsewhere. Last of all, more or less transparent from moment to moment, came a ghost dressed in Hell-Hounds' harness. It was Razkuli, dead a long time, stealing wistful glances at the old, living Hell-Hound haunts.

The Promise of Heaven was even falser to its name than usual tonight. Word of the procession had run up the street half an hour before, and the panic-stricken ladies of the night had abandoned their usual territory in favor of one more deserving of the title. Ischade strolled in past the stone pillar-gates of the park, looking with cool amusement at the convenient bowers and bushes scattered about for those who wished to begin their huggermuggering as soon as their agreements with the park ladies were struck. The cover, copses of cypress and downhanging willow, suited Ischade well. So did the little empty altar to Eshi in the middle of the park. Once there had been a statue of her there, but naturally the statue and its pediment had been stolen, leaving only a long boxlike slab of marble much carved with PFLS graffiti and inscriptions such as *Petronius Loves Sulla*.

She paused by the stone and ran gentle fingers along it.

A dog's howl went wavering up into the cloudy night. Ischade looked up and smiled.

"You're prompt," she said. "It's well. Haught, bring me what you carry. Stilcho, fasten them here."

Standing by the altar, Mriga and Siveni looked around them—Mriga with interest, Siveni with wry distaste, for she was after all a maiden goddess. Ischade put her hood back and gazed at the goddesses with her beautiful oblique eyes full of silent laughter as the frightened Stilcho tethered the ram and ewe by the altar. Haught held out one of his silken bundles. Ischade put the wrappings aside and drew forth a long curved knife of bronze, half sword and half sickle, with an edge that even in the little, dim light from the torches of the Governor's Palace still glittered wickedly keen. The flat of the blade was stained dark.

"Blood sacrifice, then," Siveni said.

"There's always sacrifice where the ones below are concerned." Ischade reached absently down to caress the ram's head. It held still in terror. "But first—other business. Stilcho, I will need your service tonight, and Razkuli's. I go on a journey."

"Mistress—"

"To hell. You are going to lend me your death, and Razkuli will lend his to this warrior-lady, and this poor creature—" she reached out to touch the wrapped bundle on the shying donkey "—as soon as I fetch him back, will lend his to the lady who limps. But you understand that while we're using those parts of your life—or death, rather—you will have to be elsewhere."

Mriga bit her lip and turned away from the sight of a dead man going pale. "Souls need containers . . . so I'll provide some till dawn; we'll be back then, and you'll find yourselves back to normal. Haught and Mor-am will stand guard till then." She stepped away from the altar, gliding past Haught and throwing him a cool look.

"Mistress—"

"Guard them well, Haught," Ischade said, not looking back at him. "I will take a dim view of any 'accidents.' I'm not done with them yet." She paced away, turning after a few seconds and beginning to walk a circle, setting wards. There was no outward sign, no fire, no sound. But Mriga felt the air grow tight, and when Ischade came about at last and gestured the circle closed, the mortals in it looked at each other in still terror, like beasts in a new-snapped trap.

"No god or man will cross that line," she said. "Goddesses, your last word. Will you do this?"

"Get on with it," Siveni said. Her spear sizzled.

Mriga nodded and looked down at Tyr. The dog put her head up and howled again, softly, an eager sound.

"Very well," Ischade said, and paused by the altar, and looked over her shoulder at the donkey. There was a wheeze, the terrible sound a corpse makes when it's rolled over and the last breath leaves its lungs—only this breath went *in*. The tethered donkey plunged and screamed as its burden abruptly began to move, a slow underwater struggling. Ischade reached out leisurely and stripped the covering from around the body. It crumpled toward the ground, collapsing to its knees, then slowly, slowly stood. It was a young woman, terribly wounded about the breast and neck; her tunic and flounced skirts were blood-blackened and her head had a tendency to slew to one side, trying to come undone from the half-severed neck.

"Well, well," Ischade said, calm-voiced, "not 'he,' but 'she.' Some poor nightwalker caught in the Stepsons' barracks, where she shouldn't have been. Pity. Haught, uncover the lantern."

The Nisi lifted up a lantern from the ground and unshuttered it. There seemed no light in it at all; yet when Mriga looked from it to Ischade and the corpse, and the altar, they all were throwing shadows that showed impossibly blacker against the ground than the midnight they all stood in. "This won't hurt, child," said Ischade. She lifted up the sickle, and swung it at the ground. A scream followed that Mriga thought would have frozen any mortal's brain. She was irrationally satisfied to glance sideways and see Siveni's knuckles going white on the haft of her spear as the corpse fell down again.

"Well, maybe it *will* hurt," Ischade said, not sounding particularly moved. She straightened, holding in her free hand what looked like a wavering, silken scrap of night. It was the shadow she had cut loose. Delicately, with one hand, she crumpled it till nothing of it showed but a fistful of darkness. Ischade held out her hand to Mriga. "Take it," she said. Mriga did. "When I tell you, swallow it. Now, then . . ."

She moved to Razkuli, who stood leaning on the ghost

of a sword, and watched her without eyes, and without a face, looking taut and afraid. "That one is nothing to me," said Ischade. "Her soul can go where it pleases. But yours might have some use. So . . . something alive . . ." She looked around her. "That tree will do nicely. Hold still, Razkuli."

The second scream was harder, not easier, to bear. Ischade straightened, shook the severed shadow out, eyed it clinically, and sliced it neatly about midway down its writhing length. One of the halves she stuffed into the rotting bole of a nearby willow, and even as she turned away toward Siveni, the willow's long bare branches put out numberless leaves of thin, trembling darkness. "Here," Ischade said. Siveni put out her hand and took the crumpled half-shadow as if she were being handed a scorpion.

"Stilcho," Ischade said.

Stilcho backed away a pace. Behind him, with a small, terrible smile on his face, Haught held up the lantern. The third scream was the worst of all.

"Maybe you *have* been suffering too much in my service," Ischade said, as she sliced his soul-shadow too and draped half of it over the branches of a shrub hard by the altar. "Maybe I should let you go back to being quite dead . . ." The shrub came out in leaves and little round berries of blackness, trembling.

"We'll talk about it when I come back," said Ischade. She tucked the crumpled shadow into her dark robes. "Mor-am, Haught, guard this spot until an hour before dawn. We won't be coming back this way. Look for us at the house, by the back gate. And don't forget Stilcho's body." She glided over to the altar, lifting the dark-stained sickle again. "Be ready, goddesses."

"What about Tyr?" said Siveni.

"She'll ride this soul," said Ischade. Her hand had fallen on the ram's head again. It looked up at her, and up, and helplessly, up; and Ischade swung the sickle. In the unlight of the dark lantern, the ram's eyes blazed horribly, then emptied, and the black blood gushed out on the altar's white stone. "Now," said Ischade, a slow warm smile in her voice, and reached out to the ewe.

Mriga swallowed the little struggling darkness, in horror, and felt it go down fighting like something itself horrified and helpless. Its darkness rose behind her eyes

for a moment and roared in her ears. The ewe cried out
and bubbled into silence. When her vision cleared, she
found herself looking at an Ischade truly dressed in
shadows and grinning like one of the terrible gods who
avenge for the joy of it, and at a Siveni robed and helmed
in dark, only the spearhead bright. Even Tyr had gone
black-furred, but her eyes burned as a beast's will when a
sudden light in darkness finds them. Tyr threw back her
head and howled in good earnest. The earth beneath their
feet buckled and heaved like a disturbed thing, as if in
answer, and then shrugged away its paving and split.

"Call up your courage," said Ischade softly, "for now
you'll need it." And she walked down into the great crack
in the earth, into the fuming, sulfur-smelling dark.

Tyr dashed after her, barking; other howls echoed hers,
above the earth and below it. Mriga and Siveni looked at
each other and followed.

Groaning, the earth closed behind them.

Mor-am and Haught looked at each other and swallowed.

They did this again later, when the donkey, frightened
and hungry past caring, stretched to the end of its tether
and started browsing on the nearest shrub. It had shied
away when the shrub screamed, and its broken branches
began to bleed.

The donkey stood there for a while shaking, then looked
hungrily over at the next nearest food, a downhanging
willow with oddly dark leaves.

The willow began to weep. . . .

The road down was a steep one. That alone would make
return difficult, if the slope on hell's far side were the
same. But Mriga knew there would be other problems,
judging by the sounds floating up through the murky
darkness. Dim distant screams, and howls of things that
were not only dogs, and terrible thick coughing grunts like
those of hunting beasts all mingled in the fumy air until the
ears ached, and the eyes stung not just from smoke but
from trying to see the sounds' sources. For once Mriga was
glad of the sharp ozone smell that came of the lightnings
crackling about Siveni's spearhead; it was something
familiar in the terror. And even if the lightnings were
burning blue, they were better than no light at all. Ischade

seemed to need no light: she went ahead sure as a cat, always with a slight smile on her face.

The way wasn't always broad, or easy, no matter what the poets said. After a long, long walk down, the sound of their footsteps began echoing back more and more quickly, until Mriga could put out her hands and touch both walls. "Here is the strait part of the course," said Ischade. One after another they had to get down on their knees and crawl—even Siveni, who grumbled and hissed at the indignity. Mriga was used to dirt and had less trouble; though the dank smell, and the way the cold, sour clods of earth seemed to press in against her, made her shudder. Right before her, Tyr's untroubled breathing and little whimpers of excitement were a comfort. At least they were until Tyr began to growl as she crawled.

The tunnel grew smaller and smaller until Mriga had to haul herself along completely flat, and swore she couldn't bear another second of it. The fifth or sixth time she swore that, the echoes suddenly widened out again. Tyr leaped out into the space; Siveni almost speared her from behind in her haste to follow.

Tyr was still growling. Ischade stood in the dimness, still wearing that wickedly interested smile. Mriga looked around, dusting herself off, and could see little until Siveni came out and held the spear aloft—

A growl like an earthquake answered Tyr's. Mriga looked up. Hoary, huge, and bloodstained, filling almost the whole stone-columned cavern where they stood, a Hound crouched, slavering at the sight of them. It was the same Hound that the Ilsigs said ate the moon every month, and sometimes the sun when it could catch it; though usually Ils or Siveni would drive it away. Here, though, the Hound was on its own ground, and Mriga's omniscience informed her that Siveni would be badly outmatched if she tried conclusions with it.

"Aren't you supposed to give it something?" Siveni said from behind Ischade, sounding quite casual, and fooling no one. "A cake, or some such—?"

"Do I own the moon?" Ischade said. "It wouldn't be interested in anything less, I fear." And she stood there in calm interest, as if waiting to see what would happen.

Siveni stared at the Hound. It looked at her out of hungry eyes, growled again, and licked its chops. Where its saliva dripped, the stone underfoot bubbled and smoked.

The answering growl startled Mriga as Tyr shouldered past her and Siveni. "Tyr—!" she said, but Tyr, bristling, walked straight up to the Hound and snarled in its face.

The Hound reared up, its jaws wide. . . .

"Tyr, no!" Siveni cried, and slipped forward, raising her spear. Too late: Tyr had already leapt. But the growling and snarling and roaring that began, the rolling around and scrabbling and biting, didn't have quite the sound any of them expected. And it all stopped quite suddenly to reveal the Hound on its back, its belly showing, its tail between its legs, and Tyr, flaming-eyed, holding it by the throat. It was as if a rabbit held a lion pinned, but the rabbit seemed unconcerned with such details. Tyr snarled again and somehow seized that throat, as wide and heavy as a treetrunk, in her teeth; lifted the Hound and shook it, snarling, as she would have shaken a rat; then flung the whole huge monster away. "Yi, yi, yi, yi, yi!" shrieked the chief of the Hounds of Hell, the Eater of the Sun, as it scrambled desperately to its feet, away from the little dark-furred dog, and ran for the walls. It went right into one, and through it, and was gone.

Tyr panted for a moment, then shook herself all over, sat down, and scratched.

Mriga and Siveni stared at each other, then at Ischade. "I don't understand it," Mriga said to her. "Perhaps you do."

Ischade smiled and held her peace. "Well," Siveni said, "she is a bitch . . ."

Tyr swung her head around—she was washing, with one leg up—and favored Siveni with a reproachful look.

"An extraordinary one," Ischade said, "but still a bitch; and as such no male dog, even a supernatural one, would fight with her under any circumstances. I suppose that even here, dogs will be dogs . . . Canny of you to bring her. Shall we go on?" And she swept on into the darkness that the Hound had blocked. Mriga followed, thoughtful.

On down they went, the light of Siveni's spear burning bluer and brighter. The sound of moaning and screaming grew less distant. Goddess or not, Mriga shook. The voices were lifted less in rage or anguish than in a horrible dull desperation. They sounded like beasts in a trap, destined to the knife, but not for ages yet—and knowing it. *A horrible place to spend eternity,* Mriga thought. For a moment she was filled with longing for her comfortable, dirty hut in heaven, or even for the real thing of which it was the image—the rough hut in the Stepsons' barracks, and her own old hearth, and Harran busy on the other side of it. *At least one of us will get out of here,* Mriga thought. *The sunlight for him, if for no one else. . . .*

Siveni glanced over at Mriga with a curious look and opened her mouth, just as Ischade glanced lazily over her shoulder at them. "We're close to the ferry," she said. "I trust you brought the fare?"

Mriga shook her head, shocked. Her omniscience hadn't warned her of this. But Siveni's mouth quirked. She went rummaging about in her great oversized tunic and came out with a handful of money: not modern coin, but the old Ilsigi golden quarter-talent pieces. One she handed to Ischade with exaggerated courtesy, and one to Tyr, who took it carefully in her teeth; another went to Mriga. Mriga turned the quarter over, looked at it, and shot her sister an amused look. The coin had Siveni's head on it.

Ischade took the coin with a courteous nod, drew her cloak about her, and continued down the path. "They will be thick about here," she said as they descended, and the darkness opened out around them. "The unburied may not cross over."

"Neither would we, if we'd left all the preparations to you," Siveni said. "Trying to make things more 'interesting,' madam?"

"Mind the slope," Ischade said, stepping downward into the shadows and putting her hood up.

The ground was ditch-steep for a few steps, and they came down among shadows that moved, like the struggling scraps of darkness they had swallowed. These shadows, though, strode and slunk and walked aimlessly about, cursing, whining, weeping. Their voices were thin and faint, their gestures feeble, their faces all lost in the great darkness. Only here and there the blue-burning lightnings of Siveni's spear struck sparks from some hidden eye; and every eye turned away, as if ashamed of light, or ashamed to beg for it.

They made their way through the crowd, having to push sometimes. Tyr ranged ahead, her gold piece still in her mouth, snuffing the ground every now and then, peering

into this face or that one. Following her, Mriga shuddered
often at the dry-leaf brush of naked, unbodied souls
against her immortal's skin. *No wonder the gods hate
thinking about death,* she thought, as the ground leveled
out. *It's an . . . undressing . . . that somehow shouldn't
happen. It embarrasses them. Embarrasses us. . . .*

"Careful," Ischade said. Mriga glanced down and saw
that just a few steps would take her into black water.
Where they stood, and other souls milled, the sour cold
earth slanted down into a sort of muddy strand, good for a
boat-landing. The water lapping it smoked with cold,
where it hadn't rimed the bank with dirty ice. Tyr loped
down along the riverbank, pursuing some interesting
scent. Mriga looked out across the black river, and,
through the curls of mist, saw the boat coming.

It was in sorry shape. It rode low, as if it were shipping a
great deal of water—believable, since many of the clinker-
boards along its sides were sprung. Steering it along with
the oar that is also a blade, was the ferryman of whom so
many songs circumspectly sing. He was old and gray and
ragged, fierce-looking: too huge to be entirely human, and
fanged as humans rarely are. He was managing the
blade-oar one-handed. The other held a skeleton cuddled
close, its dangling bones barely held together by old, dried
strings of sinew and rags of ancient flesh. The ferryman
sculled his craft to shore and ran it savagely aground. Ice
cracked and clinker-rivets popped, and Mriga and Siveni
and Ischade were pushed and crushed together by the
press of souls that strained, crying out weakly, toward the
boat.

"Get back, get back," the boatman said. He lisped and
spat when he talked: understandable, considering the
shape his teeth were in. "I've seen you lot before, and you
none of you have the fare. And what's this? Na, na,
mistress, get back with your pretty eyes. You're alive yet.
You're not my type."

Ischade smiled, a look of acid-sweet irony that ran
icewater in Mriga's bones. "It's mutual, I'm sure. But I
have the fare." Ischade held up the gold quarter-talent.

The ferryman took it and bit it. Mriga noticed with
amusement that afterward, as he held it up to stare at it,
the coin had been bit right through. "All right, in you
get," he growled, and tossed the coin over his shoulder
into the water. Where it fell ripples spread for a second,

then were wiped out by a wild boiling and bubbling of the water. "Always hungry, those things," grumbled the ferryman, as Ischade brushed past him, holding her dark silks fastidiously high. "Get in, then. Mortals, why are they always in such a hurry? Coming in here, weighing down the boat, has enough problems just carrying ghosts. Nah, then! No gods! Orders from her. You all come shining in here, hurt everyone's eyes, tear up the place, go marching out again dragging dead people after you, no respect for authority, ghosts and dead bodies walking around all over the earth, shameful! Someone ought to do something . . ."

Mriga and Siveni looked at each other. Siveni glanced longingly at her spear, then sighed. Standing in the bows of the boat, Ischade watched them, silent, her eyes glittering with merriment or malice.

". . . Never used to be that way in the old days. Live people stayed live and dead people stayed dead. You look at my wife now!—" and the ferryman bounced the skeleton against him. It rattled like an armful of castanets. "Wha'd'ye think of *her?*"

Siveni opened her mouth, and closed it. Mriga opened her mouth, and considered, and said, "I've never met anyone like her."

The ferryman's face softened a little, fangs and all. "There, then, you're a right-spoken young lady, even though you do be a god*dess*. Some people, they come up here and try to get in this boat, and they say the most frightful rude things about my wife."

"The nerve," Siveni said.

"True for you, young god*dess,*" said the ferryman, "and that's it for them as says such things, for *they*'re always hungry, as I say." He glanced at the water. "Never you mind, then, you just put your pretty selves in the boat, you and your friend, and give me your hard money. *She* don't really care what goes on out here, just so you be nice and don't tear things up, you hear? Speak her fair, that's the way. They do say she's a soft heart for a pretty face, remembering how she came to be down here; though we don't talk about that in front of her, if you take my meaning. In you get. Is that all of you?"

"One moment," Mriga said, and whistled for Tyr; then, when there was no answer, again. Tyr appeared after a moment, her gold piece still held in her teeth, and trotted

to the boat, whining at it softly as it bobbed in the water.
"Come on, Tyr," she said. "We have to go across. He's on
the other side."

Tyr whined again, looking distrustfully at the boat, and
finally jumped in.

"The little dog too?" said the ferryman. "Dogs go for
half fare."

Tyr stood on her hind legs to give the ferryman the coin,
then sat down on the boat's middle seat, grinning, and
barked, thumping her tail on the gunwale.

"Why, thank you, missy, that's a kindness and so I
shall," said the ferryman, hastily pocketing the second
half of Tyr's coin, which he had bitten in two. "They don't
overpay us down here, and times are hard all over, eh? It's
much appreciated. Don't put your hands in the water,
ladies. Anyone else? No? Cheap lot they must be up there
these days. Off we go, then."

And off they went, leaving behind the sad, pushing
crowd on the bank. Mriga sat by the gunwale with one arm
around Tyr, who slurped her once, absently, and sat
staring back the way they'd come, or looking suspiciously
at the water. The air grew colder. Shuddering, Mriga
glanced first at Siveni, who sat looking across the wide
river at the far bank; then at Ischade. The necromant was
gazing thoughtfully into the water. Mriga looked over the
side, and saw no reflection . . . at first. After a little while
she averted her eyes. But Ischade did not raise her head
until the boat grounded again; and when she looked up,
some of that eternal assurance was missing from her eyes.

"There are the gates," the ferryman said. "I'll be
leaving you here. Watch your step, the ground's much
broken. And a word, ladies, by your leave: watch yourselves in there. So many go in and don't come out again."

Looking at the dark town crouching behind brazen
gates, Mriga could believe it. Hell looked a great deal like
Sanctuary.

One by one they got out of the boat and started up the
slope. Siveni was last out, and so busy looking up at the
rocky ground that she missed what was right under her
feet. She lost her footing and almost fell, just managing to
catch herself with her spear. "Hell," she said, a bitter
joke: The spear spat lightnings.

The ferryman, watching her, frowned slightly. "We
don't call it that here," he said. "Do we now, love?"

The bones rattled slightly.

"Ah well. Off we go then. . . ."

And they were alone on the far shore.

The gates were exactly like those of the Triumph Gate
not far from the Governor's Palace, but where those were
iron, these were brazen, and locked and mightily barred.
The four stood together, hearing more strongly than they
had yet the sounds of lamentation from inside. It was
beginning to sound less threatening, the way a horrible
smell becomes less horrible with exposure. "Well," Siveni
said, "what now? Is there some spell we need?"

Ischade shook her head, looking mildly surprised. "I
don't normally use this route," she said. "And the few
times I've bothered, hell's gates have been open. Very odd
indeed. Someone has been making changes . . ."

"Someone who's expecting us, I'll wager," Siveni said.
"Allow me." She lifted up the spear, leaned back with it
like a javelin-thrower, and threw it at the gates. For that
moment, lightning turned everything livid and froze
everything still. Thunder drowned out the cries of the
damned inside. Then came a few seconds of violet afterim-
ages and ears ringing; then the darkness, in which by the
tamer light of Siveni's spearhead they could see hell gates
lying twisted and shattered on the paving. Siveni picked up
her spear, then swept through the opening and past the
wreckage, looking most satisfied.

"She does that rather well," Ischade said as she and
Mriga and Tyr followed after.

"Yes, she always has been good at tearing things up,"
Mriga said. She looked over her shoulder at the gates and
willed them back in place, as she'd done earlier with
Ischade's wards. To her great distress, they didn't reappear.

"We're on other gods' ground now," Ischade said as
they turned away from the gates, moving past the shadows
of empty animal pens and around the spur of the great
wall that sheltered the Bazaar. "Nearly all powers but
theirs will be muted here, I fear. If your otherself tries that
stunt again inside, I suspect she'll be in for a surprise, for
she was still outside hell while she did it this time."

Mriga nodded as they made their way through the
streets that led to the Bazaar. Almost everything was as it
should be—the trash, the stink, the garbage in the gutters,

the crowds. But the dark shapes moving there had a look about them of not caring where they were—an upsetting contrast to those stranded on the far side of the river, who seemed to know quite well. Looking across the city for evidence of hellfire, Mriga found nothing but the same scattered plumes of smoke and the smouldering reek that prevailed in the Sanctuary of the daylit world. Yet the overhanging clouds were underlit as if with many fires.

As they walked further, Mriga got a chance to see why, and came to understand that there was a difference here between the dead and the damned. Many of the dark people going by carried their own hellfires with them— bright conflagrations of rage, coal-red frustrations, banked and bitter, the hot light-sucking darknesses that were envy and greed, the blinding fire-shot smokes of lust and hunger for power that fed and fed and were never consumed. Some few of the passersby bore evidence of old burning, now long gone. They were burnt-out cinders, merely existing, neither living nor dead. But worst of all, to Mriga's thought, were those many, many dead who had never even lived enough to burn a little, who had given up both sin and passion as useless. They walked dully past the flaming damned, and past goddesses, and neither hellfire nor the cold clean light of Siveni's spear found anything in their eyes at all.

She soon enough found worse. There were places that seemed damned as surely as people; spots where murders or betrayals had taken place, and where they took place again and again, endlessly, the original participants dragging the passing dead in to re-enact the old horrors. Some shapes walking there were less dark than others, but wore their torments differently—serpents growing from their flesh and gnawing at it; animal heads on human bodies, or vice versa; limbs that went gangrenous, rotted, fell off, regrew, while their owners walked about with placid looks that said nothing was wrong, nothing at all—

Harran is down here now, Mriga thought. *How will we find him? Roasting in his desire for Siveni, eaten away by his guilt over the way he used me once? Or were those passions so recent that they never quite took root in his soul—so that we might find him like one of the dull ones who don't care about anything? Suppose he. . . doesn't want to come back. . . .*

The four of them passed through the Bazaar. They went

hurriedly, for they found it peopled with beasts that milled about with seeming purpose, crying out to one another in animals' voices, neighs and roars and screams. But the wares being hawked there were human beings, chained, dumb, with terrible pleading eyes. The four went quickly out into the south road that followed the walls of the Governor's Palace. "Since all this is mirroring Sanctuary somewhat," Siveni said, peering around her by the light of her spear, and looking harrowed, "I would suppose that the one we're looking for is in the Palace."

"So would I," Ischade said, quite calm. "The south gate is closed."

Mriga noticed that on Ischade's far side Tyr had dropped back to pace beside her, gazing up at her with a peculiar expression.

"What exactly *is* your arrangement with her?" Mriga said, as softly as she could and still be heard above the constant low rumor of pain that filled the streets. "You must have one."

Ischade was silent. "Please pardon me," Mriga said. "I shouldn't have asked. Power is a private thing."

"You need not come with us," Siveni said, without turning around, from ahead of them. "You've already fulfilled your part of the bargain. Though we haven't paid you yet—"

Ischade didn't stop walking, but there was a second's hard look in her eyes that was more than just the reflection of Siveni's lightnings. "Don't project your fears on *me,* young goddesses," she said, the voice silken, the eyes dark and amused. "I have no reason not to see her."

Mriga and Siveni both most carefully held their peace. Tyr, though, whined once and wagged her tail, and for the rest of the walk never once left Ischade's side. Ischade appeared not to notice.

"See," she said. "The gate."

The south gate looked much as it did in Sanctuary, and made it plain that some passions had not entirely died out here; the posts were splashed with PFLS and gang graffiti. But there were no guards, no Stepsons, nothing but iron gates that stood open. The great courtyard inside was drowned in shadow, and the wailings of hell seemed subdued here. On the far side of the courtyard lay what had looked like the Palace from a distance, but here proved itself to be an edifice not even Ranke in its flower could have built: all ebony porticoes and onyx colonnades, smoke-black pillars and porches, massive domes and shadowy towers, halls piled on mighty halls, rearing up in terrible somber grace till all was lost in the lowering overcast. Ischade never paused, but went right in toward the great pile—a graceful, dark-robed figure, small against the great expanse of dark, dusty paving: and trotting beside her went the little dog.

There on the threshold Siveni glanced at Mriga. "Mriga, quick," she said, "do all of us a favor. Let me do the talking in there."

Mriga stared. "Sister, what're you thinking of?"

"Prices," Siveni said. "Just as you are. Look. You've enough power to pay her off afterward—"

"And where are *you* planning to be?"

"Don't start," Siveni said, "we're losing her." And she went after Ischade.

Mriga went after Siveni, her heart growing cold. "Anyway, this is *my* priest we're talking about," Siveni was saying.

"'*Your*'—?! Siveni, don't you dare—"

The great steps up to the Palace loomed, and Ischade was a third of the way up them by the time the goddesses caught up with her and Tyr. Silently they went up the rest of the stairs together, and Mriga was aware of her heart beating hard and fast, not from the climb. They passed over a wide porch, floored in jet, and a doorway loomed up before them, containing great depths of still, blackness, silent, cold. Against that dark Siveni's spearhead sizzled faint and pitiful, the smoking wick of a lamp of lightnings, drowning in the immensity of night.

They slipped in.

Far, far down the long hall they had entered—miles and years down it—some pale light seethed, a sad ash-gray. It came from three sources, but details took much longer to see. The four of them had walked and walked through that silence that swallowed every sound and almost every thought before Mriga realized that the ashen light came from braziers. It was a long time more before the two onyx thrones set between two broad tripod-dishes became apparent. A few steps later Mriga's mouth turned dry, and she stopped, her courage failing her . . . for there was a shape seated in the right-hand throne.

It was not as if Mriga was unprepared for the one she

knew would be sitting there—the sweet young mistress of spring, who fell in love with the lord of the dead, and died of her love, the only way to escape heaven and rule hell by his side. But all Mriga's preparation now proved useless. Of all things in hell, only she wore white: a maiden's robe, radiant even in the sad light of the braziers. Beneath the maiden veil her beauty was searing, a fire of youth, a thing to break the heart, as Siveni's was—but there was no healing in it for the broken one afterward. Hell's Queen sat proud in the throne, cool, passionless, and terrible. She held a sword across her lap, but it was black of blade from much use; and the scales lay beside the throne, thick with dust. Hell had apparently made its Queen over in its own image, depriving her even of the passion that was the reason she had come . . . and, like those she ruled, she was resigned to it. Mriga suddenly understood that the frightful resignation on ghost-Razkuli's face was a family resemblance.

Mriga looked over at Ischade. The necromant stood quite composed with Tyr beside her, and gracefully, slowly bowed to the still woman on the throne. The gesture was respectful enough, but the air of composure still smelled of Ischade's eternal cool arrogance. *Even here there's no dominating her,* Mriga thought, annoyed, and admiring Ischade all over again.

"Madam Ischade," said hell's Queen. Her voice was soft and somber, a low voice and a rich one. There was no believing it had ever laughed. "A long time it is since you last came visiting. And you never before brought friends."

"They are on business, madam," Ischade said, her bearing toward the Queen as frank and straightforward as to anyone else she perceived as peer. "Siveni Gray-Eyes, whom you may remember. And Mriga, a new goddess— perhaps the same as Siveni: They're working it out." A secret smile here. "And Tyr."

Tyr sat down, her tail thumping, and looked with interest at the Queen of hell.

She did not say "Welcome." She said, "I know why you've come. I tried to stop you, several times, through one or another of my servants. Whatever happens to you now is on your own heads."

She looked at them, and waited.

Mriga swallowed. Beside her Siveni said, "Madam, what price will you ask for Harran's soul?"

The Queen gazed gravely down at her. "The usual. The one my husband demanded of the gods for my return, and the gods refused to pay. The soul of the one who asks to buy."

Mriga and Siveni looked at each other.

"The law is the law," she said. "A soul for a soul, always. No god would trade his life for my freedom. And it's as well, for I did not want to leave."

Ischade's mouth curved ever so slightly.

"Why would I, after I went to such trouble to come here?" said the Queen. "I gave up being spring's goddess in favor of something more worthwhile. Shipri handles spring now." She was still a moment. "Besides, even Death needs love," said the Queen at last.

Mriga could think of nothing to say.

"So." She looked down at them, grave, patient. "Choose. Will you pay the price? And which of you?"

"I will," said Siveni and Mriga simultaneously. Then they stared at each other.

"Best two falls out of three," Mriga said.

"No! You cheat!"

"You mean, I fight all-out!"

Siveni swung angrily on the Queen of hell. But anger could not survive that gaze. After a second of it, Siveni turned and said to Ischade, "This is all *your* fault!"

Ischade said nothing.

A hand shot from behind Siveni and snatched her spear out of her grasp. Siveni whirled, but not before Mriga had executed a neat reverse-twirl of the spearshaft and was holding the sizzling head of it leveled at her heart. "Don't be an idiot," she said. "Harran needs *you*. And this town is going to need all the aggressive gods it can field on its own behalf in the next year or so, with Ranke dying on the vine and the Beysib and Nisibis pushing in from two different directions. I'm mortal enough to die successfully. And with me gone, you'll get all your attributes back. Siveni, let go—!"

"Harran's right, you *are* still crazy! Suppose when you die, the attributes are lost forever—confined down here! Then what happens to Sanctuary? Haven't you noticed that I've got the fighting attributes, but you've got the winning ones?—"

There were two sets of hands on the spear-haft now,

wrestling for control: and no matter what Siveni said, they were very evenly matched. Back and forth the two of them swayed. But, "Peace," said the Queen's low voice, and both of them were struck still. Only their eyes moved and glittered as they looked at her sidewise.

"I would see this paragon over whom goddesses contend," she said. "Skotadi."

Between Mriga and Siveni and the throne, darkness folded itself together into a shadow-shape like that Ischade had cut loose from the girl-corpse and Razkuli and Stilcho. It seemed a maiden's shadow, vague around the edges, wavering but lingering in the dark air like a compact smoke. "Fetch me the shade of a man who was called Harran," said the Queen. "He will be within the walls; he was buried today."

Skotadi swayed like blown smoke, bowing, and attenuated into the paler dark. The hold on Siveni and Mriga loosened, so they could stand up. But the spear was missing. The Queen was leaning it against one arm of her throne, and its head was dead metal, smoking gently in the braziers' gray light. "Since you cannot decide," the Queen said, "he shall."

As she spoke, Skotadi came into being again and bowed before the Queen. "Majesty," she said, "there is no such man within the gates."

Even Ischade looked surprised at that. "Impossible!" Siveni cried. "We buried him!"

The Queen turned dark eyes on her. "If my handmaid says he is not here, he is not."

Mriga was out of her reckoning. "If he's not here, where else could he be?"

"Heaven?" Siveni said, plainly thinking of all the way they'd come, possibly for nothing.

Ischade looked wry. "Someone from *Sanctuary*?" she said.

"Everyone who dies comes here," said the Queen. "How long they stay, and what they make of this place while they're here, is their business. But very few are the mortals who don't have something to expiate before they move on. Still . . ." She pondered for a moment, looking interested. Mriga thought back to that look of weary interest on Ischade's face, and hope woke in her. "There is only one other possibility."

Tyr leaped up, barking excitedly, and ran a little way toward the great door: then turned and barked again, louder, dancing from foot to foot where she stood.

"Burial *enables* one to pass the frontier," said the Queen. "It does not *compel* one to pass . . ."

Tyr ran for the door, yipping. Mriga looked in shock at Siveni, remembering how Tyr hadn't wanted to get into the boat . . .

The Queen rose from her throne. "Skotadi! My Lord's chariot." Siveni abruptly found herself holding her spear: It was working again, but seemed much subdued. "Madam, goddesses," said the Queen, "let us see where the little one leads us."

Somehow or other the door was only a few steps away this time. Outside it stood a great iron chariot with four coalblack chargers already harnessed, and Skotadi stood on the driver's side, holding the reins. They climbed in and Skotadi whipped up the horses.

The chariot rolled through the courtyard and out the gates in utter silence. Outside in the streets, the cries and lamentation became muted too, and finally ceased in astonishment and dread—for not in many a decade, Mriga's omniscience told her, had the underworld's Queen come out of her dark halls. The only sound was Tyr's merry barking ahead of them as she led the way.

Mriga found it difficult to look at Siveni as they drove westward down Governor's Walk, and Siveni would not look at her at all. It needed no omniscience to hear the anger rumbling like suppressed thunder in her. "Look," she whispered to Siveni, "you know I'm right."

"No, I don't." Siveni paused a moment, watching the dark, familiar streets go by, and then said, "You wrecked it, you know that? You and he would have been out of here by now. And I would have managed: I always manage." She paused again. "Dammit, Mriga, I'm a maiden goddess! He's in love with me, and I can't give him what he wants of me! But you can. And if I stay down here, you get *my* attributes—all but that one. My priest gets what he wants—me. And you get him—"

Mriga looked long at Siveni, who would not look back, and began to love her crazily, in somewhat the same manner as she had crazily admired Ischade. "I thought you were the one claiming that the attributes would stay down *here*—"

Siveni ignored this. "I wasn't entirely myself when he called me back," she said. "I made him lose a hand for my sake. The least I could do is make sure he lives long enough to get some use out of his new one."

The chariot turned south, past the tanners' quarter. "You're a full immortal," said Mriga. "You can't die."

"If I really want to . . . yes, I can," Siveni said, very quietly. "*She* did it, didn't she?"

There was no arguing with that, whatever Ischade's opinions on the subject might be. Mriga let out a pained breath.

Ahead of them Tyr was running excitedly past the town animal pens, toward a bridge. It looked exactly like the bridge over the White Foal, where corpses had so often been nailed and gangs had scuffled over their boundaries. Past the bridge crouched the Downwind's ramshackle houses, Ischade's neighborhood. But the river running under the old bridge was that cold, black river that smoked its mists into the thunder-gray day. The ferryman was nowhere to be seen. On the far shore, in the streets among the shanties and rotting houses, milled dark crowds of the dead, but none of them used the bridge.

Tyr galloped up the curved upstroke of the bridge and skidded and galumphed and almost fell down the downstroke of it, yapping crazily. The chariot followed. Hooves that should have boomed on the planks did not. Tyr was already down off the bridge, arrowing through the crowds like a hound on a line, giving tongue. Confused, the dead parted before and behind her, leaving a road the chariot could follow. And then Tyr went no further, but they saw her jump almost up to head level once or twice, licking in overjoyed frenzy at the face of a dark form burdened with some long awkward object over his shoulders . . .

"Harran!"

Mriga was out of the chariot and running without knowing quite how she'd managed it. Beside her Siveni was keeping pace, tucking her tunic up out of the way, the spear bobbing on one shoulder and spitting lightning like fireworks. The dead got hurriedly out of their way. Mriga shot Siveni a second glance: that tunic was more gray than black, suddenly. But Siveni didn't seem to notice or care. And there, there, confused-looking, grimy, shadowed, but tall and fair and bearded, dear and familiar, *him* . . . They managed to slow down just enough to avoid

knocking him over, but as soon as his eyes cleared he
knew them, and their embrace was violent and pro-
longed.

"What—why—how are you—"

"Are you all right? Did it hurt much?"

"No, but— What's *she* doing here?"

"She showed us the way. No, Tyr, he means Ischade,
don't look so hurt—"

"We buried you, why didn't you—"

"I couldn't leave him. He's hurt. Look, there's an arrow
through his—"

"You ass, you're *dead!*"

". . . Leg—yes, I know! But he's—"

Stillness fell all around them. The black chariot stood
hard by, and as the white-robed figure stepped down from
it, Harran looked up. Most carefully he sank to one knee
in the dirty street, laid down the limp, bloodied young
man he was carrying, and kneeling, bowed himself slowly
double. He was a priest, and a healer, and had worked in
Death's shadow before: he knew her when he saw her.

Siveni looked at him, and at Mriga, and tossed her spear
away. It lay scorching the dirt, afire as if it lay yet in the
furnace where the thunderbolts were forged. Her robes
shimmered gray, and the Queen's blinding white, in its
light. Quickly, and none too gracefully—for she had had
little practice at this sort of thing—she went down on her
knees in front of the Queen of hell, and bowed her bright
head right down to the dirt. Her helmet slipped off and
rolled aside; she ignored it. "Madam, please," she said, in
a muffled voice, "take me. Let them go."

"What?" Harran said, looking up from Tyr, who was
washing his face again.

"Your goddesses have come to beg your life of me,"
said the Queen. "But you know the ancient price for
letting a soul go back up that road once it's come down."

"No!" Harran said, shocked. And then, remembering
to whom he spoke, "Please, no! I'm dead—but my town's
not. It needs her. Mriga, talk her out of this!"

Mriga could only look at him, and not steadily: Her eyes
were blurring. "She also has offered to pay the price," said
the Queen. "They almost came to blows over it. They
cannot choose. I offer you the choice."

Harran's jaw moved as his teeth ground. "No," he said

at last. "I won't go—not at that price. Send them home.
But—"

"We're not leaving without him," Mriga said.

Siveni looked up from the dirt, her eyes flashing.
"Certainly not."

The place was becoming brighter. Was it Siveni's spear,
Mriga wondered, or something else? The buildings
seemed almost as bright as if Sanctuary's usual greasy
sunlight shone on them. All around, the dead were
blinking and staring. "Let him at least go," Mriga said.
"We'll both stay."

"Yes," Siveni said.

Death's Queen looked somberly from one of them to
the other.

Tyr slipped away from Harran's side and up next to
Siveni—then jumped up and put her delicate, dusty
forefeet right on the white robes of the Queen. She looked
up into her face with big brown eyes.

"I'll stay too," Tyr said.

Mriga and Siveni and Harran all started violently. Only
Ischade looked away and hid a smile.

The Queen looked down at the dog with astonishment,
and finally reached out to scratch her behind one ear. She
looked over at Ischade. "This orgy of self-sacrifice," she
said, with the slightest, driest smile, "comes on behalf of
Sanctuary?"

"More or less, madam," said Ischade, matching the
smile. "I question whether it deserves it."

"It does not. But how rarely any of us get what we
deserve. Which may be for the best." The Queen looked
at her supplicants—one mortal and one goddess kneeling,
one goddess standing, and (apparently) one more leaning
against her and having the good place behind her ears
scratched. "No wonder you two have been having such
trouble achieving union. It's a trinity you're part of, and
without your third there's never agreement on anything.
But with him—"

"Them," Tyr said.

The Queen looked wry. "A four-person trinity?—
Assuredly, I must get rid of all of you somehow," she said.
"There would be no peace for any of us with all of you
walking around here shining and tearing up the place.
And arguing." In this warming, melting light, she seemed

much less grave and awful than she had. Mriga even thought that her eyes crinkled in amusement; but in the growing radiance, and the way it reflected dazzling from her veil, it was becoming hard to tell. "But the law is still the law. The price must be paid—"

There was a long pause.

"We could split it four ways," Harran said.

Siveni looked at him in shock, then smiled. "Why, you're my priest indeed. Each of us could spend a quarter of our time here," she said to the Queen. "We could take it in turns—"

The Queen was silent a while. "I believe I could defend that arrangement to my husband," she said at last. "But your priest is dead, goddesses. He has no body to go back to, any more than that poor child—"

"He's not a child really," Harran said, "he's about seventeen, and I keep trying to tell you all, *he's not dead.*"

"Why . . ." The Queen looked closely at the young man's soul-body in the growing light. "Indeed he's not," she said. "This soul is shattered."

Mriga stood there in shock, thinking of the young body underneath Harran's, stiff and still—but, she now remembered with amazement, not cold. "He was struck down in the attack that killed you, Harran," Ischade said, "but though his body survived the blow, apparently his mind didn't. It happens sometimes—a soul is too fragile to withstand the idea of its own demise and disintegrates. Leaving the body still breathing, but empty—"

"The arrow missed the main artery," Harran said. "The wound'll hurt, but it'll heal—"

"Go then," said the Queen, fondling Tyr's ears and smiling slightly at her. "Enough has happened for one day. Go, before my husband comes back and finds you here and starts an argument." There were nervous looks all around at this prospect. "But perhaps one of you would stay for now?" And the Queen looked down at Tyr.

Tyr slipped down, ran to Harran, collected a hug from him and slurped his face—then bounced over to the iron chariot, jumped into it, and sat there grinning, with her tongue hanging out, waiting to be taken for a ride.

"I can manage the actual transfer to the new body easily enough," Ischade said, leading Mriga, Siveni, and the still slightly bewildered Harran away. "But you will all of you owe me large favors. . . ."

"We'll repay them twice over," Siveni said, sounding somewhat grim. It was apparent she didn't like the idea of owing anybody anything.

Harran was looking from one of them to the other. "You came to *hell* after me?"

Mriga looked with quiet joy at her lord and love as Ischade led them all back toward the upper world. "They don't call it that here," she said. She was beginning to understand why.

Behind them, Tyr had her ride—the first of many—and was off about her own business when Death came home from work. The Queen of hell rose up to greet him as always, went stately to the great doors, cool and grave and shining. There her husband dropped the bare bones that were his old joke with her, leaned the blade that is also an oar up against the dark doorsill, and went to her, laughing and shedding this one of his many forms. There was none to see the dark glory that hell's Queen took in her arms, or the way her gravity dropped away in the presence of that shadowy beauty which men dare not imagine; the way her light kindled at his touch, like day in night's embrace. They laughed together, madly delighted as first-time lovers, as they always had been; as they always would be.

"Dear heart," said the Queen of hell, "a dog followed me home. Can I keep it?"

"This isn't quite how I pictured hell," Harran was saying dubiously.

"Nor I," said Ischade, sounding almost cheerful as she led them on through the under-Downwind. Indeed the place looked very little like hell just now. Downwind or not, this place was looking remarkably good: the buildings less rotten, the shanties sounder, the people all around them shadowy still, but strong and fair—and looking surprised at that. The sky had begun to blaze silver, and Siveni's robes and Mriga's own were back to normal. Mriga looked at Siveni and saw that even her 'smelly goatskin' looked fearsome and deadly-beautiful rather than ragged. Ischade's dark beauty burned more perilously than ever. And were *her* robes not quite as dark as they had been? And Harran . . .

But no. Harran looked as marvelous as he always had

when Mriga was crazy. She smiled at him. The prospect of
life with him, some kind of life—though the details were
vague yet—shone on everything, and from everything, in
a patina of anticipation and joy. The world was beginning
all over again.

"There's no garbage in the gutters," Harran said,
astonished, as Ischade led them along a little Downwind
street toward the river.

"No," Mriga said. Every minute the old decrepit houses
were looking more like palaces, and every curbside weed
had its flower. "It's as she said. One makes of this place
what one chooses. Hell—or something else. And the
upper world is the same . . . just a little less amenable to
the change. More of a challenge."

They walked down a slope, along the riverbank, being
careful of their footing. The river had brightened from
black to pewter-gray, though still it smoked silver in the
predawn chill. Across it Sanctuary rose, a Sanctuary none
of its habitués would have recognized—a Maze full of
palaces, a Serpentine all snug townhouses and taverns,
everywhere light, contentment, splendor: a promise, and
a joke.

"It could be like this, the real world," Mriga said as
Ischade led them along the riverside. "It will be, some
day . . . though maybe not until time stops. But it will,
won't it?" She turned to Ischade, her eyes shining in the
growing day.

"Not being a goddess," said Ischade, "I wouldn't like to
say." She paused by a little gate, swung it open. "Here is
the barrier, all. What is—will reassert itself. Beware the
contrast."

"But this is what is," Mriga said, as first Siveni, then
Harran, passed through the gate, and the silver day flowed
past them into Ischade's weedy back yard. Every tree
burst into white blossom; the dank riverside air grew
warm and sweet as if spring and summer had rooted in
that garden together. The black birds in the trees looked
down, and one opened its beak and, in a voice deep and
bittersweet as night and love, began to sing. The barren
rosebush shook itself and came out in leaves, then in a
splendor of roses of every color imaginable—burning
white, red like evening love, and the incomparable blue;
silver and pink and green and violet and even black.

"This *is*," Mriga said, insisting, as Ischade paused by the gate and looked through it in cool astonishment. "The waking world doesn't need to be the way it is . . . not for always. Neither do you. You could be more. You could be what you are now, and more yet. . . ."

Ischade looked down silently at what the light, the silver morning, the irresistible joy beating in the air, had made of her. Long she looked down, and lifting her hands, gazed into them as if into a mirror. Finally she lowered them and said, calm as ever, "I prefer my way."

Mriga looked a long moment at her. "Yes. Anyway, thank you," she said.

"Believe me, you'll pay well enough for what I've done for Harran."

Mriga shook her head. "Down there—you knew everything that was going to happen, didn't you? But you were trying to spare us a disaster, trying to spare Sanctuary one. Without looking like it, of course, and spoiling your reputation."

"I should have hated to lose a goddess who will be creating such wonderful disturbances hereabouts in the near future," Ischade said, her voice soft and dangerous.

Mriga smiled at her. "You're not quite as you paint yourself, Lady Ischade. But your reputation is safe with me."

The necromant looked at her and smiled a slow, scornful smile. "The day it matters to me what anyone thinks of me, or doesn't think . . . even the gods . . . !" she said.

"Yes," said Mriga. "And whoever raises the dead but gods? Let's go in."

Ischade nodded, holding the gate. Mriga went in, and with true sunrise, the influences of the underworld died away and let day reassert itself: grimy, pallid dawn over Sanctuary, reeking with smoke and the faint taint of blood—ghost-haunted, dismal, and bitter cold as befitted the first day of winter. At Ischade's back, the White Foal flowed and stank, filmed here and there with ice. But the joy hanging in the air still refused to go entirely away. She shut the gate behind her and looked up at the stairs to the house. Haught stood there, and Stilcho, swords drawn in their hands. Ischade waved them inside, assuming their obedience, and turned to regard the rosebush.

Stilcho went inside, unnerved. Haught lingered just past

the doorsill. Ischade paid him no mind, if she knew he was there. Eventually she moved, and reached out to the hedge. And if Haught saw Ischade cast a long, thoughtful gaze at the whitest of the roses before reaching out to pluck the black one, he never mentioned it to her, then or ever.

WHEN THE SPIRIT MOVES YOU

Robert Lynn Asprin

"Is he asleep?"

"Asleep! Hah! He's passed out again."

Zalbar heard the whores' voices as if from a distance and wanted very badly to take exception to what they were saying. He wasn't asleep or passed out. He could understand every word that was being said. His eyes were just closed, that's all . . . and damned hard to open too. Hardly worth the effort.

"I don't know why the Madame puts up with him. He's not that good-looking, or rich."

"Maybe she has a weak spot for lost puppies and losers."

"If she does, it's the first sign of it she's shown since I've been here."

A loser? Him? How could they say that? Wasn't he a Hell-Hound? One of the most feared swordsmen in Sanctuary?

Struggling to focus his mind, Zalbar became aware that he was sitting in a chair. Well, sitting slumped over, the side of his head resting on something hard . . . presumably a table. There was a puddle of something cold and sticky under his ear. He fervently hoped it was spilled wine and not vomit.

"Well, I guess we'll just have to carry him up to his room again. Come on. Give me a hand."

This would never do. A Hell-Hound? Being carried through a whorehouse like a common drunk?

Zalbar gathered himself to surge to his feet and voice his protests . . .

He sat up in bed with a start, experiencing that crystal clarity of awareness and thought that sometimes occurs when one wakes between a heavy drunk and the inevitable hangover.

Sleeping! He had been asleep! After three days of forcing himself to stay awake he had been stupid enough to start drinking!

Every muscle tense, he hurriedly scanned the room, dreading what he knew he would find.

Nothing. He was alone in the room . . . his room . . . what had become his room at the Aphrodisia House through Myrtis's tolerance and generosity. It wasn't here!

Forcing himself to relax, he let memories wash over him like a polluted wave.

He hadn't just been drinking. He was drunk! Not for the first time, either, he realized as his mind brought up numerous repetitions of this scene for his review. The countless excuses he had hidden behind in the past were swept aside by the merciless hand of self-contempt. This was becoming a habit . . . much more the reality of his existence than the golden self-image he tried to cling to.

Hugging himself in his misery, Zalbar tried to use this temporary clarity of thought to examine his position.

What had he become?

When he first arrived in Sanctuary as one of Prince Kadakithis's elite bodyguard, he and his comrades had been assigned by that royal personage to clean up the crime and corruption that abounded in the town. It had been hard work and dangerous, but it was honest work a soldier could take pride in. The townspeople had taken to calling them Hell-Hounds, a title they had smugly accepted and redoubled their efforts in an attempt to live up to.

Then the Stepsons had come, an arrogant mercenary company which one of the Hell-Hounds, Tempus Thales, had abandoned his mess-mates to lead. That had really been the start of the Hell-Hounds' downfall. Their duties were reduced to those of token bodyguards, while the actual job of policing the town fell to the Stepsons. Then the Beysib had arrived from a distant land, and the Prince's infatuation with their Empress led him to replace his Hell-Hounds with fish-eyed foreign guards of the Beysa's choosing.

Denied even the simplest of palace duties, the Hell-Hounds had been reassigned under loose orders to "keep an eye on the brothels and casinos north of town." Any effort on their part to intercede or affect the chaos in the town proper was met with reprimands, fines, and accusations of "meddling in things outside their authority or jurisdiction."

At first, the Hell-Hounds had hung together, practicing with their weapons and hatching dark plots over wine as to what they would do when the Stepsons and Beysib guards fell from favor and they were recalled to active duty. Exclusion from the war at Wizardwall, and finally the assassination of the Emperor, had been the final straws to break the Hell-Hounds' spirit. The chance for reassignment was now gone. The power structure in the capital was in a turmoil, and the very existence of a few veterans posted to duty in Sanctuary was doubtlessly forgotten. They were stranded under the command of the Prince, who had no use for them at all.

Both practices and meetings had become more and more infrequent as individual Hell-Hounds found themselves drawn into the ready maw of Sanctuary's flesh-dens and gaming bars. There were always free drinks and women to be had for a Hell-Hound, even when it became apparent to everyone in the town that they were no longer a force to be reckoned with. Just having one of the Hell-Hounds on the premises was a deterrent to cheats and petty criminals, so the bartenders and madames bore the expense of their indulgences willingly.

The downhill slide had been slow but certain. The whores' conversation he had overheard served to confirm what he had suspected for some time . . . that the Hell-Hounds had not only fallen from favor, they were actually held in contempt by the same low-life townspeople they had once sneered at. Once-proud soldiers were now a pack of pitiful barflies . . . and this town had done it to them.

Zalbar shook his head.

No. That wasn't right. His own personal downfall had been started by a specific action. It had started when he agreed to team up with Jubal in an effort to deal with Tempus. It had started with the death of . . .

"Help me, Zalbar."

For once, Zalbar's nerves were under control. He didn't even look around.

"You're late," he said in a flat voice.

"Please! Help me!"

At this, Zalbar turned slowly to face his tormenter.

It was Razkuli. He was his best friend in the Hell-Hounds, or had been until Tempus killed him in revenge for Zalbar's part in the Jubal-Kurd nonsense. Actually, what confronted him was an apparition, a ghost if you will. After numerous encounters, Zalbar knew without looking that the figure before him didn't quite touch the floor as it walked or stood.

"Why do you keep doing this to me?" he demanded. "I thought you were my friend!"

"You *are* my friend," the form replied in a distant voice. "I have no one else to turn to. That's why you must help me!"

"Now look. We've been over this a hundred times," Zalbar said, trying to hold his temper. "I need my sleep. I can't have you popping up with your groanings every time I close my eyes. It was bad enough when you only showed up occasionally, but you're starting to drop in every night. Now either tell me how I can help you, something you've so far kept to yourself, or go away and leave me alone."

"It's cold where I am, Zalbar. I don't like it here. You know how I always hated the cold."

"Well it's no lark here either," Zalbar snapped, surprised at his own boldness. "And as for the cold . . . it's winter. That means it's cold all over."

"I need your help. I can't cross over to the other side without your help! Help me and I'll trouble you no more."

Zalbar suddenly grew more attentive. That was more information than his friend's ghost had ever given him in the past . . . or perhaps he had been too drunk to register what was being said.

"Cross over to where? How can I help you?"

"I can't tell you that . . ."

"Oh, Vashanka!" Zalbar exclaimed, throwing up his hands. "Here we go again. I can't help you if you won't tell me what . . ."

"Talk to Ischade," the spirit interrupted. "She can tell you what I cannot."

"Who?" Zalbar blinked. "Ischade? You mean the weird woman living in Downwind? That Ischade?"

"Ischade . . ." the ghost repeated, fading from sight.

"But . . . Oh, Vashanka! Wouldn't you know it. The one time I want to talk to him and now he's gone."

Seized by a sudden inspiration, Zalbar sank back onto the pillows and closed his eyes. Maybe sleeping again would bring the irritating apparition back long enough for a few clarifying questions.

As might be expected, he slept the rest of the night undisturbed.

Zalbar awoke near midday with a fresh sense of resolve. Razkuli's ghost had finally given him some information he could act on, and he was determined to rid himself of his otherworldly nag before he slept again.

The beginning of his quest, however, was delayed until nearly nightfall. The hangover he had eluded for his late-night conference with the spirit descended on him with a vengeance now that its ally, the sun, was shining bright. As a result, he spent most of the day abed, weak-limbed and fuzzy-headed, waiting until the traditional penance for overindulgence had passed before sallying forth. He might have convinced himself to wait until the next day, but all through his recovery he had clung to one thought like a buoy on a stormy sea.

It's almost over. Talk to Ischade. Talk to Ischade and I can sleep again.

Thus it was that a wobbly Zalbar donned his uniform and ventured out into the last rays of the setting sun, determined to rid himself of his nighttime tormenter or die in the attempt . . . which, at the moment, seemed a reasonably attractive option.

It was his intention to follow the North Road, which skirted the city's walls, to the bridge over the White Foal River, thereby avoiding the streets of the city proper. It was well known that, following the Hell-Hounds' removal, the chaos in town had evolved into vicious street fighting between rival factions, and he had no desire to be delayed by a brawl. Once he had walked unafraid even in the Maze, the heart of Sanctuary's underground. Now, that was someone else's concern and there was no need to take unnecessary risks.

The further he went, the more he realized that he had underestimated the extent of the urban warfare. Even here, outside the city, his trained eye could detect signs of preparations for violence. There were boxes and barrels stacked in formations clearly designed for cover and defense rather than for storage, and there were any number of armed men lounging in corners with no apparent purpose—other than to serve as lookouts. Despite his weakened condition, Zalbar grew more tense as he walked, feeling scores of concealed eyes watching him . . . appraising his strength. Perhaps he should have taken the longer route, skirting the town to the east, then passing south along the wharfs where violence was least likely. Too late to turn back now. He'd just have to brazen it through and hope enough respect lingered for the Hell-Hounds' uniform to give him safe passage.

Dropping a hand to his sword hilt, he slipped into the jaunty, swaggering gait of old, all the while trying desperately to remember the latest whorehouse rumors of which factions controlled which portions of the town. His walk went unchallenged, and he was just beginning to congratulate himself on the endurance of the Hell-Hound reputation he had fought so hard to build when a stray gust of wind carried the sound of derisive laughter to him from one of the watch-posts. With that, an alternate explanation for his uncontested progress came to him with a rush that made his cheeks burn in spite of the cold. Maybe the Hell-Hounds' reputation had simply fallen so low that they were considered beneath notice . . . not a sufficient threat to bother springing a trap on.

It was a humbled and subdued Zalbar that finally arrived at Ischade's residence. He paused on her doorstep, momentarily lost in thought. Soldiers were never popular, and he had suffered his share of abuse for wearing a uniform. This was the first time, though, that he had been a subject of other arms-bearers' ridicule. Sometime, after he had rehoned his sword and his skills, he would have to see what could be done about reestablishing the respect a Hell-Hound uniform was due. Maybe he could interest Armen and Quag as well. It was about time they all started giving a bit of thought to their collective future.

First, however, there was the business at hand to see to . . . and in his current state his mind could handle only one plan at a time. Raising a fist, he knocked on Ischade's door, wondering at the strange foliage in her garden.

The silence surrounding the house was unsettling, and he was about to knock again if just for the noise when the door opened a crack and a man's eye regarded him with a glare.

"Who is it and what do you want so early in the morning?"

"I am Zalbar of the Prince Kadakithis's personal bodyguard," he barked, falling into old habits, "and I have come . . ." Zalbar stopped suddenly and stole a glance at the now dark sky. "Early in the morning? Excuse me, but it's just past sundown."

"We're sleeping late in this house. It's been very busy lately," was the growled response. "What is it you want?"

"I wish to speak with the person known as Ischade."

"Is this official business, or a personal matter?"

Zalbar considered trying to bluff, but could think of no way to phrase his inquiries to make them sound official.

"Personal," he admitted finally.

"Then come back at a decent hour. She's got better things to do than . . ."

"Oh let him in, Haught," came a commanding female voice from somewhere out of sight. "I'm awake now anyway."

The guardian of the door favored Zalbar with one last dark glare, then stepped back to allow him entrance.

The Hell-Hound's first impression of Ischade's sitting room was that he had seen neater battlefields. Then his eye registered the strewn items, and he revised his opinion. Once he had led an assault against a band of mountaineers busily looting a rich caravan. The aftermath had been very similar to what he was seeing here: expensive goods tossed randomly with no regard to their value.

A prince's ransom had been ruined with careless handling . . .

He decided that he wouldn't like Ischade. His time in palaces and brothels taught him to appreciate objects that he could never afford and to be offended at their neglect. At least royalty knew how to take care of their toys . . . or had servants who did.

"What can I do for you, Officer?"

He turned to find a raven-haired woman entering the room, belting a black robe about herself as she walked.

"Ischade?"

"Yes?"

Now that she was in front of him, Zalbar was suddenly unsure of what to say.

"I was told to talk to you . . . by a ghost."

The man by the door groaned noisily. Ischade shot him a look that could have been used in the army.

"Sit down, Officer. I think you'd better tell me your story from the beginning."

Zalbar took the offered seat absently, trying to organize his thoughts.

"I had a friend . . . he was killed several years ago. He's haunting me. The first time was a long time back and he didn't reappear, so I thought it was just a bad dream. Lately, he's been coming to me more often . . . every time I try to sleep, as a matter of fact. He says he needs my help to cross over, whatever that means. He told me to talk to you . . . that you could tell me what he couldn't. That's why I'm here."

Ischade listened to all this with pursed lips and a faraway stare.

"Your friend. Tell me about him."

"He was a Hell-Hound, like me. His name was Razkuli . . ."

Zalbar would have continued, but Ischade had suddenly raised a hand to her forehead, massaging it as she grimaced.

"Razkuli. That's where I've seen that uniform before. But he isn't one of the ones that I keep."

"I don't understand," the Hell-Hound frowned. "Are you saying you know him?"

"He has . . . assisted me from time to time," Ischade

said, shrugging lightly. "Now, what can I do to help you?"

Zalbar tried to digest what Ischade was saying, but his mind simply wasn't up to the implications. Finally, he abandoned his efforts and returned to his original line of questioning.

"Could you tell me what's going on? What did Razkuli mean when he said that he couldn't 'cross over'?"

"For some reason his spirit is trapped between the realm of the living and the realm of the dead. Something is keeping him from a peaceful rest, and he wants you to help him on the physical plane."

"Help him how? What is it I'm supposed to do?"

"I don't know for sure. It could be any one of a number of things. I suppose the only way to find out is to ask him."

Zalbar straightened in his chair and glanced nervously around the room. "You mean you're going to summon the spirit? Here? Now?"

Ischade shook her head in an abrupt negative. "First of all, that's not the way it works. I don't summon spirits . . . I send an agent or occasionally fetch them personally. In this case, however, I think we'll leave the spirit alone and pursue alternate methods for obtaining the necessary information. As you've probably noticed, spirits aren't particularly eloquent or informative. Besides, I just got back from a quest like that, and I'll be damned if I'll go to hell again for a while."

"How's that again?" the Hell-Hound frowned.

"Nothing. Just a little joke. What I mean is, I think we'll have better luck simply animating his corpse and asking what the problem is."

"His corpse," Zalbar echoed hollowly.

". . . Of course, someone will have to fetch it. Do you know where he's buried?"

"In the garrison graveyard north of town . . . the grave's clearly marked."

"Good. Then you'll have no trouble finding it. As soon as you bring it here, we can . . . "

"ME?" Zalbar exclaimed. "Surely you can't expect me to dig up a grave."

"Certainly. Why not?"

The thought of digging up a well-aged corpse . . . any

corpse, much less that of his friend, horrified Zalbar. Still, he found himself strangely reluctant to express his revulsion to this woman who spoke so lightly of animating corpses and trips to hell.

"Um . . . I'm Hell-Hound, part of a royal retinue," he said instead. "If I were caught, a charge of grave-robbing would be scandalous."

In his corner, Haught snorted. "Open fighting in the streets and the authorities are worried about grave-robbing? I doubt there would be any danger of discovery."

"Then *you* fetch it if you're so sure there's no danger of arrest," Zalbar snapped back.

"Yes, that's a good idea." Ischade nodded. "Run along, Haught, and bring us the contents of Razkuli's grave. With luck we can see this business done by sun-up."

"ME?" Haught scowled. "But . . ."

"You," Ischade ordered firmly. "Now."

Haught started to reply angrily, then apparently thought better of it and slammed out the door into the night without another word.

"Now then, Officer," Ischade purred, focusing hooded eyes on Zalbar. "While we wait, perhaps you can tell me what you think of the Beysib-Nisibisi Alliance."

In the next hour, while anxiously awaiting Haught's return, Zalbar became firmly convinced that Ischade was insane. The silly woman seemed to have some idea that the arrival of the Beysib in Sanctuary was somehow part of a Nisi plot . . . this opinion apparently based on the observation that both cultures were snake-cults. Zalbar's efforts to point out that the Beysib used small vipers, while military reports indicated that the Nisibisi were into man-sized constrictors, fell on deaf ears. If anything, his arguments seemed to reinforce Ischade's conviction that she was the only one who could see the true ramifications of what was happening in Sanctuary.

He assumed her mental imbalance was the result of her profession. If she was indeed a necromancer, constant involvement with death and corpses was bound to be unsettling to the mind. After all, look at the effect that dealing with *one* dead person was having on him!

As much as he dreaded viewing his friend's remains,

Zalbar's conversation with Ischade was so unsettling that he was actually relieved when a footstep sounded outside and Haught appeared once more in the doorway.

"I had to steal a wheelbarrow," the necromancer's assistant said in a manner that was almost an accusation. "There were two corpses in the grave."

"Two?" Zalbar scowled, but he was talking to thin air.

Haught reappeared in a moment carrying the first moldering body, which he dumped unceremoniously on the floor, and turned to fetch the second one.

Ischade bent over their prize, beckoning Zalbar to move closer.

"Is this your friend?"

Zalbar was still shaking his head. "I don't understand it," he said. "How could there be two bodies in the same grave?"

"It's not uncommon," Ischade shrugged. "Gravediggers get paid by the body, and if you don't watch them, they'll dump two or more bodies into the same grave rather than going through the trouble of digging several . . . especially if there are two graveyards involved and they don't want to have to drag the second corpse across town. Your friend was probably buried with someone else who died about the same time. The question is, was this him?"

The corpse was almost beyond recognition. What skin and flesh was left was dried and mummified; bone showed in many places. There was a gaping hole in the abdomen, and the internal organs were not in evidence.

"N . . . No," Zalbar said carefully. "I'm sure this is someone else . . . maybe Kurd."

"Who?"

"Kurd. He was a butcher . . . a medical researcher he called himself, but he performed his experiments on the bodies of living slaves. He died the same day as Razkuli, disemboweled by . . . a dissatisfied customer. I saw his body at the charnel house when I went there to identify my friend. They were the only two there at the time, so if you're right about the gravediggers' negligence, it stands to reason that his would be the second body."

He was babbling now, trying to avoid examining the corpse more closely.

"Interesting," Ischade murmured. "I could use a repair-man. But you're sure it isn't your friend?"

"Positive. For one thing, Razkuli was . . ."

"Here's the other," Haught announced from the door-way. "Now if you don't mind, I think I'll retire for the night. A little of this type of assisting goes a long way."

"That's him!" Zalbar said pointing at the new corpse.

"I think I see the problem," Ischade sighed. "You could have saved us all a lot of trouble if you had been more specific. Why didn't you tell me he had been beheaded?"

Sure enough, the corpse which Haught had propped against the wall noticeably lacked its hatrack.

"I didn't think it was important. Is it?"

"Certainly. One thing that will always hold a spirit in limbo is if its physical body has been dismembered . . . particularly if an important piece, like its head, has been denied a burial."

"What? You mean his head hasn't been buried?"

"Apparently not. As I said earlier, gravediggers are notoriously lazy, so I doubt they would dig a separate hole just for the head. No, my guess is that that portion of your friend's body has somehow gone astray. The reason the spirit hasn't been able to instruct you in more detail is because it can't tell which part is missing, much less where it is."

She turned to Zalbar with a smile. "This will be simpler than I thought. Bring me the head of Razkuli, and I can put his spirit to rest for you. Do you have any idea where it might be after all this time?"

"No," the Hell-Hound said grimly, "but I know some-one who might. Don't bother going back to sleep. If I'm right, this won't take long at all."

Innos, one of several grooms who watched over the military barracks and stables, awoke from a sound sleep to find lights ablaze and a swordpoint at his throat.

"Think back, Innos!"

It was Zalbar. Innos had watched his degeneration into a brothel barfly with no interest other than that there would be one less bunk for him to police. Now, however, the Hell-Hound's eyes were blazing with a savagery that spoke of old times. Innos looked into those eyes and decided that he would not lie, whatever question was asked . . . just as the street watcher had decided not to laugh at the Hell-Hound when he stalked back from Ischade's.

"Bu . . . but Zalbar! I have done nothing!"

"Think back!" Zalbar commanded again. "Think back several years. I was coming out of an audience with the Prince . . . so upset I was nearly out of my mind. I handed you something and told you to dispose of it properly. Remember?"

Innos did, and his blood ran icy.

"Y . . . Yes. It was the head of your friend Razkuli."

"Where is it?"

"Why, I buried it, of course. Just as you ordered."

The swordpoint pressed forward, and a small trickle of blood made its way down Innos's throat.

"Don't lie to me! I know it hasn't been buried."

"But . . . if you knew . . ."

"I just found out tonight. Now where is it?"

"Please don't kill me! I've never . . ."

"Where!? It's important, man."

"I sold it . . . to the House of Whips and Chains. They use skulls in their decor."

Innos was flung back, and he closed his eyes as Zalbar raised his sword to strike.

After a frozen moment, he risked a peek, and saw the Hell-Hound standing with the sword hanging loose at his side.

"No. I can't kill you, Innos," he said softly. "I could expect little better from anyone else in this town. If anything, the fault is mine. I should have seen to the head myself."

He fixed Innos with a stare, and the groom saw that he was smiling.

"Still," he continued in a friendly tone, "I'd suggest you pack your things and leave town . . . tonight. I may not be so understanding the next time I see you."

Zalbar did not even bother to knock, but simply pushed his way through the door of the House of Whips and Chains. It was his first visit to this particular brothel which catered to tastes bizarre even for Sanctuary, but his anger outweighed his curiosity. When the madame rushed wide-eyed, to confront him, he was brief and to the point.

"You have a skull here as part of your decorations. I want it."

"But Officer, we never sell our decorations. They're too difficult to replace . . ."

"I didn't say I wanted to buy it," Zalbar snapped. "I'm taking it with me . . . and I'd advise you not to argue."

He swept the room quickly with his gaze, ignoring the girls peering out from hiding.

"That brazier . . . with the hot irons in it. It's a fire hazard. I could close this establishment right now, Madame, and I doubt you could fix the violations faster than I could find them if you ever wanted to re-open."

"But . . . oh, take the silly thing. Take all of them or take your pick. I don't care."

"All of them?"

Zalbar was suddenly aware that there were no less than a dozen skulls peering at him from ledges and mantels around the room.

"You're too kind, Madame," he sighed heavily. "Now, if I could trouble you for a bag?"

The rest of the night was mercifully fuzzy in Zalbar's mind, as fatigue and shock began to numb his senses. Ischade had revived Kurd by the time he arrived back at her house . . . which was fortunate, for the vivisectionist was of invaluable assistance as they faced the macabre task of matching the severed vertebrae to discover which in the bagful of skulls was actually Razkuli's.

He buried his friend's now assembled body himself, not trusting the necromancer to do it, digging the grave far from the normal graveyards, under a tree they both knew. His task finally complete, he staggered back to the Aphrodisia House and slept uninterrupted for more than a day.

When he awoke, the events seemed so distant and bizarre that he might have dismissed them as a fever dream, were it not for two things. First, the spirit of Razkuli never again appeared to spoil his slumbers, and second, Myrtis threw him out of Aphrodisia House after hearing he had visited the House of Whips and Chains. (She soon forgave him, as she always did, her anger dissipating almost magically.)

The only other consequence of the entire episode was that a week later, Zalbar was given an official reprimand. It seemed that while engaging in sword practice with his fellow Hell-Hounds, he had broken off drilling to administer a merciless beating to one of the onlookers. Reliable witnesses testified that the victim's only offense had been to make the offhand comment: "You Hell-Hounds will do anything to get ahead!"

THE COLOR OF MAGIC

Diana L. Paxson

The sky was weeping, as if some artist had muddied all
the world's colors to gray and now was trying to dissolve
them away. Water dripped from the brim of Lalo's floppy
hat down his neck and he tried to pull his cloak higher,
swearing. The saying went that there were two seasons in
Sanctuary—one of them was hot and the other was
not—and the most miserable was whichever one you were
in. It was not a hard rain—more a persistent drizzle that
imposed an illusory peace on the town by encouraging the
bravos of the dozen or so warring factions to stay inside.

I should have stayed home too, thought Lalo. But
another hour in rooms crowded with children and the
lingering odors of wet clothing and cooking food would
have driven him into a quarrel with Gilla, and he had
sworn not to do that again. The Vulgar Unicorn was
closed to him, but last he had heard, the Green Grape was
still on the corner where the Governor's Walk joined the
Farmer's Run. He'd have a peaceful drink or two there,
and figure out what to do. . . .

Lalo ducked under the overhang where the weathered
sign with its bunch of peeling fruit knocked forlornly
against the wall. The only sign of life about the place was
the scruffy gray dog shivering against the door. Then Lalo
pushed the door open and the welcome scent of mulling

wine overpowered the more familiar odors of mildew and backed-up drains.

Lalo shrugged out of his cloak and shook it. The dog's ears flapped and its collar jingled as it did the same. Then it sneezed and followed him inside.

Lalo sat down next to the stove and draped his already steaming cloak across a chair. A skinny serving boy brought him mulled wine and he clasped his paint-stained fingers around the mug to warm them before he let the hot, sweet liquor slide down his throat. He set the mug down, glimpsed his own unprepossessing reflection in a tarnished mirror on the wall, and looked quickly away.

He had looked into a mirror once and seen a god look back at him. Had that been a dream? And he had seen all his own evil come alive on the wall of the Vulgar Unicorn. That had been a nightmare, and too many others had shared it.

The gift of painting the truth of a man had come originally from Enas Yorl. Now, he almost wished he had accepted the sorcerer's offer to take it back again. These days, Enas Yorl seemed to be chronically incapacitated by his periodic transformations—it was almost as if the sorcerer's mutations paralleled the degenerating situation in Sanctuary.

But with Enas Yorl handicapped and Lythande out of town, who was there to teach him how to use his power? The Temples were useless, and the stench of the Mage-guild made him feel ill.

Quite close to him, someone sneezed. Lalo jumped, set his mug teetering, and grabbed for it.

"Do you mind if I borrow your cloak?"

Lalo blinked, then focused on a thin young man clad only in a metal dog collar who was reaching for the garment Lalo had draped over the other chair.

"It's still wet . . ." he said helplessly.

"That's the only trouble with these transformations," the stranger shuddered as he wrapped the cloak around him, "especially in this kind of weather. But sometimes it's safer to travel in disguise."

Lalo shifted focus and saw the blue glow of power. The pride in the stranger's face was tempered by an almost puppyish eagerness, and a hint of wistfulness as well, as if not all his magic could win him what he really desired.

"What do you want with me, *Mage*?"

"Oh, you can call me Randal, Master Limner . . ." the mage grinned. He smoothed back his damp hair as if he were trying to hide his ears. "And what I want is *you,* or rather, Sanctuary does . . ."

Lalo tried to cover his confusion with another sip of wine. He had heard about the Hazard-class sorcerer who worked with the Stepsons, but during the weeks when Lalo had been trying to learn magic from the priests of Savankala, the Tysian mage had been unaccountably absent. Lalo had never seen him before.

Randal fumbled at his collar and pulled out a tight roll of canvas. With that confident grin that was already beginning to rasp Lalo's nerves, he flattened it against the table.

"Do you recognize this drawing?" It was the picture of that mercenary Niko, in whose background two other faces had so unexpectedly appeared.

Lalo grimaced, knowing it all too well, and wishing, not for the first time, that he had never let Molin Torchholder take the damned thing. Certainly no one had given him any peace over it since. It was that, as much as the conclusion that the Temple teachers didn't *know* how to train him, that had driven him home again.

"How did you get that?" he asked sourly. "I thought His High and Mightiness kept it closer than an Imperial pardon."

"I borrowed it," said Randal enigmatically. "Look at it!" He brandished the paper under Lalo's nose. "Do you understand what you have done?"

"That's what Molin kept asking me—you should talk to him!"

"Perhaps I can understand your answers better than he did . . ."

"The answers are all *no!*" Lalo said harshly. "I don't *know* what happens if you destroy one of my portraits. I've never tried to animate a portrait, and I'm not about to start experimenting. Not after the Black Unicorn. . . . You're the mage—you tell me what I can do!"

"Perhaps I will," Randal said winningly, "if you'll help us in return."

"Us? What 'us'?" Lalo eyed him warily. Badly as he needed knowledge, he was even more desperately afraid of being used.

This time it was Randal who hesitated. "Everyone who wants to see some kind of order restored to Sanctuary," he said finally.

"By kicking out the Fish-eyes? My daughter serves one of their ladies at the Palace. They're not *all* bad—"

Randal shrugged. "Who is?" Then he frowned. "We just don't want them running us, that's all. But the Beysib are hardly the worst of our problems—" His long finger stabbed at the woman's face in the picture, that searingly beautiful face whose eyes were like the eyes of the Black Unicorn.

"*She—*" hissed the mage. "*She's* at the bottom of it. If we can destroy her—even contain her—maybe we can set the rest right!"

"You go right ahead," snapped Lalo. "Just drawing her picture was bad enough. Fight your own wars—it's nothing to do with me!"

Randal sighed. "I can't force you, but others may try. You'll wish you had allies then."

Lalo stared sullenly into his wine. "Threats won't move me either, mage!"

There was a short silence. Then Randal fumbled with his collar again.

"I'm not threatening you," he said tiredly. "I don't have to. Take this . . ." From the apparently limitless compartment in his dog collar he pulled a wadded cloth. It opened out as it fell and Lalo saw a garish rainbow of red and blue and yellow and black and green. "It'll get you across town when you decide you need help from *me*. Ask for me at the Palace . . ."

He paused, but Lalo would not meet his eyes. Randal got to his feet, and as his movement stirred the drawing, shadows lifted like dark wings in the corners of the room. *Like the winged shadows in the picture,* thought Lalo, shivering. Very carefully the mage rolled up the drawing. Lalo made no objection. He never wanted to see it, or the mage, again. His vision blurred and images moved just beyond the limits of his perception. He shuddered again.

"Thank you for the loan of your cloak . . ." The words trailed off oddly.

Lalo looked up just in time to see his outer garment settle like a deflating balloon across the chair. Something wriggled beneath it, sneezed, and then pushed free. He

saw a gaunt, wolfish dog stand up, shake itself, and lift one
large ear inquiringly.

Even as a dog his ears are too big for him, thought Lalo.
Fascinated in spite of himself, he watched as the animal
sneezed again and trotted across the room. The tavern
door obligingly opened itself, then snicked shut after him.
And then there was only the crackling of the fire and the
whisper of rain against the windows to keep him company.

I dreamed it, thought the limner, but the armband still
lay before him, striped with all the colors of the lines that
sectioned Sanctuary. *And what is my color, the color of
magic?* Lalo wondered then. But there was no one to
answer him.

He dropped a few coins onto the table and stuffed the
armband into his pouch. Then he jammed his hat on over
his thinning hair and wrapped the damp cloak around him.
Now it smelled of dog as well as of wet wool.

And as that scent clung to the cloak, the mage's words
stuck in Lalo's memory. His step quickened as he headed
for the door. He had to warn Gilla—he had to get
home.

"You tell me, Wedemir—you see more of the town than
I do. Is your father right to be afraid?" Gilla paused in her
sweeping and leaned on the broom, staring at her oldest
son. Her two younger children were sitting at the kitchen
table, drawing on their slates with some of Lalo's broken
chalks. Chalk squeaked and Wedemir grimaced.

"Well, you still need a pass to get around," he answered her, "and who's fighting whom and why seems to
change from day to day. But having the real Stepsons back
in their barracks seems to have calmed the Beysibs
down."

Suddenly Latilla screeched and grabbed for her little
brother's arm. Alfi's slate crashed to the floor and he
began to cry.

"Mama, he took the chalk right out of my hand!"
exclaimed Latilla.

"Red chalk!" said Alfi through his tears, as if that
explained it. He glared at his sister. "Draw red dragon to
eat you up!" He slid down from his chair to retrieve the
slate.

Gilla smacked his bottom and pulled him upright.
"You're not going to draw *anything* until you learn some

self-control!" She glanced toward the shut door to Lalo's studio. He had said he was going to paint, but she had seen him fast asleep on the couch when she looked in a quarter hour before.

"You're going to your room, both of you!" she told her small son and daughter. "Your father needs his rest, so play quietly!"

When they had gone, she picked up the fallen slate and fragments of chalk and turned back to Wedemir, who had sat through the altercation trying to look as if he had never seen either his brother or his sister before.

"That's not what I meant, and you know it," she said softly. "Lalo is not afraid of the Beysib. He's afraid of magic."

"Name of Ils, Mother—the Stepsons' pet mage is trying to recruit him." Wedemir's black brows nearly met as he frowned. "What do you expect *me* to do?"

"Stay with him! Protect him!" Gilla said fiercely. She began sweeping again with long, hard strokes, as if she could thrash out all her fears.

"He's not going to like me tagging after him—"

"Neither of you will like it if he runs into danger alone. . . ." There was a sudden heaviness in the air. Gilla heard a faint "pop" and turned, the rest of her words dying in her throat.

Above the kitchen table hovered a sphere of darkness, scintillating with flickers of cobalt blue. As she stared, it quivered and began to drift, still expanding, toward the studio. The floor shook as Gilla started toward it.

"Mother, no!" Wedemir's chair crashed behind him as he tried to get around the table, but Gilla was already standing between the Sphere and the studio door.

"Get out of my kitchen, you demon's fart!" She jabbed at the Darkness with her broom and it recoiled. "Think you'll get my Lalo, do you? I'll show *you!*" The Sphere stilled as she spoke Lalo's name, then suddenly enlarged. Gilla blinked as colors swirled dizzyingly across its slick surface.

"By Siveni's spear, get you gone!" Gilla recovered herself and struck the Sphere with her broom. The stiff straw faded as if she had shoved it into a murky pool, then the shaft started to disappear too. Her screech of outrage was swallowed as the Darkness engulfed her. She heard the second "pop" of displaced air, and all sense of direction and dimension disappeared.

"Papa, are we going to stay here long?" Latilla looked around the courtyard of the Palace, whose usual splendor was muted by the rain, and pressed closer to Lalo.

"I hope not, sweetheart," he answered, scanning the arches of the cloister anxiously.

"I don' like it," Alfi said decidedly. "I want Mama. I want to go home. Papa, will Mama be back soon?"

"I hope so. . . ." whispered Lalo. His eyes blurred with something more than rain as he knelt to hug both children close against him, finding some deceptive comfort in the warmth of their young bodies. He and Gilla had made these children between them. She couldn't be gone!

"Father, Wedemir told me what happened! What are we going to do?"

Vanda was hurrying toward them with her older brother behind her, her bright hair coming undone from its Beysib coiffure.

"I'm going to get Gilla back," Lalo said harshly. "But you'll have to take care of the little ones."

"Here?" She looked around her dubiously.

Wedemir cleared his throat. "They may not be safe at home."

Vanda frowned. "Well, we already have some other children in quarters in the basement—that child of the Temple they call Gyskouras, and Illyra's boy—it's a regular nursery. Maybe I can work something out . . . oh, of course I'll take them!" She scooped Alfi into her arms. "Just find Mother!" She stared at Lalo over Alfi's dark head, her grey eyes so much like Gilla's that something twisted in Lalo's chest.

"I will . . ." he managed, and could say no more.

Vanda nodded, shifted Alfi onto her hip and reached out for Latilla's hand. "Come on, lovies, and I'll show you some pretty things."

"Toys?" asked Alfi.

"Toys, and other children, and everything . . ." Vanda's voice faded as she went under the archway. Then she turned a corner and was gone. _ _

"At least it was convenient to drop them here," said Wedemir dryly. "Exactly where in the Palace did that mage tell you to go?"

"I'll have to ask at the wicket. It's like the Maze inside. . . ." Lalo sighed and splashed across the courtyard.

Behind the wicket at the Gate was a little room where litigants had waited to be called to the Hall of Justice in the days when the Prince still pretended to govern Sanctuary. Lalo settled onto one of its inadequately padded benches and closed his eyes. Instinctively he reached out for that current of awareness that linked him to Gilla, but there was nothing there. He had never realized how essential her presence was to him.

Gilla—Gilla! his heart cried, and he did not realize that he had moaned aloud until he felt Wedemir patting his arm.

"You have decided to come to us after all! What is wrong?"

Lalo's eyes flew open. Randal the Mage with his clothes on was an altogether more impressive sight than the man who had borrowed his cloak in the tavern. In this setting, even his freckles seemed less visible.

"Something tried to get him and took my mother by mistake," said Wedemir accusingly. "A black globular sort of thing—it just materialized in the kitchen, and she was gone!"

"A kind of bubble shot with flashes of blue light?" asked Randal, and Wedemir nodded. The mage chewed his lip for a moment, then grimaced. "It sounds like Roxane. She has a habit of kidnaping people, and right now she's hellbent on revenge against anyone connected with Molin Torchholder or Niko. . . ."

Randal's voice had softened as he spoke the mercenary's name, and Lalo sensed the complex of frustrated love, longing, and loyalty that explained why the mage had handled Niko's portrait so reverently. But Lalo could hardly worry about Randal's feelings now. He had heard too many tales about Roxane. . . .

"But why take my mother if she wanted Lalo?" asked Wedemir.

Randal looked at the limner sympathetically. "The witch didn't expect you to give any trouble or she would have come herself. The Sphere was a Carrier, set to react to your identity. And your wife spoke your name—"

"But she must realize her mistake by now. Why hasn't she let Gilla go?"

"Roxane plays for points," said Randal gently. "As long as the woman's no trouble, she'll keep her, maybe use her as a hostage to compel you . . ."

No one needed to detail what could happen if Roxane got tired of her captive. Lalo jerked to his feet and Randal pulled him back with surprising strength.

"No, Lalo—Roxane has no honor. You could not be sure of saving your wife even if you offered yourself in her place. To strike against the sorceress is the only way!"

Lalo sank back onto the bench and covered his eyes.

"Are you with us then, Limner?" asked Randal softly.

"*I'm* with you," interrupted Wedemir, "if you'll teach me how to fight!"

"That can be arranged," said Randal. He waited for Lalo's answer.

"Help me free Gilla and show me how to protect those who depend on me," the words were dragged from Lalo's lips, "and yes, I'll do what I can to help you."

Gilla sneezed, heaved herself upright, and sneezed again. Something round and hard was digging into her side. She looked down, saw a skull, and jerked away. So much for the comfortable conclusion that she had been having a nightmare. She still gripped her broom, but she was not at home; no one had cleaned this place for quite a while.

"Ah—fat lady wake now? Fat lady sleep hard; Snapper Jo was lonely!"

Gilla stared. The voice which had uttered these words of welcome was very deep, with a kind of curdled quality that made her think of the bottom of a vegetable bin that had been left alone too long. For a moment her eyes struggled to sort through a confusion of piled boxes and dusty hangings, then she focused on a shape that was tall, and gaunt, and gray. It made a gurgling sound that could have meant anything, and lit a lamp.

Gilla blinked. The creature's general grayness was more than compensated for by a pair of purple pantaloons and a shock of orange hair. He treated her to a sharp, snaggle-toothed smile.

"Fat lady talk to Snapper Jo now?"

Gilla cleared her throat. "Does this place belong to you?"

"Oh, noooo—" The warts on his gray skin seemed to

crawl as Snapper Jo glanced fearfully over his shoulder. "Great Mistress rules here! Great Lady, very beautiful, very *strong* . . ." He ducked his head with a kind of fearful reverence.

Gilla thought he was overdoing it, but it was obvious that whoever had brought her here did have plenty of power. Beneath the dust she caught the unmistakable dank perfume of the White Foal River, so she knew she must still be in Sanctuary, and there were only two sorceresses here with that kind of power. Her skin chilled as she thought about it. It was the kind of riddle children asked in play: *Would you rather be eaten by a she-panther or a tigress? By Ischade or by Roxane?*

Suddenly the dust and clutter around her seemed stifling. Gilla got to her feet and picked her way, between a dusty carved table and a tall vase of dull brass inlaid with tarnished silver, toward the door. The vase toppled as Snapper Jo leaped with awkward efficiency to block her.

"Fat lady not to *go*—" the gray fiend said reproachfully. "Orders—Mistress says to keep you here." He favored her with a walleyed leer. "And talk to Snapper Jo!"

Gilla talked to him. She could not tell if it was for hours, really, or only seemed that way. The fiend's conversation was remarkably repetitive, and only long practice in answering the questions of small children while doing something else got her through it still sane. But the light behind the curtains was definitely fading when something moved in the doorway and Snapper Jo's patter abruptly failed.

The room seemed to brighten, or perhaps it was only that this woman left a glamor in the air around her. Local legend had said that Roxane was terrible, but had no words to say how beautiful she was. And surely it was Roxane, for everyone knew that the witch Ischade was pale as a night-born flower, but Roxane's skin bloomed like a rose.

"So, you are enjoying your conversation?" Roxane's little cat smile did not reach her eyes.

You bitch, how dare you . . . thought Gilla. Then she met that gaze, and felt her skin grow cold. She bit back the retort that ached in her throat.

"My Carrier was not prepared for such as you." Roxane looked Gilla up and down. "Count yourself fortunate that your weight did not burst it and leave you floating mindless between the planes!" The Nisibisi sorceress laughed, and Gilla's chill drove deeper. This woman reeked of evil like some deadly perfume.

Gilla found herself retreating within the fortress of her flesh; she had never understood until now how her bulk had protected her. Physically her sheer mass had made her formidable. And it had shielded her psychically from all but the most powerful personalities. But Roxane was pure power, and Gilla was afraid.

"Great Lady, I am indeed grateful," she said between set teeth. "But surely you have no use for me here—"

"No? We shall see. There is no need to act hastily!" Roxane gave a throaty laugh, as if she were savoring some private amusement. "I will keep you for a while as a companion for my servant here. But in that case I suppose you must be fed," she looked at Gilla with another laugh. "Though surely it would do you no harm to starve for a while. Snapper—leave one of the serpents on guard and get food for her."

"And food for Snapper, too, Mistress? Nice food—red, still twitching?" The fiend clutched at the air and smacked his narrow lips, his eyes glazing.

Gilla watched him and shuddered, reminding herself not to trust his apparent affability.

"Snapper, be still!" Roxane flickered her fingers casually and the fiend froze, watching her with rolling eyes.

"Great One, please let me go home," Gilla whispered, bowing her head to keep Roxane from seeing her eyes.

"Oh, you don't want to go home," Roxane smiled prettily. "Your home is going to become very damp and uncomfortable very soon. Believe me, Ilsig sow, you will be much safer here with me. Do you hear the rain?" She paused a moment and Gilla heard its soft, steady patter outside.

"You'll hear more rain soon. But don't worry, my wards will keep the water away from *here*—the rest of Sanctuary is not going to be so fortunate. Water is coming. A *great deal* of water is coming!" Roxane lifted her arms with a ripple of silken sleeves. "Oh, *they* will be sorry, when the flood sweeps their fine temples and palaces away! I will bring the great waters down from the north in such a deluge as this place has never seen!"

Gilla grew very still. If there was a flood her children

would be in danger. She had to think of a way out of here! But she had always done her best thinking when she was working; her gaze fell on the broom that had come with her through the void.

"If I am to stay, Mistress, then let me keep busy working for you." She tried to simulate humility. It did not sound convincing to *her*, but she suspected that the Nisibisi sorceress had spent too much time studying men and other beings to know much about how her own sex behaved.

"I'm a very good worker," Gilla went on. "Would you like me to clean?"

Roxane giggled. "Housecleaning? Oh yes—I with my waters and you with your broom will clean up Sanctuary!" Still laughing, she nodded to Snapper Jo. "You let her clean then, do you understand?" Bright skirts swirled as she turned, and she was gone as swiftly as she had come.

For a long moment Gilla stood utterly still. Then she seized the broom that was all she had left of home and began to sweep furiously.

And Roxane, in her witching room, set her Nisibisi Globe of Power spinning in the air before her so that the jewels inset into its High Peaks' clay gathered up the light from the candles that circled her and sent it shimmering into the bowl of water on the stand below.

Through air and water she drew the secret sigils; inhaled deeply the incense that smouldered in the corners of the room and breathed the charged air into the water until it steamed. Then she began to whisper in a language that no one in Sanctuary except Niko or Randal would have recognized.

The light grew aqueous and dim; the voice of the sorceress deepened. The Globe that spun before her focused her awareness, heightened and transformed it and channeled it into that plane of the Otherworld where the Water Demons had their home. By their secret names she compelled them, and the water in her silver basin misted away.

But over the plains north of Sanctuary great cumulus clouds began to move, at first reluctantly, and then more swiftly, as if they sensed the waiting sea. And when they met the warmer air of the seacoast they released their heavy loads of rain, and the voice of the White Foal River began to change.

"Look—there are *laws* that govern magic," repeated Randal. "If you understand them you have control. Visualize! You know how to do that, surely—when you plan a picture don't you see it in your mind before you even take the brush in your hand? Use symbols, whatever you need to focus your consciousness on the part of the Otherworld you're working with, and then do your magic!"

Lalo nodded. He could almost see the sense of it, but it was so hard to concentrate when wind rattled the window-frames and rain beat against the slubbed glass. It had been raining hard since the afternoon before.

"If you visualize a shield around you that only lets specific things out, or in, then you can control what you paint, right?" the Tysian mage went on. He sat back and looked at Lalo expectantly.

The limner nodded. "I think I understand. I don't know if I can do it, but I appreciate your effort to teach me. Worry makes me a poor student. *When* are we going against Roxane?"

"We're not ready yet—*you're* not ready. Limner, she would swat you like a fly! Even I—" He broke off, and Lalo was just beginning to wonder if even the mage feared this sorceress, when a heavy tread shook the tower stairs. The door crashed open and they saw Straton, the Step-sons' commander, standing there.

"Vashanka's rod, man, *here* you are, Randal! You've led me hell's own chase, that's for sure!" Somehow he managed to look even more formidable than usual with his hair plastered to his skull and water from wet steel and soggy leather pooling on the floor.

"Trouble?" The mage stood up, freckles suddenly dark against his pallor.

Straton spat. "Do you use those flapping ears of yours just for balance, or what? Can't you hear the rain? The river's overflowed into the Swamp of Night Secrets, and the whole southeastern promontory will be flooded soon. There's reports that the upper ford is turning into a lake and Goat Creek is over its banks already.

"The Beysa's sticking—hell, her apartments are on the second floor—but rest of the Fish-folk are heading for their ships in schools! There's nothing much we can do about the barracks or Downwind, but if we don't act fast we'll lose the main town too. I've set all the men I've got to building dykes above the bridge, but I need more!"

"Can anyone get a message to Zip?" asked Randal swiftly. "Tell him if we channel the flood maybe it'll sweep the Fish-eyes out to sea—that should persuade him! Use the same argument on Jubal."

Straton's mouth opened as if he were going to object, then it slowly closed again. For a moment he almost smiled. "It *would* solve a few problems," he said wistfully. Then he shook himself and glared at the mage.

"Fine! I appreciate the advice! But what I want from you, Witchy-Ears, is some wizard's work. You get yourself and your spells out there and do something about those clouds!"

Randal raised one eyebrow. "I will if I can. You know I'm not allowed to alter the balances if this is a natural storm."

"And if it isn't? Have you considered that possibility?"

The mage was still frowning as Straton turned and clattered back down the stairs. He sighed and grasped the knob of the balcony door.

Just a touch on the handle was enough to release it. The door banged back against the wall and a gust of damp wind swirled papers around the room. Ignoring the upset, Randal stepped outside and Lalo followed him.

The wind was coming from the northeast. Ranked banks of cloud rolled steadily seaward as if pushed by inexorable hands. Randal closed his eyes and faced into the wind, then murmured something and traced a Sign upon the air. Lalo shifted focus as the mage had taught him and glimpsed lines of violet fire that wavered a moment and then were torn apart by the wind. Then his vision was sucked upward into the clouds themselves, and he saw as he had Seen in the country of the gods.

Something moved there with, but not *of,* the clouds—shapes that were subtly *wrong,* spirits that took a malicious pleasure in manipulating the elements. Oblivious to his presence, they played—it would have taken a more compelling personality than Lalo's to disturb them. But were they demonic? Lalo had never seen storm elementals before. He knew only that he did not like these.

With a wrench, Lalo pulled back into his normal

perceptions—Randal's training had done this much for him—and looked quickly at the mage. Randal's eyes were still closed, his face set in a snarl; his hands moved, but it was clear that whatever he was doing was not enough. After a few moments he, also, shuddered and sagged back.

He opened his eyes. "Sorcery . . ." he muttered, "black sorcery, and I think I know whose! There's a Nisi stink about those demons. That bitch is working her spells, and she has reset her wards. I doubt even Ischade could get to her now!"

Lalo swallowed. If Roxane's house were impregnable, then Gilla was lost. His gaze moved numbly across slick rooftops, alternately revealed and hidden by tattered gray curtains of rain, to the muddy ribbon of the river. Mist blurred his view of the far bank below the bridge where Roxane's house lay, the house where Gilla was now. . . .

"What will you do?" he asked the mage.

"I have a Power Globe of my own," Randal said thoughtfully. "Perhaps I can use it to counter Roxane's magics. I can try." He looked over at Lalo.

"There's no way I can help you here." Lalo answered the question in the mage's eyes. "But if my hands are no use for magic, at least they can build a dyke as well as another man's. I will be down there." He gestured toward the river. If he could do nothing to save Gilla, at least he could be near her when the river swept everything away.

From the floods, at least, Gilla was not in danger. The bubble of magic with which Roxane had surrounded her house repelled the waters as it repelled all other sorceries. The personnel inside the house were another matter. So far, Snapper Jo had warned off the green house snakes— six feet long with blank ophidian stares more disturbing than the beynit's vicious gleam; undeads with empty eyes and the rotting stink of unburied flesh; and assorted thralls whose bodies yet breathed but whose souls had fled or, worse yet, were locked in some tormented reality from which an occasional gleam of awareness appealed to Gilla for a release from pain.

Even keeping a houseful of children indoors through a solid month of rain—which had been Gilla's previous definition of purgatory—paled by comparison. And of course, even when she had lived in the depths of poverty at the edge of the Maze, Gilla had never allowed her house to reach such a state of squalor.

Despite herself, she was doing the sorceress good service. For two days she had been cleaning—straightening, scrubbing, sweeping away the thick layer of dust. Already several baskets full of offal stood waiting for disposal beside Roxane's kitchen door.

But that was all that Gilla *had* accomplished. She had thought as furiously as she had worked, but still she had no plan. She stood, leaning on her broom and breathing heavily, gazing out through the dirty window and the oily shimmer of the warding shield at the incessant rain.

"Rain fall up and down the town . . ." Snapper Jo said cheerfully. "Wash everything away—shacks, Palace, all. All that fresh meat floating by . . ." he added with a sigh.

"Don't you smile about flooding—my children are in that town!" snarled Gilla. She swallowed her instinctive appeal to the fiend's nonexistent sympathy. His only response to her pleas to help her escape had been a reiteration of Roxane's command to guard.

"Fat lady is a Mama? Snapper Jo never had Mama—poor Snapper Jo. . . ." He gazed at her with dim calculation in his mismatched eyes. "Fat lady be Snapper Jo's Mama!" he proclaimed triumphantly.

Gilla looked at that inane grin and shuddered. She thought of her children. Wedemir had somehow turned into a warrior, and Vanda was growing into a beauty that she herself had never had—those two, at least, could take care of themselves now. Her next boy, Ganner, was still apprenticed to Herewick the Jeweler, and with the streets so dangerous, she hardly ever saw him. She could hope that he was safe, but he, too, was started on his own road now. It was the two little ones who still needed her. How could Lalo manage them alone? Gilla straightened with a motion as inevitable as a tidal wave rising to strike the shore. She had to get home!

One of the undeads stumped up the stairs from the basement, wiping moist earth on the remains of its tunic. Gilla wondered if Roxane's wards extended underground, but even to escape she could not bring herself to go down *there*.

The thing bumped into Snapper Jo, who snarled and shoved it away.

"Dead thing go back to earth!" The fiend pointed to the stairs.

"It is wet in the earth," the corpse said dully. "Let this one go outside."

"No, not outside—" Snapper Jo shook his head. "*She* says nothing must pass the house shield now. Dead thing try, *she* finds worse place for it than *there!*"

The tattered head turned, and Gilla could almost imagine she saw some emotion in those blank eyes. Then it sagged a little and very slowly thumped back down the creaking stairs.

Gilla sighed gustily to clear the stench from her nostrils when it was gone. She had almost forgotten that this house held worse company than Snapper Jo.

"So you want me to be your Mama?" she asked grimly.

"Mama give boy fresh *meat!*" The fiend simpered, and Gilla swallowed sickly. She had seen Snapper Jo's table habits. They were not aesthetic. Once blood flowed he became a mindless eating machine.

Mindless. . . . Somewhere in the depths of her own mind Gilla felt something stir. She looked at Snapper Jo speculatively, and slowly began to sweep once more.

The White Foal River stirred like an awakening animal, expanding through the trees on either side of the upper ford until its shining tendrils crept across the General's Road toward the Street of Red Lanterns. The alleys Downwind were already underwater, and the Swamp of Night Secrets had become a pond.

Water gurgled over the marshy ground above Fisherman's Row and tugged like some marine thief at the small boats tied up on shore. Waterfront merchants labored mightily to protect their wares or fought over the carts that could take them to higher ground. In Caravan Square water stood in muddy pools. But the river roared its frustration where the high banks narrowed it, and nibbled angrily at the supports of the bridge.

Things were not much better elsewhere in the town. Water pounded on tiles and shingles, and roofs which had been at best inadequate turned into sieves. It seeped downward and mud walls began to sag. It pooled in streets and overflowed gutters, floating away the accumulated filth of years. Block after block, the water scoured, hurrying its captured debris toward the gaping mouths of the sewers, whose hollow roar soon became a constant undertone to the drumming of the rain.

Drowned rats and bigger things were swept onward—bodies thought long buried, pieces of rotting wood, wagon wheels, cracked dishes, a mercenary's scabbard, a beggar's precious heap of rags, all became part of the stream. And presently, where pallid waterweed had rooted in the underground channels or where bricks of ancient facings had fallen in, things stuck, each piece catching and trapping more until even the force of the water could not move it forward and it recoiled back into Sanctuary.

Rising waters from the sewer that ran beneath the Maze backed up and overflowed into one of the tunnels leading from the Palace grounds. At the same time, rising river water found an outlet in the escape tunnel that ended near the ford. These waters, meeting, clashed and rose. Some of the overflow splashed into the catacombs beneath the Street of Red Lanterns, but not all, and so, as the day wore on, water began to trickle slowly and inexorably up the tunnel whose entrance was in the basement of the Palace itself.

Water seeped into the dungeons unnoticed except by those few unfortunates who were still imprisoned there. But when it made its way into the portions of the lower Palace that had been remodeled into a nursery for the Child of the Temple, Gyskouras, and Arton and their companions, it was another matter. A storm impelled by alien magics and a flood in their own chambers was not only a threat but an insult as well.

Gyskouras screamed. Arton, face darkening as his own daemon sprang to life within him, screamed louder. The other children who enjoyed the dubious honor of being their companions wept or cowered. Alfi lost completely the edge of superiority that two years' seniority should have given him and clung like a leech to Vanda, while Latilla covered her face with her hands and closed up her fingers each time the noise level rose again.

Seylalha shouted desperate orders as Vanda and the nursemaids scuttled frantically to move children and bedding up to the playroom by the roof garden while above the Palace the sky rumbled echoes of the storm-children's rage. Gyskouras picked up the vase that had been the gift of a royal ambassador and threw it; Arton grabbed a wooden horse and flung it back at him. Lightnings clashed outside and sizzled down the sides of buildings fortunately too watersoaked to burn.

Conflicting winds made a chaos of the orderly banks of cloud, shook the Beysib ships at anchor, plucked off roof tiles and uprooted trees, and folk who had watched the rise of the waters with a nagging dread now trembled with active fear.

And Roxane, sensing the chaos in the heavens, laughed, for this was more than she had hoped for. She changed her strategy, using her control of the elementals to hold back the waters, forcing them to spread sideways into the town.

Gilla could feel the force of the winds even through the witch's wards. Roxane was still secluded, but though her minions knew no particulars, they reflected her emotions, and the growing atmosphere of malicious glee terrified Gilla. What was happening in Sanctuary?

She bent over a crate into which she had dumped half a dinner service-worth of broken crockery which she had found behind the bags of mouldering roots in the pantry and shoved it across the room. What this house needed was not a broom, but a shovel! Still bent over, she glanced around her.

The two house snakes were curled contentedly in their baskets before the stove. Three thralled souls sat at the table, swaying reflexively. Snapper Jo stood between her and the kitchen door, sucking meditatively on an old bone.

He caught her glance and grinned. "Nice and clean! Mistress be pleased. Fat lady make house nice and clean and Mistress wash town!" Overcome with the wit of this observation, he began to laugh. "Wash all the children away, then Snapper Jo be fat lady's boy!"

Gilla clenched her hands in her apron to keep them from closing on the fiend's scrawny throat. At home, she would have thrown something—if she had been at home she would have been throwing things long ago! She felt fury boiling in her belly; she was a lidded kettle ready to explode. Shaking, she hefted the crate of shattered crockery and marched toward the door.

"Fat lady not go out—" Snapper Jo began.

"Great Mistress said to clean her house—I'm cleaning, you wart-upholstered cretin, so get out of my way!" Gilla said between set teeth.

The gray fiend frowned and moved an indecisive half-step, struggling to reconcile the contradictory ideas and unfamiliar vocabulary. Gilla shouldered him aside, shifted her weight, and kicked open the door. Watery light filtered through the shimmering underside of the protective bubble with which Roxane had warded her domain. Gilla took a deep breath of dank air, tensed, and heaved the crate outward with all the strength of her rage.

It arced up and outward, trailing a comet's tail of broken crockery, and burst through.

Gilla was already turning to send another load after it when she heard a sound like a tearing sheet and staggered beneath a gust of wind. Over her shoulder she glimpsed the last shards of the bubble whirling away on the storm.

The wind swept through the kitchen, upheaving the table so that Snapper Jo had to leap aside. Gilla picked up a trashbasket and flung it at one of the thralls, upended another over the serpents, saw the fiend recover and start toward her, and snatched up her broom. Another of the soul-thralls lurched forward. Her swing connected with its head and knocked it bleeding into Snapper Jo's arms.

Gilla steadied herself and cocked the broom for another swing, but the fiend's eyes were fixed on the trickle of red that crossed the thrall's skin. Bony fingers tightened and the body began to struggle. The Snapper's thin lips writhed back from his razor teeth.

"Fresh *meat*," he said thickly, and then, oblivious to the tumult around him, bent to feed.

Before anything else could come at her, Gilla kicked over the rest of the trashbaskets, launched herself through the door and slammed it behind her, and scrambled, panting, across a soggy wilderness of weeds. Before her loomed the rain-dark walls of the warehouses, and beyond them, the bridge, over the river, to home.

Lalo bent, shivering, grasped the end of the timber, and nodded to Wedemir. Together they hefted it, and staggered forward to the edge of the river where a Stepson, four burly men from the 3rd Commando, and a couple of scrawny youths from Zip's collection of toughs were trying to build a bulwark. It was a motley construction, cobbled together with wood from the market pens nearby, logs from half-drowned woods upriver, and anything else they could carry away.

Already water was lapping at the bank. There was no way to protect the low ground below the bridge, but if they could build a dyke northward from the bridge to the end of the old city wall, they might be able to save the middle part of town.

As others took the weight of the timber Lalo straightened, rubbing his back. Even Wedemir was panting, and he was young. Lalo wondered how much longer he could keep this up—it had been far too long since he had asked much of his muscles, and he feared they were betraying him now.

He looked numbly at the muddy serpent that was the river, heaving ominously as it digested what it had swallowed already and considered what next to devour. He was surprised it was not flowing faster, then realized that a south wind was holding back the waters and forcing them to spread rather than flowing harmlessly into the sea.

Witch-work, he thought grimly, and wondered how Randal was doing. It would take more than one Tysian mage to stop this. His shoulders sagged. He would have welcomed even a Rankan Storm-God's intervention now.

"Father—look at the bridge!" Wedemir shook his arm, shouting over the roar of the wind.

Lalo turned. He heard the moaning of overstressed timbers and saw the structure tremble as it was struck by an especially heavy surge. The waters were almost over the roadway now. Wedemir tugged at him again.

"There's somebody on it—someone's trying to get across!"

Lalo squinted into the rain. Wedemir must be mistaken —any Downwinder not already drowned like a rat in his hole must have sought higher ground by now. But there was certainly something moving there. . . .

Something stirred in him like a flicker of flame. He moved toward the bridgehead and the movement warmed him so that he could go faster. Wedemir started to protest, then splashed after him.

"It's a person—a woman—" panted Wedemir.

Lalo nodded and began to run. He heard the groan of tortured wood clearly now. The bridge shuddered and the woman staggered, then plodded forward again, using the broom she carried as a staff. Her soaked gown clung to limbs with the massive strength of an archaic goddess; one could almost imagine that it was not the assault of the waters that made the bridge tremble, but her stride.

Outer and inner sight were abruptly the same, and Lalo forgot his exhaustion. He sped forward, outstripping his son, knowing beyond impossibility who this woman had to be.

And then his feet thudded on the wood of the bridge; his hand closed on hers and new strength flowed through both of them. Sobbing for breath, Gilla stumbled the last few steps after him to the shore, and Wedemir pulled both of them up the bank.

And as if the will that had held it steady had been suddenly distracted, the wind disintegrated into a thousand whirling eddies. The river, no longer thwarted, raced through its narrow channel bare inches below the roadbed of the bridge and across Sanctuary's harbor in a great surge that lifted anchored vessels to the limits of their moorings and then passed onward out to sea.

As the floodtide passed the bridge it spread over the lower lands below. Spray and fragments of wood were still being tossed up by the billows, but through the confusion Lalo thought he saw something like an oily black bubble lift from beyond the warehouses and wobble through the air toward the hills.

But that was only a momentary distraction. It was Gilla he was grasping, Gilla whose warmth he felt through her wet garments, as if she were fueled by a tiny, unquenchable sun. Through the mud he felt earth solid beneath him. She rooted him against the buffets of water and wind.

They paid no attention to the babble of questions around them as they clung together, bedraggled and ridiculous, grinning into the wind.

Then Gilla's face changed. She tightened her grip and shouted into Lalo's ear. "Where are the children?"

"At the Palace with Vanda," he shouted back. "They're safe—"

"In this?" Gilla frowned at the sky. "I should be with them. Come on!"

Lalo nodded. He had done his part here, and he could see that the fury of the river was already abating. But there was still chaos in the heavens, and abruptly he caught Gilla's urgency. With Wedemir close behind them, they picked their way around the lake that had been

Caravan Square and slogged past the deserted stalls of the Bazaar.

By the time Lalo and Gilla reached the Palace Gate the terrified tantrums of two two-year-old incipient Storm Gods were bidding to do more damage to the heart of Sanctuary than all Roxane's water demons. The flashes of lightning were almost constant now, and a strong scent of ozone hung in the air. Puddles dotted the great courtyard; doors on the ground floor were open as Beysib servants tried to sweep water outside.

Lalo stopped short, gazing around in consternation, and Gilla gave him a look that said "I told you so!"

"The nursery was in the basement. I don't know where they've moved the children now."

"At least the Palace is still here," said Wedemir.

Gilla snorted, grabbed a fish-eyed female who was hurrying past with a mop and pail and began to question her. Her limited command of the language was no problem—as soon as Gilla mentioned children the maid paled and pointed upward, then slid from Gilla's grasp.

Upstairs, they found there was no need to ask directions. As they toiled up a staircase that had been well-known to Lalo in the days when he used the roof garden as a portrait studio, they could hear shrieks, punctuated by rolling thunder and the despairing murmur of female voices.

Gilla threw open the door to the sitting room and stood a moment, surveying the scene. Then she waded into the room and began smacking bottoms. Lalo stared, but he supposed that even *these* children would hold no terrors for someone who had managed to escape from Roxane.

There was a short, stunned silence. Then Gilla sat down between the two storm children and pulled them into her capacious lap. Gyskouras took a deep breath and began to hiccup fiercely, but Arton was still crying great, storm-colored tears. Illyra and Seylalha started toward Gilla just as Alfi detached himself from his sister.

Gilla motioned to the two other mothers to sit close beside her and carefully slid the children onto their laps just as her own children reached her. She was still making soothing noises, but the heavens continued their explosions outside.

"Quiet—quiet now, my little ones—see, your mamas

are here! We'll keep you safe now, you don't need to make
all this noise . . ."

"Can't stop!" Gyskouras said between hiccups. His fair
hair was plastered to his head and his cheeks were
streaked with tears.

"'Fraid . . ." echoed the dark child in Illyra's arms.

Both children were still trembling, as if only Gilla's
steady voice kept them from giving way to their terror
once more. Relative peace had returned to the room,
making the noise outside seem louder. Lalo looked
around desperately, wondering if it would help to distract
or amuse them somehow.

Toys were scattered on the floor and building blocks, art
materials, and games were stacked on shelves to one side.
Lalo's eyes widened. He remembered abruptly how his
colored flies had amused Alfi.

Painfully, for now he felt all the aches from his battle
with the storm, Lalo went to the shelves and picked up a
slate and a basket of colored chalks. Holding them as if
they might bite, he came back to the little group in the
center of the room and squatted down.

"Do you like pretty pictures? What do you like—
butterflies?" A swift stroke of the chalk laid the sweep of a
red wing; another suggested the long body and bright
eyes.

Lightning flared in the window, blinding him. When
Lalo could see again Arton's chubby hand was rubbing the
picture away.

"*Not* flutter' by! Bad bright things outside—" His dark
gaze held the limner's, and in his eyes Lalo saw the
angular, aetherial forms of the demons that lived on the
energy of the storm. "Make them go 'way!"

I won't draw them, Lalo thought fearfully, *they've too
much life already!* He took the child's hand gently, remembering how he had comforted his own children when
they had spilled their milk or broken some favorite toy,
not understanding their own power.

Now he felt Gyskouras's gaze upon him as well, filling
him with knowledge of all the powers surging in the storm.
Other images came to him too—emotions, desires as yet
formless, characteristics that sought to coalesce into a
Personality that would encompass the potential, for good
or evil, inherent in the two children before him. He
recognized the feeling—he had known it himself at the

beginning of a project, when colors and shapes and images jostled in his consciousness and he strove for the form and balance that would organize them into a harmonious unity.

But the only loss had been a ruined canvas when he failed. If these children failed, they could destroy Sanctuary.

Thunder clapped great hands above the Palace; the room shuddered and a window blew open on a sudden gust of rain. Gyskouras whimpered, and Lalo reached for his hand. *They need a mage to train them, just like me—but there must be something that we can do!* Lalo closed his eyes, driven not by fear or the pressure of a stronger mind, but by pity, to seek that part of himself that had been a god.

When he opened them again the window was still banging against the wall. Outside, clouds pulsed with a hundred shades of gray—always gray! Gods, he was so tired of this colorless world! Lalo looked down, and saw that the chalk pressed between his hand and Gyskouras's plump fingers had left a smear of yellow on the slate. For a moment he stared at it, then he reached for an orange chalk and put it into Arton's slimmer hand.

"Here," he whispered, "draw me a line beside the other—yes, just so. . . ." One by one he gave colors to the children and guided their awkward hands. Yellow, orange, red and purple, blue and turquoise and green—the chalk glowed against the dark stone. And when all the colors had been used, Lalo got to his feet, holding the slate carefully.

"Now, let's make something pretty—I can't do it alone. You both come here with me . . ." Lalo held out his hand and drew first Arton, then Gyskouras, from his mother's arms. "Come to the window, don't be afraid . . ."

Lalo was dimly aware that the room had gone very still behind him, but all his attention was on the two children beside him and the storm outside. They reached the window; Lalo knelt, his greying ginger head touching the dark child's head and the fair.

"Now blow," he said softly. "Blow on the picture and we'll make the nasty clouds all go away."

He felt the children's milky breath warm on his fingers. He bowed his head and expelled his own pent breath outward, saw chalk dust haze the damp air. His eyes blurred with the intensity of his staring, or was the blur in his eyes? Surely now there was more color in the air than they had ever blown into it, and the colors were shimmering. His ears rang with silence.

Lalo sank back on his heels and drew the two storm-children close against him, and together they watched as the rainbow arched over Sanctuary. . . .

AFTERWORD

"Mirror, mirror on the wall,
"Which is the skungiest city of them all?"
You know what the mirror replied,
with a sneer at having to state the
obvious.

SOME BLATANTLY PERSONAL

OBSERVATIONS

Andrew Offutt

Hanse and I have been in Sanctuary since the foundation stones were set, in a February 1978 letter from genius-creator Asprin. We earliest settlers (eight of us writers then, I think) received maps and descriptions, Hakiem's original background tale, copies of each other's character sketches and sort-of-maybe outlines, and letters from HQ: the Asprin mind. Everybody was excited and pretty chattery. The little description I began of a fellow to be called Hanse became three pages, physical and psychological, with footnotes and sidebars. By the time I'd written all that three or four times, I knew what the first story was about and what sort of stories he had to be in, if there were to be more.

266

As it developed, letter by letter by letter and packet of Xeroxed materials and All-Points-Bulletins to and from us beginners of that project that seemed such fun, I addressed an envelope to

"Robert L. Asprin
COLOSSUS: **The Thieves' World Project.**"

Only a few weeks later, came the next Asprin APB for us first *Thieves' World* participants . . . and derned if he hadn't made just that his *letterhead!*

Next, John Brunner, with the character sketches of his Enas Yorl and Jarveena, sent over a treatise on magic. It told us how it *had* to be in Thieves' World; a sort of logical system of rules of magic that has been ignored ever since. Then Boss Asprin was looking for a name for that first book, and I suggested *Tales From the Vulgar Unicorn*. Thank all gods he decided to call the first one simply *Thieves' World!* My title went on the second volume.

(Send *your* proposed title for the next one; Bob and Lynn just adore mail and if your title is chosen, you will receive a genuine certified Thing. Maybe a no-prize for you if you're one of my fellow comics fans. . . . If you're runner-up, your prize is a date—nocturnal only—with either Tarkle or Roxane, Zip or Ouleh the Man-killer; your choice.

(Send to *me* that detailed list of all the characters in all the books, with however brief ID for each—and whether still alive, KIA-and-dead, or Undead. I like to remember and include all those little people, such as Thumpfoot and Mungo and Shive the Changer and Frax, former Palace night-sentinel who's been out of work since the arrival of the Beysibs, and Weasel, and . . . you know. Spearbearers, many of whom don't even have speaking roles or are only referred to. Seems to me I haven't referred to York or Jubal and various other big-ikes for several stories.)

Oh, here's an Inside tip for you, Insider: go and look again at the cover of the original **TW**. Asprin long ago came up with a caption for it, and you'll love it. It's *"You're In The Wrong Place, Sucker."*

The Solid Gold 50th Anniversary Volume

It honestly seems over a decade ago when we all wrote those first stories. We were a team! We sent them in with gusto and love, having fun—for a nickel a word. That was as advance against royalties if the book sold enough copies to generate any royalties. Hey, did it ever! What now? Another S.F. Book Club volume, I hear, and is it three **TW** games or four? Translations into German and French and British and Swahili and Newjersese! Interplanetary rights up for bidding! Other publishers hot for novels about **TW** characters! Ace Books making plans for the solid gold 50th anniversary volume! Asprin and Abbey buying the state of Michigan and bidding for the Detroit Tigers!

You and we have made it quite a phenomenon. And I swear: it's still fun! Thanks, my fellow fan.

Without quite knowing why, I think I'm more comfortable in this town than any of my cohorts—the rest of the **TW** family. (Baghdad, that's the way I see it: Baghdad or the great old caravan city of Palmyra, about a year after someone put in the Interstate five or so miles away.) To hell with the invasions by Rankans and Stepsons (their big horses making an even worse mess of *our* streets and consuming so much of *our* valuable grain); to hell with the invading Beys and the Beysa and the lords 'n' ladies in their palatial manses; with vampires and walking dead and walking gods and Lon Chaney Jr.! Offutt's an Ilsig who writes about Sanctuary and its people. True, most often my people are Not What They Seem. . . .

Who is, in Sanctuary?

Hanse called Shadowspawn, and Ahdio, and the late, beloved Moonflower and Jubal are as real to me as the Maze. (I know it's real because the moment I start to write about it, very late at night usually, with soft pen and cheap lined paper and beer, I swear I can see it and hear its sounds. And *smell* it.)

I abhor any such snotty, uncultured creep as Hanse, as I loved Moonflower, also my creation. (As you probably know already, since the rules are that we can Not do in each other's characters.) Hanse would be rotten company, so full of swagger and needs. I know. I've met his sort,

time after time, at science fiction/fantasy conventions.
Sometimes even with the knives! Yet I can't help but
love my rotten thief, too, poor guy; sort of as an indulgent father. He was born of me, after all, although
Shalpa takes the credit. Now, like Tempus, he's left
town, with Moonflower's daughter Mignureal (that's
Min-you-ree-Al, and Notable must be with them too,
surely.)

As a matter of fact Hanse is up northeast a bit, standing
by to star in his own novel, *Shadowspawn*. Yes, I've
already signed the contract and this same publisher may
already have the manuscript by the time you read this
(eleven months after my writing it, a few days before
Thanksgiving '84).

Others love-hate Hanse, as he and I love-hate Tempus
and the revenant (?) One-Thumb and even the dread-
some Ischade and Roxane. (Lots of great rôle
models in *Thieves' World!*) Lalo and Gilla his wife
are people, lovable or not. No one loves Jubal except
his creator—who is now *co*-editor, because we wore
him out with gripes and late stories and plot entangle-
ments so that he married a sweet innocent woman and
now forces her to do all the work. No one can hate her
character, Illyra, who is as unreconstructably lovable as
Lynn.

Except when she imported these deleted stare-eye Beysibs and their boss stole away from me a character I'd
begun to think of as mine: Prince Kadakithis. Wait till
Lynn sees my plan for the Final Solution to the Beysib
Problem: Throde draws a picture of an M-1 tank and Lalo
makes it real.

Oh—Kadakithis is played by Roddy McDowall at age
24 and in a blond wig, did you know that? That's the way
he sounds when I read my **TW** stories aloud at conventions. I keep seeing Lee J. Cobb as Tempus, but I
haven't asked Janet who she sees. All right, "whom,"
then.

One big (A: Happy☐ B: Unhappy☐ C: Both of the foregoing☐ D: Neither☐) Family

It is enormous fun, living here in Thieves' World. We
are a *family*. Bob and Lynn have to be mommy and daddy,

obviously, and I am always Uncle Andy to anyone who knows me; the nickname started when I was seventeen. (You don't expect *un*complicated relationships in TW, do you?) There are the wayward sons, Joe and John (Haldeman and Brunner), who started with us and haven't been back; and the grievously wayward prodigal, Gordy (Dickson). There's our sweet and gentle sister Carolyn/C.J. in Oklahoma and the evil and shadowy sister, Nightshade Janet, up in New England. Her I "met" by mail years ago, when I wrote her a fan letter about her first published works, the Silistra novels. Cousin Diana, I am proud to say, first saw print in an anthology edited by me. And now we welcome Cousin Robin to the strangest familial group since the Addams Family.

Right after reading *Wings of Omen* (same time you did: last November, just before I wrote the story in this volume), I wrote Paxson and Bailey each a fan letter of congratulations and thanks. Did you? Why don't you write me, you bum!

Could those be letters to *me* that Bob brags about piling up by the bag in his home?

Like your family, we work together and separately. We get along and we argue or even fall out. When Janet Morris and I include Hanse and Tempus in each other's stories, we exchange manuscripts and say "OK, but (Tempus or Hanse) wouldn't use this word or phrase," or "wouldn't drink this much," or "he is *not* blond." (I thought Zip was, and Janet fixed that in my story last time. Zip looks like that swine who tried to murder the Pope and Hanse resembles Lee Marvin at about age 23.)

Too, Janet sent me pages and pages of lovingly machine-copied (the Xerox people keep reminding us that "xerox" isn't a verb, and is capitalized) research notes, which I filed with my own *Arms and Armor; Medieval Warfare; Smaller Classical Dictionary; Approved Tactics For Attacking and Trashing Publishing Offices;* and other valuable research sources.

She and I met once, about five years ago. We must have exchanged at least thirty words on two occasions that day. She was on her way to someplace else, both times. You don't have to know people to be friends . . . said the man who has collaborated on well over a dozen novels with people he still hasn't met!

Secret alliances, shaky relationships, and worse

Janet and I formed a secret alliance in 1980 ("Vashanka's Minion" and "Shadow's Pawn," and no I do Not
intend to write a nautical story called "Shad's Prawn" as
one darling fan suggested in '81), and sprang it on
Bob-I-mean-Dad, thus forcing him to run our stories back
to back. He got even; his Jubal "sold" Tempus to that
godawful Kurd, slicer of living humans. Then he and Janet
colluded (does that word exist?—it does now; Offutt's the
resident grammarian-linguician). The book ended with
Kurd's industriously paring and sawing this and that part
off immortal Tempus. A few months later, darling Dad-
Bob called me. (This is always difficult. He speaks a shade
faster than a Sten gun, and probably plays whole games
of *Risk* while listening to my Kentuckianly drawled
replies.)

"Andy! ThisisBob! Janet-and-Ineedyerhelp(beat)Kurd-
has-Tempus-andwe-were-wonderingifHanse'dget-himout!"

Beat, beat, beat: "Hi-i (beat) Bo-ob," I said . . .

So Hanse starred in "The Vivisectionist"—surely the
ugliest word in this or any language. Right up there next to
"edit"—in which he got the maimed Tempus out of the
dripping hands of Kurd the Turd. We all loved each other,
even Tempus and Hanse. Then H. saw how T. regene-
rated those lost parts, and got shaky. So did their relationship. Meanwhile, or rather about a year later, Bob and I
had an egregious falling out and I Left Home in worse
than a huff, Never To Return. That's why Volume 5, *The
Face of Chaos,* is Hanseless and Andyless. Seemed a
dreadfully dull book to me. . . .

(Of *course* I read it. I *had* to; another year later I came
home to Sanctuary to write a story in which Hanse split
town; returning was necessary because fans told me
rumors that Lynn and Bob were discussing Secret Plans
with Janet at the World Fantasy Con: maybe going to kill
Hanse or worse. It was a great homecoming with the
typical Sanctuary feast: Bob served up the fatted mongrel.)

So . . . we get along as all families do: usually. But not
always.

For instance . . . I fully expected UPS to bring me a
ticking package from Morris after I killed Tempus's god
and power-source, Vashanka. See, science fiction great

Edmond Hamilton had a name for destroying planets; "World-Wrecker Ed," they called him. . . . That wasn't big enough for me; *I* put the hit on a god. (Besides, I'd birthed him. Now he's in another universe, eking out a precarious living selling hamsters to researchers.) God-Zapper Andy?

Well, no bomb came. Instead, Janet ignored my wicked ploy. She was busy writing her Tempus novel, *Beyond Sanctuary*. They keep telling me that Vashanka has been reborn as an infant. Hmp. Silly dam' dodge, that; he isn't even dead!—just to keep alive a krrf-head whose body heals all wounds. (Donatien Alphons François de Sade should have thought of that. Such a person is the Perfect Victim, while by the end of the Marquis's *Justine,* she must have been covered all over in scars!)

Ils Saves!

This was not at all what I intended to write as Afterword; it was going to be a sort of history, with snippets from our back-and-forth letters. This is what poured out, though, the same way the Hanse stories have: at the last minute (or later, with Lynn & Bob pulling out their hair in great ghastly gobbets) in a rushing beery flow of hand-scribbled phrases during which I never think of style, that thing "teachers" talk about because they aren't writers and can't think of much else except maybe the mech-aniwockle dumbness of 7-2 or 5-3 paragraphs, whatever that are or them is. Somehow the style is always about the same, because that's the way the Hanse stories write themselves. I reckon we can live with this: call it an Afterword, which is "epilogue" or even "epilog" in a living language.

Yours relatively truly takes credit for all the gods of **TW;** for Kadakithis's name and his becoming a person or nearly; for the detailed map of the Inner Maze that you've never seen; for Molin Torchholder and Sly's Place; and of course for the Great Pyramid, the economic recovery, and safety pins.

"And who," the witch begged of the mirror on the wall, having nervously noticed a new line in her face, "is the fairest of them all?"

The mirror sneered again. "Is Sophia still alive, dummy?"

Yeah, you're right: the inspiration for "The Veiled Lady" is Sophia Loren, who is married to a short, homely, balding and dumpy man. Never mind the inspiration for Jodeera's name. Wonder what's going to inspire me next time?

Name of Father Ils, how I wish I'd had the idea for *Thieves' World* to begin with! Then I too could be rich and famous with a basement full of mailsacks and get to exert the editor's prerogative of writing the Afterword to Thieves' World # 7.

—Andrew Offutt
KY, USA
20 November 1984

(Note to Bob and Lynn: Try to get that Big Word in the last sentence spelled right.)